Dreamtime of an Alien God

an occult novel by

R. Douglas Burns

Magic Hat Books
14066 Creekview Trail
Tyler, Texas 75707
http://magichatbooks.com

Published in the United States by Magic Hat Books.

MagicHat Books
http://magichatbooks.com/

Library of Congress Control Number:
2012917821

ISBN-13: 978-0615702384

ISBN-10: 0615702384

Love affairs come and go, but the work of a dedicated edior may last forever. Thanks to Linda Anderson for her invaluable editing and encouragement that I continue this series.

And to S: "I love you' was my favorite of the lies you told and the promises you broke.

Preface/Caveat

I didn't set out to write an occult romance with Tantric overtones; it just happened. If you find explicit descriptions of sexual encounters disturbing, don't read beyond Chapter 1. For a more detailed explanation of how I, a freethinker and a science fiction writer, became obsessed with writing an occult fantasy, the preface to *Messengers of an Alien God*. I promise you it wasn't for money - maybe for love, but not for money.

Dreamtime of an Alien God begins where *Messengers of an Alien God* ended. A giant fertilizer bomb detonated by Sheriff John Wright and Frank Marshall failed to destroy the archangels' saucer. Worse, the bombing lets loose a flock of angel/human hybrids upon the small town of Creedance, Missouri, and causes, for unexplainable reasons, some of the recently deceased to come back to life. But the resurrected are not brain-eating zombies or vampires; they're the rejuvenated and charismatic undead, and they take living lovers. Then things become really surreal.

Laura Jacobsen has issues. One, she missed out on the first offerings of immortality by not merging with an archangel. Her quest is interrupted as she falls in love with a dead man, not just romantic love, but a heart-pounding, sexual obsession

Bryan Douglas has problems too. Not only has Laura dumped him for a dead man, he's found himself involved in the most intense love affair he's ever known. And his lover is also undead. It would be funny, he thinks, if it were not the most intense love he's ever experienced.

Things get more complicated after that.

Robert Douglas Burns
Somewhere in East Texas

1.

Requiem for the Undead

Laura.

The afternoon light was clear and soft. If Laura looked at angel Marguerite in just the right frame of mind, with a sort of mental squint, she could see the timid, kind woman who babysat her as a child, concealed like a pale ghost within the Olympian angelic form. The human Marguerite had worn full-length calico skirts with lacey blouses – even on hot summer days. That Marguerite, the prim Calvanist, would blush at the mention of a bare bosom. Marguerite-the-angel was far from proper. She was Old Testament rock and roll; she was a William Blake painting made flesh, bare flesh as she flew completely naked. Where the old Marguerite had become frumpy over the last few years, Marguerite-the-angel was gloriously, horribly beautiful, with hints of toned muscle underlying supple skin. Where church lady Marguerite's breasts had needed an underwire bra (discreetly padded, Laura suspected), Marguerite-the-angel's were perfect, large but not voluptuous, the breasts of an athlete. Her waist also belonged to that of a female athlete, slim with a hint of a six-pack beneath the skin. Her legs were muscular without looking like a female weightlifter's and were long enough as to be not quite human in proportion to her body. Something else: Marguerite-the-angel remained always poised on tiptoe when walking, standing or flying.

Laura looked away, feeling slightly aroused. She had never had any leanings that way, but Marguerite's visage drew and captured her eyes. Was it sexual or merely due to the attractive force that anything so beautifully alive, person or animal, possessed? Marguerite was luminous, and Laura wanted to reach out and squeeze an arm just to make sure she wasn't some kind of magician's trick or a holographic projection.

"Star quality," Laura said to herself. That's what Marguerite now had, which Laura Jacobsen didn't have – or had ever had.

"Someone just died," Marguerite said matter-of-factly. "I think it was John."

"John? Marguerite, do you mean your husband, John, the sheriff?"

"I mean John Wright, but he is not this Marguerite's husband, he was married to the other me."

Marguerite looked across the lake and spread her wings. Extended fully, they were at least twenty feet from tip to tip, and Laura had to step back to avoid being swatted in the face. Without further preface, Marguerite launched herself into the air. She flew around the lake, staying low just above the scrub brush. Curiously, her wings did not flap as she flew, but just remained outstretched, like a huge moth drying herself in the sunlight.

"Where's she off to?" asked Uncle Robert Jacobsen, hot dog in one hand and beer can in the other.

"To check out the source of the gunshot," Laura replied. "She said it was John Wright."

Both remained silent as they watched her fly. She glided on unseen currents, moving up and over the remains of the old merry-go-round at the edge of the lake without so much as flexing a wingtip.

"As big as her wingspread is, you know, she's still violating the laws of physics," Uncle Robert said. His real name was Simon Jacobsen, but everyone in the small town of Creedance called him "Uncle Robert." He really was Laura's uncle, but she had no idea of where the "Robert" came from. It certainly wasn't on his birth certificate.

"The laws of physics of what universe?" she asked. It was a rhetorical question. The archangels, who had merged with humans to produce hybrids such as Marguerite, did not hail from this universe. Their home universe was not ruled by the same physical laws or composed of the same number of dimensions. Human/angel hybrids such as Marguerite were evidently not bound by the same laws of gravity, mass, or action and reaction, as humans.

"I think they live partly in this universe, partly in the other. That would explain many things, like why they are so hard to see clearly," Uncle Robert said. Though in his early sixties, his eyes were bright and penetrating.

"I think these hot dogs exist only partly in this universe too," she said.

He laughed, the far-away sad look replaced by good humor. "That would make sense. The angels brought them."

At least her uncle hadn't changed. Though the hybrids had only emerged fully formed earlier today, Uncle Robert was already postulating metaphysical theories. "It all seems like a dream," he said. "We aren't dreaming are we?"

She was tempted to pinch him, but instead she said, "I don't think it matters. If you can believe the archangels, they don't even share the same god as we do. They were created and formed out of entirely different stuff."

"You're serious about becoming an angel?" Uncle Robert asked.

"No question about it. They live thousands of years. Their bodies will be perfect and never age. They see things that I as a human will never see; I bet they feel emotions I can't begin to fathom, and go places, experience things that I'm not capable of sharing as merely human. And I'm sure they don't get hung up on love."

"You're taking the angels at their word?"

"Why not? Look at the evidence. Look at Marguerite. Who wouldn't want to be like her even for a regular lifetime, and there's a chance she may live ten thousand years."

"I don't know. There's always a price to everything," he said.

Marguerite entered a bank of fog on the other side of the merry-go-around and became hidden from view.

"There you go," Uncle Robert said. Laura supposed he was being enigmatic. Most of the town people judged him as being somewhere between eccentric and just plain loony. Laura knew otherwise. He was worse. A genius, an alcoholic who drank to quell the hallucinations to which his Jacobsen brain was prone. (He used to tell her that he was a alcoholic with a crazy problem, not the other way around.)

"There you go what?"

"Nothing. Just the image of her disappearing into the fog that me reminded of something. Something that seemed important for the moment."

"One of your epiphanies?"

"Not quite. Almost, but not quite."

Almost but not quite. Laura smiled sadly. That pretty much describes my life.

A scream, inhuman in its intensity and pitch, shattered the silence. Laura and Uncle Robert stared into the fog, both startled, fearing what they might see. Behind them, the rest of the group on the shore – Deputy Jimmy Harte, Sophia Blackstone, Bryan Douglas, and Dr. Charles Jenkins –all turned in unison to look into the fog.

Nearby, the body of Frank Marshall lay flat on its back on the sandy beach and stared blankly at the overcast sky. He had suffered a massive coronary a little while earlier, either because of the excitement of bombing the saucer or from having to confront his wife transformed as an angel. Such was the spell cast by the transformed angels that no one had thought to cover Marshall's corpse.

Laura hadn't been in the least fond of Marshall. He had been a racist bigot and would-be tyrant, but nonetheless she was ashamed the neglect shown his corpse. Maybe some people were just more likeable dead than alive. If she had a jacket she would donate it to the cause, but all she had was this damn poncho made from an Army surplus blanket the angels had given her. She was naked underneath it, and modesty aside, it was chilly and damp out here on the shore of Lost Lake.

Inspiration came to her. She knelt by the old man's body and rolled him out of his khaki trench coat. It wasn't easy. Marshall had been a big man.

His bare arms were limp but still warm. With his jacket off, she rolled him back over on his back, then quickly slipped the poncho off over her head and draped him with it, then took the London Fog rain coat as her own. A fair trade for both of them, it seemed to her. As she slipped the coat on she noticed Bryan watching, looking at her like a hungry, lonely puppy. Dr. Jenkins, Uncle Robert, and Jimmy Harte hadn't noticed her exposure as they were all staring off into the fog, waiting for something to happen.

They didn't have long to wait. An angel emerged from the fog, its wings thin silhouettes and barely moving. Its body looked strangely bloated. As it neared the group, all could see that it was the Marguerite returning. Her silhouette looked bloated because she was carrying a body, a full-size human, cradled in her arms like a child. She swooped in low, her toes skimming the water, raising a misty spray.

She hit the beach running and folded her wings behind her back, stopped to kneel one knee on the sandy gravel and set the body before the group with the air of presenting a sacrificial offering.

The body was that of John Wright, the sheriff, who had been Marguerite's estranged husband before her metamorphosis. Wright's face was peaceful, his eyes wide open, as if he were merely daydreaming. A trickle of fresh blood ran from one ear.

Dr. Jenkins knelt and turned Wright over. On top of his head, a hole big enough to slip a golf ball into seeped blood.

"Amazing. There's still a pulse," Jenkins reported.

"How can that be? That's an exit wound of a bullet, isn't it?" Laura said.

"I don't know. If the bullet was from one of those high-powered magnums he uses, the inside of his head is mush."

"The hole is so big."

"Probably a dum-dum bullet. Wright wasn't one to mess around. If he was going to shoot someone, he wanted them to stay shot."

"The pulse is fading now. Fading ... Now it's gone," Jenkins said.

Marguerite looked and shrieked, startling all of them. It was a single shriek, not sustained, but a brief burst of sound that seemed to bypass the ear and rattle the soul.

"God!" Jenkins exclaimed.

"Nothing like God. It was a Bride-of-Frankenstein scream,"

Laura said.

Marguerite looked down at her with a curious expression.

How much did she remember of being human?

Laura stepped up to the angel and took her hand. It was hard and cold as steel.

"Marguerite. I'm sorry."

"I'm not. I'm angry."

"Anger I can understand. It was a shitty thing for me to say."

"Not that. I'm angry he murdered himself."

"Did you see him do it?"

"No, but May did."

"May the angel?"

"Yes, she was with him when it happened. She said he was about to shoot her, but then changed his mind and ate the gun." Marguerite stuck her index finger into her mouth and sucked on it, her intensely blue eyes closed, a strangely infantile gesture. She pulled her finger out and her eyes sprang open. "The bullet wouldn't have hurt May anyway. Not much."

"Where is May now?" Laura asked, choosing to ignore Marguerite's enigmatic comment. May had been a friend of sorts, her co-worker at Boucher's Cafe before she was transformed into an angel.

"She flew off. She is insane, you know."

"Insane?" Laura asked.

"The human May was one of the first incubators," the Marguerite said. "The animus mundi was implanted before the progenitors realized how fragile and limited is the human mind."

"And you?" Laura asked, not really expecting an answer. "Are you insane, too?"

"I don't know," Marguerite said. "I'm wholly in bliss, then I'm broken – pieces of need and sorrow."

Marguerite looked to the sky, momentarily detached, incredibly distant.

No, Marguerite apparently wasn't too stable herself, Laura decided. Which made some sort of twisted sense. Marguerite had apparently entered into an agreement with the angels fully aware of the outcome. Whereas May, misunderstanding the original angel's nature, had tried to sexually seduce one. The angel, the one May thought looked like Elvis Presley, had in turn misunderstood May's advances. The resulting implantation of the seed of the angel homunculus had been clumsy and brutal, damaging May the human both psychologically and psychically. May's mind had been transported to a place human minds were never meant to visit, and her rebirth as an angel/human hybrid had recapitulated this experience. If what the archangels had not lied about the hybrids being nearly immortal, then May might carry that baggage from her botched transformation for thousands of years.

Like a victim of childhood abuse, Laura shook off this thought.

Not now. Now was not the time to think of such things.

Dr. Jenkins interrupted her thoughts. "I agree May is insane. Do you think she will harm herself?" the country doctor asked.

Laura started to answer before she realized Jenkins had directed the question to Marguerite.

"It's hardly possible. Her body is very durable, as is mine. You know, buns of steel all over."

Dr. Jenkins and Laura laughed in unison. The original angels usually talked like out-of-work yogis much of the time, but once in a while the old, human personalities surfaced.

Intuitively, Laura asked, "Marguerite, you said that May flew away and you don't know where. Did you see who she flew away with?"

"Yes, the Sariel who merged with a human," she replied.

"*Samiazaz* taught enchantments." Uncle Robert, who had been silent until now, spoke up, "And *Sariel,* the course of the moon. And as men perished, they cried, and their cry went up to heaven."

"You're quoting from the book on angelic history you have, aren't it?" Laura said.

"Yes, the pseudipigraphical texts."

"What does it mean, then?" Jenkins asked.

"I haven't the foggiest."

"It means May is . . ." Marguerite said as she launched herself into the air with a whoosh. She accelerated rapidly out of sight into the fog, as if pulled up by an invisible bungee cord.

"Did you hear that last comment?" Jenkins said.

"No, and I don't think we were meant to," Uncle Robert said.

The men craned their necks, watching Marguerite soar into the sky. Laura looked away, feeling dizzy. At her feet lay the body of John Wright. How tortured he must have been to find his wife of twenty-some years transformed into an alien creature. But his face now looked peaceful in death, and she studied it. She hadn't realized that the sheriff had been a handsome man. He had finely chiseled features and a strong dimple-less chin. His deep-blue eyes now stared calmly into the infinite void.

In life, she and Wright had often been at odds. He had been the local authority, and she had always had issues with authority figures, probably because of her relationship with her father. But though Wright had put on quite a show as macho man, someone who wore ignorance as a badge of honor, she had met a different Wright during the conference at the Jacobsen manse. He had probably put on the country cracker sheriff act because his was an elected position. When in Crackerland, do as the crackers do. But despite his hick posturing, he had proven himself to be a thoughtful, intelligent man at times, though a bit bigoted at others.

Moreover, she had learned that he had been a friend of her family, often protecting her Uncle Robert, serving even as a kind of friend and confidant. Those times he had thrown her uncle in the drunk tank had been for his own good. Wright's letting Uncle Robert work out his personal brand of the Jacobsen demons in jail may have prevented him from being committed to Mid-Missouri Mental Hospital – as her father had been.

Bryan sauntered up with a couple of hot dogs in his hand.

"Want one?" he said.

"What? A burnt offering?" she quipped.

He reddened and looked down at his feet, a bashful boy.

"Sure," she said and smiled at him.

He handed her the hot dog and she took a bite. It tasted of hickory smoke and homemade pickle relish.

"How about we go back to the campfire?" he said, motioning to the blazing fire near where the children's playground had once been. A few people stood around the campfire – one poked it with a long stick, sending sparks into the air. It looked like a typical lakeside wiener roast. What was next? Sack races with angel/human teams?

"No, I think I need to stay here and help with Wright's body."

"Why?" he asked.

Uncle Robert and Jenkins were both looking at her curiously.

Indeed, why indeed did she feel she should sit with the body?

She tried to find an excuse, more for herself than the men. "I don't know. It just seems the right thing to do. Wright needs something. A requiem maybe. It just doesn't seem right to leave him here like this on the beach." She looked down at the body at her feet as she said this, but then let out a squeak of alarm and staggered back.

"What?" Bryan said.

The corpse's thousand-mile gaze, which had been directed straight up, now looked her way. As she drew in startled breath, the pupils constricted and focused on her, and she let out another squeak.

She grabbed Bryan's arm to steady herself. "I know it's silly, but I could swear Wright's eyes moved."

She knelt beside Wright's body and reached out to touch his hand, which was lying palm open at his side. As her hand drew closer, a zig-zag blue bolt of static electricity shot out from his fingertips and met her outstretched fingers. Instead of a jolt, she felt a tingling sensation, as though she was close to some energy field. The sensation wasn't unpleasant – quite the contrary, it was quite sensual, sending tingles up her arm, through her shoulder, down her spine and into her lower torso.

More than pleasant, it was nearly orgasmic. She'd almost wet her self.

Embarrassed, she drew away her hand, but everything still tingled. Bryan came closer and put a hand on her shoulder.

"I think we should go home," he said.

She shrugged off his hand. He appeared so young to her, now, so grounded in normality.

"Maybe . . . no, we should do something about the body," she said.

Dr. Jenkins knelt by the Wright's corpse.

"Could he – it – possibly have moved?" she asked him.

Dr. Jenkins took the wrist of the same hand that gave her the shock. He apparently did not receive a similar sensation and felt for a pulse. "I assure you John Wright is dead," he said and took a small flashlight from his pocket, one of those super-bright LED lights. He directed the beam of the light down the hole in top of Wright's head. "If I can just find the right angle — there!"

Wright's cheeks lit up.

"See the wound goes all the way through," Jenkins said. "What gray matter didn't get blown out the top of his head probably oozed down the hole in his pallet and into his throat. What you saw was the head shift – right."

She nodded.

Jenkins continued, "What you observed was probably caused by the weight shifting as the gray matter continued to drain out of the cranium."

"You're probably right," she said. "It just startled me." For reasons she didn't understand, she didn't tell Jenkins that Wright's eyes had focused on her. He'd probably have a scientific explanation for that, too.

"You're right, we shouldn't just ignore common propriety," Jenkins continued. "I tell you what. I can use Wright's police SUV to haul the bodies back to the little morgue we have at the clinic. But I'll need help from your young man, and I'll have to take one body at a time. The SUV is full of crap, and I don't want to stack the bodies on top of each other."

"Bodies – oh, you mean Marshall's too." She didn't say that she didn't consider Bryan her *young man* anymore. But why? He was a bit of nerd, but until just a little while ago, she had considered him sort of her personal nerd.

"I'll help," Bryan said.

"I think we should take Marshall first," Jenkins asked. "He's been dead longer."

"Sure."

"I'll stay here and watch Wright's body," Laura said.

"Are you sure you'll be okay with that?" Uncle Robert said. He wore that expression that said: Do we need to talk?

Did he sense something about Wright's body too?

"I'm good," she said.

He stared at her for a long moment, then walked away, heading back toward the campfire. Jenkins and Bryan walked down the beach to where Marshall's body lay. Bryan looked over his shoulder at her, a silent question like Uncle Robert's. His look said: *What did I do this time?*

I wish I knew, she thought.

But she didn't want to think too hard right now. The mystery of the energy field surrounding Wright's body posed a much bigger question.

But it was odd how these things played out. Their affair had begun with a simple, mutual physical need, then grown to something else, something approaching a spiritual union, and then just as quickly seemed to peter out, no pun intended. The sex was still good; despite his insecurities and nerdiness, Bryan was what she and her girlfriends used to call a BYM, a beautiful young man. But she had her fill of wham-bam, thank-you ma'am relationships, or rather the female equivalent, and that's what Bryan had been for her. For a long time, she thought that was all she wanted. She considered any man, beautiful or not, who wanted more commitment as too clingy, too needy, and a big turnoff. More recently, she had begun to question if happiness might not be found in a more lasting relationship, with someone who was willing to plumb emotional depths. Bryan, who was somewhere between infatuated and in love with her, which would have normally turned her off big time. But overall, he was very bright and receptive to exploration, and might have trained if she had the patience. But there was no mystery to him. She could see them settling down into a sort of post-apocalyptic exclusive relationship, maybe even having children – deeply disturbed children, of course – ensconced in a comfortable, bonded-and-shackled common-law marriage.

But that was the past. Now she had a quest: to recover the hundredth angel from the bottom of Lost Lake and merge with it, becoming an entity who though not immortal, would live for a very long time. She knew this process possible, and she was also aware that despite the archangel being under hundreds of feet of water, it was still alive, at least in the sense that the original archangels were alive. Moreover, once it was brought out of full immersion, it would be fully resurrected. She even knew the archangel's name: Samiazaz.

She looked toward the lake. Uncle Robert was back at the campfire, shrouded in smoke. There was no sign of the archangels' giant saucer, not so much as a bubble. Which in itself was a curious thing, for when she had been inside the saucer, she discovered it to be not so much as a space-going craft or even a hyper-dimensional craft, but a portal to an entirely different universe. The saucer had been blown from its muddy moorings in the forest by a fertilizer bomb built by Wright and Marshall. Dislodged, it slid into the lake and sank as lake water poured into a gash in its metallic skin. For those outside the saucer, those who had never been inside it, this must have seemed logical. The outside surface of the saucer was much smaller than the lake. Water poured in; it filled and sank. Simple.

But it was not so simple a matter for her and others who were inside the saucer at the time, for they knew there was no reason for it to sink. The inside of the saucer seemed larger than the lake, larger than the county, possibly larger than the entire state of Missouri. Its horizons stretched as far as the eye could see. No lake water had come gushing in to fill up the landscape, but Marguerite, May, Bertha and other angel/humans had suddenly gathered up herself, Jenkins and Bryan in their arms and flown out of the gash. It was only at the edge of the break in the skin that she had seen any sign of water flowing into the saucer, and that had seemed inconsequential.

Another mystery.

She sat down cross-legged next to Wright's body. She was tempted to turn his head so that he would be gazing at the sky instead at her, but she was reluctant to actually touch him. Checking to see that no one was looking, she put her open palm over his hand again, holding it a fraction of an inch away from skin without actually making skin contact. She felt no sense of an energy field this time. Had she imagined it before? Perhaps it had been mere static electricity.

Something she had once read about Tantric energy fields came back to her. She must have been only eighteen. She had considered it total bullshit at the time but nonetheless had tried out some the techniques with her girlfriends and felt nothing. There had been a detail about the way palms of sexual partners had to be aligned or whether the people were of the same or opposite sex.

Before, when she had sensed the charge, she had placed her hand so that her fingers and the corpse's fingers were parallel. Now, sitting at a right angle to the body, her fingers were at a right angle to Wright's, too. She scooted around, her hip brushing against the gun holster on Wright's right hip. Funny, she hadn't noticed it until it now, but his service pistol was in the holster. The leather safety strap was snapped. She unsnapped the strap and drew out the pistol. It was big – a Clint Eastwood, make-my-day-sized gun, the acrid smell of having been recently fired still lingered.

The question was if Wright had shot himself, what gun had he used? Certainly not this one, unless May had re-holstered it for him.

"Well, friend of the family or not," she said to Wright's corpse, "you won't be needing this any more."

She set the heavy pistol on her lap, and the metal was cold against her bare thighs where Marshal's trench coat had come unbuttoned. Wright's hands were large and the calluses on the palm slightly yellow in the dreary light. She lined up her fingers so they were parallel with his, her fingertips over his wrist. There was nothing at first, but as she brought her hand closer to his, as close as she could without actually touching, a threshold must have been crossed, and there was an immediate shock.

The effect – she didn't know what else to call it – seemed to almost burn her hand and sent a charge up her arm, across her shoulder blade, and down her spine to the private junction between her legs! It was so intense, the verge of an orgasm that reached from deep within her all the way up her spine. An inarticulate cry escaped her lips. She wanted to pull her hand away, but it was drawn to the corpse's hand a magnetic pull.

The corpse moaned, a long "AHHH" sound from deep in its throat, and the attachment was broken. She fell backwards on the gravel, her knees folded under her, the big pistol spilling from her lap.

She pushed herself up on her hands, and the trench coat fell open again. The corpse moaned again, the head shifted more until its lifeless eyes stared at her naked thighs.

Then she was running barefoot across the beach, leaving the corpse, the pistol, and the revelers at the campfire far behind.

* * *

2.

Shadows of a Last Life

Laura.

As the evening light failed, the house filled with shadows and the corners of the room faded to black. Laura's mind was dark as well, as logic or reason refused to illuminate the shadowy memory of her experience on the beach.

The electricity was out again, and she lit a candle to find her way downstairs to the basement. A musky smell permeated the unfinished basement room. Despite the smell, the basement remained dry and easy to heat because it was insulated by six feet of heavy, clay soil. Going into the basement, though, was a little like dying. Descending the steps, she entered complete darkness, shut off from even the starlight, surrounded by the smell of damp earth, the sounds of outside life deadened and remote. When summer came and the nights warmed, she would move upstairs and back to life in the sunlight – maybe.

Maybe not. Maybe this spring would be a warm one. Maybe the powers that be, whoever the hell they were, would restore the electrical power grid and the propane distribution infrastructure. Maybe she would get cold enough or become discouraged enough to let Bryan share her house and bed. Maybe, but not likely. Maybe a dog would be a better bed warmer.

Maybe, maybe, maybe.

Maybe the dead would walk the Earth again. Maybe her life was ruled by improbability and uncertainty. Maybe she carried the unstable Jacobsen gene, and someday her neighbors would find her in this basement, raving and smeared with her own feces.

Is this how Jacobsen madness began? Now that she was back in her basement the whole episode at the beach seemed like a weird, waking dream – or a hallucination. Had her father's madness begun with such delusions? He had been first institutionalized as a very young man. Uncle Robert seldom spoke of those times. But she had gathered that her father had come close to murdering Uncle Robert several times before being finally committed.

Some of the new schizophrenia medications of the time had allowed him to be released while he was still a young adult, and he had remained stable enough to convince Laura's mother to marry him. His relapse had come later, when Laura was thirteen. She remembered having to fight him off when he came into her room at night. And the culmination of the attacks one day when he had a knife. She didn't want to think about that time right now. And the murder of her mother and his suicide not long after – she never wanted to think about any of that again, but the memories would always be with her, like invisible shadows.

Suddenly the corners of the basement seemed too dark. Restoration of electric power was probably not going to happen tonight. Creedance was luckier than many towns as it had a small but operational hydroelectric generator at the Lost Lake dam. But the thing was ancient. It had been mothballed for twenty years before the Fall. Who knew where the local operators found parts for the ancient thing, but local residents were glad to get what service they could. The main power grid might never come back on again.

After the fall of the archangels' saucer months ago, most all modern electronics had died. So had the electronic ignitions of any cars or truck manufactured after the early 1970s. Newer vehicles, with their electronic ignition systems, were just so much junk. So were televisions, cell phones, radios and the electronics used to keep the country's modern electrical power grid operational.

She lit a kerosene lamp, knowing if she let it burn for too long that everything in the basement would be covered by a fine coating of soot. Even worse, her water heater was electric, so she would have to take a cold shower. But she was too tired right now to worry about it.

She undressed, climbed into the bed, and in a minute was on the verge of sleep, but though her body was leaden, her mind was a cloud of unfinished thoughts.

A knock came from the upstairs. She was immobilized for a moment, not out of fear, but from the trance-like sleep she had slipped into.

"Shit! Shit! Shit," she said.

It took a superhuman effort to swing her legs out of bed. Barefoot, still half asleep and feeling strangely weightless and insubstantial, she put on her robe and padded barefoot upstairs. There was an aluminum baseball bat she kept behind the door at the top of the stairs, and she took it with her, though she was pretty sure who was at the door and didn't think she'd need protection.

At the front door, she had to stand on tiptoe to squint out the peephole lens. (What law dictated peepholes had to be placed nearly six foot high?) She felt silly, because logically it must be Bryan as he was the only one who visited these days. A stranger meaning to do her harm would have simply kicked the flimsy door in.

She peeked out anyway. There on the porch was the shadow of of a broad-shouldered man, backlit by a pale half-moon. His proportions were grotesquely distorted by the fisheye lens. He stood without speaking, standing calmly with his arms at his side. The combination of the backlighting, the crappy optics of the fisheye lens and the moist air caused an odd lighting effect. He appeared to be surrounded by concentric bands of light from head to toe, the inner one lurid red, the outer a light blue gray.

The psychedelic sight took her breath away for a moment, then the figure stepped forward, changing the angle of the backlight and the aura disappeared. He raised a hand, elbow bent, palm forward in greeting.

She sighed; she had hoped Bryan knew it was over. Momentarily, she debated ignoring him, sneaking back down to the basement and hiding there, surrounded by the greasy smell of the kerosene lamp. But a strange mixture of feelings washed over her, composed more of melancholy and less of depression, with a dash mixed in of something she couldn't name.

She set down the bat and worked the deadbolt. Damn! It stuck, of course. Double damn! Physically Bryan was okay, more than okay as he was muscular now from chopping wood every day. Looks weren't the problem. Sex wasn't the problem. The trouble was that Bryan persisted in being so normal. Psychologically normal. She had been most attracted to him as he was recovering from a temporary psychosis induced by a too-close interaction with an archangel. But as the effects of the encounter waned, he became just an intelligent, nice young man again – no hallucinations, no psychosis – and she had lost interest.

It was almost laughable. She could never love a man who wasn't as tragic mental case as she was.

In bed, he was somewhat inhibited and conventional, but he wasn't cruel or domineering. She suspected he tended to put women on a pedestal, a characteristic that didn't foster mature relationships with codependents such as her. She had no desire to be treated like some sort of fragile goddess. And then there was the problem with his being in love with her. That kind of love always led to possessiveness, with the lover eventually, if not right away, getting around to being jealous and possessive.

Still, Bryan was hung well and trainable – like a puppy. If he could stop being so serious, he might make a nice, casual safe hiatus during these difficult times, but he thought he loved her and that made her feel claustrophobic.

Besides, if she was going to reclaim the body of the one-hundredth angel at the bottom of Lost Lake, what she needed more was a friend and ally, and not a distracting romance.

The deadbolt freed, and she opened the door to be blinded by a blast of wet, cold air.

"You can come in, but you're not staying over," she said.

"I don't want your bed. I only want to talk," the shadow said, stepping past Laura and into the living room.

"Wright!"

The sheriff turned to face her. "What's the matter?" he asked.

"I thought you were dead."

"Dead? Do I look dead to you, young lady?"

She shook her head and let the *young lady* comment pass because of his age. He looked astonishingly healthy. She'd seen corpses before. He should be gray as slate for all the blood he'd lost. But his face glistened with good health.

"At the beach. The angel . . ." She didn't dare say Marguerite's name – "brought your body and set it down at our feet. There was a bloody fucking hole in the top of your head where all your brains were blown out, and Jenkins couldn't find your pulse."

"Jenkins never was much of a doctor." He reached up to examine the top of his head, his fingers searching, then finding the hole, the index finger tracing its bloody perimeter. Laura feared he might probe the hole, like a finger in a globby nose, and the thought made the hair on the back of her head stand up.

"Damn me! How did I do that?" He examined his fingers. They were covered with blood. "Shit! I bet I look like hell," he said, and slumped down in the recliner next to the couch.

He ran his hand back up his head.

"Don't pick at it," she said as if she were talking to a small boy.

Obediently, he dropped his hand back on his lap, looked at the blood on his fingertips, then looked away. He was terrified, she realized.

"You don't look so bad." She stopped herself from adding, *considering you've blown most of your brain out through the top of your head and swallowed the remaining gory slurry.*

She started to sit down on the couch, thought better of it, and instead perched in the rocking chair in the middle of the room well away from Wright.

Silence ensued. The sheriff continued to stare at his bloody fingers, unmoving.

"Sheriff?"

No answer. He just kept staring at his fingers. Had he died for real this time? She was struck by how genuinely creepy this situation was. She was sitting in an old, dark empty house with a zombie. The chair was covered with dust. The whole room was strung with cobwebs, which were coated with black soot from the kerosene lamp. She hadn't done much except pass through the upstairs on the way to the basement since cold weather came. But it was a comical horror milieu, like being stuck as the straight man in an Adams Family movie.

Or the psycho ward at Mid-Mo . . .

"Wright?"

"What?" He said looking up suddenly, sheepishly, as if he had been caught napping on the job.

"What did you come here for?"

He squirmed in the recliner. "I was drawn here, like I was pulled by an invisible wire. I don't know for sure why I came, but I think it was to apologize."

"Apologize? What for?"

That you're about to try to eat my brains, maybe?

The thought almost made her laugh.

"Apologize for what?" she repeated.

"I don't know quite for sure. There's a memory of something I did, but which I can't quite recollect, but it occurs to me it was dishonorable, and that I should ask you to forgive me."

"You sound like you're in some sort of twelve-step zombie-anonymous program."

"Twelve step? You mean like the alcoholics?"

She nodded.

"No. At least I don't think so. I just feel like I have to make amends to you."

He reached up to touch the top of his head, thought better of it, and put his hand down.

"I was drawn here," he said. "I woke up in the woods. I felt like there was an invisible string pulling me here."

"You said that already."

"But I didn't realize I had come to your place until you answered the door."

They stared at each other across the room. A single strand of hair, jelled by coagulated blood, stood up from the top of his head. She stared at strand rather than look him in the eyes. The strand of hair amused her and alleviated some of her fear. If this was just a dream or a hallucination, why get hooked by it? Just enjoy it. Play the game. Tomorrow, she would wake up in her bed and this would just be a fading memory of a bad dream.

"So you came here to make amends?" she prompted.

He nodded. "Maybe. Why else?"

"Just to me?"

What about your wife? You gave her plenty of misery, I bet.

"No. Well, maybe other people too."

"But this is your first visit since you had this – what would you call it? – revelation?"

"Yes. I guess it is."

"Okay. Then the question arises. Why here? Why me?"

"I don't know, Laura . . . What's the matter? Why are you laughing?"

"You never called me Laura before. Not in all the years I was growing up. Not when I was grown. You always called me 'young lady,' without meaning the 'lady' part or Miss Jacobsen, or if you were talking to someone else, and didn't know I could hear, then it was that 'weird Jacobsen girl.'"

"I'm sorry about that, too. Is it all right if I call you Laura from now on?"

"Sure. I guess so." She was taken aback by his earnestness. Despite their past relationship, she found herself liking him. With this sea change of emotion his appearance became less grotesque and merely disquieting – if she didn't think about the huge hole in the top of his head.

"Thanks," he said, smiling, showing a healthy set of teeth. Again she was struck by how good Wright looked — he looked a lot better dead than she remember him ever looking when he was alive.

"You're welcome, but you still haven't told me why you came here first."

"That's the weird part," he said. "I don't know why I came here. I actually tried to resist coming here, but I had to."

"I see."

"I know what you're thinking," he said. "John Wright's gone completely off his nut, showing up in the middle of the night, asking for forgiveness."

"Not gone. Transformed."

"You say that, but you didn't know Marguerite like I did. We were married for twenty-some years, and I tell you that creature at the lake has nothing in common with my Marguerite except her face."

A little of his color came back as his voice rose with emotion. The strain must have unsettled something, broke a clot perhaps, because a thin, viscous stream of blood began to flow from his ear.

"The fucks! The goddamn angel fucks! I loved her! Goddamn them!" Wright shouted, really down deep into his anger now, and the blood stream widened and became corrupted with white flecks of tissue.

She hopped up and fetched a towel from the kitchen. When she put it in his hand, he looked at her questioningly. He didn't know he was bleeding. She took the towel back and dabbed at the blood, trying not to get any on her bare hand. Who knew what zombie virus he was host to? But as she thought about it, she realized it couldn't be all bad if it kept him walking, talking and thinking after he was dead — and looking so healthy as well.

Even buffered by the towel, touching him was electric.

She showed him the blood on the towel and gave it back to him.

"Shit!" he said. "What next?"

He got up and went back to mirror to sponge at the blood.

"Sorry," he said, "but I'm probably ruining this towel." He looked like he was about to emotionally crater. "You must think it really inappropriate, me showing up on your doorstep like this."

"Wright, you know what I think?"

"I'm not sure."

"I think you and I could be friends."

"Why do you think that? I did harass you some, you know."

"Because you confided in me. That makes us sort of friends."

He smiled at her. What was that cologne he was wearing? It was a faint smell, a bit alien and hard to place, but not miasmic. Being dead, he should smell of swamp rot or something. But his scent very pleasant. So much so, it nearly overwhelmed her. She stepped back and took a breath to clear her head.

Shit! I'm such a sucker for lost boys, even lost undead middle-aged boys.

"And as your friend," she said. "I think I should take you to see a doctor."

"There's only one doctor in town."

"That's right. I think we should pay Jenkins a visit."

"I told you what I think about Jenkins."

"Yes, I know. I used to feel pretty much the same way."

"What changed?"

She smiled. This new Wright might look be zombie, but he had a child's pleasant candor. She wanted to add she had adjusted her opinion of Jenkins as well since the two of them worked together inside the angel saucer. Jenkins hadn't been transformed into an angel, she had watched the years and middle-aged fat melt off Jenkins in a matter of hours while they had been interned together. With the age-reversal had come a shift in character. He was more tolerant now and open to other viewpoints. Which brought forth the question: Had she been transformed in some way too?

"I tell you what, Wright."

"Call me John. Please."

"Okay, John. Why don't we go visit Jenkins? You can hear him out, but nothing says you have to follow his suggestions."

"I don't know."

"It would make me feel better."

"I don't have a car."

"How did you get here?

"Walked. Didn't I say that? I don't clearly remember."

"No problem. My old Volkswagen Beetle is still running. You'll have to promise not give me a ticket because the turn signals are not working."

"I never ticketed you before, remember. I only gave you warnings. And the last one was for doing forty-five in a school zone."

"John, this looks like the beginning of strange friendship," she said, wondering how he could remember anything at all since he didn't have a brain.

She left him upstairs while she jumped into a pair of jeans, pulled on a sweatshirt and slipped on tennis shoes, not bothering to tie the laces.

She cringed when he bumped the top of his head getting in the Volks, but other than being slightly disoriented, he seemed coordinated and coherent, though more reticent than usual. In the cramped confines of the car, she was more conscious of his physical presence. Though short in stature, Wright had the shoulders and barrel chest of a professional wrestler and the manners of her Uncle Robert's generation. He hunched his shoulders to avoid physically brushing against her. The odor of cologne or whatever he was wearing was stronger and smelled really good. If he hadn't been dead or injured, if he hadn't been the sheriff and twenty-some years her senior, she would have complimented him on it.

The fog had thickened, dampening the light of the old Beetle's headlights to a fuzzy yellow glow. They were at the small clinic in fifteen minutes. As Laura expected, Jenkins' Chevy pickup was the only vehicle in the parking lot.

They found Jenkins asleep on his back on one of the orange vinyl sofas in the waiting room. No nurse was on duty at the tiny admitting desk.

She was going to shake Jenkins awake, but Wright stopped her.

"Let him sleep," he said. "He's probably pulled another all-nighter."

"I think we should get you looked at right away."

"I feel fine, just kind of light-headed," he said.

Was he making a joke about his brains drooling out his ears?

She glanced at him and decided he wasn't. He was obliviously unaware of his own condition.

"Really, I'm just sort of cold and damp," Wright said.

"Not real. None of it real," Jenkins said, making both of them jump. Then the doctor emitted a long snore. He had been talking in his sleep.

Wright chuckled but stopped when he looked to her.

"Listen, I appreciated your concern, but do you really think we need to be here? I don't think it's bleeding anymore." He reached up to feel the top of his head.

"Stop!" she said and grabbed his wrist to pull hand away before he could stick a finger in that gory hole again.

"Okay! Okay!" He seemed amused now and a little more awake.

Her fingers tingled at the touch of his skin, and she let go.

"So it looks that bad?" he said.

She nodded.

"All right, I'll make you a deal," he said. "Get me a cup of coffee – hot coffee – and a warm blanket, and I'll hang around for while until the doctor wakes up."

"Yeah, I guess. But Jenkins is in another world. He could sleep for hours unless we wake him up."

"Then I'll nap out here until he does," Wright said. His mood changed. "There's nothing to go home to anyway."

He looked on the verge of crying. Laura realized at that moment that he had really loved Marguerite, and her heart softened a little more.

"Let's go back into the admitting rooms," she said, taking his hand. He followed as she tugged at him. "It'll be warmer back there."

"Another thing," Wright said. "Don't try to get me into one of those stupid gowns that are open at the back. I'd rather be muddy and wet than walking around with my butt out for everyone to see."

The main room in the emergency section of the clinic was circular with small examining rooms around the circumference. In the middle of the room was a corpse on a gurney. A sheet, its edges frayed, had been pulled back to partially reveal the face of Frank Marshall. Both the nurses who had worked at the clinic had become angels, so Jenkins was probably keeping the clinic open by himself.

Still holding Wright's hand, she led him to one of the examining rooms. He was surprisingly compliant. When she knelt to take off his boots, he protested.

"Hey! I said no hospital gown."

"I wouldn't dare, Sheriff," she said. "But let's get you out of these wet boots. I'll stuff them with paper or towels or something, and they can be drying out while we wait for Jenkins."

"I'm not one of the geezers you used to tend to in the nursing home," he said, but he let her proceed. She wondered why she bothered. For some reason, she found it comforting to help him.

Despite the boots being damp and ice-cold, Wright's toes were pink and warm, nothing at all like a corpse's. She couldn't get him to lie down, but she found a clean blanket in a cupboard, and he let her drape it over his shoulders.

"I'll go see if I can find some coffee," she said. It went without saying that there was no guarantee about the coffee because the fall of the angel saucer had severely disrupted interstate commerce.

After she found only burnt residue in the coffee maker, she decided to wake Jenkins without telling Wright. But as she passed the examination room, she met the doctor coming from the front.

"Hello. What brings you two here?" Jenkins said. He looked surprisingly neat and tidy for someone who had been sleeping in his clothes a few minutes before.

"You don't look surprised to see us," Laura said.

"Not really," Jenkins said and stepped up to examine Wright.

"Hmmmm," Jenkins said, and reached out to touch the wound, making Laura cringe for about the umpteenth time this evening.

Wright drew back, and Jenkins said, "Relax, Sheriff. I'm just going to have a look-see."

He pulled a battery-powered penlight out of his pocket and peered down at the hole in the top of Wright's head. After a few seconds, he sat down in a swivel stool next to Marshall's corpse. "Amazing," he said, shaking his head.

"That's it? You're not going to take his pulse or anything?"

"What for? We're living in a dream. All of us. What good would it do?"

"A dream?"

"Yes. That's the only explanation. Wright, why don't you lie down?"

"I'm not tired."

"That doesn't surprise me either. The dead, you see, don't need rest."

"Dead! What is this bullshit?" Wright said in a near whisper. He seemed to be ready to topple from the gurney, and Laura took his arm to steady him.

Jenkins ignored Wright and spoke to Laura. "As I suspected from my examination at the beach, the hole on the top of his head is obviously an exit wound from a large-caliber bullet. The wound has dried out now, the light is better here, and I can see deeper. Quite a bit deeper. The bullet's passage liquefied most of the brain tissue. There's not enough undamaged brain tissue left to manage an eye blink, much less to maintain bodily functions such as a heartbeat or breathing, which explains why Wright has neither a pulse nor respiration."

"Bullshit! Hey, Jenkins, I'm talking to you! I'm not dead!"

Jenkins looked a little wary as he swiveled on the chair, as if he expected Wright to strike him. "Whatever is animating the body of John Wright is not the brain of John Wright. It's just so much bloody mush – and there's not much left of that!"

Wright seemed frozen in the middle of the emergency room, a statue.

"Show me," he said.

"Sure, why not. It might be edifying for the living. Come with me."

Wright, padding barefoot on the linoleum tile floor, followed Jenkins to the clinic's small operating room. The room was equipped with mirrors on stands, which Jenkins quickly arranged at the end of a gurney.

Again, Laura was amazed at how nimble this Jenkins was when compared to the one she knew only a few weeks ago. He had lost his potbelly, his wrinkles and that flabby double chin. She knew he was in his late fifties – a month ago he had looked in his seventies – but now looked a very fit forty.

He sat Wright down on the end of the gurney. The mirrors were positioned so Wright could see the top of his own head. Jenkins slipped on a latex glove, directed an examination light at the top of Wright's head, and began tugging at bloody strands of hair around the wound. "Does that hurt?" he asked.

"No," Wright said.

"Ah, here we go," Jenkins said as he lifted the strand up. With it came a large chunk of scalp. The piece of scalp was still attached to Wright's head with a flap of skin, and Jenkins laid it on a stainless steel table next to the gurney. Laura gasped. She could see deep into Wright's skull. It looked like a hollowed out jack-o-lantern.

"See," Jenkins said, "it's like a soup bowl and his brain is cream of tomato."

She forced herself to step closer. Close up, she could see down through Wright's cranial vault and into what looked to be his mouth. His tongue moved in the shadows like a dead fish in muddy waters.

"So what do you think?" Jenkins asked.

He's right. We must be dreaming, she thought.

Instead, she said, "I'm astonished. I had a complete conversation with him. He listened, responded, blinked his eyes, but I can see there's nothing in there – Oops! Sorry, John, I guess I shouldn't be talking about you in third person as if you're so much meat."

"It doesn't matter," Jenkins said. "Look." He waved his hand in front of Wright's face. There was no response.

Laura knelt to look at Wright's face. His face was relaxed and his eyes closed. He appeared to be sleeping sitting up, then he began to slowly topple forward, threatening to take her down with him. Jenkins grabbed his shoulders and together they managed to get him safely down to the floor.

"Why didn't you just let him fall?" Jenkins said.

"I didn't want him to bash his head," she said but stopped when she realized how silly that sounded. "Is he breathing?"

"Probably not. I doubt he was breathing before when he was walking about. He didn't even seem to need to take in air to talk, but what's a minor impossibility like that compared to his animation."

"Then you're saying he really is dead now, finally?"

"To answer that question requires some convoluted rhetoric, which I'm not up to right now. He was dead when he walked in. I'm sure of that, unless he's got a second brain hidden away in his butt. But then so was Marshall when he regained consciousness a couple of hours ago in the emergency room. I took him in there to prep the body for burial as the morgue's filled up. I'm doubling as mortician these days, you know. I had just finished draining the blood and was pumping in the embalming fluid when Marshall sat up and asked me what the hell I was doing to him. I thought I had made a terrible mistake, but when I couldn't find a pulse and his temperature measured barely 80 degrees, I knew something else was going on.

"Frank, like Wright, argued that he wasn't dead," Jenkins continued. "I explained, very convincingly, I think, that he was. Funny thing, debating death with a dead man. In life, Frank, despite all his bluster was an intelligent man. Frank-the-dead was no less a formidable debate opponent. He nearly convinced me I was mistaken, but in the end I won out. Frank couldn't dispute his own death. The moment he accepted the facts, the exact moment he realized he was dead, that he was an animated corpse, he blacked out, just as Wright did now."

"Blacked out? Is that all it is with Wright?"

"If he follows Frank's pattern, he'll come to in about a half hour remembering everything except the shock of learning of his own death. I've argued Frank into immobility three times since I brought his corpse to the clinic this evening."

"Why?"

"Why what?"

"Why hit his reset button three times? I'd think you would have established the pattern by the second time."

"Pretty much. I wasn't quite sure though, and I had the bone saw out . . ." Jenkins patted his shirt pocket as if looking for something. "Funny thing, the cigarette habit. I've quit months ago, and don't miss the things at all except at times like these. What was I saying?"

"Something about a bone saw."

"Oh, yes. I wrestled with the idea of performing an autopsy each time he went out, but I just couldn't bring myself to do it. Is it murder to open up a corpse when it's still walking and talking? I don't know. I had questions that I wanted answered. You see, for some reason, I suspected that Frank was just the tip of an iceberg, that there would be others. I suspected I would have to try to understand the physiology of what was happening. That's where I was when you and our good sheriff's walking corpse showed up on my doorstep."

Laura started to tell him that he was sleeping when she and Wright came to the clinic, but Jenkins wouldn't let her get a word in edgewise.

"Staring into Wright's empty skull while he was talking was a revelation. Frank's cause of death is not so readily apparent, but I suspect I could do a full autopsy on him, put all his internal organs in a bucket, even pop his top and remove his brain, and he still would wake up eventually – perhaps even while I was cutting – and argue his own existence. Hell, he might even win the argument."

Laura found herself speechless. She felt the need to defend Wright – in a few minutes he had shown her a human side that she cared about – but she had to admit Jenkins was right on target. Wright simply could not be alive. He had to be some sort of zombie or illusion.

The shabby little medical room suddenly became a place of hard, cold light. The walls, the floor, the door and all the equipment took on hard metallic edges as sharp as razors. The surgical equipment, the gurney, which by design were metallic with distinct edges, became so sharply defined as to be impossible to look upon. She studied Jenkins. He seemed made of dull aluminum foil, two-dimensional; he moved about with purpose or reason. She was crushed by the faux nature of her surroundings.

The emotional affect dissipated as suddenly it arrived. The room was a normal room, not a crushing enormity. Jenkins was speaking words, not non-sensible syllables, and his body was three-dimensional. She felt as if she were rising from some great depth. She gasped for breath. *Had it been a prelude to a schizophrenic episode?*

She slammed her hand so hard against the metal gurney it rang like a bell.

"What is it?" Jenkins asked.

"Nothing. Just a bad moment. It passed."

"It appeared to be more than a bad moment. You looked at me like I was some kind of monster. You were truly horrified."

"I was overcome by the terribleness of Wright's situation. It was nothing." But it wasn't nothing. It was the Jacobsen genetic schizophrenia, an inheritance that passed to many Jacobsens in their mid- to late twenties. Like many of her cousins, she had brief previews during adolescence and her late teens. Such episodes had been the reason she hadn't finished college. But upon leaving college and adopting a working-class lifestyle, the episodes had become less frequent. She hadn't experienced one since she was twenty-one.

She excused herself to use the restroom. At least the toilet still worked. But she didn't leave after flushing. Instead, she switched out the light, put the seat down and just sat in the cool darkness.

She would not let her father's destiny become hers. She would not let madness take her. She would find the lost angel in the lake. She would cross over into the world of the angels and become safe from the errors of human flesh, bad genes and unbalanced brain chemistry. It was her only hope.

When she left the bathroom, Wright's body was no longer on the surgery room floor or anywhere else in the clinic. She found Jenkins asleep again on the admitting room couch, looking as frumpy as before.

* * *

3.

Metathesis of Love

Wright.

When Laura gripped his arm the clinic room shimmered and spun. Then he was in a high, dry place, lying on his side on a white-sand desert plane peopled with crystalline plants. He could see the clinic room far away, with three of its walls unfolded in the fashion of a diorama, all the sharp edges softened, the corners rounded, everything seen as if in a mirage, shimmering in the heat waves rising from the sand. And he could see his body, and that too was a cardboard cutout. And there was a two-dimensional Laura Jacobsen, still holding his arm, trying to keep him from falling.

Jenkins and Laura laid him on the floor, and he was at once in his body and looking at it from the outside. The mirage-like effect had passed. He was back in his body, but it felt dried out. His lungs were filled with dead leaves, his eyesockets inhabited by brittle insects, his nose a fossilized alien creature. He tried to take a breath and couldn't; nor could he redirect his gaze or so much as blink.

Is this what it feels like to be dead?

Jenkins and Laura leaned over him and above their heads small clouds – no, puffs of smoke as if from a chimney – floated in and out of his field of vision.

Laura's lips were moving, but he couldn't hear what she was saying. He felt the same attraction he had felt earlier, not so much sexual as magnetic, as if he were being pulled toward her by some irresistible, invisible force.

She looked as if she were about to cry.

Jenkins reached down and drew a hand across his face – and Wright could no longer see. Before he could panic, the darkness was filled with dancing sparks of light, like embers flying from a fire. He felt his feet becoming cold first, then the chill spread upwards through his legs, his torso, filling his chest, his lungs, numbing them. But he could still feel his heart and the top of his head.

No joke, I'm really dead.

Sparks filled the darkness. No, they were not sparks at all, but some small creatures akin to fireflies dancing in the dark spaces of his mind. In sync to a choreography all their own, the sparks condensed into a single flickering, dying flame like a guttering candle. The center of the flame was yellow, surrounded by a dark line, then an aura of blue flame. Wright would have felt at peace except for a magnetic pull that tugged at him, swinging his attention back and forth. Though he remained blind, he recognized the pull was coming from Laura Jacobsen as she moved about the room.

Why her? Why now?

The flame flickered out but instead of darkness, his mind filled with a vivid white light. The light was the quality of moonlight, except it had no center, no graduations of intensity, just an even, serene glow. Wright was without memories, without a past, without a future, but still something distinct, something apart from everything else – an "I."

The light of the mind intensified, becoming orange and bright, the mind itself becoming more vivid than anything it had ever experienced. The sense of being apart from everything faded but didn't quite disappear.

Now, the orange light deepened until it was nearly black. But it was not the black of an absence of light. The darkness glowed, as if it were on the verge of turning into a clear pure light. The mind yearned for this clear light, this ultimate pureness. The light became the mind, the mind became the light, and . . .

Wright awoke with a start. He was staring at the ceiling. He was able to look around the room now, happy to be back in his body.

But it was a bittersweet happiness because he yearned to return to that clear pure light of being again.

He found he could move his hands, too. Had it all been a dream? He brought a hand up to his head, his fingers searching his scalp until they found the blood-crusted hair, then the edge of the hole.

His impulse was to stick a finger down the hole and find out if indeed his skull was truely empty, but the thought of doing so made him reel. As beautiful as the world of clear, pure radiant light had been, he felt he had unfinished business in this world and didn't want to go into another fugue.

The vision faded more. He felt the hint of a memory of another time, before he had awakened on Lost Lake beach. He had walked across the woods after he left the beach; he remembered that well enough. And the strange thing was that as he remembered a time of stumbling through undergrowth and around downed trees, then he "remembered" himself "remembering" his journey from the stage of mirage to smoke and clouds to the moment of clear light – but he couldn't remember it directly. There was something about clowns, but they seemed as alien to the crystalline desert as he was. He became "removed" from the memory, only able to access it by remembering himself remembering it. It was a memory twice removed, like something read in a journal he had written but then forgotten.

So seemed the memory of his last life, right up to the time before his wife had become an angel, before he had stuck the cold steel of the .357 barrel in his mouth. If he tried, he could remember the taste of the steel barrel, so it seemed like someone else's memory. His mind reeled again and he suppressed the impulse to fade out. Evidently a memory once or even twice removed was enough to trigger the mind fugue.

Which brought up an interesting question: Where did his mind reside if indeed he had blown out all his brains? Again, he felt dizzy and shut off the speculation. His mind, wherever it was housed, cleared as soon as he let the question drift away unanswered.

There seemed to be a technique to avoiding the fugue. He had to be sensitive to just how much he could dwell on his situation. Evidently, quite a few areas of speculation were off limits. But if he paid attention, sensed the onset of a fugue, and stifled the line of thinking in time, he would be okay. The trick was not to get so hooked by a train of thought that he could not let go of it before he passed out.

He sat up on the gurney, swung his legs around, and hopped to the floor.

For a dead man, I feel really good.

He was losing weight though. His pants were about to fall off, and he had to tighten his belt. How long had it been since he'd eaten? Could he eat? He wasn't really hungry, but he made a mental note to try to eat something later.

Someone - probably Jenkins or Laura – had taken off his boots and set them at the foot of the gurney. He bent over, careful of his degenerated lower lumbar, but found he didn't need to be concerned. The pain that had nagged at him for years was gone. He started to think about how no brain meant there was nowhere for the pain signals to reach, but stopped this introspection when he sensed the beginnings of the fugue. He pulled his mind back to the here and now, and just concentrated on putting on his boots on, focusing on the pleasure of having limber, painless joints, the feel of air entering his nostrils, of ironically, on just feeling so alive, even though he might not be . . . *wait, why should he even be breathing?*

Don't think of it!

He found his boots were stuffed with newspaper. He remembered now; Laura had convinced him to take them off because they had been sloshing wet. The newspapers and towels – both scarce items these days – had soaked up most of the moisture, but the leather was still soggy.

He left the examination room on squishy steps trying to maintain an even state of mind. The clinic halls were empty. Were they avoiding him? Judging from the light streaming in the hall windows, it was mid-morning. He left by the front doors, finding the parking lot empty except for the sheriff's department Chevy Blazer. *Who had driven it from the beach and why here? Jimmy.*

There were no keys in the ignition, but he checked his pocket and found his wallet. Behind the badge was the spare key he always kept as protection for when he absent-mindedly locked his keys inside the vehicle.

If this isn't a case of absent-mindedness, I don't know what is.

But he had to be careful not to think too much about this little pun. Or the other joke that came to mind, such as being guilty of DWAB – driving without a brain.

He laughed despite the morbidness of the thought.

The laugh echoed strangely in his sinuses.

It was a ten-minute drive to his house. He found it locked up tight as he had left it, but he had a spare key for the back door as well, this one left under a stone paver in the back patio. He let himself in and stepped into the kitchen. It had been a week since the kitchen floor had been mopped, but the house still smelled of the pine-scented cleaner that Marguerite had been so fond of using.

He tried not to think of what Marguerite had become; to do so was too painful.

He ran the sink faucet and got hot water in a couple of minutes, happy he still had propane for the water heater.

In the refrigerator he found a raw round steak that was brownish but smelled normal. There was also deer meat jerky that he had processed and dried himself. Evidently the power had been on most of the time he'd been . . . where ever he had been.

But though the meat wasn't spoiled, the thought of eating it disgusted him; so did the thought of the taste of the jerky. He settled on a couple of locally grown apples and opened a can of red beans. A chilled beer was in the fridge, but he took one sip and spat it out in the sink. It tasted like gasoline. He settled for tap water – the local supply was fed by an artisan well. It tasted wonderful.

He felt his energy building with each bite and sip of water.

The only weird part was that the red beans kept getting lodged in the hole in his upper pallet where the bullet had entered. After a near-fugue episode, he learned to rinse the beans out of the hole with a kind of snorting/gargling action. Visualizing them ending up inside his empty skull, rattling around in there, like pebbles in a maraca, both made him laugh and become fugue-prone again, so he concentrated on chewing and swallowing.

With his hunger satisfied – and feeling happy that it had been so easy to do so – the next step was to clean up.

He undressed silently in the bathroom. From the look of his jeans he must of spent one his blackouts crawling on his knees. There were briars embedded in the denim, but the skin of his knees seemed to have escaped unscathed. He took off his blue shirt and found the back of it covered in dried blood. He tried not to think about the little breadcrumb-sized bits of gray flesh stuck to the blackened stain.

He stripped off his shorts and panicked: All of his pubic hair was gone. He was as bare as prepubescent boy. Most of his chest and leg hair was gone, too. Was there some reason they might have shaved him at the clinic? His skin didn't feel stubbly or raw.

He found most of the lost hair in the legs of his jeans and on the inside of the shirt. He hadn't been shaved; he had shed.

What next? Would he be coughing up hair balls?

He turned on the shower, and while waiting for the water to get hot, he looked for soap and shampoo. He found a bar of soap in the medicine cabinet amid Marguerite's numerous bottles of facial creams and lotions. The soap was lilac-scented, but it would have to do. The smell of her before she became an angel was also in the medicine cabinet, and it elicited a feeling of profound loneliness, a feeling so strong that his knees weakened and he had to sit on the edge of the bathtub until it passed. The spray of hot water on his back was calming, and he stepped into the full stream of the spray.

I'm forgetting something . . .

Hot water immediately began gushing out of his mouth and down his throat.

He danced out of the streaming shower, bent over so the water would drain, and coughed up gouts of water filled with chunks of clotted blood and tissue. The sight and sound of water sloshing around in his head almost sent him into another fugue. He caught hold of the plastic shower curtain and shook his head until a red bean came out with the blood and tissue. The bean was caught in the vortex of the whirlpool at the bottom of the tub and went round and round, hypnotically, until it disappeared down the drain.

In another minute the water cleared of blood, and he continued showering, concentrating on the image of the swirling red bean to keep his mind off the surrealism of his situation. He tilted his head back so he could wash his face and shoulders but keep the water out of the hole in his head. Then he did the same with his back, this time tipping his head forward.

He would have liked to shampoo his hair but didn't care.

By the time he finished, he almost felt like a normal human being. His mind kept wanting to return to the question of how he could be conscious, how he could think, how he could feel the pain of lost love, without a brain. Was this just a walking dream? Had he never pulled he trigger? Or had he pulled the trigger and somehow bungled the job? Perhaps he was lying in a hospital ward now, brain-damaged but not brain-dead, dreaming a brain-damaged dream.

He shook his head. It should feel light without the three pounds of gray tissue, but it didn't. He entertained this thought for a while before he realized it should have triggered a fugue.

He toweled dry, including his hair, and dressed in clean jeans and shirt. Marguerite, with her perpetual house-frau sense of responsibility, had apparently washed and ironed all his clothes before running off with one the angels.

Combing his hair caused him to pause for a moment. He avoided looking at the top of his head in the mirror and settled on a kind of comb-over style to cover the hole. Luckily this was possible as he had a full head of hair.

Now what do I do with myself?

Without Marguerite, the house seemed as empty as his head, and he was overwhelmed momentarly with heartbreak and loneliness, and his deathwish returned. But he had tried to die and failed, so what was left?

The answer came immediately: his job. He used to take satisfaction in being a sheriff. Early in his career, he felt lhe was a good one, an honest one, before the compromises to get re-elected had become too great. There was a time he thought of himself as performing a public service, not just a stop-and-ticket cop, but a protect-and-serve public servant.

He pulled on his boots over freshly laundered white socks. He was about to strap on his service revolver but on second thought left it on the couch. What would the bad boys do if they wanted to resist arrest? Shoot him in the head?

As he drove back to town, he concentrated on the sound of gravel crunching under the tires and the sky, which was now clear and blue.

He found the door to the sheriff's office ajar. Inside, Jimmy Harte, his deputy, was slouched in an office chair, his alligator-skin cowboy boots up on the desk, and his Stetson tipped down over his eyes.

"Kind of early in the day for a siesta, isn't it?" Wright asked.

Despite himself, Wright laughed when Jimmy fell backwards and went sprawling.

The deputy picked himself up and looked forlornly at his crumpled Stetson. Wright noticed a piece of white tape had been stuck on the Sheriff's lanyard badge where "John Wright" was printed. "James Harte" had been scrawled on the tape in blue ballpoint ink.

Wright pointed at the badge and said, "Kind of presumptuous, don't you think?"

"I thought you were dead."

"The reports of my death were NOT greatly exaggerated," he said.

"What?"

"Never mind," Wright said. "Let's just say that I was injured but, as you can see, I'm still walking and talking."

"Yes, sir."

"Any calls?"

"Just one, but the phones haven't worked good today."

"What was it?"

"I don't know. Maybe thieves stole the phone lines to sell the copper."

"I meant what was the call about?"

"Oh, that." Jimmy's hands were nervously trying to push the

dents out of his hat. "Just some off-his-nut farmer. Something about his cows giving birth to little angels – cherubs, he called them."

"You didn't believe him?"

"No. Would you?"

"I don't know. A lot of weird shit has been happening lately," Wright said.

Funny, a hundred seven-foot tall archangels crash-land outside of town in a huge flying saucer. They abduct women and men, implant homunculi – seeds of themselves – that turn the humans into angel/human hybrids, and my deputy has trouble believing that dairy cows can give birth to cherubs.

For a moment he considered having Jimmy peer down the one-inch diameter hole in the top of his head and into his empty braincase. Would he believe that?

Wright paused. Odd that the thought of the hole in his head didn't cause him to fall into a fugue now. Was he becoming acclimated? As for Jimmy, he was one of those people who were in a permanent fugue. They appeared conscious, but were oblivious to anything they couldn't fit into their concept of reality, sort of a zombie state as well — if you thought about it. Maybe that was the secret. He had come to accept the hole in his head as just one of those unexplainable facts of life, such as love or the nature of consciousness itself.

This last thought surprised Wright. Where had that come from? He was beginning to sound like an intellectual; like Uncle Robert.

"Who was it that reported the cherubs, Jimmy?'

"Ben Cartwright."

"Ol' Bonanza Ben, huh?" Wright knew the man well. They had been buddies in high school. Ben had taken ribbings daily because of his name and the television show, which was only in reruns even then.

The odd thing was as Ben grew up, he began to look like an over-sized version of his television namesake. Big, broad-shouldered, with craggy features, like the father, but more the size of the son, Hoss.

Ben had a bit of the conspiracy theorist in him. The federal government was usually the conspirator, the force behind anything he considered unusual or unfair. Communist plots were a strong second string. But Cartwright wasn't a liar. He didn't make things up, he just misinterpreted.

"Yep."

"Well, I tell you what, Deputy." He put extra emphasis on the word "deputy."

"Yes, sir." Jimmy seemed more or less satisfied with his hat and put it on. It still looked as if it had been tromped on by a thousand-pound steer.

"I'm going to drive out and talk to Cartwright. You stay here and mind the shop."

"Yes, sir."

"And, Jimmy, one other thing." It was all he could do to not laugh at his deputy's sad-looking hat.

"Yes, sir."

"Take that piece-of-shit tape off my ID and give it back to me."

* * *

4.

Your Heart, a Secret Document, Lies

When I saw that clumsy crow
Flop from a wasted tree
A shape in the mind rose up
Over the gulfs of dream
Further and further back
Into a moonless black
Deep in the brain, far back
–T Roethke

Bryan.

Bryan Douglas walked the three miles to the Jacobsen Manse with dread, knowing with certainty what Laura was going to tell him. How did he know? The simple fact that she wanted to meet him at her Uncle Robert's house instead of her basement apartment was a sign. There she could break up with him safely. She probably feared a scene – maybe that he would toss furniture about or threaten her physically. Violence in connection with sex was a deep-rooted fear for her. He had repeatedly tried to assure her that he was not the kind of man whose brain's wiring for sex and violence were entangled. He just was not the violent type, period. He had never struck a woman, even in self-defense.

But he knew enough about Laura's history to know why she would reflexively fear violence from a man, particularly a lover, particularly someone whom she had learned to trust. He didn't know all the details, but it had something to do with her being abused as a child by her schizophrenic father. There had been violence, confinement for days in a closet, a knife held to her throat. He wasn't sure if there had been rape, but he assumed so.

The wounds of childhood abuse by a parent go deep, and though he wasn't a student of such things, the signs were plain enough to see in Laura long before they became involved. For example there was her need to either completely control her lover – or be completely controlled by him. There seemed to be no middle ground with Laura.

And he had his own personal demons, too. Why else would he fall in love with someone so emotionally flawed? Was he in love? It didn't seem a manly thing to admit that he might be prone to loving women who would ultimately reject him, but there was no mistaking how this relationship patterned ones of his past. The difference was, where he could just walk away from previous lovers, he couldn't think about anything else but her. As painful as it was to be with her, he didn't feel complete without her. And he was in tune enough with her emotions at this point that he didn't need any overt signs to know that the end was coming.

What troubled him just as much as losing her was the illumination his obsession cast upon his own psychological makeup. He was beginning to suspect that he was attracted as much as anything to her dark troubled soul and further shackled by the constant threat of her rejection. Would he have been so attracted to exactly the same Laura but without the neuroses, one who hadn't been abused as a child, a Laura who could loved and accept him as he was – as he did her?

What the hell was wrong with him? Why did he have to be so needy?

And there was the fact that he was attracted to her not just on a physical level before she had said a word to him. He had an unshakeable impression that he had met her before. What was that all about?

He remembered the first time he had admitted to himself that he was in love with her, not just attracted, not just in lust, but an old-fashion, chest-beating, throw-himself-off-a-cliff-to-please-her love.

The affiar began back in Columbia, a year before the angel saucer fell to Earth. They had just come out of a journalism class, that day, but their paths had crossed several times before. It was a large campus, host to more than forty thousand students from September through May.

They also had another class together, an introduction to Buddhism, and they both visited a meditation hall where they often showed up at the same time for the group sits. Neither of them bought into the reincarnation thing, but they joked that they were karmically entwined. (The joke was that they were 'komically' entwined.) He was drawn to her then, but she was involved in an exclusive relationship, one that for a while she expected to lead to marriage. There was the unspoken understanding that she and Bryan were just to be good friends, that is to say, friends without benefits, intimate confidants all the same.

He knew whom she was involved with: the professor of their journalism class. Moreover, the professor, who was in his late forties, had become increasingly possessive and controlling to the point of being abusive. As time went on, she wanted out of the relationship but feared what he would harm her academic career out of revenge. She had told Bryan all this and more.

Standing in the middle of the hallway, she had told him how now her professor-lover had ridiculed her interest in Buddhism and meditation, things that had been her last sane refuges. Also, he had learned of her history of childhood abuse and used it as emotional blackmail. She was deeply unhappy.

"It's not my business to tell you how to run your life," he said to her on that day as other students passed by in the hall, "but I think you need to find someone – I mean some way – to have time for yourself, just yourself, each day, whether for meditation or whatever."

Her face softened, her eyes moistened. There was a foot of distance them as they stood to talk, and he was at least eight inches taller than she was. She seemed to be straining toward him, trying to close that distance by will alone. Conversations continued around them, people talking in twos and threes, but their voices came from far away. Something primal, a mixture of lust, compassion and protectiveness, stirred in Bryan asin response to her yearning; it took all his will power NOT to step forward and kiss and hold her.

All he had meant to do was express concern for her welfare.

Despite all her successes, her perfect grade-point average, despite her hovering on the edge of being beautiful, despite her coming from a family with some means, despite a promising career in whatever she chose to do, she was miserable and starved for affection, for understanding, for a touch, at least the affirmation that she was desirable. He reminded himself that her professor-lover was a powerful figure on campus. The professor posed no problem for Bryan personally because he was planning to drop out of college even then. But for Laura, his vindictiveness could spell disaster. It was a kind of karmic realism: A kiss here in public or even an intimate hug, and her promising academic career might be ruined by the jealous, vindictive professor.

He forced himself to take a half-step back. Disappointment flickered across her features to be replaced by her usual calm resolve – and a hint of resentment.

A movement high above caught in the corner of his eye and brought him back to the here and now. The sky was aqua blue, not a cloud in sight. An angel flew sluggishly toward the east, so high as to be nearly indistinguishable. No, wait. He counted wings. There were at least two angels and they carried something large. They were either struggling to hold onto their burden or fighting over it. As he watched, they seemed to hang motionless for a moment. Then they dropped whatever it was they carried. They both raced after it, and caught it about a hundred feet above the ground.

They hovered again, their wings entangling, as they battling over a large black, white and red blotch against the blue sky.

Bryan guessed what it was before he heard it moo.

Without warning, they dropped the cow, and the animal picked up speed as it hurtled toward an inevitable impact in the distant woods. Its bellowing moos were distorted by the Doppler effect as it fell.

The angels flew higher, passing out of the range of his vision. The cow crashed in the woods a hundred yards away. It mooed no more.

He didn't know whether he was amused or frightened. Why would angels be fighting over a cow? It was ridiculous; they had looked like giant pigeons squabbling over a piece of bread. On the other hand, some of the angel/human hybrids were rumored to be insane, which was a terrifying thought. The cow they had tormented and then abandoned to gravity could have as well been a human being.

He scanned the sky, but there were no other angels in sight. A robin chirped to the right. From far off, came the chug-a-chug sound of a farm tractor. The gravel crunched under his feet as he began walking again. It was as if the surrealistic scene he had just witnessed had never happened, and he trudged on, his mind pulled back to that time in Columbia when he had tried to do the right thing for Laura. An unspoken contract had been formulated at the moment he had stepped back from her. They could not return to be even casual friends. No more conversations in the hall after class. They gave each other perfunctory nods in the meditation hall and sat in different rows in their common classes, but never said anything more than "Hi" or "Hello."

He felt he had cast himself into hell by an obscure sin of inaction.

Then one night, while he was systematically getting drunk at Shakespeare's Bar and Pizza, Laura had come in and sat next to him. He didn't recognize her at first. She had cut her long black hair short, almost boyish short. And instead of baby-doll tight blue jeans, she wore a suit – not a women's business power outfit, but a young man's black pinstripe jacket and slacks, complete with skinny black tie. He was sitting by himself in a booth large enough for four, but instead of sitting on the other side of the booth, she sat next to him, close enough that their thighs touched. She put an arm around his waist and leaned her head on his shoulder. They sat that way, silent, not speaking, for an hour, finishing off a bottle of cheap nouveau red wine.

Leaving Shakespeare's, they walked the five blocks to his apartment, still not speaking, more tipsy than drunk, holding hands and sharing a joint.

At his tiny apartment, she broke the silence with an abbreviated laugh when he unfolded the Murphy bed out of the wall. She sat on the edge of the bed, bouncing up and down a bit, smiling at the squeaky springs. They undressed quietly, watching each other. She stopped at her bra and bikini panties; surprisingly, both garments were pink with little embroidered roses, very girly-girl in comparison with the mannish suit that had hidden them.

He stripped all the way, glad to free his erection from the confines of his boxer shorts.

When he tried to help her remove her panties, she slapped his hands away and took the panties off herself as she sat on the edge of the bed. He sat beside on the bed and tried to kiss her, but she turned away so quickly that the kiss landed on her cheek. By the way she suddenly tensed up, he expected everything might stop right there, despite their being naked together; that she would say, something like "This is a mistake," or "I can't do this." But she surprised him by quickly standing up and pushing him back on the bed. It wasn't a gentle push. She was strong, and it was more like a shove from a man trying to start a fight, and it triggered a primordial anger in him. He repressed the anger, let himself be pushed back, and was rewarded for his passivity by her straddling him in a quick, athletic move.

The mood of tenderness they had shared in the bar was history. She grabbed his penis but didn't impale herself on it. Instead, she pushed it flat against his stomach, and with one hand on the tip and other spreading her labia, she squatted on top of him. He was in the grove of her sex, but not inside her. Thus positioned, she leaned forward and worked her hips so that her clitoris, now the size of a hard pea, rubbed right up under his glans.

"Lie still!" she commanded, with the tone of a dominatrix.

And he tried, but his hips had a will of their own, and he thrust back hard, almost bucking her off. She slammed her open palm against the center of his chest, nearly knocking the wind out of him.

"What the . . . ?" he tried to say, but she put a hand on his mouth, pressing down hard enough to hurt a little. He could have knocked her away – he was at least fifty pounds heavier than she and strong from spending afternoons in the student commons gym – but he just laid there, entranced by her intensity.

She lifted up her arms, laced her fingers, and rested her hands on top of her head. The posture raised her breasts and, though she supported part of her weight on her knees that still straddled his hips, put considerably more pressure on his penis. Her clit further enlarged, emerging from its little hood; her breasts flushed, and her breath came in short gasps. She held her arms out like wings.

He was lost. Her intensity was hypnotic. She was his dark angel. He came to the verge of orgasm again and again but didn't ejaculate. Was he was restrained by something in her posture or in the actual physical threat that the hundred-and-ten-pound woman now manifested? His level of arousal was so intense it was painful, but he couldn't cum. Laura seemed to be enveloped in a sheen of golden light. Maybe if he closed his eyes, if he couldn't see her breasts gently swaying as she ground the vestibule of her vagina against the underside of his penis, he would be able to cum and thus be set free.

Laura began to spasm. There was no other word for it. The grinding until now had been restrained to her hips, but the undulations spread up her entire body, making her slowly writhe like a belly dancer. She rose up and slipped him inside her. Her vagina clenched tightly around him; he came almost immediately, and she rolled off him just as quickly.

He gasped for breath. He hadn't been breathing but didn't realize it until now.

Laura said, "He's dead."

"Who's dead?" His mind was fuzzy from the orgasm, and the truth was at that moment he really didn't care.

"Professor Stephens. He died of a heart attack this afternoon. He was jogging with one of his adult sons and died in mid-stride." She said this as if reporting that her car had a flat tire.

She rolled away from him and pulled a sheet up over her shoulders. "This was the son-of-bitch's wake."

Bryan knew if he had been wise, he would have gotten out of bed then, pulled on his pants and shirt and left. Maybe he would have if they'd not been in his apartment. No, that wasn't it. At that moment, he had an epiphany: The very fact that Laura was so darkly disturbed made her irresistible. If he turned his back on her now, he would never feel complete again. He was hooked, and the lovesick feeling in his gut and chest terrified him.

CLUMP! A large mass of bloody red flesh, laced with even darker red veins, fell at his feet. He had been standing still in the middle of the gravel road, lost in the memory of the first time with Laura. He stared at the lump of bloody flesh. It appeared to be a sort of bloody sack.

Something inside the bag twitched and squirmed.

As he watched a tiny hand with chubby fingers and black nails – almost but not quite human – pushed its way out a hole in the sack. The hand clenched into a tiny fist, squishing out semi-congealed blood between the fingers. The fist clenched so hard Bryan could hear the tiny joints pop before the hand went limp.

He heard laughter from above, and looked up to see angels again, this time flying from the woods where the cow had landed. Were they the same angels who had dropped the cow? He couldn't tell and didn't want to wait around for the perverse flying motherfuckers to show him.

Laura.

Laura watched from an upstairs window as Bryan ran up the driveway toward the house. He wasn't jogging but running full speed. He stopped about halfway, red in the face, his shirt soaked with sweat, and turned to look behind him toward the woods. Then he looked up, cringed, and began running again. She tried to look where he had looked but the awning over the window obscured her vision, giving her only a brief tantalizing glimpse of wings high in the sky. He had seemed to bring out the worse in the archangels, and now no doubt he was having an issue with the hybrids.

She mentally sighed and started downstairs. The front door was locked. She would have to let him in before he had a seizure. He would be an emotional basket case again, which stirred something in her, something akin to what made her take in lost puppies. But she was determined to make a clean break with him today, even if he was on the verge of a nervous breakdown. Besides, she reminded herself, if his psychoses were angel-induced, all he needed to do was stay away from the creatures. Which was all the more reason for her to end the relationship. She planned to spend a lot of time in the company of angels. As Bryan couldn't tolerate angels, better that he wasn't around her.

Besides all that, she actually liked him, but knew that she would hurt anyone who tried to get too close. Face it, she didn't love him. Not romantically. The chemistry wasn't there.

She reached the front door and unlocked it just as Bryan trod up the porch steps. The hinges squeaked, grating on her nerves, as she opened the door.

He stepped in, smelling of sweat and road dust. It was a smell she was getting used to. With the breakdown of modern commerce, such things as mass-produced deodorants and colognes were in short supply, as was hot water for showers and baths. His smell wasn't that unpleasant, but for some reason, the odd odor that John Wright's moribund body exuded came to mind. Bryan's odor was just a mild musk, and though not repulsive, it wasn't pleasing either.

Wright's smell, in contrast, had been more a fragrance than an odor, like the hint of a man's expensive aftershave, one that seem locked in her memory and recalled from the back of her mind, like a forgotten dream, unearthly yet fecund with associations. *Curious.* But whatever Wright smelled like, it was certainly not the effluvium that one would expect a walking corpse to have. Perhaps the scent was something that had rubbed off from Marguerite. She made a mental note to check if any of the angels exuded a compelling scent the next time she was close to one.

"What was all that about?" she asked.

"Fucking crazy angels," he said between gasps for air. "I think one of them was May. They tried to drop something on me."

Before her conversion to an angel, May Tyre had been a waitress at Boucher's, the same restaurant Laura where had worked at when she returned to Creedance after dropping out of school. May had very little formal education and had worn enough blue eye shadow to paint a car. Yet she and May had developed an odd kind of friendship, unlike any other girlfriend-type relationship she'd ever had. Why? May was unabashedly without shame; without shame about sex, without shame or guilt about practically anything. It was a state of mind that Laura had been trying to cultivate most of her life, and May came about it naturally.

But May had seduced an archangel before the creatures had

fully understood the physical and spiritual nature of humans, and the implantation of the angel homunculus had been bloody and painful. May's mind had been damaged in the process, but it had not been an intentionally evil act by the angel. The creatures did not know evil, at least not in the way humans did. Instead, it had been an act of incompetence, but May had suffered terrible consequences nonetheless.

Laura walked past Bryan and stepped out on the porch. She scanned the sky but saw no signs of angels. Too bad. She wondered if May the angel, though deranged, would recognize her.

"What do you see?" Bryan called from the doorway.

"Nothing. Nada," she said.

"Come inside. Lock the door. They might come back."

Actually, crazy or not, she hoped they would come back but didn't say so. Disappointed, she stepped back in the house. Bryan closed the heavy door behind her and latched the deadbolt. She thought of reminding him that the angels were so strong a mere two-inch-thick oak door wasn't going to stop them. Moreover, if they had wanted to do him harm, they could do so. But he was so overwrought and vulnerable, which reminded her why she wanted to break up with him. He brought out conflicting emotions in her; first she felt nurturing toward him, then turned-on, then angry enough to want to hurt him.

"Bryan . . ." she started.

"What?" he gave her that lost puppy-dog look.

"Follow me," she said and led him up the stairs. Something about him clumping along behind her, his scent now stronger than ever, the slight rasping of his accelerated breathing, made the fine hairs on the back of her neck stand up.

"You know," he said, "I'm so glad you let your hair grow back out. That time you bobbed it after the professor died – I don't know – it was like you were mutilating yourself." He reached up and stroked the back of her head.

She turned without thinking and knocked his hand away, then slapped him hard. He started to fall backwards, but caught hold of the banister.

He should have hit her back. Most men in her life would have done so. But not Bryan. He just stood there looking shocked and hurt. His cheek was red from the slap.

"Why?" he asked.

Why indeed? Maybe what made her angry was that he knew as well as she did that the relationship wasn't working. That in the long run, the relationship wasn't good for either of them.

If he were any kind of a man, he would be strong and end it himself. More than that, if he were smart, he'd realize that she was inherently flawed and that she was eventually going hurt him a lot more than just slapping him around.

"Sorry," she managed to say. "That time, back in college, I was extremely angry. Angry with myself for putting up with that sap, angry with him for taking advantage of me after I confided in him, angry at everything. I guess you brought back all that anger just now."

She had meant to lie to him, but this felt too close to the truth.

"I understand," he said, rubbing his cheek. "I should have known better than to stir up those memories. I'm a real idiot."

And he was an idiot all right. A idiot for buying that load of shit from her in the first place.

Now she was more determined than ever to end it with him. Given her family's history of abusing those they cared about, if she truly was becoming schizophrenic, he might even get killed. It was up to her. Things had to end today or they would end very badly later on. He needed – deserved – to be let down gently. She just didn't know how to do it. She felt out of control again. What had she intended to do with him upstairs? Fuck him as part of a farewell gift? Show him that fucking had nothing in common with intimacy and trust? What the hell was she doing?

She sat down on a step, facing him.

"It's over," she said. "I never want to see you again."

He just stood there.

"Aren't you going to say anything?" she said.

"We went through this before, back in college."

"Yes."

"It was exactly like this. I thought things were going well, that we were moving beyond just fucking. That we were getting closer. You told me you loved me. Then almost immediately afterward, you threw me out, dumped me hard."

"Yes," she said. "But it's different this time. This time, I mean it. I've told other men I loved them and thought I meant it. This is different. You should leave me, because I'll totally mind-fuck anyone I love. That's what Jacobsens do.

"Different?" he asked.

"What?"

"You said it's different this time."

"Yes, different," she said. "This time I know I'm doing it for your own good."

"How is it for my own good? Tell me the fuck that."

"Bryan, just leave. Or if you're afraid of the angels, you can wait downstairs. I'm going to take a nap now, and I don't want you to follow me." She turned and walked across the landing, half hoping he would follow her. "I just don't want to play nursemaid to you anymore."

She took the second door and entered her grandmother's bedroom and flopped down on her back on the big king-sized bed. Above her head, was her Aunt Sophia's mural opus, her equivalent of the Sistine Chapel. The dominant colors were pink and baby blue. Off-center, to the right of the light fixture, a pair of lovers, the woman as big as a cow, the man dark and animal-like, were entangled in an acrobatic tryst. Around them, Raphael-like chubby cherubs hovered, laughing, pointing fingers at the lovers.

A few minutes later, she heard the front door being unlocked, then slammed shut.

The ceiling was like a prophetic vision. Sophia had painted it nearly a decade before the archangels arrived.

Laura and Bryan had made love – not just fucked, but bonded somehow – in this room less than a week ago. She had thought that the Jacobsen curse – more specifically, her personal demons – might have been exorcised then. Did she really know what she was doing?

Something pounded into the bedroom window. She got up to check, expecting to find an angel. Instead, she found a small blood spat-ter on a cracked windowpane. A dead dove lay on the sill, its head torn off. She felt like she living an Emily Dickinson poem: *Hope is the thing with feathers that perches in the soul.*

* * *

5.

Under a Swarm of Cherubs

Wright.

Wright's drive to Ben Cartwright's ranch would have been uneventful except for the terrorist sparrow.

He had been driving down Old Buffalo Road with the windows down, enjoying the feel of the fresh morning air, the disturbing shower scene nearly forgotten, when the attack happened.

The sounds of spring overlaid the crunch of the gravel beneath the SUV's tires and the roar of the engine. As he rounded a corner, a flock of sparrows flushed from a roadside hedge. Four or five sparrows rushed through the open passenger-side window and flittered about, panicking, madly chirping about the inside of the SUV.

The sparrow invasion startled him, but not so much he was in danger of losing control of the car. The SUV had never been properly converted to a police vehicle and had no divider between the back and the front seats. All but one of the birds quickly flew to the back of SUV, bouncing mindlessly off the back window. One sparrow, either by chance or by having a few more sparrow brain cells, perched on the rearview mirror, cocked its head to one side and stared at him.

The power back windows still worked, and Wright rolled them down with a touch of a button. The birds in the back made their escape in an instant. The smart-ass sparrow, however, remained perched on the rearview mirror, and seemed more interested in Wright than escaping.

"What's the matter, bird?" Wright said. "Tired of flying? Want to hitchhike? Careful, I'm the law in these parts; I might have to arrest you for vagrancy."

He could have sworn the bird winked at him. He laughed and was surprised at the sound . His laugh had a booming resonance, almost a reverb, and seem to project from above his head. The tonal change must have had something to do with sound waves from his throat passing through the hole in his head and resonating inside his skull. This thought should have cast him into a fugue but didn't.

What would happen if he put his hand on top of the hole in his cranium when he laughed? Could he do that thing that trumpet players do?

The sparrow continued to stare at him, cocking its head one way, then the other.

"What do you think, bird?" he said. "Do you think I could make my laugh go whah-whah?"

In lieu of an answer, the sparrow hopped from its perch to the top of his head. Wright grabbed for it, but it dropped through the hole and into his empty skull.

He slammed on the brakes, nearly broadsiding into the ditch. He sat there as the dust settled around the SUV, afraid to move, afraid to think. He had the weirdest impression of his eyeballs turning backwards and watching the sparrow inside his skull. The bird was just sitting there in the middle of a pool of light that spilled down from the hole. The background to this scene – whatever was left of his brain, if anything – was in shadow, which was a good thing.

The impression of his eyes actually looking into his skull – of getting stuck that way – was so strong that he had to check his eyeballs in the rearview mirror to make sure they were not turned around backwards. He was relieved to find his eyes staring back at him, apparently normal except for a deer-in-the-headlights look. As he watched, the fucking sparrow popped up out the top of his head like a sprung jack-in-the box. He grabbed at it agin, but it retreated too fast and all he succeeded in doing was to give himself a Three-Stooges slap on his head.

He laughed aloud, and that seemed to make the bird flutter

about wildly in there.

What to do? He couldn't have the thing in there, flitting around in his head, dropping little runny white globules of bird shit everywhere. Another strange idea sprang to mind: of his head splitting open like a huge egg and a hundred fledglings flying forth, all of them with little human faces – his face. The thought made him gag. He shook his head violently, in part to dispel the hatchling vision, in part to evict the god-damned bird.

All the shaking did was to make him dizzy.

Another idea came to him, this one more to be his own making. He would drown the little fucker! He climbed out of the vehicle and opened the back hatch. Good, the blue and white beer cooler he had set in the back more than a week earlier was still there. Now if Jimmy hadn't discovered the remaining beers inside.

Yes, there were two long-necked bottles of Schlitz sloshing about in a few inches of tepid water. He opened one – they were twist tops, thank God. He put his left hand up to find the hole in his head. The hole seemed smaller than he remembered it. Brushing aside the hair, he hesitated for just a moment, then upended the bottle into the hole. The warm beer glugged down into his skull. In a second, he tasted the beer as it drained through the hole in his palate.

Chirp! Chirp! Chirp!

He couldn't feel it, but he could hear the bird fluttering its wings inside his head.

The taste of the beer changed, a flavor he couldn't identify. What was the bird doing in there?

Throwing the bottle aside, he knelt and put both hands down on the gravel and dropped his head forward, like a monk kowtowing to a heathen god. The beer drained out slowly, forming a sudsy pool on the road, but no bird; no sign of his inner tenant, not so much as a feather or a bird doodle.

Wright got off his knees – the gravel hurt – and sat with his back against the Blazer's rear tire. The sun, though still hidden by the forest, spiked the aqua-blue sky with a radiant rays of golden light. The birds in the roadside bushes had been quiet after his near-accident but now started up their daily ministrations of chirping and singing. Another sparrow perch on a nearby limb hunging out over the ditch. It was indistinguishable from the one that had flown into his head, and it was examining him. Wright watched it with trepidation. He wanted to put his hand over the hole to prevent a second bird from setting up housekeeping, but still hoped the current resident would tire of the confinements and check out.

Was it still in there? He tried looking inward again and was rewarded with a vision of a bird rustling its feathers to rid itself of drops of beer. To support this vision, a trickle of tangy liquid dribbled down from the hole in his palate to his tongue.

He spat it out.

The absurdity of his situation overwhelmed him, and a chuckle rose in his throat, grew to a chortle, then blossomed into a booming laugh he couldn't control. The tonal quality of the laugh was hard to describe; it was in part like something a whale might emit but mixed with the laugh of an grossly obese man, raising in volume until the woods echoed with it.

With an audible POP! the sparrow exploded out of the hole, expelled by the booming laugh.

Still laughing, Wright rose to his feet and retrieved the other bottle of beer from the cooler. He couldn't decide at first whether to drink it or use it to flush out anything the bird had left behind. After some thought about the scarcity of bottle beer these days – hot or cool – he decided to drink it. He climbed back into the driver's seat and sipped on the longneck bottle. It was violation of police ethics, but he felt he deserved a respite, and besides, it was the best beer he had ever tasted.

The taste was still with him all the way at turn-off to the Cartwright farm. And the fact that he had no brain to house the mind that remembered the pleasure no longer bothered him. Who cared where memories resided as long as he had them.

More sparrows were flushed from the brushy roadside as he drove. He considered rolling up the windows. But the cool, clean air on his face was too refreshing to give up. He pulled over and rummaged in the back seat until he found a blue baseball cap from the sheriff's department baseball team, a leftover from a past life. The slogan, "The Authority," was embroidered across the front in gold thread.

Wright was still wearing the cap as he pulled into Cartwright's drive. The house and barn were set about a hundred yards back from the road. As Wright neared the house – really a doublewide trailer with a log facade – Cartwright stepped out on the porch and waved.

Over the front door was a wooden sign with "Ponderosa" carved on it and painted in red letters. Originally it had been a joke on Ben's name, but the name had stuck, and the ranch had become know locally as the Ponderosa, though local wits often called it "the Ponderous" with a smirk, a reference not to the size to the ranch but to that of the ranch owner.

Cartwright was a big man, more than six feet, six inches tall. He and Wright had gone to junior high and high school together, even buddied-up for a while, tipping beer cans together on country roads, way back when they were too stupid to do much else with their time. They had fallen out when Wright had gone away to college for a couple of years. When Wright came back to Creedance, Cartwright had settled down to run a full-time beef cattle operation.

Cartwright was bipolar, what was called manic-depressive when they were in school. The latter term was much more descriptive. He had been diagnosed in junior high after feeding all his father's prize-winning, pedigree basset hounds through a wood chipper while in a manic state.

Later, on bipolar medication and over a beer, Cartwright had confided to Wright that he hadn't meant to be sadistic or cruel. Nor had he done in to get even with his father.

"I really thought I was doing the ugly, misshapen creatures a favor," he had told Wright over a Miller's High-Life beer on that simmering summer evening. "I felt they had been screwed by some fuck-up god, and by chipping them I was giving them a chance at rebirth."

Which was a funny story in itself. Cartwright's parents had been Southern Baptists of the no-nonsense, dancing-is-the-devil's-work, fundamentalist genus. But along with the tendency of fate to digress to extremes, the mind Ben Cartwright had been born with was of the free-thinking, dreamer style. He had been a self-professed Buddhist long before his brain chemistry disorder had manifested itself.

Cartwright was an odd sight, even for rural Harmon County. Tall, with shoulder-length prematurely white hair and beard, he dressed in knee-high rubber boots and blue bib overalls. He wore a Bowie knife strapped to his belt.

Knife was a misnomer. About fifteen inches long and with a cross piece, the weapon was more like a short sword than a knife.

Cartwright leaped off the porch and trotted over to the SUV. With his long hair swaying as he ran, he looked like an aged, rampaging Viking warrior. Before Wright could come to a complete stop, Cartwright opened the door and leapt inside in one quick movement.

As he slammed the passenger door, he said: "Hi! Took you long enough to get here, turn right at the gate, good to see you, after all these years, John, I have to say, there, there, no there! You can see the carcasses over by that big oak tree, shit, what a mess!" Cartwright said all this in about one second, but with each syllable clearly enunciated.

"Ben, Ben, slow. . ." Wright started.

"Found them this morning just like that, their jaws gone, their assholes gone, cut like with a cookie cutter, and no blood, can you imagine that, all that cutting and no, no, no blood. . .?"

"Ben, shut the fuck up for a minute – if you can!"

Cartwright looked at Wright, shocked.

"Are you off your meds, Ben?"

"No, no, no, not entirely."

"What does not entirely mean, Ben?"

" I was 'fraid of running out, only had three months supply." He took a deep breath. "Shit, I wish I could slow down."

"So what did you do?"

"About what?"

"About your fear of running out of meds."

Ben took another deep breath. "I started taking it every other day; worked for while."

"Well, it's not working now."

"I thought it was until Suzanne left," Cartwright said. He fished a prescription bottle out of his pocket and put a big pink and green capsule into his mouth. Wright winced as Cartwright swallowed it dry.

"You look different somehow. Younger," Cartwright said.

"I've been sleeping better," Wright said. It was a lie. Except for the fugues, he didn't remember sleeping at all since his suicide.

"You look fitter too, jewel in the lotus, man, you look ten – no fifteen years – younger; I hear Marguerite became one of those things, flew off and left you, zoom, zoom; shit, I feel for you man; Suzanne and I had a fight and she left me two days ago – did I tell you that already? – Anyway, I'm worried more about her than these fucking cows – do you suppose the angels had something to do with Suzanne going away?" Cartwright's voice cracked as the words came rapid-fire.

It had been an odd marriage between a prosperous farmer with an IQ supposedly in the genius level, bipolar or not, and an exceptionally pretty redhead high school dropout, also of high IQ, but more inclined to religiously follow popular music stars than long-dead eastern mystics, a rock-and-roll diamond in the rough. Despite his idiosyncrasies, Cartwright was a thoughtful man in his late thirties at the time Suzanne had moved in with him. Wright had given the relationship a few months, a year at the most; he predicted Suzanne leaving his friend and taking half his assets with her as soon as they passed the common-law marriage time limit.

But he had been proven wrong. The marriage had lasted years, and despite the oddness of the match, seemed relatively stable. Suzanne, at Cartwright's encouragement, had gotten her GED, and before the fall of angel saucers, had been commuting to Columbia to take a college-level class now and then. Though Wright and Cartwright hadn't spoken much for years, he had been happy for his old school chum.

Now this.

"What do you think? Do you think she went away with one of those winged hungry ghosts, voluntary or involuntary or what? Shit!"

"I think you need to calm down a bit, my friend," Wright said, patting him on the shoulder. "How long before your meds take effect?"

"Shit, I don't know. I'm rambling aren't I?" Cartwright scratched his head. "I need all this trouble like I need a hole in the head!"

Wright winced.

"Hey, that's some hat," Cartwright continued, now on a roll. "I thought you didn't like to wear hats. That you believed they'd make you go bald or some such nonsense."

Wright withdrew his hand from Cartwright's shoulder and compulsively straightened his hat. "I thought it would make you respect my AUTHORITY," he said, giving a bad imitation of Cartman.

Cartwright laughed politely, but the joke lost on the big man. Wright remembered now. Ben didn't watch TV at all, even serious stuff, so he wasn't likely to know anything about cartoons.

"I get it. I get it. South Park," Cartwright said.

Feeling like a forty-something retard, Wright was tempted to show his old friend the hole his head, to have him shine a flashlight down into the allegedly empty space between his ears and get him to explain in Buddhist metaphysics how he could have a mind without a brain to house it.

He didn't dare, however. His friend needed his help; he didn't need something else to feed his intellectual mania. Besides having a hole in his head wasn't likely to get Wright any respect.

"Now, Ben, here's what I want you to do. I want you to sit here in the Blazer and try to calm yourself down while I go look at the carcasses. Okay?"

"But John. . .?"

"Shut the fuck up and listen to me, okay?"

Cartwright smiled at him, but his eyes blazed. For moment he seemed to be outlined in a red light, as if God had taken a neon crayon and traced him.

Wright rubbed his eyes and looked again. The aura was gone.

"Something wrong with your eyes, John?"

"No, just allergies, I guess."

"Yeah, Suzanne has problems this time of year. Last year she got a sinus infection and had to take antibiotics. I'm kind of worried about her."

"You used to tell me," Wright interrupted, "something about your Buddha meditation practice."

"Zazen," Cartwright corrected him.

"And another thing I always wondered about, though it's none of my business."

"What?" Cartwright said. His every muscle seemed strained to the point of snapping, like guitar strings tuned too tight.

"I thought Buddhists didn't eat meat, but here you are...?"

"A rancher?"

"Well, yes." Cartwright smiled, relaxing a bit. It was a familiar question, as Wright guessed, and he tried to look puzzled though he knew the answer.

"I don't slaughter. They're thoroughbred animals. Or at least they were." He nodded toward the carcasses and sighed. "Now, they're just thoroughly dead."

"So they're still meat on the hoof whether raised by a Buddhist or not, aren't they?"

Cartwright laughed. "Yes and no – did you know you sometimes speak in koans, John?"

Wright just looked at him, and Cartwright said, "I just harvest their sperm. I have a machine that jacks off the bulls – well, actually, it gives electric shocks to their prostates, but same difference. I freeze it and sell it – or at least I used to. I can no longer ship the sperm. But I don't as a rule eat meat. Not unless I was starving. Maybe not even then."

"So this comes from your zazoom practice?"

"Zazen, not Zazoom." He laughed good naturedly, reminding Wright for the umpteenth time of Hoss. "It means quiet thinking. But I get your drift."

"Whatever," Wright said. "You once told me that it worked sometimes as well as the medication." He waited for some sort of affirmation but got none.

"Anyway, try that while I go do my AU-THOR-IT-Y *thang*," Wright continued. "It'll solve two problems. One, you getting too worked up, and two, my not being able to concentrate with your mouth working a fucking mile a minute. Got me?"

Cartwright took a deep breath and let it out slowly. When he didn't say anything for a minute, Wright realized his friend had done exactly what he'd suggested. His eyes were half-closed and his hands were relaxed in his lap. He was meditating.

Impressed, Wright wondered if Cartwright could go into a trance state at the flip of a mental switch. If it hadn't been such a weird day already, he would be more than a little creeped out right now.

But whatever worked.

He got out the Blazer as quietly as he could. He wanted to tell Ben that they could talk about Suzanne's disappearance after he examined the cow carcasses, but didn't want to startle his old friend out of whatever mental state he was in. It might not be helping – he might be in total turmoil inside that seemingly serene outer shell – but at least he was quiet.

A huge, dying single oak tree dominated the center of the pasture. Underneath the tree were the bodies of two cows and two bulls. The four carcasses were arranged with their snouts touching, and their rear ends pointed outwards so that they formed a sort of cross.

Once upon a time, cow mutilations had been big news. Somewhere in his office file cabinet, Wright had a one-hundred-and-twenty-eight-page report from the FBI titled "Animal Mutilation Project." At that time, there had been a lot of conjecture that government black opts were behind the incidences, and the title of the report could be read two ways.

But Wright nonetheless remembered the salient points of the report. And of course, by there had been numerous television documentaries on the subject. The basic details included the removal of eyes, udders, sexual organs, the anus to about a depth of twelve inches, and a single ear. Sometimes soft organs were taken. And the cuts were done with surgical precision. Blood loss, though it had to be excessive, was never in evidence. Scavengers such as buzzards wouldn't touch the carcasses.

As Wright walked toward the cows, a black crow, its beak red with clotted blood, walked out of the gapping wound in the rear end of one of the bodies. So much for scavenger pickiness.

"Squawk!" it said and flew off.

The grass was sticky with blood, and although large sections of the carcass where the sexual organs would have been were missing, there was nothing surgical about their removal. The missing parts appeared not to have been cut out but torn out.

So much for the rest of the FBI report.

However, one similarity was clear: Except for the paths in the ankle-high grass, one that Cartwright had made earlier and another Wright had made to investigate, there was no sign of passages leading up the carcasses. The cows were lying in depressions in the dirt. He couldn't say for sure, but the animals appeared to have been dropped from some height, and their impacts had pounded imprints deep into the hard soil. He looked up: nothing but blue sky. The FBI reports posited helicopters. He wondered.

He looked back at the Blazer. Cartwright remained in the same position, sitting upright, his chin tucked in a bit and his eyes closed. Wright would have liked to ask him when he had found the cattle or if he had heard anything, but Cartwright looked so peaceful, *Buddhistic* even in his bib overalls, it seemed better to leave him alone.

Wright walked around the perimeter of the scene. His boots made sucking sounds as walked through the blood-soaked ground. Closer up, he could see a similarity in the wounds. In all cases, the sexual organs had been brutally scooped out. That much was apparent from a distance. But up close he could see that the wounds did not appear to have been inflicted from the outside. Instead, it appeared as if they had been blown out by explosive force.

This thought occurred to him because he had once arrested a drunken redneck for doing exactly that. He and his buddy had stolen several sticks for dynamite and some blasting caps from the construction site where they worked. Barely able to walk after an all-night drinking spree, which they had supplemented with hits of crystal meth, they had managed to drive several cows into a corral with an attached working chute.

Sobering up the next day in jail, one of the perpetrators had said he and his buddy were rolling on the ground after one of the cows looked at them funny when the stick of dynamite they had shoved up her ass had gone off.

"I ain't never saw a cow look surprised, but she fucking did. No moo, just a confused sorta look before she died."

The redneck said the game had continued to be a hoot until a stick of dynamite went off prematurely while his buddy, Joe, had his arm up the elbow in the next cow's rectum.

"Even then it was funny," he said, his pupils still the size of teacups from the residual crystal. "Both the cow and Joe had the same surprised look on their faces when it went off."

He seemed only mildly concerned that Joe had died there in the pasture from blood loss and shock.

Wright picked up a dead limb. Squatting on his haunches and using the stick as a prod, he flipped back a flap of loose cowhide and peered into the cavity. This wound didn't fit the dynamite theory. First, there was no smell except cow shit. Exploded dynamite left a long-lingering, bitter, hot-metal smell.

But more important, the inside of the wound was not charred. It wasn't smoothly cut either. Instead, it was as if the inner organs had just disappeared. Wright was reminded of the erupted perimeter of a blown-out tire.

What about the bulls?

Wright got up and started to walk toward the business end of a bull before he realized his bum knee hadn't hurt as he stood up. Only a few days ago, if he had squatted and stood up quickly, his knee would have popped and crackled like broken glass. Now he felt like he could do a hundred-yard dash in ten seconds.

Who needs a brain? Maybe I'm better off without it.

The bull had fared little better than the cows. Its balls and dick were still there, but like the cows, it looked like its rear end had blown out.

"The question is, where are the insides?"

Wright jumped. He turned to find Cartwright standing behind him.

"Don't sneak up on me like that!"

"Isn't it curious, though: What happened to all the insides, I mean." He lifted a foot. His knee-high rubber boots were splattered with clots of blood.

"I wonder if everything was liquefied. Maybe we're walking in the leftovers," Wright said.

Cartwright studied his foot. Wright was amazed how calm the man was now. Had the medication kicked in already or was it the meditation?

"I don't think so," Cartwright said, finally. "Ever slaughtered a cow?"

"No, I can't say that I have."

"Well, there's really not that much stuff here on the ground. A couple of gallons at the most. It just looks like a lot more." He adjusted one of the straps on his bib overalls. "Anyway, I saw you looking inside. There's a lot of stuff missing: tripe, colon, uterus in the cows. If the insides were liquefied, we'd be standing in a couple of inches of the stuff."

"Maybe it soaked into the ground."

"Not here. It's all hard clay pan."

"You don't have a camera, do you, Ben?"

"Only a digital one that hasn't worked since the saucer fell. What about the sheriff's department gear?"

"It was digital, too," Wright said.

There was no reason to say anything more about electronics.

"I'm going back in town to see if I can find a film camera. Maybe the newspaper still has one," Wright said. "I want to document this."

He started walking back to the SUV. Halfway there, he realized that Cartwright wasn't following.

"Ben?" He turned to find his friend standing with both hands on his face, his mouth wide open in a terrified grimace. "Ben?"

Cartwright didn't answer so Wright jogged back to him. "Ben?"

He still didn't answer. Was he in some sort of trance? Wright grasped the big man's forearm and shook it. Cartwright shrugged off Wright's grip as he might shoo away a fly. He raised an arm, and for a moment Wright thought he might have to defend himself. But Cartwright only pointed to something pink and glittery on the ground. Wright looked but couldn't quite make out what it was. The object lay partially covered in congealed blood, and it took him a moment to realize he was looking at a severed human ear. The metallic glitter came from one of those big ear piercings that the kids were getting these days. One piercing was a little silver bar about an inch long that went through the ear's outer rim in two places. It had little silver balls on both ends. The other piercing was something that he used to only associate with National Geographic and aborigines. It was a large tube, perhaps a half-inch in diameter that went completely though the lobe. The kids called them "gauges." The official police report term for them was more descriptive: "flesh tunnels." Whatever, the flesh tunnel in this ear was black with a rim of rhinestones. He recognized the jewelry and guessed at the owner of the ear.

"Is that Suzanne's ear, Ben?"

Cartwright nodded.

"Do you have any idea how it got here?"

Ben nodded and stuttered, "God, how we argued about her getting that thing. I didn't mind the bar thing, but she kept wanting to get larger and larger gauges."

Big tears were streaming down his face. "I couldn't nibble on her ear lobes anymore."

Wright felt he needed to do something for his friend but was too embarrassed for him to say anything. Instead he knelt by the ear. "Hand me that pencil you've got in your shirt pocket, Ben."

Cartwright knelt on the other side of the ear and passed the pencil over. It was a yellow No. 2. His hand shook. Wright couldn't look him in the face.

Still wishing he had a camera so he could take a picture before disturbing evidence, he used the eraser end of the pencil to flip the ear over. Then he used the eraser like a swab to wipe away the gunk.

The morning had turned hot, and he was sweating. Without thinking he removed his hat and used his forearm to wipe his forehead.

Cartwright made an odd sound, and Wright plopped the cap back on. Had Cartwright seen the hole in his head?

"Why don't you go over to the Blazer and see if there are some plastic bags left in the glove compartment?" Wright said.

Cartwright didn't reply; didn't move. Wright stole a glance at his friend's face. The look of horror was now replaced with an odd expression one not quite readable. Curiosity? Amusement?

Wright took a deep breath. The edges on the ear where it had joined to the head were ragged and torn. Wright stole a glance at Cartwright's Bowie knife. If the ear had been cut off, the edges would be smooth, wouldn't they? Nonetheless, he wished he hadn't left his sidearm behind.

"Never mind," Wright said. "I'll get the baggies myself. Don't move anything – okay?"

He was back in a minute with the baggie and a spiral-bound notebook. He squatted, poked the pencil eraser through the earlobe gauge – there was plenty of room – and lifted it gently into the baggie. Holding it up to the light, he could see the ear was lightly freckled – as a redhead's ear might be. It was almost certainly Suzanne's.

He sealed the baggie and tucked it in his shirt pocket. As he stood up, Ben's gaze followed the pocket, the same amused look on his face.

Wright wiped the blood off the pencil on his sleeve and opened up the spiral notebook. "When did you say Suzanne left you?"

"I don't rightly remember," Ben said. "I just remember waking up and she wasn't beside me in bed. She always – always – slept in a lot later than me, so that was strange. I searched the house; she wasn't there. I went out to the fishpond – she used to like to sit on the pier and watch the blue gill strike the water in the mornings – but she wasn't there either. She didn't take the van. She didn't take any clothes. I found her purse on top of the dresser. She just left, I thought."

"Didn't you find that strange?"

"Find what strange?" Cartwright asked.

"That if she left you, she didn't take any extra clothes or money."

"Well, John, you know Suzanne; she was a free spirit, as they say."

"I guess you could call it that," Wright said, instantly regretting his words.

"There's no need to be insulting."

"I wasn't," Wright said. "I simply meant that since you lived with her for what . . . ? Three years?"

"Going on four."

"Exactly. Then you should know her moods better than anyone."

Cartwright scratched the top of his head and nodded. Wright started back to the SUV. Cartwright walked behind.

"So what's next?" he said.

"I'll put the ear on ice; I'll write a report; before the Fall, I would have put out a bulletin but with most electronic communications down, I think I'll just put up posters around town. That reminds me: Do you have a picture of Suzanne – a big one? Maybe we can get the newspaper to print up something up. I think they can still do that."

"Aren't their electronics fried too?"

"Doesn't matter. Except for a couple of old Apple computers, they were pretty much operating like a mid-20th century newspaper anyway. They even have a hot-lead typesetting machine, right out the 1900s. But I was thinking of a mimeograph. I think it might destroy the picture, though." Wright climbed in the SUV. Cartwright got into the passenger's side, his big knife clunking against the door as he shut it. The man seemed calm now, almost cheerful. A few minutes ago he looked like he was on the edge of a nervous breakdown.

"I have a studio portrait in the bedroom," Cartwright said. "Stop at the house and I'll get it if you think it will help."

Back at the doublewide, Wright waited in the SUV while Cartwright went indoors. If Wright had been armed or if he'd his deputy had been with him, he would have followed Cartwright into the house. If the murder had happened inside the house as he suspected, there would be signs. Even if the house and floors were recently scrubbed clean, that would mean something. But Wright didn't want to be unarmed in tight quarters with a two-hundred-and-fifty pound man who might have murdered his common-law wife. Wright didn't know much yet about the finer points of being undead, but he suspected having his bones broken would still hurt like a son-of-a-bitch.

Cartwright came back out with a framed picture.

"Do I need to come in town with you?" he said passively.

"No, I don't think so. Not now. Maybe later," Wright said. The truth was, given the evidence of foul play, Cartwright should have been brought in for questioning. But Wright wanted to put some distance between himself and the big man.

"I'll see if I can organize a search party to walk the woods, Ben."

"Sure," Cartwright said, grinning.

As Wright drove away, Cartwright called out: "This is some kind of lucid dream, isn't it, John?" And he patted the top of his own head.

Maybe it is. Maybe it fucking really is just a dream.

Strange thoughts took up residence in his mind; flittering impressions that he had no more control over than he had over the trespassing sparrow.

* * *

6.

You Say Undead Love is Harder

What's madness/but nobility of soul/At odds with circumstance – Theodore Roethke

Laura.

Laura didn't want to serve coffee to undead Frank Marshall, but she was the only waitress on duty, and Salman, the manager, was giving her crap. She enjoyed her independence and didn't want to mooch off of Uncle Robert and Sophia. She needed to keep this job.

Marshall had come in late in the evening, looking much his old, alive-self, dressed in what almost constituted a uniform for him: khaki pants and a dark blue shirt. Under one arm he carried the brightly colored poncho she had used to cover his corpse as it lay on the beach at Lost Lake.

He had slung the poncho over the coat rack near the door, paused, given the garment a long curious look as if it were an alien artifact — which in a way it was — then snorted and sat down in his usual booth, his head bowed a bit, his hands steepled on the table.

This is where she was supposed to slap a menu down on the table and ask if he wanted coffee, as she had done nearly every day for months - before he had died.

Marshall had been coming to the cafe every day sitting at the same table for the last month or so, ordering the same thing. This schedule had begun when his wife of nearly forty years had run away tomerge with one of the archangels and become immortal, and continued right until the day before Marshall's death.

From across the room, he didn't look corpse-like. His color was good for a man in his late sixties, and his comb-over was neatly done. His shirt and slacks, however, were wrinkled today, which was a departure from his normally tidy look. He usually wore spray-starched, ironed shirts and neatly creased slacks, even after the Fall when starch and electricity to power irons had become scarce. Men of his generation rarely knew how to do such unmanly things as washing and ironing, but he had kept up appearances even after his wife disappeared. She suspected he was some kind of hoarder, stashing away cardboard boxes of cans of spray starch and maybe a gasoline-powered electric generator just so he could maintain the old-soldier look.

Marshall wasn't the only undead in the cafe. There were the bubb-ettes and then there was the undead farmer and his undead wife. The former were accidental deaths. The later most likely murder-suicides.

The undead were hard to tell from the living at first sight, but you knew something was off-key with them immediately. It was a subtle impression, a sense of there being something not quite right about them. She couldn't put her finger on it; whatever quality was lacking was ineffable. She would have been at a loss to describe it to one of the living who hadn't encountered one of the undead. But any living person had met one of the undead up close knew immediately something was askew. Even the usually clueless Salman sensed the weirdness.

More than once, she saw the living become a little uneasy when one of the undead came near. This reaction was apparent even when the living didn't see the undead enter their space, as from behind, a raising of the hair on the back of one's neck. Laura felt it immediately as two undead bubba-ettes entered the cafe earlier.

The women had been roomies when living and still were now that they were undead. They were of a type, what Laura called the small-town mean-girl class. They were relatively young; had probably been pretty in high school, but cigarettes, fast food and too much beer had dulled the pretty veneer by their early thirties. They used a lot of make-up, particularly blue eyeshadow; smoked a lot, drank plenty of beer at the local pub – when there had been beer – picked up men on occasion, usually of the species *bubba sapiens*, but seemed to enjoy, more than anything else, talking about what "shits" men were.

These two bubba-ettes in the corner booth had wandered into Boucher's shortly after their deaths. The vent of the propane space heater in the doublewide they shared had become clogged, and they had died together in their sleep. Laura imagined them lampooning some bubba-boy right up to the time they lost unconscious.

The next morning they had come into Boucher's disoriented, their big hair disheveled, and their faces cherry red. Their eyes, irritated by the colorless gas, had watered so much that their mascara had ran in streaks down to their chins, giving them a tribal-tattooed look. Seated, they had ordered coffee, and when Laura had accidentally touched one of their hands while serving them, the flesh had been ice cold.

The cherry red coloration disappeared by the next day, and the two women now sat in the corner booth behind Marshall, one talking excitedly, moving her hands about as if to hold an over-sized big beach ball as she said, "of course the big oaf loved her little tight buns this much, but he was such a stupid jerk, and he smelled of cow manure . . ."

For all appearances, they were the same as they had been alive. But up close, one could feel there was something eldritch about them, as if surrounded by an unearthly light.

Maybe it was their eyes. Or rather their gaze. The impression was they weren't really being themselves, but rather were reading a script written by their living selves or one relayed from their real selves from some distant universe by a cosmic radio signal.

Generally, except for that slight feeling of unease that registered on a somatic level, Laura could ignore the two undead bubba-ettes. Marshall was different. She had known Marshall on the waitress/customer level before he had died. And then there was the connection, perhaps only in her mind, between Marshall and Wright. They had all been members of an ad hoc task force to deal with the archangels and the disappearance of humans. The same task force that had decided to make the fertilizer bomb that had caused the archangels' saucer to slide into Lost Lake three days ago.

It was stupid, but she feared that Marshall would have the same effect on her that Wright did. The thought she might find herself sexually attracted to another middle-aged man totally creeped her out.

She had tried to tell Salman that Marshall disturbed her. She couldn't tell him why, of course, but had asked him to serve the old man himself. No luck. Now here she was. He was still clunky old Frank, he wasn't Wright, there was no supernatural draw to him, which was a relief, but there was still the association he had with Wright.

But she couldn't explain any of this to Salman, of course, and he had just asked rhetorically, "Does Marshall have money? Can he pay his bill? If so, it's your job to sling the hash, pour the coffee. Go do it."

What an asshole! She was surrounded by asshole men! Or clingy men. Or needy men. Or undead men. Or . . . what exactly was Wright?

"If he tries to eat your brain, I'll take care of it," Salman had said, not being clear exactly what he would take care of? Her chewed-up brain?

In answer to this unspoken question, he had pulled out the aluminum baseball bat he kept on a shelf under the cash register and slapped it hard into his meaty palm. "Good customer or not, I'll bash him if he tries to latch his dentures onto your head."

She suspected it was her soul not her brain that was in jeopardy, but Salman didn't believe women had souls, or at least possessed souls equal to those of men, and she didn't try to explain such a fine point to him. As she walked over to Frank's booth, her hands were shaking so badly that the coffee cup was clinking on the saucer.

Last night, John Wright had been in her dreams. And the dream was dark and disturbed – even by her standards. Details of the dream had faded upon waking, but she remembered strong erotic overtones. That was what had really given her the heebie-jeebies, the cloudiness of the dream, the parts hinted at and the details left to her waking imagination: a slight hint of her bare flesh, of being simultaneously incredibly excited and indescribably repulsed, of being entered by a member as cold as the bubba-ette's hand. She didn't want to think about it anymore but couldn't get the dream out of her head.

A shudder rose from the base of her pelvis and traveled up

through her spine to her head, a rushing river mixture of pleasure and fear, that almost made her drop the coffee cup.

She managed to set down the cup in front of Frank, and he looked up at her and smiled as naturally as anything as she poured the coffee from the carafe.

By the standard waitress script – unwritten but binding nonetheless – this was where she was now supposed to chat the customer up a bit – especially if he was an old man alone – and say something like, "You're looking chipper today." Instead she said, "I have your trench coat."

"I wondered what happened to it."

His eyes were blue and a bit bloodshot, but he didn't have that combination of Ben-Gay ointment and unwashed goat that old men often had. He was just an old man after all, even though he was undead, and again she was thankful he didn't have the effect on her that John Wright did.

She relaxed a little. "I borrowed it. I didn't think you'd mind at the time."

"Well, at least you're an honest thief," he said.

She waited for him to ask her why she thought he didn't need his coat anymore, wondering what his reaction would be when she tried to explain he had been stone-cold dead when she took his coat, but she avoided the issue.

"I couldn't figure out how I wound up in that hippie contraption."

"Would you like something to eat this afternoon?" she said.

"I'm not hungry – wait a minute." He scratched his head, disturbing the comb-over. "I am hungry. What do you know about that? I haven't been hungry since . . ."

His eyes rolled until all she saw were the whites, and Laura thought he was going into one of his undead fugues. She hesitantly shook his shoulder.

"Stay with me, Mr. Marshall," she said. There was no electric spark or so much as a tingle when she touched his shoulder. The erotic weirdness was apparently confined to Wright. She wasn't sure whether to be relieved or creeped-out even more.

"I guess I'll have the meatloaf special," Marshall said. "I'd like to have the potato, but the doctor said I shouldn't have butter and sour cream – any of that stuff – because of my heart, you know."

"Oh, I think you can chance it once in a while, Frank," Laura said. She barely restrained herself from saying something like: "What the hell, Mr. Marshall. You've already died from a heart attack."

"You're right, sweetheart," Marshall said. "What the fuck – pardon my French – what does Jenkins know anyway? You know he tried to tell me that I di. . . di . . . die . . . "

Marshall's eyes turned up again, and Laura shook him again.

"That was the meatloaf special, with baked potato, extra butter and sour cream?" she asked as if nothing had happened.

"Yes," Marshall said, but his voice came from far away, a dispatch from wherever the fugues took the minds of the undead.

"I'll have it right up," she said.

She filled out the order on the little green pad and was walking toward the kitchen when the bell on the front door jingled behind her.

She knew it was Wright without looking.

She made a quick detour to the bathroom because she had become so aroused that she was afraid of fainting. Once there, she was afraid to leave then bathroom.

Silly. He's just a man and an undead one at that. But as she stepped out of the bathroom, the café landscape took on a dreamlike quality. Everyone except for John Wright, who was sitting alone at a booth, seemed to be frozen. She heard the patrons. They were still chatting and bickering away, but their voices were muted. She couldn't do anything but just stand there, unable to retreat to the kitchen, unable to make herself go back out into the café.

Wright looked up, smiled sadly, and the spell was broken. The sense of being immersed in wet cotton dissipated, and she was pulled toward him. She barely stopped herself from trotting over to him like a damn dog. Only with the greatest exercise of will did she manage to turn and go back to the kitchen.

Wright.

After returning from Cartwright's farm, Wright went back to the sheriff's office and sat down at his salvaged Oliveti typewriter, a bottle of correction fluid in reach. He fully intended to make complete reports on both Cartwrights's mutilated cattle and the missing Suzanne before doing anything else.

For a while, the click-clack of the antique typewriter was reassuring. As he thought about it, didn't seem that long ago that he filled out reports on a typewriter, albeit it was an IBM Selectric with a correcting feature built in. How did that work? Even without a brain, it only took him a moment to recollect the special backspace key would automatically erase the last few characters typed via a built-in correction feature. But the Selectric had been all mechanical, not digital. He still had the Selectric in the storage closet, but the ribbons and correction tape had dried out, and there were no replacements to be found. The Oliveti was so simple that he had been able to re-ink the ribbon using paste ink from the newspaper's print shop.

Typing clean copy on a typewriter had marked the beginning of his career; shortly thereafter the personal computers and printers had appeared on the scene. Typewriters were regulated to typing up envelopes addresses and formal letters for a while, then banished to closets and junk rooms as the digital revolution progressed.

But a crime-scene report was still a crime-scene report, whatever it was written on. In the his years in law enforcement, he had written hundreds of such reports. For the most part the process was highly formulaic and required little more than recording the facts as he found them.

Now he couldn't concentrate. Several times he had started typing, only to have his attention lapse.

The office chair squeaked as he leaned back and took stock of himself. It wasn't so much his mind wouldn't behave. The facts he needed to record were there, brain or no brain. His body was the problem. He felt pulled toward the door. Worse. He felt on the verge of falling toward the door. As if he were poised over it, and the horizontal was really vertical, with the door was at the bottom of a deep pit, and if he leaned just a bit further forward he would fall.

He knew this feeling. He had felt the same way the night after waking up in the woods near Lost Lake. God! That was only one night ago, but it seemed like another lifetime. But the force then felt the same as it had drawn him to Laura Jacobsen's house.

He pushed away from the desk, the office chair's wheels complaining as they rolled over the unevenly tiled floor. He felt the force might grab the chair itself and make it roll him in it toward the door, but instead it pulled at him alone, forcing him out of the chair and to his feet.

He got up from the chair – or rather the force nearly lifted him out – and he started toward the door, grabbing his cap on the way out. Outside, the force pulled him to the right and across the street to Boucher's. As he approached the cafe's front door, he feared he might be pulled through the glass panels before he could grab the doorknob, but the force weakened within a few feet. He tried veering away from Boucher's but the strength of the force renewed.

Decades ago, before the Wal-Marts devoured all small-town retail stores, Boucher's had been a clothing outlet. When the owners converted it to a café, they had hung curtains in the display windows and the front door to shield customers from the afternoon sun. But on days like today, the curtains were often kept drawn back. Now as he looked in, he could see Frank Marshall and the two women behind him in a corner booth sitting perfectly still, watching him through the glass with blank eyes. Wright had the unsettling feeling that they were just manikins arranged in a store-window diorama, put there to model the clothes they wore.

Then Laura Jacobsen came into view, lithe, dark, full of nervous energy, her long, black hair down her back. She set a coffee cup down in front of Marshall and filled it from a carafe it in one smooth motion. He watched as Marshall came alive, back from the Twilight Zone where people were frozen manikins. Frank smiled at Laura. The feeling of being pulled subsided as he watched Laura take the older man's order.

Some sixth sense made Wright look up just in time to step out of the way of a falling pigeon. The bird hit the heaved-and-cracked sidewalk at his feet. It was obviously already dead because its head was missing, but the body still twitched .

A chirping, childish laughter came from above, and he looked back up, seeing nothing but an expanse of aging brick and blue sky. Topping the brick facade was a circular cast concrete frieze of a compass and square. He had forgotten that half a century or more ago, years before it became a mercantile store, this building had been a Masonic lodge.

The infantile laughter came again, this time from behind the facade. Were a couple of local juvenile psychopaths perched up there on the flat, asphalt roof raining beheaded pigeons down on him? He could imagine their fat, imbecilic faces grinning at their own imagined cleverness.

Before he could think further about this, the pulling force resumed. Laura had disappeared from view, and he quickly stepped inside.

The bell on the door tinkled, and everyone stopped chattering for a moment and looked up to see who had entered. As he was a regular at Boucher's, and therefore boring, they all went back to gossiping, eating, quarreling or whatever the were doing before. Except for Laura. She stood half-turned toward him, one hand on a hip, one foot behind another, accentuating the curve of her hips. She wore a mid-thigh orange skirt, right out of his memories of what waitresses used to wear twenty years ago. Her tennis shoes and college sweatshirt spoiled the vintage effect, but her legs were good – great, really. Athletic without being so muscular to be feminine. She stared at him with an expression he couldn't quite read. There was fear in her face, and she frowned at him, but the frown was mixed with a strange enigmatic, almost teasing Mona Lisa smile.

She was, he realized with a start, both happy to see him and scared to death of him, but not only did she not want him to know this – she didn't want to admit it to herself. She turned and jogged away on her tennis shoes toward the kitchen. He looked around for a booth away from other customers, but the place was nearly full. With no TV or radio stations working there was little for folks to do at home.

Boucher's had become a regular watering hole, bringing everyone from bored farm wives who ordinarily would be home watching soaps, to right-wing bubbas who would be listening to hate-talk radio, to the local marijuana-grower mafia who now watched his every move, cat-like, their eyes moving but their heads not turning, as he walked toward the only open booth.

He settled into the booth, hoping Marshall wouldn't notice him.

No such luck. Without asking permission, Marshall got up and slid into the booth across from him.

"Hello, John," the old man said.

"You doing all right, Frank?"

"I've been better," he said.

There was something different about the old man, but he couldn't quite figure it. It was as if he was slightly out of focus.

"Me too," Wright said, but as he thought about it he knew it wasn't that case. The feeling of extreme well-being was still with him. He felt like doing cartwheels. He felt like doing them for Laura, like some fool teenager showing off for his puppy love.

Marshall stared at him curiously, and for an instant gave him a foolish, affectionate grin. The grin cut off in a second, to be replaced by his usually sour countenance. What was that all about?

Wright realized it he who was wearing the foolish grin because he was thinking about Laura. Marshall had just mirrored Wright's grin, misinterpreting it, thinking it was for him.

"I feel like I'm in a dream," Marshall said. "One I can't quite wake up from." He scratched his chin. "Sometimes, I feel like I'm going to wake up, but I black out, and then when I come to, I'm back in the dream again."

Wright was surprised by this insight. Marshall had never seemed a profound-thinker type, more the knee-jerk reactionary type.

"That's exactly how I feel; like I'm living on the edge of the dream. It's exhilarating – when you get used to it," Wright said.

Marshall leaned forward, his forearms on the table, his hands clenched so tightly the knuckles cracked. "I think it's goddamn terrifying!"

Two booths down, a woman who Wright remembered her as

Margie, a barfly, stared at him with a curiously empty expression. She was looking at him and through him at the same time, as if he were as transparent as a ghost.

What's there to be afraid of? We're both dead; what worse thing can happen to us?

He stopped himself from saying this aloud. How did he know Marshall had died and come back? But he did. And it was the same with Margie and her crony at the far booth. He knew they were – there was no other word for it – undead.

They were all undead! And he laughed aloud at this thought, a concept out a comic book or some B-movie.

"Are you laughing at me?" Marshall asked. His face had turned red, almost cherry red, like it used to when he was living. Any time he encountered any idea or concept that he didn't understand, he took it as a threat, as an attack.

"No, Frank. I wasn't laughing at you. I was laughing at myself."

The old man didn't seem convinced. His fear had been replaced by anger, and where once Wright would have found this threatening, now it was only a bit sad. That was Marshall in a nutshell: scared shitless of a world that didn't think or behave as exactly as he did. In response, he turned that fear into anger. It was a kind of a coping process. Anger made Marshall feel in control. Fear, for Marshall, was not being in control. That was why the man had spent most of his life pissed off at something.

"Bullshit!" Marshall said. It took Wright a second to realize Marshall still thought he was being laughed at.

"No, not bullshit!" Wright said and surprised both himself and Marshall by reaching across the table and patting the old man's clenched hands.

Marshall relaxed a minute, his face looking relieved. But then the anger came back like a dark cloud suddenly appearing in a clear sky, and he slid out of the booth, his fists clenched at his side.

"What have you done, Wright? Gone queer? I would have never thought that of you."

A sense of sadness overwhelmed Wright. Was he going to have

to fight the old man?

"None of that in here, boys."

They both turned. It was Laura, a tray in hand.

"You two looked like you were going to start screaming at each other," she said.

The steaming chunk of meatloaf was surrounded with green beans and buttered potatoes – Boucher's perennial blue plate special. She set the plate on Marshall's table, started to leave, then took a step back, looking at Wright. Though pretty, she couldn't be more different from the blonde or redheaded modest women Wright had pursued all his life. And she was too damned young, but he couldn't take his eyes off her.

He tried to find that same sense of amusement at the absurdity as he had with the idea of being undead, but his lust was too strong. He knew if he tried to speak right now, it would come out as gibberish.

"What's with the hat?" she asked.

"Covers a small bald spot," he managed to say.

"Can I see it?" she said, wringing her hands together.

Wright wanted to say no, but instead he said, "Not here."

"Do you two need to be alone?" Marshall said.

As an answer, Laura picked up his plate and silverware and set it on the adjoining booth where Marshall was originally seated. The old man gave her a look that slid from angry to hurt. He looked at Wright questioningly.

"Go enjoy your food," Wright said. "Ms. Jacobsen and I need to have a private word." Pulse or no pulse, he felt his heart beating hard in his chest.

Marshall scooted out of the booth, mumbling something about *perverts* to himself. Laura stepped aside for him to pass. Before sitting down, Marshall stood and quietly stared at them, as if waiting for an explaination. Wright and Laura simply returned his stare, and finally the old man shook his head and sat down with his back to them, shoulders hunched.

Instead of sitting across from him, Laura slid beside him. He gasped as her knee brushed his with an electric shock. He didn't have to ask if she got the same reaction.

"What the fuck is going on?" she said before he could ask the same question.

"I don't know," he said. "I'm sorry."

"Sorry for what?" she said. "You probably think of me still as a snot-nosed girl, but I'm a grown woman."

"I feel as if I'm stalking you. Shit! This is crazy. I'm the one who feels like a teenager."

She leaned back in the booth, looking relieved.

"So you feel it too?" she said.

"I feel something," he said. "Look . . . I'm not good at this; at talking about such feelings." He tried to look nonchalant toward her but suspected he was failing.

"Maybe you'll grow into it," she said.

"Now you're toying with me." He tried to get angry but failed. She actually looked hurt by his accusation.

"I don't toy with people. Well, not so on a conscious level," she said.

"What does that mean?"

"It means I have issues from my childhood, but you know that."

Wright took a deep breath and let it out slowly, hoping it would clear his mind. What was she talking about?

"The abuse thing by your father?" he said.

"Yes."

"I thought you went to therapy for that."

"I did, but the scars go deep when that stuff happens to you as a child. You never quite get over it. That's what the therapist taught me. The trauma goes right down to muscle memory." She shook her head, causing her long hair to swing. Her scent travel from his nose right down to his groin.

"That's why I always cut you a lot of slack, you know," he heard himself saying.

"Pardon me?"

"When you were dealing marijuana and that other stuff," he said. "I figured you were entitled to be a little crazy, so I looked the other way, hoping you wouldn't get mixed up in meth or crack. If you had, then I would have had to do something. I figured you were smart and you'd eventually grow out of it, and you did."

"I didn't know that," she said, smiling at him. "Anyway, sometimes things trigger me, and I'm like another person, watching myself mess over people who try to get too close to me." She brushed her hair away from her face and over an ear. How many piercings did she have in that one ear alone – four or five? He wanted to touch them. Restraining such impulses was getting harder and harder. Did he even have the will power to get up and walk away? He wasn't sure and didn't want to try.

"With you it's different," she said. "That same unconscious thing that makes me run off from other people is making me . . ." She looked around to see if anyone was close enough to hear. He followed her gaze. The two big-haired women in the second booth over were staring at them. She turned toward him, resting an elbow on the table, a hand cradling her chin, her face inches from his, so close he could see the brown flecks of color in her dark eyes. The universe came to a complete stop. He was aware of her and her alone.

". . . want to run toward you," she finished.

He tried to tell her something similar, perhaps even stronger, was at work on him, but he found himself tongue-tied. It was all he could do not to grab her and kiss her right there in front of the whole cafe, dead and undead alike. He was petrified.

"I thought," she continued, "that maybe you reminded me of my father, and it was some sort of weird childhood sexual-abuse trip messing with me."

"I am old enough to be your father," he managed to blurt out.

"But you're nothing like him. Or even like my Uncle Robert, who was more a real father to me than my psychotic biological dad. Besides, you're looking a lot younger today. Too young to be my father. Did you know that?"

He shook his head. "I feel really good, more fit than I have for years," he said. "But when I look in the mirror, it's still me – or was the last time I looked. Except for this, of course." He tapped the top of his cap where the hole was hidden.

"I thought that might have something to do with it," she said. "I used to have this kind of love affair with the whole concept of death and nihilism." She leaned closer. Can I see it?"

"What?"

"Will you take off your cap for moment?"

"No, I'm wearing it for a good reason."

"Why? Everyone knows you're undead, anyway."

"Really?"

"Really," she said, smiling that Mona Lisa smile. "The living sense that you are not quite right. Just take it off for a moment and put it right back on."

He shook his head.

"For me?" she asked

"No."

"Why not?"

And he told her of the episode with the sparrow.

She laughed. "So instead of sparrows springing from your forehead like dreams they fly back in."

"That's some kind of literary reference – right?" he said. "Oh, I get it, something about Greek gods."

"Sheriff Wright, you do surprise me at times." She got up from the table. "Look," she said. "Salman looks like he's about to blow steam out his ears."

"Ignore him," Wright said.

"Salman will fire me," she countered.

"Not if he knows what's good for him."

She looked at him questioningly.

"Salman lives in a glass house, and I, as the local representative of the law, have the stones that can shatter it."

"I suspected you had stones, Sheriff Wright, but that sounds like an abuse of power to me."

"I'm tired of being good all the time. I'm ready to be selfish," he said, surprising himself again.

She put a hand on her hip. "I had the breakfast shift, and I get off in a couple of hours – at six," she said. "Maybe we could go somewhere and talk. Maybe you can show me the top of your head in private – do you think?"

"I don't know," he said.

"You're not scared of me, are you?"

His eyes met hers, and he almost got lost in them. "Honestly what I feel for you scares the hell out of me, but I don't want it to go away either."

"I can't get you out of my mind," she said.

He didn't add that it sounded like love – that would be ridiculous. Instead he said, "It's like some kind of supernatural thing. It's hard to explain."

She laughed. "They say undead love is harder."

"I beg your pardon?"

"It's from a poem I wrote years ago," she said. "You remember; my goth/suicidal phase."

"I'll be at my office," he said.

"You can stay and have coffee."

"No, I need to get out of here," he said. "I feel like everyone is staring at me."

"They are, you know," she said.

"Because I'm undead?"

"That maybe part of it, but you're not like the other undead."

"How's that?" he said, getting to his feet.

"You glow; you almost shine. You look so healthy it hurts to look at you. You really aren't aware of how hot you look, are you?"

Before he could answer, she was off toward the kitchen, using both hands to tie her long black hair into a ponytail as she walked.

"Go look in a mirror," she said over her shoulder.

She had left the check for coffee on the table, and written on it was "No charge for a hot old man." Underneath that: "I'll meet you at your office at six."

Her scent and the memory of those brown flecks floating in the lucid depths of her dark eyes were still with him as he crossed the street to his office.

* * *

7.

But I Say it's Only Rigor Mortise

Wright.

Wright's feelings were divided as he stepped out of the café. He felt as if a part of himself was inside, still sitting at the booth, still talking to Laura.

He turned and looked through the large plate glass windows, half-expecting to see a ghost of himself sitting in the booth, and Laura there in her waitress uniform, her little green order pad in hand, rapidly scribbling as he ordered from a lascivious menu.

"I'll have touch of your breasts, stroke of your legs and a smell of your dark hair on the side," his imaginary doppelganger would say. And Laura would jot it all down with her No. 2 pencil without so much as a blink.

"And how would you like my hair? Up like this," and she stopped writing to gesture at her hair, now in a prim French braid, "or down?"

"I'd like it down," his ghost would say, "on the side, in bed – not in a braid, but loose on the pillow, fanning out beneath your face so I can run my fingers through it."

"Can do, but I'm afraid the menu items may not be as fresh as you'd like; there's the risk of some other STDs – all that self-destructive behavior when I was a teenager, you know – is that okay?" she said.

"No problem," he would say. "I'm undead already, remember? What worst thing can happen to me."

"Oh, yes," she'd say, and pat the top of his hat where the hole lay hidden. "You look so sexy and young in your cute little blue macho uniform that I almost forgot you were a walking middle-age corpse."

"It wouldn't matter. Even if I were alive, the way I feel now I wouldn't care if you had AIDS."

He shook his head, the stupid little daydream faded, and the only ghost he saw was his dim reflection in the dirty glass. His imaginary Laura had been right about one thing. He did look younger, a lot younger. Or was he imagining it because Laura had suggested it?

But one thing was certain: The relentless pull had relaxed somewhat. Now it was more like a gentle though persistent tug. Was it because he had seen her, gotten his 'fix' from her proximity? Whatever, he could live with the pull if it got no stronger than this.

He took the shortcut across the town square. As he walked past the brass eyes of the statue of Laura's great-great grandfather, a Civil War hero and founder of Creedance, gazed at him admonishingly. The brass horse upon which he rode also gave Wright a hard look.

He found the door to the sheriff's office unlocked, which was disturbing because there was a rack holding three shotguns and extra loads for the hand pistols were in plain sight. He wanted to blame Jimmy for the unlocked door, but he suspected the culprit was himself. A quick inventory showed nothing was missing, and once again he was thankful to be living in a small town.

Or would that be 'un-living' in a small town?'

He busied himself stirring the fire in the cast-iron potbelly stove, enjoying the pop and crackle sounds and smells of the burning blackjack oak. This building, like most in town, had once been a store. It had twelve-foot ceilings. All the warm air rose to the ceiling, and it took a lot of wood to keep things warm at floor-level. A piece of wood spat a cinder at him as he turned it. The wood was a bit green; he needed to have the chimney cleaned. Green wood emitted more tar and unburned sap that could start a fire in the flue. He'd have to double-check the next load of firewood Bryan Douglas sold him.

He was happy the tug toward Laura was weaker – had just talking to her helped? Whatever, he settled himself at his desk, determined to finish his report on Cartwright's missing wife. He worked steadily for a few minutes. Laura remained on his mind, but not to the degree that he couldn't finish the report. The mystery of the attraction remained. She was dark and willful. He had always been attracted to women who were fair and demure. Even May Tyre, the young woman he had been tempted to have an affair with before she became an angel, had been blonde.

But even now, as he thought of Laura, a surge of desire raced up his spine, making him stretch like a cat. As he leaned back in the chair , he looked up at the ceiling and found the angel May Tyre staring at him from the ceiling.

"Hello, John," she said. Her wings were spread out behind her against the ceiling tiles. Her eyes were open, but her pose was that of a sleeping woman curled up on her side. Her arms were folded across her breasts, and her knees and hip turned, presenting an alabaster flank.

There was no sign of anything holding her to the ceiling. He was momentarily disoriented, feeling as the room was upside down and that he was defying gravity, not her.

"Hello, May," he said. He should have been shocked – even fearful – but all he felt was mild wonderment, akin to opening a drawer and finding a mouse inside.

These were strange times indeed when finding a naked female angel hanging from the ceiling spawned only mild surprise.

"You don't look happy to see me, John," she said.

"As I recall, our last meeting ended with me killing myself," he said.

Without speaking, May stretched out her legs and twisted her hips. The move had a yoga-like quality to it, and there was a faint crackling sound, like static electricity, as she peeled off the ceiling. She descended feet first, slowly and with grace, and Wright moved back against the wall to make room for the expanse of wings.

But he needn't have bothered because as she came down she folded her wings, bringing the tips up like an inside-out umbrella. She landed on her toes on the shuffling of documents and reports on his desk. Despite May the angel being at least a foot taller than May the human, and therefore by all the laws of commonsense therefore much heavier, her splayed toes didn't so much as dent the sheets of paper.

Those toes were webbed, with nearly translucent skin tattooed by a filigree of fine, blue veins. A similar tracing of veins ran though the somewhat thicker skin of her outstretched wings. Unlike the angels of Christian lore, the wings had no feathers.

The effect should have been bat-like; instead the overall impression was of a large beautiful insect. Not a butterfly, though there was a moth-like quality to her wings, but of something unique in itself, something at once ephemeral and eternal, yet reminiscent of a human flesh.

She sat, her legs folded in the lotus position, giving him full view of her genitals, which were hairless and entirely human in appearance. Her folded wings stretched several feet above her head. A brief quiver ran across their surface, like ripples in a still pond, and she seemed to settle more, but her full weight still did not compress the papers on which she sat. He was reminded again that angels were not subject to such mundane physical laws as gravity.

"It was warm up there," she said, smiling as she caught him looking between her legs.

He looked away, embarrassed, though in truth he had been held in awe by the strangeness of her alien beauty, not transfixed by lust. That kind of attraction was apparently now reserved for Laura; he could the pull of the invisible cord stretching out to her growing, stronger now than only few moments ago.

A silence opened up between May and him, expanded by the ineffable emotion she elicited in him. Was that emotion fear, loathing or wonderment?

It was, he realized, a mixture of all but mostly awe. He wasn't afraid of her in the usual sense. He should be fearful, he supposed. May the Angel could shrug off a bullet. He guessed she could probably pull his arms off without batting one of her beautiful eyelashes.

But these thoughts didn't frighten him. May's eyes were as cold blue as they had been when she was human, but to look into those eyes now was to stare into nameless depths. He kenned she knew something about him and his place in this reality that he wasn't ready to know.

"You seem calmer than I remember," he said to fill the dreadful vacuum of silence. But it was true. She didn't seem as frenetic as the last time they'd met.

She shrugged, causing the folded skin in her wings to tremor like sailcloth snapping in the wind.

"I think it's the baby," she said.

"The baby?" he said. "What baby?"

Did he really want to know?

She patted her bare abdomen. "This baby."

Her stomach was flat and smooth. A ripple of abdominal muscles was hinted at but not prominent under the skin. There was no sign of a pregnant bulge, but it would be too early for that wouldn't it?

"Really? I didn't know angels could get pregnant," he said and immediately felt gullible. May might look saner, but obviously she was still clearly delusional.

"You didn't know? What made you think we couldn't?"

"Well . . . for one thing," he said, "the original archangels – the original one hundred – were sterile and sexually ambiguous. Who's the lucky father?"

"Why, John," she said and batted her eye lashes, looking for a moment ever-so-much like the old May, the waitress with the big hair and thick blue eye shadow, for whom seducing men was a kind of hobby. "You are."

"Beg your pardon?"

"You're the father, John. Don't you remember our being together at the lake – it was only a day ago?"

A shiver traversed Wright's spine. Unlike the shiver of passion he had felt for Laura, this was a wave of fear that ran from his head down his spine, rather than up from his groin. And this shivering left him feeling weak-kneed where the other had strengthened him.

He gathered his breath and said, "No, I can't say I remember much."

But that was a lie. He remembered that encounter, but it seemed a whole lifetime ago, not just a day.

He had been sitting by the remains of the wrecked merry-go-round at the shores of Lost Lake. He remembered crying over the loss of his wife – he hadn't cried over anything since childhood and he was embarrassed. As he stood crying on that desolate shoreline, cold hands had reached from behind and wiped the tears from his face.

The voice was alien, but he remembered thinking it was his ex-wife, and decided to try to find some remnant of her in the beautiful, monstrous creature she had become.

He turned, the cold, wet gravel crunching under his feet, to find not Marguerite but May the angel, just as terribly beautiful as she was now, but her eyes crazed, darting to and fro.

"What do you want from me?" he had asked.

May had muttered something incoherent and leaped fifteen feet straight up to perch on an overhanging cornice of the old merry-go-round. He could recall the vision of her as clearly as he saw her now: She had perched unsteadily on the cast iron beam like a circus high-wire walker, her eyes blazing with madness.

"I'm not sure," she said, "but I think I wanted you to remind me what it was like to be human."

In one of those instant transitions angels could do, he found himself wrapped in her frigid arms. She spoke in a high-pitched accelerated voice and told him the human/angel hybrids were able to make love like ordinary humans. He remembered her being so tall, making him feel like a child in her arms. One of her cold breasts was against his cheek. That touch of bare angel breast had been electrifying, but the lust had been mixed with despair and his hand found the handgrip of his pistol. He remembered the reassuring feel of the pistol's handgrip, its weight as he pulled it from the holster and brought it up between their bodies. He had looked up the thick gray sky, his tears cold on his cheeks, then – nothing. No sound of a gunshot. No recollection of a gunshot or pain or sex, just a dreamless darkness until he awoke alone and cold in the woods near the lake, his face covered in his own blood.

"You don't remember what we did?" May asked, bringing him back to the present.

"I remember nothing," he said. "I think you wanted to fuck, but

I think I shot myself instead."

May laughed, a deep throaty sound, without taking her eyes off his face. She unfolded her legs and stepped down off the desk to stand before him. She didn't seem as tall now as in his memory, and was even shorter than she had been as a human for her eyes were level with his.

"Death becomes you, John Wright," she said. "You used to be such a prude. Before, you would have never used the F-word in front of a woman."

He restrained himself from telling her that she was no longer a woman.

"We didn't do anything," he repeated and took a deep breath, hoping he wouldn't slip into a fugue. "I blew out my brains rather than do anything with you."

"That's not true, John." Her hand snaked up his back, a finger flipped off his hat, and the hand cupped the top of his head, enfolding the exit wound. He tried to resist, but a force flowed from the hand into his open skull, and an electrified warm flow of energy transfixed him, paralyzed him.

"You remember as I remember," May said.

And he was treated to a vision of his face – his old face before his transformation. Through her eyes he could see his bare arms thrust out, supporting his weight, the expanse of her wings quivered with pleasure and occluded the gray, wind-swept clouds above. He could feel the cold, wet gravel press into her back as he thrust. He watched through her eyes, his face grimaced in the momentary gasp of ecstasy and near pain. There was blood trickling from his ear.

"Let me go, May," he said, snapping back into the here and now.

Was there such a thing as 'here and now' any more?

"It was only afterwards that you pulled your gun," May said, ignoring his request. "I thought you were going to shoot me, and I was waiting to see what would happen, but then you shoved the gun in your mouth and the top of your head," – her hand massaged his cranium – "exploded!"

He tried to push her away, but her arms, despite looking soft and womanly, were as hard as steel. She lowered her wings and wrapped them around him. He became enclosed in a blanket of human-like skin.

"Release me!" This time he shouted.

Had he spilled his seed inside this creature? No, it had to be a false memory. He closed his eyes, hoping the vision would disappear. He heard the front door open, and then Laura's voice.

"Well, isn't this cozy," she said.

Still holding him, May turned her head nearly one hundred and eighty degrees to look behind her.

"Oh hello, Laura. Long time no see," she said, showing no sign of letting go of him.

Laura.

As she crossed the town square on the way to the sheriff's office Laura felt more alive, happier, than she could remember. It was like being a child again and waking up on Christmas morning at Uncle Robert's house. More than that, she felt a mixture of the same excitement as when she had developed her first schoolgirl crush on her hippie English teacher. Later in life, she had felt the same exhilaration when she thought she might be loved and be able to love in return. The only problem was that John Wright was such an unlikely candidate for either a secret crush or a mutually loving relationship. Yet what she felt now was stronger by far than any of those previous experiences.

Amazing that she was even thinking about it

Her step was light as she stepped up on the curb and reached for the door. She was being pulled by the same invisible cord Wright had described. Perhaps the pull on her wasn't as strong as the one on him, but nonetheless, it was a tangible force. She felt it, knew it was unreasonable but was nearly powerless to resist it. The invisible cord seemed attached not to her mind but to a spot near her navel, connecting to some mysterious, unmapped country cradled in her pelvis. She felt the pull grow stronger with each step toward the sheriff's office, and with the stronger force, her sense of vitality and joy increased. She imagined she could lean backwards, walk on her heels, and yet be kept from falling by the mystical tether leading to John Wright.

The sound of voices – first John Wright's, then a female voice

– came from inside. She felt slight twinge of jealousy, which was silly. It was probably just someone filing a complaint.

She opened the door and stepped inside to find John Wright wrapped in the wings of an angel.

The angel's back was to her, but she recognized the voice and the honey blonde hair: May Tyre.

May's wings wrapped tighter around Wright, making a sound like the rustling of dry leaves.

"Release me," Wright said, but though he raised his voice, it didn't sound to Laura as if he wanted to be released.

"Well, isn't this cozy," Laura heard herself say. And jealousy overcame her with such intensity that her hands shook.

May turned her head all the way around to look behind her. The effect should have been like something from the movie, *The Exorcist.* Instead, Laura, though her vision was blurred by jealousy, was stunned by the beauty of the creature who, when human, had been her friend and co-worker.

"Oh hello, Laura," May the Angel said, still holding Wright.

Laura tried to say something but the words came out as a croak. In an alchemical manner, like transmuting lead into gold, the fiery jealousy changed into bittersweet melancholia.

The illogic of this emotion did not escape her. John Wright should mean nothing to her romantically. He was at least twenty years older and definitely not her type. He seemed to really care what society at large thought of him, or at least he had before his death. He probably saw Marguerite specifically and women in general as back-ups, as support staff for his own aspirations. She, on the other hand, ran on her own internal governor and had little use for what people thought of her, but kept looking for someone – and it made her feel stupid and weak to admit this –who would be a soul-mate.

No, John Wright and she couldn't be more different, yet since he had returned from the dead, she was consumed by some unnamed craving that was much more than just simple lust.

She couldn't call it love – that would be ridiculous. Besides she had been in love before, and this thing she had for Wright was more powerful. It was a sense of being fundamentally connected with someone.

Worse, she had instantly become addicted to this feeling.

And now, her old friend May, who had been transformed into this hideously beautiful goddess, was in between her and Wright.

"May, let me go!" Wright said.

"You're not going to shoot yourself again if I do, are you?" May said with a coyness that reminded Laura of her old friend before the metamorphosis.

"Of course fucking not," Wright said.

This time, the angel complied, unwrapping her wings from around him and dropping her arms. Wright stepped back and reached down to pick up his cap from the floor. He smoothed his mussed hair – it seemed blacker than it had only a few hours later – and tried to put the cap on, but it wasn't quite large enough to fit his head. He took it back off and looked at it curiously. It had fit just fine a couple of hours ago in the café.

"It's not what it seems," he said, which made Laura wonder if it really wasn't like what it seemed, why was it his first impulse to explain it away?

"Oh, but it is. Sheriff Wright and I have a special connection," May said, patting her tummy.

Wright winced.

Laura closed the door behind her with shaking hands. "So what does that mean? You two been getting it on?" The jealousy returned along with equal portions of anger and cold ratiocination.

Why the fuck should I care if they had? But she did.

"May claims," Wright volunteered in a shaky voice, "that she's carrying my baby."

"Are you, May?" Laura said.

But she thought, feeling ridiculous as she did so: *How could you do this to me, John?*

"You betcha! We had union," the angel said. "And it feels wonderful to have trapped a little bit of him inside me!"

She sprang up on the desk and did an impossible slow-motion

pirouette on one toe, folding her wings in just enough so the tips barely missed brushing Wright in the face. She held her arms out in front of her as if she were hugging a big beach ball. One revolution took nearly twenty seconds, and though her toes rested on the desk, the papers underneath them did no so much as crinkle.

"It's not possible," Wright said. "I remember." His eyes fluttered and Laura thought he was going to pass out, but he took a long, deep breath through his nose and let it out slowly between his lips. "I think I remember dying – I remember shooting myself – as you took me in your arms. And the memory of yours that you showed me through your eyes when you touched my head . . ."

"What about it?" May said.

"What ARE you talking about, goddamn it?" Laura shouted.

Wright looked at Laura and the grimace left his face to be replaced by a smile. This calmed her somehow. "When May grabbed me just before you came in, she did something that let me see the time of our being together as seen through her eyes."

"So did you fuck her?" Laura asked.

"No, she fucked me!" Wright shouted back. "God! Why is your generation so crude?" He looked at her with a wet-dog expression. "Anyway," he continued, "I was already dead and unconscious. I could see the blood pouring out of my ears and nose as she was on top of me. So it's impossible that she's pregnant by me."

"Doesn't matter," May said. "Rigor mortise."

"That doesn't make any sense."

Laura stepped forward and and reached up to take one of May's hands. The skin was cold but gave her a tingling sensation like a mild electrical shock, but the sensation was quite different from touching one of the undead bubba-ettes.

This creature used to be my friend.

"May, you remember me, our talks over peach moonshine when . . .?" She had started to say *when you were still human.*

May looked at Laura's hand on hers like it was an alien creature. But her expression gradually changed. "Like drinking syrup. We gagged. We laughed. We cried. Hah!"

"You do remember!" Laura laughed in spite of the graveness of the situation. "Now remember what happened on the beach with you and John."

May looked at her curiously.

"Right after he shot himself. What happened?" Laura prompted.

May's expression became what Laura could only describe as 'transcendental.'

"He still had his gun in his hand, his pistol and his side. He was just standing there, the blood running out of his mouth. I knew he wanted me though, so I pulled his pants down, and . . ." She smiled.

"Go on," Laura said. She stole a glance at Wright. He was standing there, his hands at his side, blushing.

Who would have thought the undead could blush.

"He had a hard-on," May said, "I laid him down on the beach and I took it in my hand and slipped it inside me."

"How did you do that?" Wright said, his voice breaking."

May leapt off the desk and was in front of him in a flash. Before he could react, she brought a leg up and encircled his waist while standing on one foot. "Like this."

Wright struggled to free himself of the snare of May's leg and move closer to Laura. She could see now how terrified he was of May, and she reached out and gripped his hand. Without taking his eyes off May, he squeezed her hand – hard.

"See?" Wright said. "She's crazy or lying or both. She can't be carrying my child."

"Maybe, maybe not," Laura said. "Ever heard of 'angel lust'?"

"I don't lust for that creature," Wright said.

"It's something I learned in nursing school," Laura said. "May, what happened when John shot himself?"

"He got even bigger inside me, and," she smiled, and this time the expression was lascivious, "came inside me. I felt it. Warm. All the way up!"

"What nonsense!" Wright said.

"No, John, it isn't," Laura said.

"I know corpses can have erections, but that's only from blood settling, and that's long after death, usually when all the muscles relax, so whatever I had would have gone right away, unless I was strangled or hanged."

"No, that's not always true. The muscles at the base of the penis have to relax to let blood fill it. And in violent death, the last beats of the heart fill the lower extremities with blood, and - I've read this in a medical text - and severe brain or spinal cord trauma can make ejaculation take place."

Wright let go of her hand and looked at her as if she were betraying him.

"Priapism in living men - you know, erections that won't go away - has been associated with brain trauma."

"He stayed hard for a long time," May said unabashedly. "I milked him of every drop." She did a slow pelvic thrust to demonstrate.

Wright turned away. "You raped a corpse," he said. "My corpse."

"It was a trade. A bargain," May said.

When Wright didn't respond, Laura said, "What did you give him in return, May?"

"Energy," May said.

"You mean you brought him back to life?"

"No that would have happened anyway," she said. "All the rules of dying have changed, you know. Many still walk, but others get a little of the same bargain we got from the archangels."

"He would have been undead anyway?"

"Undead." May smiled. "I like that. Didn't you and I watch a movie like that once?" And again, for just an instant, she seemed like the human May.

"I've forgotten the title, but yes."

"What I gave him was a little bit of me, a little of us, the new angels." She focused on Laura's eyes for the first time. May's eyes were blue. They had been blue before, but they had been a warm blue. Their blue this time was as cold as ice.

"You can see and feel the difference, can't you? How special he is compared to the other undead."

"Yes, I can," she said. "He and I are connected somehow. Can you tell me why?"

"Not in a way you can understand yet," May said. "Later when you become . . ."

But she didn't finish her sentence. She cocked her head as if she heard something they didn't. Without another word she was out the door, movig so fast as to be almost a blur.

"They move so quickly, or do I see so slowly?" Laura said, but when she turned she found John Wright lying on his side on the floor. She knelt and put a hand under his neck, another to his cheek and turned his head toward her.

He was warm now, and she could have sworn she felt a pulse on the carotid artery on his neck, but as she searched for confirmation, it was gone.

Unthinking, she ran a hand through his hair. What gray hair had been there before was now entirely black. The texture of his hair was fine, slightly wavy, not oily at all, and had the sheen of good health.

As with May, the touch of his skin imparted an electric tingling. But with May she had only felt it in her fingertips. This sensation traveled right down to the base of her spine.

His eyes were closed, his chest gently rose and fell, but when she put a had to his face, she couldn't detect any sign of breath.

As she looked at his face, she experienced a curious double vision. He was still the John Wright she had known for years, fit but aging, mildly attractive except for the stern set of his mouth. However, overlapping that visage, he was the most handsome man she had ever seen. Undead or not, he emanated a vitality and virility magnetically drawing her lips to his.

She restrained herself and instead of giving him a hard kiss, she merely brushed her lips across his. The sensation was so erotic that she almost ha an orgasm right there. She took a deep breath and pulled away, afraid of what she might do.

Her hand glided across his scalp and to the crown of his head to find the hole had completely closed. Her fingers found only a small patch of scar tissue covered by hair.

R. Douglas Burns

* * *

8.

Styxian Sue, Oh How You Complete Me

Bryan.

Bryan's chainsaw sputtered, coughed, and stalled as it ran out of gas. He set the chainsaw down and sat on a knee-high stump and let his thoughts drift. Felling trees had become a kind of moving meditation for him.

The spring mornings had been alternating between unseasonably warm and unusually cold. This was one of those unusually cold mornings, and now that he had stopped working, the chill immediately began seeping through his coveralls. His skin was damp with perspiration, and he was shivering in moments.

He got to his feet and, using the side of his boot, he brushed the leaves and twigs away to make a small bare patch of dirt. In minutes, he stack enough rocks to make a fire ring and in a few minutes more, he found some crumbly dry tender in a nearby dead log. He dribbled a few teaspoons of gasoline from the can onto the tender, and when he flipped a lit match into the tender, it flashed into flame with a whoosh.

A lot of available dead limbs were lying about, but they were still wet with dew. He layered them on the fire, making a small pyramid with the smaller pieces at the bottom, and he was soon rewarded with a smoky fire.

The smoke stung his eyes and by some sort of cosmic law which reinforced his Lovecraftian impression of the basic inimical nature of the universe, curls of smoke sought him out no matter where he stood on this windless morning.

As the flames grew hotter, the smokiness of the campfire diminished, and he was able to sit back down on the stump and warm his feet and hands, but his backside remained cold. So he squatted with his back to the fire, which helped, but the rest of him quickly developed goose bumps again.

He needed a bigger fire.

And he also needed to get Laura off his mind. He had always walked as if on broken glass with her, so why did he miss her so much? It wasn't even a proper dumping, but more like she had fired him from a job. He had suspected from the start that things would end this way. But despite all that, his longing for her was a cold, dull pain centered in his chest that no fire would warm.

What bothered him most was though he had lost something irreplaceable, he felt relived. It was confusing. The relationship had been emotionally exhausting from the time it began back in college. She would be sexually aggressive one moment, and in a heartbeat she would recoil if he tried to do so much as pat her on the shoulder. The sex had been intense but at times creepy. He had felt as if someone was watching them, hanging over them, as if she were putting on a sex-show for the ghosts of her unhappy childhood.

But the intensity had given the sex almost an addictive aspect, and he had begun to identify so much with her needs that his own will had been gradually fading.

Why was he mulling over all this? He needed to get his head out of his ass and get something accomplished.

Today he was working on the west side of his grandfather's farm, a plot of wood bordering the Cartwright place. The fences had been down here for much of the winter, and Cartwright's goats had infiltrated his woods, vacuuming up most the small shrubs and vines that would now be useful as fuel. All of the wood Bryan had cut the last few days was still too green to burn; he had already hauled off the bigger pieces of cured wood to sell.

However, across the fence on Cartwright's place, Bryan could see a large pile of old fence posts. He mulled over the idea of pilfering a few and decided that Cartwright owed him a bit of firewood for the trespassing goats.

Most of the posts were of treated oak, but the creosote had long since departed and the wood was riddled with termite tracks. He pulled a couple off the top of the pile and dragged them, one in each hand, to his burgeoning fire and threw them on top. In a couple of minutes the fire changed from a smoking mound to leaping, crackling yellow flames. He warmed himself for a bit, rotisserie-style, standing close and turning slowly so the blazing hot fire boiled the moisture out of his clothes.

But as with people who burn too brightly, fires from rotten wood do not last long. His thoughts turned to Laura, who fit this metaphor better than anyone he had ever known. He tried to build an imaginary mental scenario, one where Laura hadn't dumped him a second time, where things had leveled out emotionally, where they stayed together and built some sort of life. But no matter how he manipulated the details, it always played out the same. Whether he made money or not, no matter how attentive he tried to be to her needs, no matter how good the sex was, she would always be running away, seeking some sort of catharsis he couldn't give her. She was incomplete at some fundamental level of her psyche. She would never be satisfied with just him, and he doubted she ever did or would feel as completed by him as he had by her.

He let out a growl, a sound born of anger, pain and loss that worked its way up from his gut and rushed from his throat like an animal let loose from a cage. He actually felt the loss of her in his chest, and he now understood what people meant by heartbreak. A fragment of a poem came to mind – by Rilke, maybe – something about random chance putting his heart in the hands of someone who didn't care about his yesterdays, much less his tomorrows. His memory of the verse was faulty, but that was the general idea. Laura wasn't cold-hearted, she just couldn't be distracted from her quest. She was looking for completion and she hadn't found it with him.

The fire was already dying down, and cold seeped through his denim coveralls. He felt stupid and emotionally lame, as if his love for Laura was a simple puzzle that he was too clueless to solve.

This thought depressed him even more. Maybe he should just sit back down on the stump and allow the fire go out and let himself die of hypothermia, a sort of slow lover's leap via exposure.

But this idea was so stupid it made him laugh; the morning wasn't cold enough to do anything but give him a bad cold.

Stupid.

Unless he wanted to be both heartbroken and sick, he needed to build a better fire or go back to the farmhouse. He had noticed a scattering of cedar posts mixed in with the oak ones in Cartwright's pile. Cedar wood contained a natural preservative, and though the posts were as old as the creosote-treated oak posts, they would not be so crumbly and should burn slower.

He trudged over to the pile, still trying to purge thoughts of Laura, but she remained a smoldering ache in his heart.

The universe wasn't fair. In fact, it was downright hostile, built to a cosmic blueprint that would deny him such a basic need as love. The cedar post was buried under a couple of layers of oak posts – another symptom of a contrary universal order – and his anger growing, he pitched them off two at time. His eyes watered; he wasn't sure if from the smoke or with tears.

Fuck you, Universe! Fuck you!

And the universe answered by causing the top half of the interwoven stack collapse.

The posts rolled down, pounding his shins. As he stepped back to get out the way, a post rolled under his foot, and he fell backward, landing hard enough on his back to knock the wind out of him.

He lay there for a minute, stunned, staring at the sky, gray clouds with patches of blue, then sat up slowly, looking for any damage. A broken bone or a deep laceration could be a death sentence these days as antibiotics and other essential elements of medical supplies were nearly nonexistent in Creedance. A pile of wet leaves had cushioned the back of his head from the fall, but just inches to the left was a chunk of limestone the size of his fist and vaguely pyramidal in shape. He had been spared for some reason, probably just dumb luck, but he wasn't sure he cared. As he got to his feet, the empty feeling of deep personal loss that had been exorcised by fear came back with a vengeance.

What now? Maybe he should figure out some way to get drunk and stay that way for a long time; a definite option.

Another post rolled off the pile, catching his attention.

Then another fell.

Something was moving within the pile. Some animal must have made its home in an empty gap between the posts, and that home had now collapsed thanks to him. Now whatever was in there was trying to get out.

He could decide whether to help or just watch. He could see movement now, as something white snaked up to push fragments of rotten wood out of the way.

He jumped back as a woman's hand emerged to flutter in the cold air. The wrist was slender, the hand stark white with bloody fingernails. It gave a come a come-hither wave. After the initial shock, his first impulse was to rush forward and clear the logs off the buried woman. But his previous experiences with angels who seemed inclined to entomb themselves in old wood made him wary.

The hand waved again, and a muted cry like that of a hurt kitten escaped from the woodpile. Did it mew a "help-me!" or was that his imagination? "Come here, come here," the wave said, and now he could see a multi-colored tattoo on the pale skin of the inner wrist. The tattoo was composed of a series of concentric five-pointed stars, each inked a different color.

He recognized the tattoo and by it, the wrist – both belonged to Suzanne Zimmerman, Ben Cartwright's wife. He had met her a couple of times, had coffee and even a drink with her once at Shakespeare's Bar and Pizza in Columbia when she was taking a few classes at the university. That was before Laura, and he had tried to pick up Suzanne, really wanted to pick her up, even though Goth, tattooed girls weren't his type. She was at least twenty years younger than the farmer she had lived with. She had multiple piercings, including ear gauges and eyebrow studs. She had started talking about it being her common-law wedding anniversary and showed him a ring. It had been a turquoise and silver ring, not at all like a wedding band, and he had decided she was just blowing him off. He remembered trying to shrug off the rejection, failing, and getting shit-faced drunk on cheap draws.

Face it. He had never dealt well with rejection.

Later he learned she really was married, by common-law rules, unhappy, but faithful nonetheless.

Gingerly he began removing the posts one at a time so to as not to injure her further. As he tossed the posts aside, she gradually came into view. First her shoulder and hip, then her head and legs. She was curled up on her side in a fetal position. After he tossed a few more posts aside, she turned her head and looked at him with terrified eyes.

"Help me," she said, her voice barely more than a whisper.

"I'm trying," he said. "I'm wondering if I should try to lift you out of there."

Her face looked terrible with a huge bruise under one eye. And her neck! He remembered her having more tattoos, but if so, they were obscured by large bruises, purple turning to black and yellow, that circled her neck like a noose.

"Maybe I should go get help," he said. "I might hurt you more lifting you out."

"Don't leave me here. I'm freezing!" She struggled to sit up, which set another post rolling off the pile. He hopped over the falling post, then stepped back to the pile to put a hand on her shoulder. She was wearing a skimpy blouse with fishnet sleeves, and her skin was ice cold. She shivered under his touch.

"Get me out of here," she repeated in a rasping whisper and tried to stretch out a leg. The pile of posts shifted again, threatening to collapse entirely.

"Okay, okay," he said. "Just lie still, and I'll see if I can lift you out."

Moving slowly, he worked one hand under her shoulder and another under her bent knees. He had to bend awkwardly at the waist, but she seemed so tiny he wasn't concerned about straining his back.

"I'm afraid this wood pile is going to come down like a house of cards when I pull you out," he said. "So I'm going to yank you out quickly. Try to keep your body in this position with your knees folded up when I pull. Okay?"

"I'm freezing," she repeated.

Not waiting for a direct answer, he heaved her body up to his chest in one smooth motion and stepped back quickly, almost tripping on another post lying on the ground. She lay limp in his arms and let her legs stretch out, her head fall backward.

He could now see that the other side of her face and her shoulder were covered in caked, dried blood and dead leaves. She brought a hand up to brush away the blood and leaves. He was shocked to see one ear was entirely missing. She dropped her hand weakly down to her side, and said in a faint voice, "If it wasn't for the cold and the pain, it would be almost like I don't exist."

"Is that a song lyric?" he asked.

"I don't think so," she said, then lifted her head a little and added, "Maybe."

He hated to set her down on the cold, wet ground but had little choice. The blaze from the dead wood had died, and the fire was mostly smoke.

"I'll be right back," he said and went to fetch some cedar posts.

"Don't leave me again," she said, but seemed to be talking to someone else.

Coming back with two cedar posts, he plopped them crisscross on the fire, sending up an encouraging flurry of sparks. A few of the sparks landed on her, but she was so wet they quickly went out. A wave of shivering passed over her body, starting from her bare feet, rolling up her legs under the ripped fishnet hose and across her uncovered stomach and torso.

He now wished he had brought the pickup. But to save precious gasoline, he had left it back at the farm house, a good half-mile away, thinking he would just cut wood and pile it, leaving it to be hauled another day.

The cedar posts caught fire and burned with blue and yellow flames. The resulting fire was not as hot as the one generated by the oak posts but was enough to create a circle of warmth.

Thinking the work of cutting wood would keep him warm, he

had only worn shorts and a T-shirt underneath his coveralls, and the chill was now seeping in. Despite the radiant heat from the fire, Suzanne's shivering had increased until it looked like a seizure. He realized he had no choice. He unlaced his work boots, unzipped his coveralls and stepped out of them. Now wearing only boxer shorts, wet socks and a damp T-shirt, he began shivering himself.

He draped the coveralls – they were dry everywhere but the seat – over Suzanne, then quickly put his work boots back on.

When he tried to take the coveralls back for a minute, she clung to them weakly.

"Let go, Ms. Zimmerman," he said. "Just for a minute."

"They smell good," she said, delirious.

"Look, we don't have time to be subtle," he said and jerked them out of her hands. She looked at him as if he had betrayed her.

He spread the coveralls on the ground beside her and unzipped them all the way. Stepping briefly between her and the fire, he lifted her up and on top of the coveralls. The fire threatened to sear the backs of his legs, but he felt the cold of the damp air sink into as he moved to her feet. Grabbing both feet in one hand, he pushed her legs up to her chest. Again, she was too weak to give much resistance. With the other hand, he managed to get one of her legs into the coveralls. Both of her feet wanted to go into the same pants leg. Cursing and shivering, he struggled with her until both legs were in separate pants legs.

His teeth chattering, he sat her up and got one arm and then the other into the sleeves. She had stopped fighting him and was looking at him curiously.

"I hardly know you," she said. "Why are you doing this for me?"

He ignored her question as he zipped up the front of the coverall. One of her nipples was exposed, pink in contrast to the stark white breast and black fabric of the remainder of her blouse.

He held her by her shoulders and looked into her eyes. When she didn't focus on him, he shook her gently. When her eyes found his, he said, "I'm going to carry you back to the house where it's warm, but it's a long way away, and you're going to have to help me. Understand?"

"It's a long, long way away," she parroted.

"You're hopeless," he said. How was he going to do this? He couldn't carry her a half-mile in his arms. Without thinking more about it, he turned, squatting so that he straddled her legs with his back to her. Then he reached behind, grabbed both her arms and crossed them in front of his chest. When he stood, her legs dangled. Worse, as he tried to walk, her long legs flopped against his legs, and nearly tripped him.

"Suzanne?"

When she didn't respond, he shouted, "Suzanne! Wake up!"

"What?" she answered.

"It's time for a horsey-ride," he said, feeling silly.

"I don't want a horsey-ride," she said." My arms hurt."

It was a good sign that she could feel anything at all.

"Wrap your legs around my waist." He managed to get one hand over her crossed wrists then reached behind with the other hand and pulled one of her legs up around his waist. To his surprise, Suzanne obeyed, lifted the other leg and wrapped it around him, crossing her ankles, gripping his waist hard. Her breasts pressed firmly against his back; he could feel her erect nipples through his damp T-shirt.

"You really smell good," she said. "I could eat you up." She nuzzled his ear, which gave him the heebie-jeebies.

Because the propane that fired his water heater was scarce, he hadn't had a bath in two days. He suspected he had the ambience of a homeless person but didn't argue with her about smelling good. Whatever delusion encouraged her to hold onto him was better not questioned.

The fire was still blazing, but the ground around it was covered in wet leaves and pine needles, so it should burn itself out eventually. Whatever, Suzanne's condition was so serious, he couldn't wait for the fire to die.

He began a slow lope through the woods towards the farmhouse. Suzanne laid her head on his shoulder, her cheek brushing his. He could see where the lost ear had been. There was just a hole there, surrounded by a ring of clotted blood. He tried not to keep looking – he should keep an eye open for roots or deadwood that could trip him up – but not to stare down into the little hole in the side of her head was impossible.

Suzanne was could only be described as "willowy." Though she was tall, perhaps five-foot eight or nine, she was all legs and arms. She probably weighed no more than 110 pounds. As long as she kept her legs tight around his waist, her weight didn't affect his balance, and the chances of getting her back alive to the farmhouse now seemed possible. The jog quickly warmed him up, but blackberry and green briar played hell with his bare legs. After a few hundred yards through the woods, his shins were streaked with blood. However, the wounds were not deep and looked a lot worse than they were. The biggest threat was green briar vine, which grew close to the ground and wrapped itself around trees and shrubs; natural barbed tripwire.

Deeper in the woods, the oaks were fewer oaks and more loblolly pine. The pine had never been thinned – it wasn't really suitable for firewood and there were no local pulpwood factories. The result was a lot of scrub trees bunched together, competing for sunlight and moisture and choking out each other in the process. Amid these pitched biological battles, a few giant pines, fifty feet to seventy feet tall, had long ago won the battle. They overshadowed the runt trees, making their fight for survival that much more difficult. And both the giants and the runts made the going harder. The runts grew too close together for him to do anything but zig-zag around them. And the giants formed a dense overhead canopy, blocking the already limited daylight, making it hard to see the snares of green briar.

He knew he should slow down, but to do so threatened defeat in another way. His pace slowed by the scrub pine, he was getting cold again. Worse, he felt his energy waning.

The toe of his boot snagged on a strand of green briar, and he went stumbling, catching his balance at the last moment but not before slamming his shoulder into a tree.

From above came laughter. He looked up into the shadowy expanse to catch a fleeting impression of several large white birds. Though no wildlife expert, he was familiar with these woods and couldn't think of any fowl that might fit what he glimpsed. They were too small to be angels. Wild guinea hens perhaps? No, those birds were nearly flightless and – except for an occasional clucking – mute. A neighbor had once raised peacocks, one of them albino, but such creatures were rare, and their call was a screech, nothing like the twittering sound he'd heard.

The sound came again, most definitely a chirping, infantile giggling. A lone pinecone, dislodged by whatever moved above, fell at his feet. Then another, the size of a softball, missed his head by inches. Another supersized pinecone whizzed by, and another, this one bounced off his chest and hurt like a son-of-a-bitch.

And the giggling rose as three huge pinecones came down simultaneously.

"They're back!" Suzanne screamed.

Without thinking he ran, picking his feet up high, jolting his back and knees with every step. Behind him, he could hear more pinecones hitting the ground. Above, the movement in the upper branches paralleled his path. He had to grab Suzanne's wrists with both hands and pull them down to keep her from choking him.

In minutes he was out of the piney woods and into a stretch of scrub oak. Suzanne had slipped down on his back. Her already limited reserves of energy were apparently weakening too. He broke into a clearing shaded by old-growth oaks, ringed with brush. A small, stagnant pond filled with green algae and light-starved weeds occupied the center of the clearing.

Only about a week ago he had come into this clearing to find an angel – one of the hundred original archangels, not a human-angel clone – seized by paroxysms of pain and convulsions as it gave birth to an enormous cocoon. Was it only a week ago? It seemed like years.

On that day – on another cold day like today – he had made the mistake of following the archangel as it burst from the clearing carrying the cocoon. Reconstructing the events later with Uncle Robert's help, he had apparently witnessed the rebirth cycle of one the angels, something that took place partially in a dimension alien to human consciousness. But at the time, he hadn't known that. Though not religious, he had stared into the face of a giant blue god with a thousand eyes and a thousand senses he couldn't even name. The experience had shaken the foundations of his sanity.

The clearing was free of angels today – hybrid or otherwise –

and despite the memory of that soul-shaking experience, he felt more secure here. At least he could see his attackers.

Or could he? He pivoted slowly on one heel, scanning the tree-tops for any movement.

None came.

The woods beyond the clearing looked forbidding now, but he had no choice. Other than turning back the way he had come, he had only one way out of the clearing. Without looking up again, he took a narrow break in the ring of the brush. He pushed himself into a brisk jog, hunching over to keep Suzanne from slipping further down. In minutes, he was winded, his muscles cramping, his knees aching, but he kept trotting. After what seemed an eternity, he emerged from the dark woods into the open pasture without any attacks from above. He wanted to set Suzanne down in the tall dead grass and rest. But he feared if he sat down he wouldn't get up again. Moreover, Suzanne was shivering violently again. The house was less than a quarter mile away. Over the gentle rise of the pasture, he could see the upper story, white paint peeling away to gray clapboard, its windows like dead eyes but nonetheless welcoming.

He took a deep breath and let it out, marching now rather than jogging. Suzanne let out a long sigh, and he felt her grip around his neck sliding off and her leg-lock loosening. He grabbed her wrists again with one hand. The work in the woods over the past year had thickened his fingers, and his clamping grip on her thin wrists would probably leave bruises, but he had no choice. With his other hand he grabbed one of her ankles.

The posture was unbalanced, and he had to slow down to a weak wobble. When he reached the front porch of the house, he could barely make it up the steps. He backed into the porch swing and unloaded Suzanne in it, which set the rickety structure swaying and its chains squeaking.

The door was unlocked – no sense locking it when he wasn't here as it would be easy to kick in – but the latch was old and he needed both hands to jiggle it until it turned. With the last vestiges of his strength, he picked up Suzanne and entered the house like a groom carrying his new bride over a threshold, and kicked the door closed behind him.

Inside wasn't much warmer than outside. He dropped Suzanne on the couch and pulled off his soggy boots. From the downstairs bedroom, he retrieved two of his grandmother's handmade quilts, both old and frayed, one of which she had made as she was dying of breast cancer. The dying-quilt's patchwork pattern was of angels in various sizes and poses, each painstakingly stitched by hand. She had made it from old dresses, cast-off clothes, even pieces of one of his plaid childhood shirts. She had called it her "heavenly dreams" quilt, for she had known death was certain and soon. She had died only days after finishing it.

He covered Suzanne with the angel quilt. She was now even paler than when he had discovered her in the woodpile. He wrapped himself in the other quilt.

When he laid his hand on her forehead, she was ice cold and didn't move. Suspecting the worse, he felt for a pulse and found none. Yet he could hear her breathing, a small miniature snore, and he decided his pulse-taking technique, which he had learned from Laura, was flawed.

The first order of business was to get both of them warm. He left her on the couch and went to the kitchen. His grandparents' house had been built in the early 1900s, and had not originally been plumbed for water. The propane water heater was housed in a small add-on closet in the kitchen. Its pipes ran outside the wall, fastened against the fading floral wallpaper by wooden braces.

Checking that the pilot light was still lit, he turned up the thermostat. After a few seconds the burner flared up, emitting a blue glow through the little window.

Returning to the front room, he found Suzanne as he had left her, and took time to go back to the bedroom to trade his quilt toga and shed his wet jockey shorts and T-shirt for dry underwear, a pair of dry jeans, wool socks and a flannel shirt.

His shivering subsided, and he returned to the living room and dug in the fireplace ashes with a poker. Underneath a layer of ashes was a bed of hot coals. He pushed the ashes to the side, stirred the coals, and added some dry kindling. When that blazed, he added some fully cured blackjack oak. In a few minutes, the fire was blazing. In a few more minutes, the room was noticeably warmer. Now warm and dry, he felt better, stronger, and his mind clearer. His original intention had been to run a hot bath and warm up Suzanne. Now that he was thinking clearly, he decided it would better just to take her directly to the clinic. Jenkins would be there – he was always there – and would be better equipped to tread hypothermia.

He uncovered Suzanne and removed the coveralls. He should get her out of her wet clothes, but the thought of doing so made him feel uncomfortable. Instead, he covered her again with the quilt and went outside to start the truck. The truck's engine turned over when he tried the key but would not start. Checking under the hood, he found nothing obviously wrong. His grandfather had been a mechanic, and long before the fall of the saucer had converted the truck to a dual-fuel vehicle that ran on either gasoline or propane. Gasoline was hard to find these days, so Bryan had sacrificed the propane from the furnace to fill the large cylinder in the truck bed. The dial gauge on the propane cylinder showed half full. There was a valve under the dash that switched fuels, and he checked that as well. There was no reason the piece-of-shit truck shouldn't start, but it didn't.

Cursing aloud, he returned to the house and started filling the tub in the bathroom just off the kitchen. The water wasn't hot enough to steam, but he didn't feel he had time to wait. He carried Suzanne, still wrapped in the quilt, to the bathroom floor.

Spreading out the quilt, he stripped the coveralls off her as the faucet continued to fill the antique porcelain tub. He pulled off her miniskirt – it was leather, no less. She didn't open her eyes, but lifted her legs to aid him. The fishnet hose disintegrated as he tried to pull them off. She wore no panties and the sparse strip of pubic hair proved she was a true redhead. As tired as he was, he got an erection, which he tried to ignore.

He had to sit her up to remove the remains of her blouse, and she opened her blue eyes and laid both arms on his shoulders in a kind of loose embrace.

"I'm trying to help you," he said , more to convince himself than her.

"Men!" she whispered. "You always say that, but you're always undressing me, babying me, or hurting me."

"Okay, then," he said. "Be my good baby." He lifted her blouse off over her head. He could see the tattoos on her neck now. Had the bruises faded already? No, it had only been an hour or so since he found her. It must be the light. Her breasts looked larger than he had expected.

"I'm going to lift you up now and put you in the tub, Suzanne."

She looked at him slightly amused, an eyebrow cocked. The missing ear was on the same side as the cocked eye, and the action gave her face a lopsided look.

"It would be good if you could grab hold of the edge of the tub and steady yourself."

She didn't respond, but she didn't resist either as he turned her sideways and slipped one forearm under her butt and the other around her back and in her armpit. To his surprise as he lifted her she did indeed reach over and put a hand on the opposite side of the tub. The water only warm, but she cried out, "Hot!" as he lowered her into it.

"See, you're hurting me," she said and pushed herself halfway up and out of the water with her arms.

"No, Suzanne. It's only lukewarm."

She shook her head at him.

"Really it is," he said. "It only seems hot because you're half-frozen. Trust me."

She stared at him, her eyes focusing on his. She reached some decision, perhaps based on the sincerity of his gaze or more likely on some past experience. Whatever, she relaxed and let him lower her into the water.

Her toes were toward the faucet, and he freed his arm from underneath her and turned off the water. It was running cold already because the temperamental water heater took forever to heat water above tepidity.

She was tall enough so with her feet against one end of the tub and her legs straight, her back leaned against the other end, leaving her sitting up, the water only up to her waist. He lifted her knees so her legs bent and gradually scooted her down so the water covered her breasts. Little twigs and bits of leaves floated to the top of the water. He scooped them up and threw them into the toilet, then got a washcloth and some soap.

She closed her eyes and remained passive as he washed her. He truly wished his erection would subside. It didn't though, flagging the fact that he was indeed a male animal despite all his good intentions. He grabbed a more-or-less clean towel from a shelf near the tub and tied it around his waist, but the towel seemed to highlight the bulge in his pants instead of hiding it.

He continued washing her shoulders, her neck, avoiding the bloody patch where her lost ear had been. He had no shampoo, just the skimpy bar of Ivory soap, so he used it on her hair, too. More twigs and leaves and a few little black beetles floated to the top. He scooped them up and dumped them in the commode as he had done before.

The soapy water ran down the side of her head and began to color the water red as it dissolved some of the clotted blood. But the wound still looked nasty and he could see dirt and more detritus embedded in the clots. Steeling himself, he soaked a washcloth in the water, wishing it were warmer, soaped it and pressed it against the wound.

"Does that hurt, Suzanne?" he asked.

"No, feels good," she said, a little smile on her lips. "It all feels good."

"Okay. Can you hold the washcloth against your head while I rinse your hair?"

"Yes," she said, but he had to take her hand and position it. When he let go she kept her hand there.

He used a small plastic bowl to dip water from a cleaner portion of the tub water.

"Close your eyes or the soapy water will sting," he said and realized he had never washed another human being before. Somewhere in memories almost primal he remembered these words being uttered by his mother. Or was that an imagined memory?

She closed her eyes tightly, and he poured the water over her head. Then he pulled her hand away and poured another bowl over the wound. He was rewarded with clean skin, but shuddered at the place where the ear had been. It appeared that it had not been cut off, as he had originally presumed, but gnawed off. In fact, he could see tooth marks lower on the jaw line like a bloody hickey. It was a child-size bite mark though, leaving him to ponder what had attacked her. He had his suspicions, though they didn't make much sense; he didn't know if such creatures as he imagined actually existed.

The tub water was now truly dirty and it had cooled considerably.

"Do you think you can stand if I help you?" he asked her.

As an answer, she rose, holding the edge of the tub and taking his offered hand. She stood there for a moment, her skin rosy now from the warm water, lit by the pale yellow hue of the bare lightbulb, her wet, red hair streaming down, hiding the lost ear and lying gently on her pale shoulders. He must have been staring, because she modestly moved one hand to cover her mons and the other to cross and cover her breasts. But she didn't look embarrassed; she looked rather amused, as if sharing a private joke. Slowly he got it: Botticelli's Birth of Venus.

He laughed and felt like Igor tending to a goddess as she steadied herself on his shoulder and stepped out of the tub.

The quilt that he had used to cover her before was wet, so he led her, naked, into the living room. By now the fireplace had heated the room, and he stood her near it while he retrieved the other quilt from the bedroom. When he came back, she was turning slowly in front of the fire, her wet hair still dripping down her back. He draped the quilt over her shoulders and led her into the bedroom. He pulled back the covers and sat her on the edge of the mattress. She just sat there, looking at him with expectation.

"Get under the covers," he ordered, holding up the blankets. She did so.

He tucked her in and noticed her looking at the towel still rolled around his waist like a kilt. He looked down and saw a still-noticeable bulge. As tired as he was, his penis had a mind of its own.

"Look. No, I mean listen. I know you're probably hungry, but I'm about to fall down. I'm going to go sleep an hour or so on the couch.

Do you understand?"

She nodded. "I'm not hungry. Not at all."

"When I get back up, I see about bandaging you ear."

"What about my ear?" She tried to pull her arm out from under the covers.

He stopped her. "Never mind that now. If you feel like it, you can find some canned food in the kitchen cupboard, but I think mainly what you need right now is rest. I know that's what I need."

As he left, she said, "Don't leave me alone."

"I'll be in the next room," he said.

"You could sleep in here, next to me," she said.

"That's not a good idea," he said. "I'm leaving the bedroom door open so you'll get some heat from the fireplace."

He went back into the living room and collapsed on the couch. As he fell asleep, he heard something large crawling on the roof. But the sound came as if in a dream, and he couldn't rise to do anything about it.

Maybe it was only squirrels in the attic.

But some part of his brain knew better. Where was his grandfather's shotgun? In the broom closet in the kitchen. It was a real blunderbuss, not a pump action, but double-barreled, loadable with only two shells at time.

He forced himself to get both feet on the floor, then stumbled toward the kitchen broom closet, twice forgetting what he was looking for, not remembering as he laid back down on the couch.

* * *

9.

Kiss My Empty Braincase

Laura.

Laura sat on the edge of the bed and kicked off her shoes. Wright, modest by old school standards even in death, was undressing in the bathroom. She heard the heavy police-issue belt buckle clank on the tile floor as he dropped his pants. Even if he had been completely silent, she would have known he was there, sensed him in the way a migrating bird knows which way is south. He was another part of her, lost from the beginning of time, now found.

She wasn't sure, but it felt like a lot like love as well as lust, which was exactly what she didn't want to be with anyone, alive or undead, certainly not with a reincarnation of the aging sheriff who had shadowed her during her self-destructive teens and early twenties.

She was compelled to consummate whatever it was she felt, which was why they were in Wright's house. He had driven his police SUV here, and she had followed in her Volkswagen, a half-hearted attempt to be discrete. Common sense told her that she should get up and leave right now; her crazy heart, which seemed to have the majority voice these days, told her to sit tight and wait for Wright to come out of the bathroom.

Marguerite had left behind many traces of herself: cosmetics on the dresser, lace curtains, a lingering smell of lilac perfume. The room was overwhelmingly feminine and gave the impression that Marguerite had truly lived here while Wright had been just a tourist, his maleness barely tolerated.

She stood up, unzipped her skirt and let it drop to her ankles, then kicked the garment, a pale-orange ugly thing with side pockets and streaked with ketchup, into the corner. She examined her legs, running a hand over her calves. They could use shaving, but razors, like every other disposable consumer item, had become very scarce.

She knew with absolute certainty that a little stubble wouldn't deter John Wright, just as she knew that if he smelled like a rotting corpse, she would still be obsessively drawn to him.

She shivered at the thought. He might really smell like a walking corpse. He most certainly was dead. No one could live with his brains blown out through the top of his head. But she was under some sort of spell, and he smelled and looked irresistible. She could smell him even now, from fifteen feet away and through the bathroom door, a sensory feat that should be impossible even for a dog.

But everything about Wright was impossible, and while her actions were idiotic and self-destructive, she was compelled to continue.

She pulled off her panties but left on her sweatshirt for John to have the pleasure of removing. The sweatshirt had been a necessity for the cool weather; she wished she had worn something more feminine to work, but she knew Wright would enjoy finishing undressing her as much as if she had worn a lace teddy. She knew this as surely as if they had been lovers for years and this wasn't the first time for them.

Suzanne.

Suzanne Zimmerman woke from a lucid dream based on what she remembered as a real event. The day the angel saucer had slid into Lost Lake, she and Ben had rowed out in his canoe to watch the sinking close up. As they neared the ship, a huge, glowing air bubble rose from below like a radioactive Godzilla fart, illuminating the depths, rising slowly and fascinating them at first by its size, luminosity and violent churning. It was so beautiful and hypnotic they were slow to realize it might be dangerous. They had tried to paddle out of the way, but time slowed to the crawl of a living nightmare of frantic, useless splashing of wood paddles, and then the monstrous bubble ruptured, and the resulting waves had flipped them out of the canoe and into the cold, dark waters of Lost Lake.

Neither she nor Ben were swimmers, and, idiotically, they hadn't been wearing life preservers. As the deep, dark cold water closed over their heads, all rational thought abandoned both of them until they became panicked animals, scrambling over each other, grasping for handholds on clothes, flesh, hair as if the other's body was a ladder to safety. But it was an unequal survivor contest, for he was stronger. She became indignant that he, in his drowning panic, was not ready to sacrifice himself for her, that he had tried to use her as ballast – exactly as she had done to him – and she remained indignant though she knew they were both at fault in their selfish and separate acts of self-preservation.

They had survived only because the canoe had drifted close enough for them to cling to it and paddle to shore. The canoe had been empty in the Real-Life Event – she whispered repeated this aloud to herself in the darkened bedroom, "Real-Life Event, Real-Life Event," turning the phrase over and over as if it were an odd knickknack, trying to find its meaning or purpose.

Her dream closely echoed the events of the Real-Life Event: the sound of the canoe sliding through the water, the feel of the cold water, the way the water stung her eyes. Everything was the same — with one exception. In the dream from which she had just awoken, Bryan Douglas had been in the canoe, and as she struggled to climb in, Ben had grabbed her ankles, then rose up, his massive head above water, his weightlifter's arms wrapped around her waist, a ponderous weight pulling her back under the surface to a cold death. In the dream, Bryan had grabbed her wrist with one hand and with the other had used a paddle to wallop Ben on the head. The paddle met Ben's head with a solid *thunk*, like a fast-pitched baseball hitting a catcher's mitt. Ben's eyes rolled up in his head, and he let go of her.

As she looked back – still lost in this dream with a false history

– she had been paralyzed, turned to salt by the vision of her husband's bloody face as it sank into the depths while Bryan pulled her aboard.

"Rescued you," Bryan said in the dream. But she hadn't felt so much as "rescued" as "set free" by this act, and though she knew the Bryan-version was only a dream, that in the Real-Life Event, once the mindless panic had passed, she and her husband had worked together to right the canoe and paddle to safety.

But the dream held more sway; on an emotional level, it felt more real than what had happened in the Real-Life Event.

This intimation persisted, making her feel nothing but fear and disdain for her Ben, while for Bryan – a young man she barely knew – she felt what only could be described as love and passion and deep personal connection. It was like an addiction, and for that reason alone, she should get up while he was still sleeping and run from this house, run from him and what she felt for him. She feared the unquestioning trust that he engendered in her. Yet what she felt for Bryan made her feel a complete person for the first time in her life.

She could hear Bryan snoring gently in the next room and desperately hoped he might feel the same way for her.

She sat up in bed and examined herself in the large dresser mirror across the room. How could he? Even in the dimming light, she could see she was a mess, an aberration, a freak. Yet the way he had looked at her – or rather had tried to avoid looking at her – as she had stood in the tub and let him towel her dry – and the huge bulge in his pants – revealed he saw her in another light.

Had he really been too tired to do anything then and there or had he been trying to be a gentleman? His All-American Boy Scout morals might be getting in the way.

Her hand stole up to examine the place where her ear had been. Maybe all she needed to do was spiff up the packaging a little bit.

Byran.

Bryan was not surprised he awoke on the couch with Suzanne sitting on top of him. For reasons that weren't entirely clear, he had a dream of her doing exactly that, dressed exactly as she was now. He had been sure it was a dream then, and had got up to feed the fireplace with more chunks of split wood. That had been the late afternoon. The fireplace blaze had dwindled but still cast enough warm, rosy light to illuminate her face. The windows were dark, which meant he had slept the last of the day away.

Suzanne, on her knees with her legs astraddle his hips, was staring at him with the same self-absorbed, amused look she had given him while she was in the bathtub. He didn't remember taking off his jeans, but he could feel the taunt skin of her inner thighs against his hips.

Her skin was not cold as he expected but was warm to the touch.

"I feel a lot better," she said. "Like a new woman."

She looked ethereally beautiful and cute at the same time? She wore an old, dead woman's gown, a diaphanous thing with little faded pink bows at the shoulders. On her head was something that looked like a cross between a hat and a hair band. Made of a glossy material, it had several folds and was wider on one side of her head than the other. She had pinned a large rhinestone broach over the wider side to hide her missing ear. While he slept, she must have rummaged through his grandmother Bess's armoire. His grandfather had kept his wife's clothes and jewelry undisturbed in the bedroom closet after her death, which had been nearly a decade ago. Weird, it was like making love to the beautiful, young ghost of his grandmother. *If that wasn't a goth thing, what was?*

She looked at him curiously. "You want to ask me something. I can tell," she said.

"Someone beat the holy crap out of you, and …" He stopped himself from talking about the hacked-off ear. "And left you for dead there in the woods. Do you remember who it was?"

"I don't remember much of anything. I remember being cold and in pain, but I don't remember who did it. I don't think I woke up completely until you started digging me out."

"So what's the last thing you remember?"

"I don't know. It's as if everything was a dream before you carried me over to the fire. I'm not sure I can tell the dreams from the real thing anymore, but. . ."

"But what?"

"I remember flying. And I remember having a big fight with Ben. He was throwing things around, screaming, and his eyes empty of thought, but that could be a dream too."

"Who's Ben?"

"Ben Cartwright, my husband. You know. You've sold him firewood."

"Oh yeah. I only know him as 'Mr. Cartwright.' Anything else?"

"I also remember something about slaughtered cows, but that could be a dream, too. I don't know. It really warps me," she said.

What disturbed Bryan was not that she was someone else's wife, but that she should by all rights be dead. Yet here she was, sitting on top of him. Her husband was allegedly a Buddhist and non-violent, but he outweighed Bryan by at least eighty pounds and was built like a pro football running back. He was also reputedly bi-polar, and, in a manic state, might might have bitten off Suzanne's ear and tossed her into the woodpile like a broken doll.

Bryan knew that if he had even a little common sense, he should be discouraging what was about to happen for the sake of his survival. But he felt disassociated, as if this was another dream-moment and his real body lay asleep somewhere. Any thoughts of caution evaporated as she began thrusting her hips back and forth as if she were riding a horse. Something sharp, like a small rock or piece of gravel, painfully poked in his back, and the house suddenly smelled of damp, rotten leaves, but these impressions slid by like gray, scudding clouds. He became so aroused that his concentration was confined in his lower abdomen and his dick. His hands automatically slid up under the thin gown, over her thighs and up to her flat tummy to cup her small, firm breasts.

She sighed, and leaned down to kiss him, oddly strong for a small woman, pushing his elbows against his chest and pressed his hands harder against her breasts. Her nipples were small hard pebbles under his palms. Her hand sought out his dick, and with her thumb and index finger, sheencircling it at the base, her other three fingers cupping his scrotum.

I'm lost in her; this is sure to end badly.

But the pain of loss that had possessed him since Laura dumped him now faded as if into a past life, and he didn't care about the consequences.

Wright.

Wright sat on the closed lid of the commode, staring at his feet, afraid to come out of the bathroom.

Like the rest of his body, his feet didn't look like they belonged to him. He wasn't as hairy as he used to be, and what little body hair he had left had changed in texture. Before, black, coarse, curly hair had covered most of his body, even his back, a physical trait that had grossed out Marguerite. Too bad the human Marguerite no longer existed and could see him now. His old body hair had fallen out this morning when he had showered, though he hadn't noticed any re-growth of hair at the time, he certainly had it now. The re-growth was finer and neither curly or thick. And he was abolutely sure his scrotum had been completely bald after the morning shower. Now it was covered with fine, straight short hair, perhaps only a quarter-inch long. Like all his new body hair, the scrotum hair lay close to his skin, like thin fur on a new-born animal.

Would it continue to grow out at this accelerated rate? Would he look like wolf boy the circus freak by morning?

Right now, the hair wasn't thick enough yet to cover his skin. It was actually quite sparse, as if his natural body hair was growing back, just finer. His skin seemed to be changing too, becoming smoother, rosy with health. An old eye-shaped scar on the back of his right hand, the reminder of an infected insect bite from childhood, was gone. He could see the blue veins just below the skin on his hands. But he still couldn't find his own pulse.

All these changes – this rejuvenation – should have elated him, but instead made him feel like a stranger in his own body.

And when he ran his hand over the top of his head, he found that the hole had closed up completely. The hair there hadn't grown back, though; a small bald spot remained, about an inch in diameter.

With his fingertips he could trace a series of concentric ridges, like a bull's-eye, with raised rings underneath the skin. In the exact center of the bull's-eye was either a small depression or a tiny hole, he couldn't tell which.

Should he ask Laura to look?

Maybe, but first he would have to summon up enough courage to leave this goddamn bathroom.

He could sense her out there. He knew instinctively that she was naked except for the sweatshirt she had worn at Boucher's. Right now, she was nervously pushing it down just enough so it covered her sex, but high enough to show off her legs and a bit of hip. He was as certain of this as he was of sitting here in this stupid bathroom, contemplating his toes. He also knew she was in her own way just as conflicted about this situation as was he, that she desperately wanted him, but knew how crazy it was to do so, and yet felt powerless to resist.

But the sense of alienation went beyond the miraculous changes in his body. The hunger he felt for Laura did not seem to belong to him. With a combination of resignation and excitement, he decided not to put his trousers on before he went out. They would not hide his enormous erection anyway.

As he reached for the doorknob, the bitter taste of burnt gunpowder came to him as if in a lost dream.

Laura.

Laura's heart leapt as Wright came out of the bathroom looking silly wearing a woman's purple bathrobe.

'Her heart leapt.' What a silly-ass cliché. But there was no other way to describe it. Her breathing quickened, and she could feel her heartbeat speed up. Her heart seemed be higher and more to the front of her chest as if trying to burst free. She was elated and hated herself for being so out of control. All this despite John looking a little ridiculous in a woman's robe that was too small in the shoulders him.

"I feel weird," he said.

"Well, you look weird." But in truth she thought he looked fantastic – irresistible.

He gave her a hurt look.

"So what are you doing here?" she said. In this light, he didn't look twenty-some years older than she.

"You invited me. Remember? Besides, this is my house, as I recall." The robe fell open as he brought up his hands in a kind of what-the-hell gesture. She gasped. He not only had six-pack abs, he was nearly hairless.

He hastily closed the robe and looked around the room as if for an escape route. The question was, what was *she* doing? Back at the sheriff's office, he obviously wanted her, but was just as obviously struggling with their situation as she was. Besides all their emotional baggage – his love for his wife, her romantic history – he was old enough – to be her father.

Was she unconsciously recreating the dynamics of the abusive relationship with her father, doomed to make the same mistakes over and over?

Back at the university, before Bryan, the relationship with her professor had at first been wonderful and exciting. It had been her first sexual liaison with an older man, and he had been protective and nurturing at times, demanding and smothering at others. But she had been powerless to walk away from him. It had not been a matter of the professor threatening to damage her academic career as she had told Bryan. She had become emotionally dependent upon the abuse itself. Bryan had offered her a way out. He had been so eager to please, and, before he became a woodsman, a bit soft and infantile, like a big puppy, someone who didn't threaten her and loved her despite her mood swings. She had used Bryan as a bridge not to escape the professor, but to defuse her own obsession with the older man.

Now here she was again, making the same mistake with another older man. Or was she?

Wright was so different from anyone she had ever imagined being with. Was it the dim light of the basement that made him look as if he were in his mid-twenties? But looks seemed to have little to do with it. She had been attracted to him even when she had found what she believed was his dead body on the shores of Lost Lake.

Was necrophilia somehow connected to childhood sexual abuse issues? She couldn't imagine how.

Trying to look nonchalant but failing miserably, Wright sauntered across the room and perched on the edge of the bed. Then he just sat there, his hands on his lap, two feet away.

Do something, you idiot!

She patted the spot on the bed beside her. John Wright just looked at her timidly. And although she usually didn't like insecure men, his bashfulness pushed her across some previously uncrosssed boundary.

She kneeled beside him. The sweatshirt rode up and she could feel the cold air on her butt. He put his hands on her waist. She was relieved that his hands were warm, not cold as a corpse's as she had feared. She pulled the robe away from his lap to find he was fully erect – and now she could see he wasn't hairless but covered with fine, black, short, silky hair. She ran her hand over his chest, his stomach. It was like petting a short-haired cat.

Holding her waist, he picked her up as if she weighed nothing and sat her down slowly on his erection. She had a moment of fear that he would be too big for her and that it would hurt, but as she settled onto his member, she found it was a smooth fit, not stretching her, but filling her nonetheless. She let out an involuntary sigh, felt tears coming to her eyes and was surprised to see as he kissed her that he was crying too.

She licked his tears and they tasted delicious.

"This is bound to end with one of us, maybe both of us, getting hurt," he said, as she pulled away from the kiss.

She had a deja vu moment of Bryan saying the same thing, but she couldn't remember exactly when.

"I know," she said, laughing, breathless. "But right now I don't care. Fuck me. Fuck me hard!"

I don't even care that I sound like a slut.

As she began moving up and down on him, losing herself in the rhythmic rocking of sex, she didn't care if he was some sort of ghoul. She didn't know what this was, love or lust or something else, but she had never felt it before and never wanted the feeling to pass.

Bryan.

Sex with Suzanne was completely different from any Bryan had before. He'd had enthusiastic lovers before, most notably Laura, but Suzanne was the first woman who seemed consumed with hunger for him. Not just for the sex, but for him personally. She didn't stop at kissing him, but licked his face and neck. No degree of physical or emotional intimacy seemed to embarrass her. Like small, scurrying animals, her hands grabbed his shoulders that had become heavily muscled by cutting wood. Her hands worked at the muscles as if she were kneading bread.

"God! You taste wonderful," she said as she licked sweat from the hollow beneath his Adam's apple. "How I love you, love you, love you," she said as she rocked on top of him.

And the most amazing thing was that he felt the same way for this strange willowy redheaded goth girl he barely knew.

She was all legs and slim waist. Her breasts were larger than he remembered from bathing her. Was that another illusion? He soon forgot the hat or headband, or whatever it was, covered a missing ear. She radiated a light of her own, hints of red light shot through with purplish sparks visible between flickers from the fireplace.

The vision was hypnotic and incredibly erotic. He didn't want to cum yet, so he closed his eyes and held his breath with his mouth open, a Tantric technique Laura had taught him.

Suzanne reached down with both hands and, using her thumbs, gently pushed his eyelids open.

"You must keep seeing me!" she said.

"Why?" he asked.

"Am I so ugly you can't bear to look at me?" she said.

"No, you're too beautiful. I feel I'm losing myself in you." And it was true. He had never had a thing for punk or goth girls, and she was a lot of both. But she seemed to emit this glow of absoluteness, as if she were the perfect ideal punk/goth girl, the one by which all others were just imperfect imitations.

She stopped moving and settled on him. It was like being wrapped in a moist, steamed towel.

"I'll lose it; I won't last long enough if I don't close my eyes."

"I came already – twice – didn't you notice?"

He shook his head.

"Besides, it doesn't matter. It only matters if you see me. If you're not looking at me, I don't even feel that I'm real. Earlier, in the bedroom while you were sleeping, I was afraid to look in the mirror; I was afraid I wouldn't see myself."

"You're real," he said and patted her butt to prove it.

"Harder," she said. "Slap it hard. Make it hurt."

"I don't think I can do that."

"Go ahead. I feel like this body is no longer mine, so it doesn't matter what I do with it or what you do to it. It's as if my real body was laying dead somewhere, and this is just a duplicate – what's it called?

"A clone?"

"No, not that. Like I'm a ghost double of the real me."

He didn't tell her that he had the same feeling, that this wasn't quite real, that he wasn't the real Bryan Douglas. Where they both living in someone else's dream, and if so, whose?

If this was a dream, he didn't want the dreamer to awake. He sat up and swung his legs off the couch. Suzanne locked her legs around his waist and he stood, pulling her to him. He had intended to take her back into the bedroom, but halfway there passion overcame him, and he backed her up against the wall. The headband fell off as he thrust inside her, and the wound where her ear had been was like a bloody, smashed rose, a livid pressed flower on fine paper. A trickle of blood ran from the side of her head and mixed with their mutual sweat. He came at once, and she gasped as he ejected warm semen deep into her. But he didn't lose his erection, and they continued to work their bodies against each other in a slow languid, autonomous rhythm that made him think of frothy waves of some primordial ocean. The bloody sweat made her breasts stick to his chest with little sucking sounds, and she laughed, finally embarrassed about something, but she didn't cease grinding back against him. He was careful to continue staring into her eyes so she wouldn't disappear, and he sank into their depths, drowning in her.

Wright.

"I'm happy, but I need you more than I've ever needed anything or anyone, and I hate needing anything or anyone," Laura said.

For the first time he could remember, Wright regretted not being able to sing or compose poetry. Ordinary words were inadequate to express how he felt. All he could manage was, "Me too."

Which seemed to be enough for Laura. She smiled at him and kissed him long and deep, then pulled away, laughing.

"What's so funny?" he asked.

"I hate this," Laura said. "It's so good, and I love you so much, but I hate it. You should have nothing I want, but you complete me, and I hate it because it doesn't make any sense."

"I think all men feel incomplete without a woman," he said. *Without the right woman*, he wanted to add, and Laura, by all logic, should be exactly the wrong woman for him.

"What about you? You say you like being alone. Don't you feel incomplete?" She ran her hand over his chest gently, then drew back and slapped his pectoral muscles hard. "You're so solid. You're like a furry Chippendale dancer. Who would have guessed?"

"I've just become accustomed to feeling incomplete. Used to it."

"What about Marguerite?"

"I loved her. She loved me too, at first, I think. But that was over long before she turned angelic. Anything I said, anything I did, was wrong. I made a mistake with her, a selfish mistake, one she could never forgive."

"I can't imagine you being so selfish that you couldn't be forgiven."

He ran a hand over the graceful, soft curve of her breasts; the feel of her skin was food for his soul. It was more than a sensual fulfillment. She had said exactly what he needed to hear and made him believe it: That he could be forgiven. And he suspected that there was nothing Laura wouldn't forgive him of. For the first time since the end of his marriage, he felt as if Marguerite was part of an old life, and this life with Laura, if he could be said to be alive, was the start of a new one.

Suzanne.

Waves of multiple orgasms washed away the past and future, suspending Suzanne in a timeless place. Breathing hard, Bryan backed away from the wall. She had the fleeting impression they were encased in a large soap bubble. The surface of the bubble shimmered with iridescent colors she could not name.

With an audible pop, the imaginary bubble burst and disappeared. Had Bryan seen the same thing? Before she could ask him, time returned and with it a vision of the past – at least it seemed like the past. She was being carried through the air by soft little puffy flying babies – cherubs, like on Valentine's Day cards. But where the Valentine's Day cherubs always precious babies with innocent faces and the wings of doves, these were cruel things, naked, pink-skinned, hairless flying monkeys, with sharp little teeth and tiny hands that pinched her butt and punched her breasts. In the dream, they were flying over the pasture near Ben's house. There were dead cows below. One of the cherubs whispered something nasty in her ear; its breath smelled of raw meat and shit, and she tried to slap it away, but it hurt her.

"Wait here," Bryan said, rescuing her from the vision. He sat her on the bed. When she clung to him, he said "You'll have to let go of me if I'm going to get us something to eat."

"Don't leave me," she surprised herself by saying. She sounded clingy, but the truth was she was deathly afraid to be alone. She used to love solitude and now was afraid to be by herself even for a moment.

"I'll be right back," he said.

She untwined her legs from around his waist but held onto his shoulders. "Can't I come with you?" she said.

"I'm just going to the kitchen and cook something – if I still have propane left."

"I'll come with you. I can cook," she said.

He smiled. "Don't trust my cooking?"

"Something like that."

After more than two hours of lovemaking, after having multiple orgasms, she still wanted him. It was just so wrong. First, he was too young – she usually preferred men much older – and he was so retro. He wore funky Clark Kent black horn-rimmed glasses, just not her style. And he would probably do sweet, Boy Scout things such as hold doors open for her if they ever went out together. She hated Boy Scouts. He didn't even have any tattoos. Even Ben had tattoos!

But now, as they walked through the cluttered living room and he took her hand and held it as if they were children crossing the street, she knew she loved him – Boy Scout or not – like she had never loved anyone before.

He pulled on a pair of jeans and gave her one of his heavy wool shirts, the tails of which came down to her knees. She hadn't thought of him as tall until then. She had just wanted him more than she had ever wanted any man – or anything for that matter. Now she could see he wasn't a Boy Scout after all, but a young, muscular man. The light brush of his hands was sexually charged as he straightened the shirt to cover her behind. Ben's hands had been callused from farm work too, but she had been somewhat repulsed by their paw-like nature. What had really turned her off was his remoteness. He had often not seemed to even notice she was there, even when looking directly at her, except when they were having sex, and sometimes not even then. When Bryan looked at her, she felt no one else existed his universe but her. The next moment he seemed embarrassed, not a Boy Scout, but a guilty little boy caught with his hand in the cookie jar.

Her free hand sought out that moist mound between her legs. It was as if that was the only part of her still alive, as if that's where her consciousness now resided, not in her head, not in her heart, but in her cunt. Her lust was like some sort of tropical disease, a cancer she had developed in a foreign country, a curse she would never be rid of.

Suzanne, you are now completely, completely mental.

Something skittered across the upstairs floor, making click, click, click sounds on the hardwood floor. Then came a crash of glass shattering. She was about to ask him if he had a dog when she saw the fear on his face.

Laura.

Laura needed to get up to pee, but her legs were trembling and she was afraid if she stood up they would collapse underneath her. Wright lay on his back next to her. He was covered in a light sheen of sweat and breathed slowly and deeply. She knew he had reached orgasm several times, but he still had an erection. If she wasn't so exhausted, she would have climbed up and mounted him again, but she feared if she had sex with him again, she might have to go to the clinic.

When did you become such a crazy, horny bitch, Laura Jacobsen?

Wright turned his head to look at her.

She surprised herself again by saying, "I love you."

He sighed. "Me too." And ran a hand over her stomach, down to the mons. A light touch, a caress not a grasp. "Crazy, isn't it? I had to die to find this with you, and now I'm scared shitless it's some sort of dream."

She didn't want to meet his eyes because she was afraid she would start crying, so she looked past him, hoping she wouldn't seem fake and coy, and the wallpaper opened a set of pudgy eyelids and stared back at her.

She rolled over quickly, putting her back to the hallucination. Wright must have sensed something was wrong and turned on his side and hugged her spoon fashion.

"I do love you," he said. "Like no one ever before."

She lay there, afraid of opening her eyes, afraid of what she might see.

If you knew just how crazy I am, John Wright, you'd run away as fast as you could.

* * *

10.

And I Die All Over Again

Wright.

As Wright drove along the Old Buffalo Road to Cartwright's ranch, his mind kept returning to the previous evening. Just the thought the time with Laura brought him so much pleasure that he found it hard to keep his mind on the road.

The scar atop his head throbbed, and he rubbed the tip of his index finger around the perimeter, then in to the center. It was still completely closed, though still a little soft. His fingers explored it: The concentric circles were remained but seemed more like horny ridges of callus than scar tissue. And running across the circles, was a small ridge that bisected the circle. He hadn't noticed the ridge before. He had hoped hair would grow back to cover it, but it was still a bald spot.

It throbbed as much with pleasure as pain.

He should have had Laura look at it, but like an adolescent in love, he didn't want to bring her attention to any of his imperfections.

He really needed to concentrate on the question at hand: what to do about Ben Cartwright. The ear was immersed in a jar of formaldehyde in the evidence locker at his office. But did it constitute evidence of a murder? People could live after losing an ear, but there had been great deal of blood at the crime scene. Either way, there was enough probable cause to at least hold Cartwright for questioning, but the situation was complicated in this post-Fall world.

Before the fall of the angel saucer, he would have taken Cartwright in and asked the district attorney in Columbia for advice as to the legality of holding him without clear proof of a murder. Now, he was pretty much on his own. With the long-distance landlines down and cell phones not working he had no backup whatsoever. Who knew if law still ruled in Columbia?

And even if he could legally hold Cartwright, Wright wasn't sure he'd be able to board him in the jail. Not unless he wanted to move into the jail himself. Jimmy wasn't around much; without a regular salary since the Fall, the deputy, as was Wright, was subsisting on donations from the local citizens. And those donations had been few and far between of late, so Jimmy was spending more time planting a garden at his place and hunting the woods for white-tailed deer to keep food on the table.

But the biggest issue was the tendency of some of the recently departed not to stay dead, himself included. Suzanne Zimmerman might be walking around somewhere, without an ear and without a pulse, undead. How does one take a murderer to trial if his victim is still walking and talking?

Still, it rankled Wright's sense of right and wrong to do nothing. Hence this trip to see Cartwright today. He'd just play it by ear, he thought, wincing at his own unintentional pun.

The gate to Cartwright's drive was open, which was unusual. Ben usually kept it closed and padlocked when he wasn't expecting anyone. And Wright hadn't phoned to tell his old friend he was coming; he wanted to catch Cartwright unprepared – unrehearsed – for questioning.

More troubling was seeing the front door of the doublewide open. Wright hadn't wanted to carry a sidearm since his suicide; in fact, though he had been a gun collector before, now he had almost a visceral aversion to any firearm. But as he got of his SUV, he became more suspicions, and his cop instincts told him he should at least take the shotgun from the back seat. He opened the back door and reached for it, but the touch of the gun sickened him.

What the hell? What's the worse that could happen? Someone in the house ready might kill me? So what? I'm already dead.

This rationale seemed straightforward in a bizarre way, but he remained apprehensive as he climbed up the metal stairs to the small porch. As he stepped through the darkened doorway, he was possessed by a vision of Laura's face, her forehead beaded with sweat, her features transformed by ecstasy. He stopped, halfway in and halfway out of the light, and waited for the vision to release him. It would be tempting to go sit under a tree somewhere and relive the moments of last night. The passion and love – he resisted calling it 'love' but had no other word for it – had been the most intense, the most all-consuming experience of his life.

I have always been ruled by obligations, not love. Even at best, I thought love something selfish, a need to fulfill a hunger. Now there's the hunger again, but stronger than ever before. And something else, a feeling of being complete for the first time in my life. Now I know what's meant now by my other half. Laura, of all the women in the world, is my other half.

But he had responsibilities, not just to the community as a sheriff, but to find out if his friend was okay. Laura would have to wait.

From the roof came the scurrying sound of an animal, its claws scraping on the composite shingles. It sounded too large for a squirrel, but what else could it be? Ben alleged he had seen cherubs, but didn't those things fly rather than scurry? He was a bit foggy on this point. He didn't remember any pictures depicting cherubs as having claws.

Maybe it was a fat momma possum he heard, though it would be odd for one to be out during daylight.

His eyes gradually adjusted from the bright outdoors to the darkened room. The curtains were not drawn as he first assumed. Instead, unfinished pine boards had been nailed across the windows. Small furring strips had been tacked over the cracks between the boards to completely close out the light. What light there was came from the doorway where Wright stood.

Cartwright's roper boots sat inside, left of the doorway on a small welcome mat. Red clay mud covered the toes and heels. A pair of nearly new Nike tennis shoes sat next to them. Both pairs were precisely lined up as if for inspection. Cartwright never wore boots or any sort of shoes inside the house.

"Ben?" Wright called. "Ben, it's me, John Wright."

No answer.

The living room floor was uncluttered except for a few rugs and small stuffed pads. From earlier visits with Ben, Wright knew these were for sitting on the floor, Buddhist-style. There was one large overstuffed chair that Cartwright kept for visitors who didn't want to sit on the floor.

Wright stepped over the cushions and entered the hallway. The hallway was narrow, stretching the length of the doublewide, and even darker than the living room. There was only one local supplier of such factory-built homes. Wright had been in several of them, most often in his official capacity. They all had pretty much the same floor plan.

The first door on the right was always the second bathroom. There were doors to two other bedrooms: The door to the master bedroom was at the end of the hallway. Wright decided to try that one first.

He found Cartwright sitting in the full-lotus position on the edge of a large, blue futon. His hands were folded on his lap, his elbows on his knees, his head bowed so his chin rested on his chest. He wore his standard outfit: bib overalls, T-shirt. One sock had slipped down and dangled on the big man's toe. It was a white sock with red strips around the top, a gym sock.

"Ben?"

Getting no answer, Wright leaned over and gently shook his old friend's shoulder. The big man toppled over on his side before Wright could catch him.

"Shit!" Wright said aloud. He knelt and felt for a pulse on Cartwright's neck. The man was heavily muscled with very little fat. Wright had no trouble locating he carotid artery; he felt for a pulse but didn't find it. Ben's skin was room temperature.

He studied Cartwright's face. His eyelids were partially open, and he had a slight smile on his lips. His complexion was ruddy, not ashen; he looked neither dead nor asleep, just very relaxed. If it hadn't been for the lack of a pulse, Wright would have guessed he was only drugged or comatose.

Would Cartwright become another undead? And if so, how long would the resurrection take? Would it be a nearly immediate transformation like in a zombie movie? Would Cartwright's eyelids suddenly pop wide open as if spring-loaded, a horror movie cliche? Or would it be a gradual process, as if he were waking from a deep sleep?

Wright didn't remember much about his own revivals, neither the first one in the woods nor the later ones after a fugue. The first time, there in the woods, he had become aware almost instantly. He remembered nothing of a twilight sleepy time. Nor did he remember any dreams from the time of his death until that first awakening. He had opened his eyes, completely awake, and had found himself on his back, aware of the cold, wet leaves and the starry sky above him. He remembered thinking that there was something odd about the constellations and trying to figure out what it was, when he realized he had no memory of entering the forest. And at the same time he had been conscious of that irresistible force, the invisible cord that made him get to his feet and dragged him out of the forest towards Laura's house. Stumbling along, confused and compelled to jog by the force, he hadn't had time to look up at the sky again.

Turning back to the matter at hand, he continued his search for an obvious cause of death. Ben had no obvious wounds, no contusions. At this point, the protocol was to call in the coroner and order an autopsy. But the coroner had resigned two weeks ago, citing no paycheck for months, and told everyone he was switching to subsistence farming. Wright had no doubt the man was growing a few vegetables and selling them at the farmers' market, but he suspected coroner, who was also an avid horticulturist, had taken up growing a more lucrative barter: hybrid marijuana.

Too much to worry about right now. Chalk up another one to the open market.

Not really wanting to, Wright rolled the big man over on his back. He unsnapped the overall shoulder straps and unfastened the big brass buttons along the side. Then he turned Cartwright over on his stomach and pulled down the overalls below the butt. Cartwright was wearing tidy-whities, and he had to pull down those, too.

Cartwright's butt was white. Wright knew from watching the coroner work that blood should have settled in the buttocks if he had been dead very long. Moreover, he should be already stiffening from rigor mortis. Cartwright's skin being at room temperature indicated he had been dead for some time, but the big man was limp as a drunk.

Wright pulled the underpants back up and draped the back of the overalls over his old friend's shoulders. He then rolled the body over on its back and began searching the overall pockets.

He found a brown legal-size envelope stuffed deep in the right-side pocket. Inside the envelope was a single sheet of white paper with a few lines of type on it, justified to the right, one short sentence to a line, like a poem. Wright's first thought was that it was a suicide note, but as he read it, he wasn't sure.

Buddha said evil is merely Ignorance,
Masquerading as anger, desire and Fear
Pagans believe Satan is God's other Face
Playing Trick-or-Treat every day of the Year

Wiccans, I don't know, but I Suspect
Wickedness to them starts with looking Up
Instead of down an inward to Gaia
And I? Who do I think lives at the cruel Crux?

I thought Evil was nothingness made real by Desire
The Self, that chimera of smoke and fire –
Was the cause of all human delusion
Now I know something else is the case

It's treat or threat; those Pagans got it only half-right
For cruel fat, flying infant terribles rule the night
However I have found a way out of this haunted house,
The exit is found looking inward, toward the light

Ben Cartwright had added his signature below the last line.

Underneath that was what looked like a hastily handwritten scrawl of a sentence, barely legible, like an afterthought. It was addressed to him.

"John, I'm going, going, gone before this place turns me into one of you undead. Ben. P.S. I think the little flying fuckers got Suzanne."

Wright read the note a second time. Surprisingly, he understood much of what Cartwright was alluding to. In a conference led by Uncle Robert – was that only a few days ago? – he had learned of the Gnostic bent of the archangels. They believed that they had been created by an amateur god, a screw-up demiurge. The creator had made them and their universe, but made it imperfectly. The archangels believed they had been designed so they couldn't reach higher levels of existence. And since the creator made them immortal, they were doomed to an eternal purgatory. Their escape was to merge with humans in this universe. The results of the merging, such as Marguerite or May as angels/human hybrids, might live a thousand years, but would eventually die and escape the existence that the original archangels had come to feel was an unbearable prison.

The last stanza didn't make sense at all. "Flying infant terribles?" He read the last stanza and the handwritten scribble one more time before folding the letter and putting it in his shirt pocket. He would deal with it later. Maybe he could confer with Laura – if they could keep their hands off each other long enough to talk next time they were together.

He smiled at this idea and felt pure pleasure to be alive – or undead – or whatever.

But now he had to decide what to do with Cartwright's body. Wright didn't want to spend the day – or even a few hours – sitting with Ben, waiting to see if he was truly dead or just in the process of being resurrected. What he needed was some way to get the body in the back of the SUV, but Cartwright was a big man, two hundred and sixty pounds at least. Even if Jimmy was inclined to leave his farm, there was no way to call him for help.

Wright wondered if he could drag the body to the SUV. Once at the vehicle, perhaps he could cantilever it up in the back. Maybe slide it up on a plank.

He folded the thick, padded quilt the corpse lay on around the body like a shroud. Using the quilt as a kind of sled, he grabbed the edge and slid the corpse off the futon. Having moved corpses before, he expected it to be an ungainly job. After all, that's were the expression "dead weight" came from.

But it wasn't. Cartwright's huge arms were surprisingly light. Without thinking, Wright knelt on one knee, put his shoulder below Cartwright's sternum and stood up. He now had Cartwright's body, still wrapped in the quilt, in a fireman's carry. Wright knew his knees should be buckling under the weight. Instead, the huge man seemed light as a child.

Was Cartwright now made of goose down and Styrofoam instead of muscle and bone? A bathroom scale sat near the door to the hallway and Wright stepped on it. Together, he an Cartwright should weigh more than 400 pounds, but the scale pegged out at 300 pounds, its limit. So much for that idea.

But Wright suspected it wasn't a matter of Cartwright becoming magically lighter. More likely he had become stronger, a whole lot stronger than he ought to be, alive or undead.

He walked down the hallway. Cartwright's sock feet slid along the narrow passageway with a whispering sound. As Wright stepped through the trailer door, Cartwright's head bumped into the doorframe with a dull thud.

"Sorry, old friend," Wright said.

He laid the body in the back cargo section of the SUV. It fit after folding the legs and head so the body lay in a fetal position. Moving Cartwright's body had been so easy Wright briefly considered bucking it into the front passenger seat so he could keep an eye on if it revived. Instead he decided to pull over a couple of times along the way back to town to check it.

Nothing change had occurred on either of the two stops on the way back to town, so Wright decided to check his office before he took the body to the clinic for Jenkins to look at.

A sheet of yellow legal pad paper was tacked to the door of his office.

"Marshall has gone crazy. He's in the old cemetery. You need to do something. I've got to weed my tomatoes. – Jimmy"

Wright took a deep breath and let it out slowly. There were too many issues, and he needed help, but he couldn't blame Jimmy for needing to feed his family. Thinking Cartwright's body would keep, Wright drove to the little cemetery on the west edge of town. It was a small cemetery, encompassing about only about an acre. On the far side, he could see Marshall, easily recognizable from his khaki trousers and navy blue shirt, standing by an open grave, leaning on a shovel with a bright yellow handle.

He crossed the cemetery, trying to avoid stepping on graves. No one had been buried here for thirty years. Many of the monuments dated from the early 1900s, a time when more art was put into their construction. Some tombstones had faded daguerreotypes behind cracked, mossy glass frames. Much of the marble stonework had held up well, though a few had been vandalized. A few years ago, a old hippie and would-be Michelangelo had taken up residence in the abandoned caretaker's house and had begun carrying off the larger pieces of broken marble for his sculptures. He had been easy to trace because he'd used a wheelbarrow to haul off the stone, and it had left a single wheel track through the soft soil back to his shack. Wright had looked the other way for a while, thinking the stones had already been broken, but then the intact monuments had begun disappearing.

One day he had arrived at the caretaker's house with a warrant to find the sculptor hauling one the monuments back to grave sites. He hadn't been stealing the stones for raw material, but had been "refreshing" the original stonework, deepening and sharpening the inscriptions, even adding the names of grandchildren and great-grandchildren born long after the deceased had been buried.

Wright had torn up the warrant and found a few extra dollars in the local budget to name the hippie as deputy in residence at the cemetery. But the sculptor had disappeared the next year, a victim, Wright suspected, of the marijuana mafia, the heavily armed growers who had farms in the nearby Mark Twain National Forest.

Wright stepped over a limestone cherub, no doubt broken off

the top of a pyramidal-like monument by some jackass's baseball bat.

Marshall had returned to digging a grave next to a six-foot-tall obelisk.

"Hey, Frank," Wright said.

"You can't stop me," Marshall said. The hole was about waist-deep. It looked as if the first few feet had been easy digging. Marshall was now down to wet clay, and the going was hard. Marshall stomped on the edge of the shovel to sink it into the clay. The shovel'syellow fiberglass handle bowed as he put his back into prying the lump of clay from its bed. Wright was about to warn the old man not to strain his heart digging but reminded himself he was as dead as himself.

"Got a ways to go until you get to the standard six feet," Wright stated. He had to dodge the lump of clay Marshall pitched out.

"You can't stop me," Marshall repeated.

"Wasn't going to try. This is your family plot, right?"

Marshall looked up at him, the angry squint fading for a moment. "Right."

"Tell me one thing, though, as a friend," Wright said.

"What?" The angry squint returned.

"Whose grave ya' diggin?"

"Mine, of course."

"Got immediate plans on dying?"

Marshall stood on the shovel again; this time he had to rock it back and forth to get it to sink in despite putting all his weight on it. Wright waited. After a moment, Marshall said, "You should know as good as I do that's not a valid question."

Marshall's eyes rolled up and he wavered on his perch on the shovel, and Wright worried the old man was going to go into a fugue. But Marshall recovered, wigwagged his shoulders like a dog shaking off water, then steadied his grip and jumped up and down on the shovel until it sank into the clay.

You may be a bigot, but you're a smart old bigot. You've learned the trick of acknowledging death without looking it straight in the face.

"The dead should be given a proper burial," Marshall said and threw another shovel-load of clay out of his pit. The clump of wet muck landed at Wright's feet with a *schlepp* sound.

"You know, Frank, if you keep pitching those shovelfuls of shit next to my feet, I might begin to think you're trying to hit me and I'll have to run you in for aggravated assault."

"You just happen to be standing where I'm pitching," Marshall said in a gruff voice, but a smile crept across his face. "Maybe you should move."

"Maybe I should," Wright said. "But maybe I don't want to. Besides, what about the undead?" Marshall had another near fugue, tottered a bit but recovered.

"What about them?" he said.

"If they're undead – still walking and talking – shouldn't they be unburied?"

"Don't know about that. Ain't no sky pilot." Marshall shook his head slowly and looked at Wright out the corner of his eye. "I know that I can't stand this," he said.

"This? What's this? You mean this beautiful spring day?"

Marshall looked up. Wright could see his eyes were wet; the old man was holding back tears.

"This . . . " Marshall let go shovel, and it stayed upright, the blade wedged in the thick muck. He spread his arms wide as if to encompass the graveyard, the sky, everything. "This uncertainty. This not knowing."

"I get your drift, Frank." Wright caught himself scratching his chin and stopped. "But it's not that much different than before this happened to us, is it?"

"What do ya' mean?"

"We didn't know what life was, what our place in the world was, why we were here, before. Did we?"

Marshall looked him, the angry squint returning. "I never suspected this of you, Wright."

"Suspected what?"

"I knew what life was about. We all had our place. Some people might not have known it, but they all had their places. There were rules. Now the rules have been broken. I don't have a place in all this playacting. I'm going to exit."

"Suspected me of what?" Wright repeated.

Marshall went back to working his shovel in the muck. Wright gave it up.

"Frank, I'm not going to try to stop you from burying yourself alive, though I don't know how you're going to cover yourself up."

"I'll figure it out. Pay somebody, if I have to."

Wright shrugged. "But you know what, Frank? I think if I was still aware, alive or undead or whatever, I wouldn't want to have a ton of clay on top of me, oozing into my nose and throat, keeping me from even moving my toes. I think I'd rather be up and about here in the light and air where I at least had a chance to take my mind off my situation."

Marshall didn't answer, but as Wright walked he heard the shovel land on the ground and sucking sounds as the old man pulled his feet loose from the muck. Wright glanced over his shoulder to see the old man climb out of the pit and sit at the edge of the grave. He was still sitting there, staring into the hole he had dug for himself, as Wright drove away.

Wright had driven halfway back to his office before he remembered to check Cartwright's body in the back. He pulled over, and when he opened the back hatch of the SUV Cartwright's body was gone.

* * *

11.

But Immortality is Only a Waking Dream

Laura.

Laura woke in John Wright's bedroom, disoriented from a dream so vivid it made the real life seem a pale two-dimensional copy.

She was dreaming of being back inside the angel saucer before it had slid into Lost Lake and sank. In the dream, she was watching herself sleep in one of the Army surplus cots the angels had appropriated. Around her, lying on similar cots, covered by gray woolen blankets up to their necks, were the ninety-some women and men who were still in the process of becoming angel/human hybrids.

Her viewpoint in the dream was out-of-body, from about eight feet above her own sleeping body.

Dr. Jenkins came into the room and methodically began lifting the blankets to check the developmental stages of the angel homunculi attached to the humans' bodies. The homunculi had begun as small, doll-sized creatures, more like colorful tattoos, nearly two-dimensional. Now, without exception, they were toddler-sized, glistening with life and color and extending above the skin of their human hosts by several inches. They stared back at Jenkins, blinking, alien emotions rippling across the deep pools of their eyes.

Jenkins came to the sleeping Laura's cot and tried to pull her blanket down. But the sleeping Laura clutched it tightly around her neck. Jenkins gave the blanket a savage yank, and it came away, but before the out-of-body Laura could see if her sleeping body had a homunculus attached too, she had woken up here, in John Wright's bedroom.

The odd thing was she felt more as if she were in a vivid dream now that she was awake than when she had been actually dreaming.

Did that make sense?

Wright's presence lingered about her like cologne. Her memory of his last words before they had fallen asleep also persisted. She remembered exactly. He had said "Crazy, isn't it? I had to die to find this with you, and now I'm scared shitless I'm only in some sort of dream."

Shitless. John Wright might not be the most eloquent lover she had ever had, but his observation was right on target. This thing she had for him scared her *shitless,* too. She didn't know why, but he was the first lover to ever make her feel complete. They'd only been lovers for a day but already felt she could tell him anything about herself and he would still accept her unconditionally. She didn't know how she knew this, but she was certain of it. And the pull – that's what she had come to call it – whatever had pulled Wright to her was now pulling her toward him. The pull was more than a sexual thing – lust she could deal with. It was – she hated to use the word – *spiritual.* Or it was *love?* – another word she hated to use.

But it felt so right.

And even more surprising: She trusted him. Usually, the more she became emotionally intimate with a man – or a woman for that matter – the less she trusted them. She knew this was because of the childhood abuse she had suffered from the very people she should have been able to trust implicitly. But knowing did not seem to help. The wounds given her as a child seemed to go right down to muscle memory. That's where she felt it first, in certain parts of her body, a cold sense that she was disassociated from her own breasts, her own thighs; even her own vagina became an alien thing, something to be disowned and disparaged.

That was what had happened, she now realized, between her and Bryan. He had given no reasons for her not to trust him, but the closer they became, the less she trusted him, and the more she mistrusted her own feelings. It was an unfocused, feeling of deep misgiving.

It had been this way in her relationship with the professor. He had never threatened her. Nor had he initiated the relationship. He had been fatherly at first, serving as her counselor, setting boundaries that excluded physical love. She had been the one to insist that the relationship go further. His own marriage had recently dissolved, so seducing him had been easy. She had simply visited him at his house, took off all her clothes, and lay on his bed.

Then as they became closer, both physically and emotionally, she began distrusting him. In fact, she remembered the exact moment when she began to fear him: When he had professed his love for her.

With John it should have been the same. But it wasn't. The closer they got, the more she trusted her feelings and the more she trusted him. Hearing him say he loved her had been like a drink of clear, cool water.

Yes, a dream it must be! She had seen John's body on the beach soon after he had shot himself. Later, at the clinic, she had peered into his empty skull with Jenkins' penlight. Both times he had been obviously dead. Whether he was dead or undead was a fine point. He had most certainly died. He most certainly was not living, but *undead* didn't seem an apt description.

A mess of conflicting emotions, she got out of bed to a chilly room, clad only in a sweatshirt and panties. Only cold water came out of the bathroom faucet, and she was tempted to return to the warm bed, but she really needed to talk with Uncle Robert. She had told John she was going to visit her uncle, and he had been understanding, promising to meet her there after checking on Cartwright. There was something about the rancher's wife having gone missing that he had to investigate. But she missed him already and considered putting off seeing Uncle Robert.

Goose bumps rose on her arms and legs as she pulled off the sweatshirt and took a quick sponge bath with cold water. Shivering, she toweled herself, patting dry the area above her pubes because it was tender from lovemaking. Her breasts were sore, too, but she suspected that was because she was getting her period. Good news actually, for she hadn't been using birth control. If she got pregnant by the undead, what sort of child would she have?

She still had a supply of birth-control pills. She had condoms, too, in her purse. Why hadn't she used them? Unconsciously, did she want to get pregnant by John? It all seemed too banal: Did she want to have his baby, whether he was undead or not?

She slipped on her panties, wishing for fresh ones, and pulled on a sweatshirt. Her bra was nowhere in sight. As she stood on one leg to step into her waitress skirt, some small thing fluttered into the room, bouncing about the ceiling right over her head. She jumped, a scream rising in her throat. The thing chirped a panicky little melody, and she saw it was only a sparrow. The bird landed on the bed, its wings at its side, its breast rising and falling in rapid little swells. It was speckled with blood and bits of gray goo.

John had told her about the episode of the sparrow flying about inside his empty skull, but she had only half believed him at the time. Was this the same sparrow? The skirt was still in her hand, and she threw it over the bird. The little thing fluttered as her hand found it under the skirt, then gave up the struggle as her fingers wrapped around it, its bird brain now resigned to death.

She pulled the handful of bird out from under the skirt. She could feel its rapid, fluttering heartbeat. Its eyes were like tiny black coals. How had it gotten into the house? An open door or window? No matter. She stepped to the window, bird in hand, intending to set it free. Before she could open the window, something too large to be another bird flittered past the glass. With her hands full of feathered heartbeat, she peered close to glass, bird in hand, to see a only a back yard that needed mowing. She had been holding her breath, and she let it out now.

"False alarm," she said aloud, glancing at the little bird's terrified eyes. But as she looked back out the window, bright fierce eyes and a pudgy, pasty face stared back at her. Startled, she stepped backward from the window and fell on the bed. The sparrow escaped from her hand in an explosion of motion, the window glass shattered, and the sparrow returned, darting about her head, tweeting in alarm. She tried to rise but was overwhelmed with a paralyzing sense of hopelessness. Immediately, she was engulfed in a multitude of buzzing wings, and small, cruel fingers grabbed at her arms, legs and feet. One tiny hand clutched her breast through the sweatshirt. Stubby teeth nibbled at an ear. She tried to scream but could get not even manage to gasp as was lifted into the air.

Ben Cartwright.

Cartwright woke feeling cold and damp in the back of his Chevy camper van. Suzanne lay beside him, her head partially buried in a pillow, a smile across her face.

"Bry," she said in her sleep and turned onto her back, pulling the gray blanket from him. He was relieved to see that both of her ears were intact, piercings and all. The inside of the van was cold, and he was wearing wet blue denim overalls. He didn't remember getting into the van wet and hadn't a clue as to how he had come to be here.

He swung his bare feet out of the camper's bed. His toenails were purplish and the skin of his feet was as white as ivory soap. Thick ice-cold blue veins traced the contours of the tendons. He wiggled his toes and clapped the soles of his feet together. Despite having the feet of a corpse, everything in his body worked. He was still himself. His mind was up to the same old tricks.

A shiver washed over him. Though wet, the wool blanket had been keeping him warm. Now he noticed his breath was fogging in the cool air. He needed to get some warm dry clothes. Last he remembered, the camper's propane tank was half-full. Was this the same reality or an alternate one?

"Lordy, Bryan!" Suzanne said, this time punctuating it with another pelvic thrust, the blanket outlining her hips, the curve of her legs and the small mound between them.

Bryan? The poet journalist turned woodcutter? Unless she had taken up reading 18th century romantic poetry, "Bryan" must be Bryan Douglas. He didn't seem Suzanne's type. But neither did he, a forty-four- year old Soto Zen Buddhist cattle rancher, seem Suzanne's type.

No, Bryan Douglas was the obvious candidate, but the question was, was he her lover only in a dream world, or in this reality where he shivered in wet coveralls?

Was there a difference between the two worlds?

He watched her smiling in her sleep as he stripped off the wet overalls and underclothes. The rest of his body matched his feet. Vampirish white skin with blue veins tracing the contours of his muscles like some sort of tribal tattoo. His pecker was blue too. Serious shrinkage down there: His scrotum had shrunken to something that it looked like a dried bulb of some exotic tropical flower.

"Ahhhh!" Suzanne moaned.

"Oh, Suze Q, I love you," he said, standing naked beside her. His pecker sprouted and his scrotum relaxed, rooting him in the moment though not in her. Even when breathing some other lover's name in her sleep, she was the whisper of spring, the remembrance of the passion of his young-buck twenties, when lust mixed with love could push out all other phenomena from his mind.

He had always known she would leave him one day, but he had allowed himself to give into love, to become attached to another human being, though had known full well letting himself become so involved would eventually bring him pain.

He knelt beside her. He could smell a scent uniquely hers overlaid with the muddy water odor from Lost Lake. His hands dug under the thin mattress until they found the large plastic bag he kept there for emergencies, such as boating accidents while fishing. Though he didn't remember any such accident, something of that order must have happened for him to be soaking wet now.

Inside the bag were a clean pair of jeans, socks and a T-shirt. He sat on the edge of the bunk bed, his back to Suzanne, and dressed.

She moaned again, a whisper of passion.

All the surfaces in the van, the tiny sink, the munchkin-size refrigerator, the cooking top, the painfully polished surfaces, even the rounded edges of the handles and knobs on the stove, looked scalpel-sharp, gleaming with rainbows of refracted light. The sharpness increased until everything became imbued with life and mysterious purpose.

He turned to look at her while she slept. She was still the young red-haired girl who had moved in with him three years ago, piercings and all. She had been the little red-haired girl to his Charlie Brown. Now there was something else, something impossible to ignore, that overlaid the young woman like an invisible sheathe, not seen but sensed. The world had suddenly lost familiarity and took on an ineluctable quality that he couldn't name.

"Threat" came close but wasn't quite it. As he struggled with a world that both had form and formlessness, a line from the Platform Sutra came to him, the writing as clear in his mind as jet-black calligraphy on rice paper.

"Successive thoughts never cease; all thoughts from the past through the present to the next moment of the future follow one after the other like goats on a mountain path. If one instant of thought is cut off, the Dharma-body falls from the physical body, and in the process of falling into the abyss, is separated from the past and the future, there will be no attachment to anything."

That was how he had left the other world. He had managed to cast aside all thinking – though only for a few moments – and the other realm had dissolved. The next thing he knew he was here, in bed with Suzanne, in a realm that was a half-forgotten memory.

But the question remained, a nagging itch of a thought: Which realm was real? Which was a construct of the mind? This one, where Suzanne lay sleeping, dreaming of a new lover? Or was the real world where her severed ear had been found among the bodies of mutilated cows?

"All life is the creation of the mind," he said out loud, imperfectly quoting the Dhammapada. But the objects of his mind, the grass, the blue sky, the dirty windshield of the van, the busted spring in the seat cushion, seemed all too real.

The pain he felt at losing Suzanne was also all too real, and he began to weep softly, embarrassingly, as he drove back to the ranch. He reminded himself that the pain he felt was not Suze's fault, but his own for letting himself become attached. He wasn't much of a Buddhist. What he really felt was that he had been visited by abandonment, the cousin of betrayal.

Suzanne.

She awoke on Bryan Douglas' couch haunted by the memory of a dream where she was back with Ben, sleeping with him in the back of the conversion camper van.

She hated that van, with its peeling Formica counter, dollhouse-size cook stove, and persistent smell of fish.

The odd thing about the dream was that she was watching herself sleep with Ben. Then Ben got out of bed, and she had been two places. No, three places. Still lying in the bed but watching herself as if she were a fly sitting on the camper's ceiling. And at the same time, she had been asleep here, on Bryan Douglas' couch, dreaming about making love to him again.

God! It had been hot! Like nothing she had ever experienced. Despite what the Creedance townspeople believed, she had not been a slut before she married Ben. As a teenager, she had a couple of lovers, one-night stands both of them, and a lot of crushes on boys that started and ended with heavy petting, sometimes fingering her, a trembling palm underneath her bra, but no real sex, only those tentative seductions which were about as far as the bashful wannabe punk boyfriends dared to reach unless they were drunk – and she hated drunks. She wasn't exactly a virgin when she married Ben, but was nearly so by the standards of a lot of nineteen-year-olds, including quite a few church-going girls.

Her friends had wondered why she had moved in with a man twice her age. He had seemed so different then. She had grown up in a household where God was used as an excuse for all sorts of abuses. Her earliest memories were of her father, a preacher, screaming at her mother about God. *Humble yourself! Obey his will. You must humble yourself!*

It had been like a chanting liturgy of domination and submission. What her father had really wanted – she figured this out at about age twelve – was for her mother, her brother and herself to humble themselves before *him*. It was all about submission to *his* will, not God's. It was all bullshit!

When she was seventeen, her mother, never stable, a martyr to love by nature, had finally had a mental breakdown and bludgeoned

Suzanne's little brother to death while he slept, then shot herself. She had left a rambling note about her guilt, about letting the demons take over both her children, and about God coming to her in a vision, telling her she would have to sacrifice her immortal soul in killing both of them to save them.

Why her mother had not murdered her while she slept too she would never know.

Her father had not blamed himself for his wife's collapse, but had pointed his self-righteous finger at her, the surviving daughter.

Suzanne had escaped by running away, living in her car for awhile, working part-time at as a waitress, and partying with university hipsters. When her car had broken down, she had been forced to return to Creedance, where she met Ben for the first time. He used to come to the sandwich shop there, where she worked to save up for a proper escape. It was the only place in town where he could get a vegetarian sandwich, a confession that had made her laugh because she had known what he did for a living.

Ben was an odd contradiction. A cattle rancher who was built like the Hulk and who practiced Buddhism. And he was kind when he wasn't in one of manic states.

But what had really attracted her to Ben was his lack of bullshit; that and that he wasn't Christian. She had enough of that brand of guilt, thank you very much. When it came to his religion – or just about anything – he'd tell her that she didn't have to believe what he said but encouraged her to think for herself. "All religions are based on guilt," he said, quoting someone. "They just have different holidays." He had been shelter from the storm, a way to escape control by her father. He had been freedom.

Ben's manic times had come less frequently during the last year. But there had been no passion in the marriage, at least not on her part. Sex with Ben was like keeping house –a routine, daily chore.

Bryan had made her feel like a virgin all over again. Better, she knew instinctively the sex had been nearly a religious experience for him too. She longed to touch him now, but where was he?

She sat up with a start. The last thing she had remembered was his going upstairs to investigate a sound. She had been awake, almost delirious from making love, but she didn't remember going to sleep or his returning. She remembered the fear on his face at the sound of scurrying feet and the sound of breaking glass from upstairs.

Her memory came to a permanent stop at that point, like pages torn from a journal. A chill stole up her back, and she was transported back to a time when she would hide in her room to escape her father's ravings with no one but stuffed bears and tigers to protect her.

"Bryan. . .?" she called, meaning to shout, but producing a squeak.

She cleared her throat and a little bit of bloody phlegm came up. Swimming within the scarlet glob were glittering specks of blue, green and silver. Broken lungs! Broken memory? What else was broken about her? Tears welling in her eyes, she stole a hand up to where her ear had been, a tentative touch, expecting the bite of savaged nerves, but instead of the clotted ragged wound of before, her fingers found a helical swirl, a labyrinth of ridges overlaying smooth skin, like a new ear trying to burst through from underneat the skin. It frightened her more than finding the bloody phlegm.

"Bryan!" This time her shout was un-caged, a scream to drive away demons.

No answer. More sounds came from the room directly overhead, not little toenails on hardwood, but of something large and heavy being dragged across the floor. Then a gargled cry – Bryan's – followed by a childishly wicked snickering. She was off the couch without thinking. Carried along on a wave of panic, she fled to the bedroom. The fear possessed her, dragged her into the large closet where she dived behind the old gowns, calico dresses and wide lapel gray suits, hiding in someone else's memories.

She crouched among the smell of mothballs and dust, her breath coming in rapid pants. Her view of the room was overlaid with a vision of being carried through the air, the same brief vision she had before, the spring grasses in the pastures below, the terribly cruel little hands, only this time she wasn't watching it happen from afar. She lived it and felt terrible pain, as a soft, pudgy, baby face came into view and grinned at her, showing teeth like needles.

Glass broke again from upstairs, and the vision flickered out. Her fear for herself was transferred to Byran.

Had those nasty little things been real?

Her hand went to where her ear had been. They were up there now.

Her hands shaking, she parted the clothes and stepped out of the closet. Her legs nearly collapsed under her, and she had to steady herself by grabbing the edge of the closet door. She desperately wanted to go back into the dark womb of the old clothes and close her eyes and her mind, but the mental image of what the little devils might be doing to Bryan mutated her fear to a red-hot anger that magically washed away the weakness in her legs and hardened her shoulders and arms.

She tiptoed back into the living room, naked, conscious of the cool air on her bare breasts. She needed a weapon. Leaning against the fireplace was a convenient collection of tongs, an ash-covered shovel and a poker with three tines that looked like a trident.

She lifted the poker, shuddering when it made a weak squeal as the point dragged across the granite stonework. The poker was made of iron, and its weight and the devilish-looking trident point was comforting. No further sounds came from upstairs, just a deathly stillness that was a sound unto itself. She wished she had time to dress or at least find a shirt to cover her breasts, but feared she might be too late already to save him.

As she went up the stairs, she realized that she had never risked her life to save anyone before. But the baby angels, if that's what they were, didn't seem that intimidating. Singly, they might weigh twenty pounds. Like killer bees they were dangerous only in swarms, but how many could be in the room? And in the confined space, their natural advantage of flight and surprise would be limited.

Emboldened by this logic, she took the stairs two at a time, carrying the poker before her like a lance. She was Joan of Arc, consumed by visions, risking her life for someone she had only spent one night with!

Crazy!

But she discovered being crazy was effing exciting; the promise of doing something radical and violent, like slam dancing. That was it! She was going to slam-dance the poker into little fat-ringed eyes, knock little piglet teeth out of snickering mouths. In her mind's eye, she saw the poker swinging, the creatures' teeth flying through the air like broken buttons, the evil little grins smeared with blood. The vision erased the fear that had paralyzed her in the closet.

She paused on the landing. There were three doors. Which one? The staircase had taken a right turn halfway up and now she was disorientated. She tried the middle door and found an empty room, smelling of dust and mold. As she started to close the door, the hinges made a tormented squeal, and she stepped away, holding her breath.

Had they heard her?

She walked flat-footed to the farthest door and grasped the knob. The knob was brass with some kind of ornate carving. The doorframes had carvings too, roses and vines traced their way up the sides and ended in little faces at each corner, their lips pursed as if whistling. Odd, she hadn't noticed until now that the whole house was like that: like an art deco museum with everything covered with a coat of varnish turned black with age.

Should she open the door slowly or charge in? If it wasn't the right door and she made a lot of noise, it would alert the little bastards. On the other hand, if it was the right door and she opened it slowly and found them chewing off pieces of Bryan, she might lose her nerve. Best she kick the door open. No, wait. She was barefooted. What a silly bitch she was. She'd break her toes; then what good would she be?

But she turned the knob slowly until she felt the latch release with a too-loud click. She froze, then took a deep breath and pushed the door open with the poker.

She had expected a darkened room, but she stepped into a space so bright she was momentarily blinded. Something large and white glided slowly toward her from within the light. As her eyes adjusted, she first thought it a white bed sheet blown by the wind, then saw it was one of them, one of the fat, nasty flying babies!

It was just as fat and puffy as she remembered from her vision but it was by no means baby-sized but as large as a big man. It's naked skin glowed incandescently, a shimmering cold blue aura outlining the details of its face. She could see it was male, but its genitals were shrunken, baby-sized; if it had a scrotum it was hidden by the rolls of fat on its thighs. It had curly hair, so blonde as to be almost white.

Its face was smeared with blood. Bryan's blood?

It glided toward her, a big glowing balloon suspended on an invisible tether, with baby prick dangling and tiny wings flittering, a giant hodgepodge of unlikely parts, like a cheap, fast-food store gigantic windup toy, its eyes glittering malevolently. The wings seemed too small to support anything so large. They were skinny with a blue sheen, like those of a hummingbird, but they didn't buzz or even flap, just slowly fluttered. The fleshy blimp of a creature moved through air in a leisurely motion, and should have taken minutes to reach her, so she felt she had plenty of time to bring the poker up. But it shared the ange's space/time warp ability, and was upon her in an eyeblink. A pudgy hand the size of a shovel reached out for her. Its fingertips ended not in claws as she remembered from the dream but in straight nails filed to a point.

Her mind was frozen, but her arm came up of its own accord and sank the ash-covered point of the poker into the cherub's left eye.

It made no sound, but the grin faded slowly from its face. It drew back a shovel-size hand as if to swat her, and she felt something warm running down her leg. She had peed on herself in terror, but she didn't withdraw. She pulled the poker out of the eye socket – it made a slurping sound – drew it back and stabbed the other eye.

This time the thing let out a scream that she felt as much as heard. It swung a hand at her, and she ducked just in time. The great paw missed her and slammed into the doorframe, sending wood splinters and plaster flying.

The creature made another roundhouse swing, but it was now blind, and the punch came nowhere close. It flew forward, barely fitting through the shattered doorframe. One of its wings made slap-slap-slap sounds against the wooden molding. She moved to the side, waited until it was all the way out, then stepped behind it. The creature screamed again, a giant, angry baby's howl, and continued moving until it crashed halfway through the railing, and stuck there, its silly wings still fluttering, suspended over the open stairwell. She moved closer, brought the poker up with both hands and drove the iron spikes down into the top of its head. The spikes sank through the creature's curly hair and into its skull with a thunk.

The cherub jerked away, pulling the poker out of her hands, did a slow blimp-like turn in mid-air, and rushed toward her with amazing speed before she could react. But it was totally blind and bypassed her, slamming into the wall to the right of the door, propelling plaster into the air. The floor bounced under her feet with the force of its collision. Momentarily off balance, she stepped backward, her foot trying to find solid floor. But her bare heel landed on a big piece of the shattered doorframe. The piece of wood rolled under her foot, and she lost her footing to fall hard on her back, her head hitting the floor. She lay there dazed as the monster did another blimp-like slow turn toward her. Though blind, it must still be able to hear, and had notice the sounds she had made as she fell. In a split second it was hovering over her, its clawed paws windmilling like wood chipper blades.

Time dilated as in a dream or as, or so she'd read, when you're about to die.

But I'm already dead.

She had known this when Bryan had pulled her from the woodpile.

I'm undead, like those ladies they talk about in town.

But she hadn't been able to face that fact until now. Now, nothing seemed to matter. Life, death, they were two sides of the same coin. But distantly, she wondered if it would it hurt terribly to be shredded into pieces if she was already dead. Would her severed arms, legs, head remain undead or just become plain dead? If undead, would the parts be aware? Would each piece be her? Or would her thoughts and memories be shared among the bloody parts?

The monster's blade-like hands buzzed closer. She could see the ruined remains of its eyes running down its face. Rivulets of black blood traced along wavy curls of hair, and the poker, still stuck in its skull, waved in counterpoint to the swinging of its arms.

But I hurt you, you fucker. You'll never be the same.

She closed her eyes and felt a breeze as one of the huge hands barely missed her face.

Then the world exploded, and her face was wet and sticky. She wiped the blood away from her eyes to see the angel suspended above her, its hands dangling and its tiny wings still flittering. But now everything above its eyes, including its brow and its curly-topped head, was gone.

Another explosion, a hot wind blew against her cheek, and the rest of the creature's head disappeared. The little wings gradually slowed and stopped flapping and the huge mass of fat, white skin fell, enveloping her.

* * *

12.

Once More into the Waters of Illusion, My Love

Wright.

Wright felt like an idiot for losing Cartwright's body, though strictly speaking, he hadn't lost it. It had mostly just got up and walked away.

In another time, another reality, Wright would be out rounding up drunks or meth heads – the usual suspects in these parts – who might have stolen a body. But Wright was reasonably certain that Cartwright had awakened as a new citizen of undead Creedance.

He'll probably show up at the coffee shop tomorrow asking for a cup of green tea.

What bothered Wright was that he hadn't heard the SUV's rusty door hinges squeak when Cartwright opened the back hatch. True, Marshall had been talking to him, but he still should have heard Cartwright's exit.

A stranger thing was Cartwright had left his clothes behind. So he was out there somewhere, not only undead but undressed. Wright chuckled at the thought of Cartwright runing around bare-assed naked.

Before this angel business, Marguerite had gotten the Rapture bug, the belief that the End of Times was coming and that chosen Christians would be lifted into heaven. In her local pastor's interpretation, "raptured" Christians would leave all their earthly possessions behind, including their clothes, when their physical bodies were taken to heaven. Not just their souls, but their actual bodies would be lifted up. He used to tease her about how uncomfortable she would be, what with her being so modest, being carried up to heaven without any clothes.

"Just shut up, John. Just shut up," she would say, not amused at all.

"If you're driving when the Rapture comes, would you please pull over to the shoulder before you're taken up," he'd say.

"Shut up, John!"

Some compulsion, not cruelty so much as obstinacy, drove him to poke at her beliefs like picking at a scab on a wound.

He shrugged off the memory and the nostalgia associated with it. Now she was flying around the county naked and not giving it a thought. More failure. What had happened to the marriage? Had such little jibes caused her, a God-fearing woman, not just to become alienated from him but to choose to forfeit her humanness and be transmuted into a monstrosity?

But back to here and now, had Cartwright been "raptured," transported somewhere by forces unknown? Or had the angel/human hybrids been responsible? He turned the idea over in his mind but couldn't get a handle on it. That just didn't seem like something they would do, crazed creatures or not.

Then there were those "little flying fuckers" Cartwright had written about. The angel/human hybrids could by no means be called "little." Marguerite had been five-foot-two before her transformation. Now she was six foot or better. Was there another type of angel flying about? What were those little things called? Cupids? No, that wasn't right.

There was one person he could ask: Simon Jacobsen, whom practically everyone else knew as Uncle Robert. Laura said she was going over to visit the old man today, who really was her biological uncle. And though Wright had only left her a few hours before, he longed to see her

Besides, in addition to information, the old man might also have something stronger than beer on hand. Yes, what he needed more than anything now was a stiff drink, but whiskey was a scarce commodity in Creedance these days. Before the Fall, Uncle Robert had bought Scotch and Irish blends by the case.

The only problem was gasoline. He checked the gas gauge. He should fill up first but the need to see Laura became an unquenchable thirst. Was it the pull again he felt now? No, the physical tug of the invisible string that had drawn him to her in the first place was gone. What he felt now was something else entirely.

Fifteen minutes later, when he pulled into the Jacobsen driveway, the gas gauge on empty. He parked beside Uncle Robert's Land Rover, thinking what a waste to have abandon such an expensive vehicle to bird droppings and the elements. No one answered his knock but the door was unlocked, and he let himself in.

"Hello?" he called. When no answer came, he walked from the foyer to the main dining room, which he knew Uncle Robert used these days as a kind of study. On either side of the double doors that led to the room were two life-size busts on pedestals: one of an old man with shoulder-length hair whom Wright didn't recognize. The other was recognizable enough: Elvis Presley, though he wore a do-rag and large hoop earrings. It was probably an Elvis in a role from some movie, but which one? Wright thought he knew them all because his mother had worshiped Elvis, but he couldn't think of one where Elvis played a pirate or a gypsy. Someday – not today – he'd get Uncle Robert to explain.

He stepped between the busts into the oversized room illuminated by the light of a large picture window. The room was a bibliophile's wet dream. It was lined with wall-to-wall bookshelves, some which were ten feet high, whose top shelves could only be reached with a rolling ladder. Uncle Robert had taken many of the books from the shelves and stacked them in piles about the room. Some of the piles were waist-high, others were higher, and they clogged the floor space, leaving narrow winding paths just wide enough to walk through.

He could see the top of Uncle Robert's white-haired head from the doorway, but not all the paths led to him. Feeling like a mouse in a maze, he worked his way through the various paths, running into dead ends and having to turn back and retrace his steps. Finally he came into a little open space among the stacks where the old man was sitting on a white plastic lawn chair, one of those ubiquitous things that are popped out of injection molds by the millions and sold for $9.99 each at Walmart – when there had been such things as Walmarts. Uncle Robert's back was to a large walnut table, also covered with stacks of books. Lined up around the table were ornate antique captain's chairs, expensive-looking things with carved legs and rich upholstered seats. But those chairs were full of books, too. Uncle Robert sat perfectly still in the cheap plastic chair with his eyes closed, hands in his lap, feet planted squarely on the floor.

"Uncle Robert?" *He should remember to call him by his given name.* "Simon?"

No answer. He stepped closer and tapped Simon on the shoulder. The old man did not respond, yet his eyes were partially open. Wright felt for a pulse the second time in a day on a motionless body and couldn't find one.

"Shit! Not another one," Wright said to the now all-too-quiet room.

"Well?" Simon said, making Wright jump.

"Shit! I thought you were dead," Wright said.

"I get that a lot, lately," Simon said. He stood up and lifted the plastic chair to reveal it was not one chair but two, the top one nestled on the other. He set the chair between two stacks of books precariously balanced to shoulder height and motioned for Wright to sit.

"Just this morning," he continued, "Sophia woke me up screaming bloody murder. I said, what the fuck? And she said, 'I dreamed you'd died, and your body was in bed with me.'"

Simon shook his head and sat down in the other chair. "You don't want to hear such things from a woman who is subject to prophetic visions."

He hadn't bothered to cut his mane of white hair since the fall of the angel saucer, and it was now shoulder-length. He'd also lost weight. Before the Fall, he had reminded Wright of a sort of eccentric and jolly Santa Claus. Now his face was lined and weathered, and he looked more like Willie Nelson after a hard night.

"If this keeps happening – if y'all keep mistaking me for a corpse – I'm going to start wondering myself."

"Sorry. I found Ben Cartwright in a similar state just this afternoon – only he really was dead – I think." He told Uncle Robert about Cartwright's body apparently disappearing from the back of the SUV.

"Are you sure he wasn't in a meditative trance?"

"Meditating? Is that what you were doing? Putting yourself in a trance? What's that got to do with it? You think he came to, got up, took off all his clothes and walked away into the woods?"

Simon looked at him quietly for a moment, his bright eyes unblinking under thick white eyebrows. "Not a trance," Simon said. "Just zazen – quietly thinking. The world doesn't so much as disappear as lose importance."

"So you knew I was here all along?"

"Yes and no. I wasn't sure if you were real or just a delusion." He smiled. "I still don't."

"Now, Simon," Wright said. "You know it's those kinds of statements that cause people to think you're whacked."

"You used to think that yourself."

"Who says I stopped?" He was rewarded with a belly laugh from the old man.

"You're a jokerman today, sheriff," he said. His face lost its haggardness, and he momentarily turned back into a jolly Santa in bib overalls, stained white shirt and wrinkled tweed coat.

"It's been a long time since I had a good laugh," Simon said, wiping a tear from the corner of his eye. "But I doubt you came over just to bullshit and cheer me up. What can I do for you, Sheriff?"

"I just came over to talk to you about Cartwright."

"And . . .?"

"That's about it. I guess he's wandering around undead somewhere, naked I suppose."

Simon scratched his chin and stood up from his white plastic chair. "Do you still have his note?" he asked.

"It's here somewhere," Wright said.

While Wright fished in his pockets, Simon stepped gingerly around the back of his chair and shuffled in a column of books. He handed a bottom book to Wright. The title was "Chronicles, Volume 1." Before Wright could read the author's name – Bob something – Simon handed him a bottle of Bushmill's Blended Irish Whiskey. The bottle was full, the seal on the cap unbroken. Wright traded him Cartwright's note for the bottle and set the book down.

"Water of life," Simon said. "I don't have any glasses in here, but you can drink from the bottle."

"Do you have a whole case of this?"

"You betcha. Also, I have a couple of cases of Scotch tucked away in the cellar. And you know what, Sheriff? You can take all of it with you if you'd like." He turned his attention to the note.

"What's the catch?"

"No catch. I've stopped drinking," Simon said without looking up as he unfolded the sheet of paper and began reading.

"You? On the wagon? Why?"

"Go ahead and pop the cap, take a swig, and I'll explain."

Wright twisted the cap until the seal broke. He set the cap aside on a nearby set of books, raised the bottle to his lips and took a sip.

"Well?" Simon said.

"Real smooth stuff. Nice and warm going down," Wright said. "How did you know I needed a drink?"

"You just looked like it. Take another swig, a deep one."

"Trying to get me drunk?"

"You've always struck me as a man who can hold his liquor. More important, one who knows when to stop, unlike many of us Jacobsens."

Wright nodded. It was the first time he remembered Simon admitting outright the Jacobsens were apt to end up as sots. He tipped the bottle and took a deep drink, letting the liquid roll down his throat. When he brought the bottle down again, he saw that he had swallowed a third of the fifth. He rarely drank hard liquor. He was going to pay for this.

"Notice any effect?" Simon said. "Got a buzz?"

"No, now that you mention it. It was like drinking water, only it tasted like Irish whiskey and burned a bit going."

Wright gave the bottle a closer look. The label, the glass – everything looked authentic. "What is this? Some kind of joke whiskey?"

"If it is, the joke's on me. I bought three cases, a dozen bottles in each, right before the Fall and paid full price. I can testify that the bottles I opened last week were the real stuff. Bushmill's or not, I got a terrible hangover. Now, I don't know. But if you don't believe me, pour some on a plate and light it. It burns blue just like eighty-proof whiskey should."

"Last week? You mean . . . ?"

"Yes, before you nut cases tried to blow up an interstellar, trans-dimensional flying saucer with a fertilizer bomb."

"Well, we might have been off our nut." Wright felt his anger rising. "But we did manage to make the abomination slide into Lost Lake. I think you'd call that a partial success at least."

"If you were so successful, why did you stick a .357 magnum pistol in your mouth and blow your brains out?"

"Who says I did?"

"I do. I heard the shot. I looked inside your skull with a flashlight. You did a thorough job." Simon grinned at him. "Are you going to bash me in the head with that bottle or what?"

Wright looked at his hands. Unconsciously, he had been gripping the bottle's neck in a clenched fist, holding it like a cudgel.

"If so, then I don't have any brain cells left to lose. Is that why I can't even get a buzz?"

Simon winked at him. "I drank a whole fifth and all that happened was I had to take a long piss."

Wright's anger evaporated and he laughed. "I guess you're trying to make a point, not really trying to find out why I killed myself. I don't know why I did it. I really don't remember."

"No point really, just an observation," Simon said.

"So drop the other shoe."

"Nothing very astute, I'm afraid," the old man said. "Just that we are living in a reality where the usual rules don't apply. Dead men don't stay dead. Eighty-proof whiskey has no alcoholic effect. So why should we think it odd that a Buddhist can translate out of this reality and leave his clothes behind?

"Is that what you think?"

"I don't know what to think," Simon said. "I do know there are a lot of odd things going on since you sank the saucer, and I'm not just talking about you undead people. Have you heard about the giant cherubs?"

"Cherubs? What are cherubs?"

"Sheriff, sometimes you surprise me. One moment you seem like a bright, well-educated man. Then another, you seem a lot like – never mind."

"If you're talking about gaps in my education, maybe it's because I didn't have a rich family to give me a Club Med college experience."

"Or a lot of time to sit in a mental ward and read a lot," Uncle Robert said as if reading his thoughts.

"I had to work my way all through what college I got. I didn't have much time to read for pleasure," Wright said instead.

"You're quite right, of course. We Jacobsens have been both blessed and cursed by circumstance." Simon cleared his throat. "A cherub – more properly a cherubim – is another type of angel. Technically, it's a second class of angel, below the archangels, but in art they are usually represented as babies with wings, with an innocent or chubby face."

"Like a cupid?"

"Yes, but they don't necessarily carry bows and arrows."

"'Cruel fat, flying infant terribles – not God – rule the night.' That's what Cartwright wrote," Wright said.

"You have a good memory, and I like the description in the addendum better: 'little flying fuckers.'"

Simon looked at Cartwright's note again. "'However I have found a way out of this haunted house. The exit is found looking inward, toward the light.'"

"What does that mean?"

"Not sure, but it sounds like a meditation thing: locking inward."

"So he thought good thoughts and flew away?"

"Hah! Maybe that's what he did. Makes as much sense as anything. Life is but a dream."

"Then who's doing the dreaming?" Wright said. "You or me?

"Maybe neither of us. Maybe it's someone or something else," Simon said.

"So what happens if that someone wakes up? Do we all disappear?"

"Good question, but one I don't want to think about," Simon said. "Can I keep Cartwright's note?"

"Be my guest, but hang onto it. If his body shows up, I'll need it as evidence."

"Evidence of what?"

"Good question."

Simon folded the note and put it a pocket, then took the bottle of whiskey from Wright's hand and took a long drink. Wright could see the old man's Adam's apple move up and down under his beard as he swallowed.

"I never realized how bad this stuff tastes without the promise of a buzz," he said, and tossed the bottle over the stack of books where it shattered unseen.

"Aimed for the fireplace," Simon said, as if that explained anything.

They sat not talking, not looking at each other. Wright toyed with the idea that this reality – what he saw, smelled, heard and felt – was a dream. For a brief moment he saw himself as a tiny figure, not from on high, but like he was a toy man walking around in a dollhouse. The colors of the vision were over-saturated, muted toward a cold green as if seen through dirty water. But everything seemed so real, from the odor of the musty books to the press of the hard plastic chair he sat in, just reduced to a miniature set.

Something scratched at the window, and for a moment he saw a huge version of Laura's face looking in the picture window.

It was only a tree branch, blowing in the wind. He an the room were back to normal size.

He relaxed and was rewarded with a memory of Laura, not the giant Laura face of the momentary vision, but her face from last night, flushed with passion and animal happiness as he had worked in and out of her.

"Your niece?" he asked Simon.

"What about her?"

"I was supposed to meet her here."

"Why?"

"Police business," Wright lied.

"Crap! What did she do now?"

"Nothing. I just wanted to talk to her about the other undead who frequent the café," Wright said. He wasn't used to lying. But once started, one lie led to the next and the next.

"Really," Simon said. "Is that so?"

Maybe I'm not that good at lying.

"You know," Simon continued, "there's something different about you now."

"Really," Wright said. "Is that so?"

"Yeah. For one thing, you talk smarter," Simon laughed. "The other thing is that you look pretty good for a man your age – how old are you again?"

"Either forty-two years or about three days, depending upon your perspective."

"Beg your pardon? Three days? Oh, I get it, when you revived after your accident."

"I thought we agreed it was no accident, but what I remember is intending to shoot May."

"May the Angel? Why would you want to do that?"

"I don't remember, but she came by the office yesterday evening and laid some cock-and-bull story about me getting her pregnant."

"My, you have been a busy boy," Simon said. "Offhand, I'd say your life has improved since you killed yourself. First knocking up an angel; now seducing my niece, who, by the way, is young enough to be your daughter."

Wright felt his face flush.

"You don't really think that I'd to that, do you, Simon?"

"I don't think the old John Wright would have – he wouldn't have had a chance with her anyway. But this person you've become – well, maybe you don't realize it, but you look like a man half your age, and you're sort of a pretty boy at that."

"I know I've changed, but I feel like the same person – inside."

"It's not only your looks. There's something else about you. Sophia saw you in town this morning and mentioned it. A mixture of 'charisma and animal magnetism' is how she described it. Sex appeal is what she meant, though she claims to be beyond such things, but I read between the lines."

"Simon, I would never. . ."

The old man waved him off. "I know. I think you're still an ethical man, dead or undead, and Sophia, despite the attraction, has too much sense. But she was curious and watched you for a while and saw you and Laura leaving your office yesterday. She said you two kissed at the doorway – 'long and hard.' Then Laura followed you out of town in her old white Beetle."

"Simon.?"

"She's of age, but the mystical sex appeal aside, I couldn't imagine a more unlikely couple. Not to insult you – personally, I like you, John. But despite you having turned into pretty boy, I still can't for the life of me see Laura falling under the spell of a man like you. Again no offence intended."

"None taken, but it's not like that. I really didn't set out to seduce her," Wright said. And he briefly described the irresistible force that pulled him to Laura's front door the night he had awakened undead in the woods.

"Moreover, your niece later confessed she felt it too; though I don't think the pull on her was a strong as it was on me, it was definitely there. We were like moths being drawn towards the light, and the light was each other." He paused. "I'm not explaining it very well."

"I get the idea," Simon said. "You're describing just another one of these odd things that have been happening since the saucer sank in the lake."

"Things were pretty weird even before that, what with arch-angels flying about and hopping across dimensions, embedding those little things . . ."

"Homunculi proxies, is what I've come to call them."

"Whatever," Wright said.

"Yes, I agree. *Whatever* about sums it up." Simon got up from his chair. "But the level of weirdness definitely went up a few notches right after."

Wright could hear the old man's knee joints popping, reminding him of how his own knees used to sound.

"To answer your original question, Laura is not here. She was supposed to come for lunch but never showed."

"Is that like her to do that?"

"No, not really, but you know she was always the creative one. Sometimes she'll get become completely absorbed in something and lose track of time – like me you know. But today, who knows? It could be car trouble. She's always been too proud to let me replace that VW of hers. Or maybe she has *other* man problems and is laying low," He winked at Wright.

"You can joke, but I'm worried now about her now, what with those 'little flying fuckers' out there."

"We don't know that they're a danger – or that they really exist," Simon said and began tracing his way through the narrow aisle that led toward the foyer.

Wright took this as a hint that the visit was over. He got up and followed.

"I don't know," Wright said. "I saw some weird stuff out at Cartwright's farm. Did you know that Cartwright's wife, Suzanne, is missing?"

"That little goth girl? She wasn't even half Ben's age. Maybe she ran off with a musician." Simon turned and looked at him for a moment.

"I get your drift," Wright said. He knew as well as anyone why middle-aged men chased women young enough to be their daughters. As much as anything, they hoped to recover their own lost youth. Such things were usually mistakes for old-man lovers. "But there are some things you don't know."

The two men stepped out on the porch, and Wright further described the state of the severed ear, the absence of tracks, and Laura's telling him of the angels dropping cows out of the sky.

They both looked to the sky, the treetops, as he spoke, but it was left unsaid that neither found anything but phantoms of their own minds. Uncle Robert took Cartwright's note out of his pocket and read it again.

"If this is a dream, then there must be some way to wake up," he said. "Still need gas? I have a tank in the garage. Take what you need."

Wright borrowed five gallons of gasoline from Simon, slopping the fuel from the red plastic can over the fender in his haste to get back on the road and check on Laura. He invited the old man to come with him.

"No, I should stay here. She'll probably drag her rear end over here eventually. She's a realistic country girl and is not likely to become an accident statistic." Uncle Robert smiled as if enjoying a private joke, but Wright could tell by the set of his eyes and how he hunched his shoulders that he was worried, too.

Wright drove through town without stopping when he didn't see Laura's Beetle parked near the square. He should have breathed a little easier when, ten minutes later, he pulled up behind her car still parked at his house – but something didn't feel right. The birds chirping in the trees seemed to be off key. The breeze from the south smelled almost syrupy sweet. Even the crunch of gravel under his feet, which should have been reassuring in its familiarity, grated on his nerves.

He entered the house through the front door, his stomach now a hard knot.

"Laura?" he called, not really expecting an answer.

The bedroom floor was cluttered with torn sheets and the remains of the window. The window was not merely broken. The entire frame and part of the wall had exploded inward, splintering the two-by-four pine framing, leaving a round hole where the rectangular window had been.

He was reminded of the broken windows at the clinic when the archangels had abducted Laura and Dr. Jenkins.

Laura's orange waitress skirt hung on a bedpost, the little green pad she wrote orders on sticking out of a pocket. Her tennis shoes were mixed with the bloody sheets, splintered wood and shattered glass on the floor.

Wright retrieved his twelve-gauge shotgun from the closet and searched the yard outside the window for any signs of Laura, angels or cherubs. Just an all-too familiar looking sparrow lying on the soggy leaves, now dead, but still splattered with Wright's blood and dried brains.

He drove back to town, as if lost in a bad dream, the shotgun in easy reach in the passenger's seat. He looked up for a sign, for a clue of what to do next, where to search for her, but found none, neither in his heart or the sky.

* * *

13.

And as the Curtain of Dreams Rises

Laura.

She was back in the saucer, back in the damned Army surplus cot, back under the scratchy wool blanket.

This dream again; what does it mean that I keep having it?

She counted her breaths to calm herself and took note of her dream surroundings.

The dream was different this time. It seemed just as real, a lucid dream like a detailed stage setting. Everything in this dream – the walls, the wooden frame of the cot, the funky discolorations in the fabric of the huge tent – was in sharp detail and brightly illuminated, just as it had been in the dream where she was being attended by Dr. Jenkins. And now her awareness stretched well beyond her peripheral vision. She felt she could see around corners.

This dream was different in other substantial ways. There was only one other cot in the huge tent, where before there had been dozens. The person on the other cot was shrouded from toe to head under the blanket. Was it a dead body or another human with a gestating homunculus? He, she or whatever, it was motionless and too far away for her to hear if it was breathing.

Jenkins was nowhere to be found in this dream; in the other, he had been trying to snatch her blanket away. And she didn't remember odors from the other dream – in fact, she couldn't recall ever smelling anything in any dream. But here the air reeked of dead fish, mud and something fetid and rotten.

And in the previous dream she had been out of her body, floating near the top of the tent, watching herself struggle with Jenkins to keep the blanket. Here she was most certainly locked in her dream body, she just had the preternatural wrap-around vision.

A memory coalesced – something about glass breaking and wicked little hands– then dissolved, leaving her feeling disconcerted. Was that another dream? A dream within a dream? She didn't want to slip into another dream realm; she wanted to explore this one.

There must be a reason she kept returning here.

She swung her feet off the cot and found she was dressed only in panties and a sweatshirt. Her feet had caked blood between the toes, and this alarmed her until she reminded herself this was a dream. She lifted a foot and examined the sole. There were no huge wounds, just a lot of small gashes. Something was lodged in one cut, and she plucked it out: a small piece of glass. It hurt. Things shouldn't hurt in a dream.

The body on the other cot stirred and turned on its side, exposing bare feet. She gasped. The feet were large and white as marble: an archangel's.

He – for the creature was in its male form– sat up on the cot. The blanket fell from his face. His features were sculptured, as handsome as a male model's, beautiful, with slight feminine hints, but not effete. She knew the archangels were native to a realm where time was just another dimension like height, width and depth, and their human-like beauty was an illusion. Even so, his beauty still took her breath away. It was as if Michelangelo's David had come to life. The angel opened his eyes. The violet irises looked brilliant in contrast to the marble-white skin. As she watched, a pink flush rose, giving the marble skin a rosy hue.

"Who are you?" she asked.

"I am Samiazaz," he said. There was a muted distorted quality to his voice as if her ears were full of water.

"I remember your name," she said.

Samiazaz was one of the two angels who had collided with a small plane over Lost Lake. His companion's body had been recovered by Wright, then a living man, and Jimmy Harte, the deputy. But Samiazaz had become entangled in the wreckage of the plane and sank to the bottom of Lost Lake. Submerged in water, the archangels went into a kind of hibernation. This archangel was the only one of the original one hundred left. He was her last chance at a kind of semi-immortality. But did she really want that now – now that Wright was in her life?

Of course, she did. Why shouldn't she?

Muddy water trickled from his left ear and ran in a rivulet down the broad expanse of his hairless shoulder. Hypnotically, it traced a thin line between his pectorals, then zigzagged down his washboard abdominals like a snake's shadow and disappeared under the blanked that still covered his waist and groin.

Samiazaz stood, clutching the blanket to his waist. More dark water poured from of his ear. Absentmindedly, he wrapped the blanket around his waist, giving her a momentary glance of what looked like male organs. Now she was certain this was a dream. Male angels were supposed to look like big Ken dolls down there, not like human males. They had some other organ there. Something sharp as a crystal, something that penetrated and implanted the homunculi seeds.

Samiazaz rolled the blanket around his waist and tucked in a corner. He walked to the end of the tent and lifted a flap, exposing an exit. A cold blue light filtered in. He looked back over his shoulder and motioned for her to follow.

She stood, and a chill breeze washed over her. She imitated Samiazaz, wrapping the blanket around her waist to make a kind of skirt.

Outside the tent, she found a familiar sight from her time inside the alien saucer. The craft was only a saucer in three-dimensional space. In the archangels' reality, it was a trans-dimensional portal – sort of vestibule – that led to their home universe. She had gathered from her previous talks with angels that their extra senses saw an entirely different sight than her limited human eyes, which interpreted the reality of the angel realm a form into some her mind could accept.

But despite the four-dimensional filter of her human consciousness, the landscape still appeared alien. Miles away, cloud shadows sped across a painted desert landscape, but though the clouds were white and the alien sun a bright spot in the emerald sky, the shadows were white as well. And the colors of the painted desert were all wrong. They shifted into hues that made her nauseous if she stared at one spot too long.

Nearby boulders of all shapes and sizes littered the desert. Some boulders were shaped like toadstools, and she wondered if they were boulders at all. Crystalline things shaped like barrel cacti erupted in the spaces between the boulders. When she wasn't directly looking at one, the crystalline structure seemed to mutate to some other shape. But when she looked directly at one, it seemed as stable and still as any Earth plant.

The ground trembled perceptibly under her feet. The sky momentarily flickered from emerald green to blue, then back to green.

Beyond the boulders a broken-back range of ancient mountains stretched from horizon to horizon. Occasional straight lines – arrow-straight lines – ran at odd angles across and up the sides of the mountain. The lines glowed neon green.

Everything seemed so real but couldn't be. Samiazaz wasn't in the saucer when it sank. He was interned with the body of the human airplane pilot on the other side of the lake, submerged in at least a hundred feet of water. Then again, she reminded herself, that the archangels were not subject to the same physical laws of time and space as were humans. Maybe Samiazaz was in both places at once.

It gave her a headache to think about. She could ask Samiazaz where his body really was, but maybe she should start off with something innocuous as a kind of lead-in to the nitty-gritty. If this was some kind of altered reality – and not an ordinary dream – she might narrow down his real resting place. If it was truly just a dream, then she would be simply tapping into her own unconscious. Either way, it would be enlightening.

"Samiazaz, you're the angel who sank to the bottom of Lost Lake with the small plane – is that right?"

"Yes."

"Well, I thought you guys went to sleep when immersed in water."

"Yes, that's correct too, though we didn't know that until we traveled to your plane of existence."

"Then how come I'm talking to you? How can this be?"

"We sleep a dreamless sleep when we're deep underwater. But when the water is shallow, then we dream."

"You didn't answer my question."

"Yes, I did," Samiazaz said and used a smaller boulder to step up to the top of one the taller mushroom-shaped rocks. To get to the higher rock, he had to bring one leg straight up so his knee nearly touched his nose – like a cheerleader doing a high kick. But once he got his heel on the mushroom rock that was enough. It was odd to watch; for an instant the world went topsy-turvy as he stepped not up but down from the small rock to the larger one.

She rubbed her eyes and looked again. There he was standing on top of the big rock as if it were a dais, and the world was right-side-up again. Her feet and the ground were down and the sky was up instead of vice-versa.

"If you're asleep and dreaming how can I be talking to you?" she said.

"Obviously, because you're dreaming too. The dreamtimes of our species, of our worlds, overlap here in this place. "

"Yes, obviously," she echoed, meaning to sound sarcastic, which of course was lost on the angel. "And this dreamtime," she started to say but her train of thought was interrupted by a memory.

She remembered Uncle Robert once telling her about the indigenous Australians' "dreamtime." He had used the phrase 'everywhen' when trying to explain it to her. That was all she could remember now, for she had been smoking hashish daily then and thought her uncle had been trying some sort of mind-fuck rehabilitation game on her. She did recall his saying something about the dreams of dreamtime being the real, objective world, while the walking-around world, the world where their physical bodies lived and breathed, was only a faded copy, a kind of aboriginal Platonic vision.

Samiazaz stared at her, patiently waiting for her to finish her sentence. "So we're in different dreamtimes together? Isn't that like going to different high schools together?" she said.

"I don't understand what you're asking."

"Me neither, really. It's just a stupid saying."

He stretched out a hand to pull her up.

"I can't get up there," she said.

"Step on the small rock and lift your arm," Samiazaz said.

She struggled onto the rock – it only looked small in comparison to the other. It was the size of a doghouse. She reached up, but his hand was still several feet out of reach. Then his arm stretched out impossibly long; height, length, up, and down became all mixed up again. This is just a dream, she reminded herself as her stomach turned inside out. And then she was standing next to Samiazaz atop the rock.

From the high vantage point, she could see more of the desert floor. The mushroom rocks were spread across the visage for miles. Here and there were open spots filled with the crystalline cacti. Even from a distance, the cactus form was dependent upon whether she was looking directly at them.

Samiazaz pointed behind her. She steadied herself by holding onto his arm and turned to look. A column of water fell onto the desert floor from about ten or twelve feet up. There was no cloud, no geological formation, from where the waterfall originated. It came out what appeared to be a ragged crack in thin air. The terminus of the waterfall on the desert floor was shrouded in mist and spray. But a small river snaked out of the mist and flowed toward the mountains.

"The shell of our craft was breached by your explosives," Samiazaz said. "Lost Lake is draining into our realm. Soon the lake will be dry and my body in your world will be uncovered, and more than only our dreamtimes will merge." He smiled at her, triumphant.

She looked down to see a thing of diamonds and razor sharp edges projecting through the blanket. Like the cacti, it was both organic and crystalline.

"But you don't have to wait. In this time or out of this dreamtime, you could be reborn to live for millennium," he said.

Terrified, she stepped back. Her heel found only air, and then she was falling backward.

"I am your last chance," Samiazaz said, watching her fall.

Dreamtime or not, it's going to hurt when I land on that boulder.

Bryan.

Suzanne lay on her side on the green sheets, facing away from him, her red hair tucked under her head on the pillow. She had kicked off the sheet, and her bare back traced a sinuous curve reminiscent of rolling waves and highland hills. In the soft morning light, her skin was as white as foam, and the freckles that washed along her waist lay in pattern reminiscent of a Celtic motif.

He lay behind her, leaving a few inches between them, wanting to touch her but was afraid if he touched her, he'd break the dreamlike spell she cast as she lay there. But a greater fear was he would find she was dead, really dead this time. When he had pulled her out from under the giant headless cherub he hadn't been able to find a pulse. Blackish, tarry blood had streamed from the angel's neck onto her face. He had wiped her clean and carried her downstairs, back to his grandparents' king-size bed.

That's the second time I've found you for dead and had to clean you up.

However, the first time, when he had found her in the woodpile, she was still talking; cold as ice, but moving. This time, after he'd heaved the massive lifeless hulk of the cherub off her body, she had lain motionless. He had looked for signs of breathing and found none. Listening, he could hear only the nervous rasp of his own breath. Neither could he find a pulse.

At first he feared she'd been hit by a stray pellet from the same shotgun blast that had taken off the angel's head. He had fired from across the room – had been able to do so only because Suzanne had drawn the angel away from him by pounding on it with the fire iron.

He searched for an entry wound, running his fingers through her red hair, fearing he'd find fresh blood – human red blood, not the black shitty stuff from the angel – on his fingertips. He found none, and she gasped and smiled as his thumb traced the delicate convolutions of her ear – wait! Only hours before, there hadn't been an ear there!

Cupping one hand under her cheek, he gently turned her head to the side to see if he had been mistaken as to which ear she had lost. There indeed was an ear on that side of her head, identical to the undamaged one on the other side, except . . .? He turned her head back and re-examined the new ear. What was different? He saw it now. The old ear, the one she had lost, had had extensive piercings, beads, a short bar going through the upper part, and a gauge big enough to pass a pencil through. The new ear had no piercings, no signs of ever having any. A virgin ear.

She kissed his hand without opening her eyes.

"Are you awake?" he asked.

"No, I'm dreaming," she said.

"It's been so long since a strange woman has slept in my bed, that I feel like I'm in a dream too."

Not to mention, that this strange redheaded woman is undead.

"Who's dreaming who?" she said. "Am I dreaming you, or are you dreaming me?"

"Whom?" he countered without thinking.

"Huh?"

"Never mind," he said.

"No, tell me."

"'Who is dreaming whom' is more grammatically correct. Sorry, it's habit. I didn't mean to sound so pedantic."

"No, don't apologize. I want to learn better English – at least I want to learn it from you." She smiled at him. Her cheeks were flushed and her smoky blue eyes flashed. "What does 'pedantic' mean?"

"Sort like of the worst asshole teacher you can think of – everything by the book."

"I don't think you're like that at all," She reached out and brushed the side of his cheek with her fingers, a Braille kiss. She glowed with good health, exuded energy and life. He found it hard to believe that she was undead.

"I lost my train of thought," he said. "What were we talking about?"

"Dreaming. Were you an English major or something in college?

"No, not for long anyway. I was a journalism major, which is a worse kind of asshole," he said. "We used to call ourselves 'jerk-o-lism' majors."

The smile she gave him told him she didn't care if he shoveled manure for a living. He felt that whatever he did would be okay with her. And amazingly, he felt the same about her and wanted to tell her so.

But she's undead, he told himself and said instead. "Maybe someone else is dreaming both of us. Or maybe we're equal partners in this dream, I don't know."

"I like that. Equal partners, but I doubt it. I don't think I've ever been an equal partner in anything."

"Never?"

"No, I've always been someone's stubborn child, someone's runaway daughter," she said. "Most recently, I've been someone's wife. I've always felt as I was typecast in a movie from the moment I was born. I don't think I've ever been just me."

She sat up and pulled the quilt around her shoulders. From the corner of his eye, he saw something scurry across the quilt. It was a lizard or a newt, one of those slick, scale-less things that lived in mud. The lizard ran across an area of the quilt that looked like lily pads, a movement that was part four-legged gait, part slithering, made visible more by the shadow it cast than its body. It ran past a sewn-in felt frog and stopped in a patch of brown suede cut to resemble dead, wet leaves. He reached for it, but his hand came up empty.

Where had it gone? He was sure his hand had closed over it. He leaned over to stare closely at the quilt. There he found the lizard among a cluster of little stars, but it was sewn into the quilt, part of the pattern made of bits of red and green fabric, not a living thing at all. Had it been a trick of the light? It must have been, but he was sure he had seen it move. He traced the little creature's outline with his fingers. His grandmother's stitches were precise, exact. The eyes were little buttons sewn on with green thread. Suzanne grabbed his hand and squeezed it hard. Her inner thigh was underneath the patchwork lizard.

"I had another dream," she said.

"It wasn't a dream," he said. "That big fat fuck of an angel was real."

"Oh, I know that," she said. "I figured it out before I passed out. I'm not stupid, or a dumb redhead or a druggie, despite what people say."

"I don't listen to what people say, and I know you're not stupid; far from it."

"How do you know it?"

"This may sound like New Age bullcrap."

"Shoot." She sat up, exposing a breast, then modestly pulling the quilt up.

Something had changed between them, but he couldn't quite say what. Last night, he had felt fated to be with her. A match, maybe a lifelong one. He had never felt that before. And it wasn't just the sex. It was like he couldn't do anything wrong; couldn't say anything wrong. But now everything had changed. She was the same woman. She was still beautiful, more so now that her ear had grown back. But he didn't say this. Instead, feeling vulnerable and defensive, he said, "Never mind. I was going to say something about us being soul mates, but you don't feel that way do you?"

She blushed the way only redheads blush, not just her cheeks but her whole face, and turned away. The blush faded; she was obviously struggling with a reply.

"It was like a dream inside a dream, but I dreamed of my husband," she said.

His heart sank a little at the word "husband," which was stupid of him.

Her red hair shimmered in the morning light. He had the oddest impression that the room was a under water, an octopus' garden drawn in with colored markers, and that she alone was three-dimensional in a two-dimensional world. Pale freckles swam like tiny minnows across her skin.

"And . . .?" He braced himself, knowing what was coming, reminding himself they had only spent one night together.

"I know I said a lot of things last night, and I meant them when I said them," she said.

He waited.

"But I'm going to have to go back to him." She paused, looking away again. "In my dream he was crying; he was crying for me." She looked back to him. "I'd rather stay with you, fat angels or no fat angels, but it's a karma thing. Understand?"

"I think so. I've sort of been through this before." He put on what he hoped was an indifferent expression but felt his eyes watering. He could understand now why her husband would cry over her absence. A concern overcame him.

"I don't know how to ask this," he said. "It's going to sound weird."

"It's been a weird day anyway."

"When I found you in the wood pile, you'd been beaten up, left for dead."

"Undead," she corrected. "Don't be afraid of the word. You and I both know it's true. "

"But you look so good. And your ear has grown back," he said.

She pulled her arm out from under the quilt and touched her new ear. "Not only that, look at my hand," she said. "I nearly lost this thumb when I fell through a window. There was a scar that wound all the way around and there was nerve damage too. The scar is gone now." She held up her hand and touched the tip of her thumb quickly to all the tips of the fingers. "And I have 'full range of motion,' as the doctors would say."

"You didn't answer my question."

"You didn't ask one."

"You said something about the last thing you remembered was having a big argument with your husband."

"Ben."

"Excuse me?"

"Ben, that's my husband's name."

"Yeah, I forgot. Anyway, you said he went crazy and started throwing things around."

"Not things. Furniture. A sofa, you know."

"He's a big man."

"But he was kind most the time. He's bipolar. After the Fall, his medication was running out."

"Whether he meant to or not, it doesn't change things," Bryan said. "It might have been him that damaged you."

He couldn't bring himself to say "murdered you."

She smiled sadly. "I can't believe it was Ben who did it. But there's no *nearly* dead about it. You tried to take my pulse and didn't find one, did you?"

"No, but I thought maybe I just didn't know how."

"We both know that's not the problem."

"Yes," he admitted. "The angels have changed the rules of life and death."

"They've changed the rules of love, too," she said and ran a hand through his hair. "We don't always get what we want. It's never as simple as it should be. I don't want to, but I still have to go see Ben."

"Why?"

"I know something bad has happened to him. I don't love him but I owe him. I'm obligated."

"I'm going with you. I'm going to drive you."

"How would I explain you?" she said.

"You can think of something. I'm not afraid of him."

He had more to tell her. "It's not just your ex-husband I'm worried about. Look up," he said, pointing to upstairs landing. The bloated white flesh of the cherub's body pressed against the balustrade. A viscous stream of black blood trickled over the edge of the upper floor and dripped on the floor below. The body looked smaller, as if it were melting. "If there's one of those things, there could be more."

"So you want to protect me?"

"I guess so. It's mutual isn't it?"

She leaned forward and kissed him again, this time on the lips, the quilt falling down on her lap. As his hands found her breasts, the patchwork lizard ran a zigzag course across the quilt. He ignored it as he would an LSD hallucination.

Suzanne took his penis and slipped it inside her, and it didn't seem to matter anymore whether this moment was real or an hallucination; whether his lover was dead or undead, whether it was to be a short-lived love or one that lasted forever.

* * *

14.

I See You for What You Are

Laura.

Again, she was back inside the saucer, back inside the tent, back on the Army cot, and as before she didn't remember how she had gotten here.

Diluted green light streamed in from a rip in the tent's ceiling and pooled upon a clutch of angels/human hybrids in the center of the tent, near one of the main tent poles. They swayed gently in unison, their faces blank, their eyes closed, the gossamer filigree of their own wings wrapped around them like robes.

The angels Marguerite and May Tyre were among the twelve, and impulsively Laura gave them a little parade-queen wave, all wrist, no arm action. Neither angel showed any acknowledgment of her wave.

A small tree with blood-red flowers and metallic green apples sprouted through the tent's canvas floor next to her cot.

Good dream, like walking around in a Salvador Dali painting, she thought. *No construction in baked beans, but more than hint of dyspepsia.*

Last she remembered, she had been talking to Samiazaz about Dreamtime atop one of the mushroom rocks, and he had extended the crystal spar – and then what? Oh yes, she had fallen backwards. She must have been knocked unconscious, and Samiazaz had carried her back here like a good Boy Scout.

She laughed out loud. What was she thinking? That this was real and not a dream?

But if it wasn't real, why was she still here?

"If this is a dreamtime," she said. "Why can't I wake up?"

"It is a dream," said a familiar voice behind her.

She let out a little scream. Jumping up from the cot, she found Uncle Robert standing behind her.

"But you're not the dominant dreamer, so it takes a special technique to escape it," he said. He had a fishing pole draped over his shoulder.

She hugged him, careful to avoid getting tangled in the pole's fishing line, then stepped back to survey him.

She was pleased with what she saw. His beard had been neatly trimmed and he looked fitter than he had for years. He was as she remembered him when she was about twelve, and she had lived with him and Sophia after her father's death. For a moment, she was that little girl again, back in a time when her real daddy had turned into a monster and Uncle Robert and Aunt Sophia had been there to remind her that there were good people in the world, good people who genuinely cared about her.

"Been fishing?" she asked.

"Yep, and I caught something big," he said. With his free hand, he tugged on the pole's line, taking up some of the slack. The line glistened, a fat, milky silver cord, stretching out through the doorway of the tent then out of sight.

"There are fish out there?" she said, pointing toward the desert.

"Yeah, they just have to take the bus to get anywhere," he said, grinning that sad-eyed way of his. "Did I hear you use the word *Dreamtime?*"

"Yes, it was a word Samiazaz, the archangel, used."

"You were talking to him?"

"Yes ...no. I don't really know whether if it was a dream or reality or a mixture of both."

"Well, that's the nature of dreamtime, isn't it? Life is but a dream, tra, la, la, la," he said and laughed.

His laugh was contagious and she laughed along with him and gave him another hug. "You're a good dream," she said.

"Dream or not, you should cover yourself a little better, child," he said, kissing her on the forehead, then pushing her away at arm's length.

She realized she was still only in panties and a sweatshirt. As in the dream with Samiazaz, she grabbed the wool blanket from the cot and wrapped it around her waist like a skirt. Uncle Robert looked away as she modesty adjusted the blanket.

"Better?" she asked.

"Yes," he said, looking at her again, smiling. "I know that we're in what was the birthing tent for the homunculi. But what's with the angels over there?

"I don't know," she said. "They've just been standing there."

"They remind me of a church choir. I expect the organ music to begin at any moment."

As if taking a cue from Uncle Robert, the angels began to sing in unison:

We sing a requiem for your undead
Whose shadows of a last life linger
As the metathesis of love reveals a truth
That opens the secret document of your heart,
Its pages blown by mad, beating wings. . .
And you cry:
'Undead love is harder, a cruel parody of life'
But we say it's a metaphoric rigor mortis
A stiffening of the limbs, a paralysis of the mind
Gradually becoming familiar, a transition to something higher

Ask Styxian Suze,
Ask how she completes him
And he completes her
Or ask yourself as you kiss your lover's empty braincase,
Then think 'father' and die all over again
But even now, immortality is part of your heritage

As you dive once more into the waters of illusion,
And as the curtains of Dreamtime rise, my love
Let him see you for what you are:
The other, dreaming you whose innocence ran
As blood runs in troubled waters,
As light fades at dusk

But our calls come from the deep
As we resurrect our lost souls for this last refrain
And then, even then,
'It's not over!' you scream
'Oh, you dismal waste of flesh!'
'Always but a breath away from death!'
Transformation comes quickly,
And then you will be powerful indeed
Powerful enough to save what you love
And lose it at the same time
But another level awaits those left behind

The angels abruptly stopped singing, leaving the tent deathly silent. They closed their eyes and began gently swaying in unison again. Their languid motion reminded Laura of underwater plants embraced by unseen currents.

"What was that all about?" Laura said. The song – half chant, really – had seemed nonsensical, mere jabberwocky, but with an underlying hint of significance.

"I'm not sure what the meaning was. I wish there were a replay button," Uncle Robert said. He scratched his chin. It was so odd seeing him looking young again. "But I think it was meant to be oracular."

"Oracular?"

"Sorry. Fancy, two-bit word; means like an oracle."

"You mean a prophecy? Was that someone's future they were singing about? Mine?"

"Maybe," he laughed. "But it's hard to tell. Oracles are by nature obtuse. Besides, keep in mind this is a sort of dream-made-real. Come on, I want you to show me what's outside this tent."

As they walked out of the tent into the alien landscape, Uncle Robert held the fishing rod in front of him, reeling in the silver line as they went.

The sky was a shade darker green now than when she had come out with Samiazaz, but the same stark-white stretched-thin clouds raced across the sky. The alien sun hung low on the horizon, not white-hot now but bluish and cold, out-of-place in the green sky. Shadows of the clouds still played across the desert floor, but now they were bluish-gray.

The barrel cacti had retracted their crystalline thorns but were shrunken, wrinkled. They were still hard to focus on. At the base of most of the cacti were now roundish little baseball-sized plants that looked related to the larger plants.

"It looks different from when Sophia and I were here before," Uncle Robert said.

"Before?"

"Before Wright and Marshal set off their fertilizer bomb," he said.

"It's constantly changing," she said. "Samiazaz didn't so much as out-and-out say so, but I got the impression that the part we can see is modified by who's looking at it."

"More Dreamtime stuff," Uncle Robert said. He kicked a baseball-sized cactus, sending it flying out over the desert floor. The cactus screeched like a cat whose tail has been stepped on, and neon-glowing text appeared on its surface, fading and eventually disappearing as the ball's flight slowed. The text was tantalizingly familiar yet unreadable. The cactus ball hit the desert floor and disintegrated into a dust cloud.

"Did you see that?" she asked.

"The words?"

"Yes, if that's what they were. Could you read it?"

"No, but there was definitely meaning. Everything here seems encrypted, the whole place is a message just beyond the limits of my perception."

"Kick another."

"No, I don't want to hear it screech like an abused cat again."

Uncle Robert walked on, following a barely discernible path across the desert floor, which was a mixture of flat rocks and open patches of sandy dirt. He continued to reel in the silver line, which showed no signs of ending.

An infinitely long fishing line? Everything else here was so strange. What if it were only an ordinary fishing line? How weird would that be?

The rocks and sand were cold under her bare feet. The sandy areas were marked by footprints that led toward the angel encampment. It took her a moment to realize the footprints matched those that Uncle Robert's old black-and-white tennis shoes, and he was retracing his path to the tent. He had obviously not just 'woken up' in the tent as she had, but had walked in from somewhere in the desert.

"Where are we going?"

"There's something I have to show you, something that will deeply disturb you – at least it disturbed me," he said. "It's not far from here, but first we have to talk about some things."

"Like what?"

"Like how you got here. What you remember immediately before waking."

He stepped off the path and sat on a large flat outcropping of rock.

"Come sit," he said and brushed the sand and crystal-looking thorns from a spot, then leaned the fishing pole on a cactus. She winced when his hand brushed across the razor-sharp thorns, but when she sat down beside him, his hand looked uncut.

"It's really quite beautiful here – once you get over the weirdness."

"It makes me nauseous if I stare at anything too long," she said.

"It did me too at first. The trick is not to try to make things fit your expectations; to relax a little. You know those optical illusion poster-pictures where there's a hidden picture in an abstract pattern?"

"Yeah, but I could never see them," she said. "I never had the knack."

Uncle Robert laughed. "Well, then look at me. Take your mind off the place."

She did as he suggested. He smiled at her. Was it something about the light? He seemed to fade in and out, his outline first in crystal-sharp relief, then out of focus.

Her stomach churned, and she put a hand over her eyes.

"What's wrong? Am I that ugly."

"No, no, it's not that. You're part of this place, aren't you."

"Perhaps I am now. Permanently part of the Dreamtime. Locked here in this plane of existence. Maybe. I don't know. Try looking at me now."

She peeked at him through her fingers, feeling like a little girl playing hide-and-seek. He laughed, the deep throaty Santa-Claus laugh she remembered from childhood. It relaxed her, and she took her hand away. His image was stable, but seemed in extra-high definition, which made her a bit uncomfortable but not nauseous.

"It's like you're a digital image. Too sharp and bright to be real," she said. "Do I look the same to you?" She examined her own hands.

"No, you look perfectly normal," he said. "Now tell me. What do you remember immediately upon waking up here?"

"The first time?"

She briefly told him about her encounter with Samiazaz and her fall from the rocks. "But the first time, I woke up in one of the cots, just staring at the ceiling. I don't even remember opening my eyes," she finished.

"Ahhhh, that's encouraging," Uncle Robert said.

"Why?"

"Why what?"

"Don't mess with me, Uncle Robert. When you do that, I know you're trying to stall and change the subject. Why so you think it's encouraging?"

"I can't get much past you, can I, Scout?" he said.

"Just answer me."

"Well, it's encouraging because – wow! Look at that! The sky just flickered emerald!"

"Uncle Robert!"

He laughed, again, but his laugh cut off prematurely, leaving a sad note.

"Because," he said, "My waking experience here was completely different, and I'm afraid the implications aren't very good."

"What exactly happened?"

"All in good time," he said and patted her on the shoulder. "Let's talk about what happened before you woke up here, before you found yourself in the saucer."

She paused to think, then stuttered, "I don't exactly remember. I was at John Wright's house, and, and . . ."

"I know all about you and the good sheriff," Uncle Robert said.

"You do? What do you know?"

"Now it's you who's stalling. And you're blushing. I don't think I've seen you blush since you were a little girl."

"I don't think I was ever a little girl."

"Oh, but you were. I remember one time very well. It was not long after the episode with your father, with the knife. Maybe I shouldn't stir up old memories."

"It's all right. You taught me it's better not to bury those things." But it did hurt to think about that time, even now – what, twelve, thirteen years later? Her father had caught her plucking her eyebrows – she feared she had been growing a unibrow. In one of his psychotic episodes, possessed by private demons, he had started screaming at her that it was against "God's law." When she had defied him, he had knocked her down, sat on her and held a knife at her throat.

She could still remember the feeling of the blade pressed against her neck, just under her chin. The blade had been warm for he carried it folded in his back pocket. His sweat dripped on her as he stared at her; his eyes had been so dilated they were black pools bordered by thin blue halos.

"Go ahead!" she said. "Do it, Daddy. Just get it over with!"

His eyes had softened then, and she saw the red rings underneath, felt how exhausted he was, felt his hatred for himself. She knew then that's what it was all about. He was consumed with guilt and self-hatred. In some sort of twisted sky-pilot fashion, he had been projecting all his own self-hatred and guilt to her.

He stood up, folded the knife, put it back in his pocket and walked away. It took her a minute to catch her breath, but she felt amazingly calm. She had picked herself up off the floor and gone to her room. When she looked in the mirror, she saw her throat was bleeding from where the blade had nicked her. Though only a superficial cut, there was a lot of blood, and it was smeared across the front of her white blouse. Without changing or washing off the blood, she had stuffed some clothes, her portable CD player and a book of Roethke poetry in her backpack and walked the ten miles or so to Uncle Robert's house. He had put her under the care of Sophia and called John Wright, who had put her dad in jail. But her father had a trust fund and a high-priced law firm on retainer. His lawyers had gotten him out the next day, but everyone in town knew Wright had spent the night in the jail, probably sitting outside her father's cell with the lights on, talking quietly to him.

Her father killed himself a week later. She often wondered what had transpired between her father and the sheriff that night in jail. Had he been on a suicide watch? That's what was assumed. Or had the sheriff been working a different agenda?

"Whoa, come back to me," Uncle Robert said.

"Sorry, I was thinking. What made me blush all those years ago?"

"There was a little boy in school with you – I think his name was Bob – pathetic little guy, thin as a rail and with bad haircut. He showed up on our doorstep one Valentine's Day with a card and a single flower – a bedraggled rose. You broke his heart and sent him packing. But you kept the card, and would take it out of your pocket and look at it when you thought no one was watching."

Uncle Robert laughed, this time a full and throaty laugh. "You blushed every time you looked at the card, and you're blushing like that now."

"Despite what you think I'm not still a child; I'm grown woman."

"That may be, sweetheart, but I suspect you still have that little girl's heart. Tell me what's going on with John Wright. I can't think of a more unlikely lover for you."

"Neither can I, Uncle Robert. Neither can I."

"Then what is it?" He said."Wright would stoop to extortion. He has his faults, but . . ."

"It's magnetic."

"You mean passion, lust?"

"That, but it's more. It's like we're connected by an invisible cord. I barely know him, really, and yet it's we've been lovers for years."

"You're blushing again. I thought you were a modern woman and nonchalant about such things," he said.

"You mean about sex?"

He nodded.

"Me, too," she said. "But it's not the sex – which is really good, by the way – it's — oh, I don't know what to call it – now you're blushing, Uncle."

"Maybe it's love," he said, clearing his throat.

"Maybe. Whatever it is, I feel complete when I'm with him. And worse, I feel incomplete when we're separated for any time at all." She shook her head. "And maybe I should just chalk that up to one of life's mysteries. But goddamn it, Uncle, he's fucking undead. I looked down the hole in the top of his head at the beach. He blew out all his brains! Now, he's walking around looking like some stud muffin off the cover of a romance novel!"

". . .as you kiss your lover's empty braincase," Uncle Robert said.

"Yes," she said. "The angels reference in their song wasn't lost on me; nor was the line, 'then think father, and die all over again.'"

"We're certainly in strange territory here, in a sort of post-apocalyptic world or plane of alternate reality, or whatever," he said.

She didn't reply because she didn't have an answer. They sat on the rock in silence for a few minutes.

After a few minutes, he said, "I can understand strange attractions. You know I love Sophia. I didn't love her on first sight – I thought she dressed like a hooker – but within moments of our first conversation I was hopelessly in love with her. And I still do love her, but there couldn't be a more unlikely couple than we are, with the possible exception of you and Sheriff Wright."

"Why do you think that was? I mean, why did you fall in love with Aunt Sophia?"

"I've thought about it a lot, and it's still a bit of a mystery to me after all these years," he said. "It was not just the fact that she had legs like Tina Turner's, though there was that. Maybe it was about her heightened consciousness."

"Really? You fell in love with her mind? Why, Uncle Robert, that's sort of romantic, in a nerdy sort of way."

"Yes, I guess it is," he said. "I know this sounds weird to you. I was a professed atheist before I met Sophia. Under her influence, I've become a bit of a Buddhist - thought I still don't hold to all the teleological arguments."

"I'm not following you."

"My mind is wandering, so it wouldn't be wise to follow me. We both might get lost," he said, laughing again. "But what I'm trying to say is, I have always been looking for some higher meaning to life, some intimation of a higher level of awareness. Sophia promised that. Not implicitly, you understand, but just that she always seemed to be connected to something beyond the mundane. She saw beyond the level of what I called cause and effect, and seemed privy to some sort of secret knowledge. I guess I was always hoping she'd share the mystery with me, maybe she'd tell me where to find the secret document that would explain everything. But either she doesn't know how to explain the way she does some of the things she does. But in the long run, it didn't matter. It was enough to know that she knew of something beyond the boring, everything-is-broken world that I saw. She saw – and still does see – connections to everything, connections that cause the world to make sense.

"But back to your getting here. You said you were in John Wright's house. Is that right?"

"You're not changing the subject again are you, Uncle Robert?"

"Yes, but for good reason. Think hard. Or rather, relax and let the memories come back."

"I can't."

"Can you at least remember which room you were in?" Then he

said something she didn't catch.

"No, I told you I can't – wait, I can! I was in the bedroom! Why is it I can remember now?"

"What do you see?"

"It's morning. Sunlight is seeping through some flowery curtains. I'm sitting on the edge of the bed, wearing the same sweatshirt I'm wearing now. It's John Wright's bedroom. I remember now. We spent the night together, but I woke up alone because he had to go to work. Why can I remember this now?"

"Because I hypnotized you," Uncle Robert said.

"I don't feel hypnotized."

"It's a very light trance. I was only able to do it because you trust me. You do trust me?"

"Yes," she said.

"Now remember what happened. Let the memories come in; don't try too hard. Let them drift by your consciousness like clouds on a warm summer day. The memories are far up in the sky, but you can see them clearly, can't you?"

"I'm holding a live sparrow that I've caught in the room, and I'm about to put it outside." She gasped at the memory and what followed. Then the little nasty creatures were all around her, bloated little angels with pudgy fingers that ended in claws. She was screaming, then slugging one of them in the face. Its nose caved in as if she had struck soft clay, but then more of the abominations were on her, their hands pinching, grasping. Her vision spun into a dark well; then she was only conscious of her heart beating.

She came to in Uncle Robert's arms. "There, there, it's all right," he said, gently rocking her side-to-side.

"What happened?" she said, her breath came in short gasps.

"You started screaming and fainted. Do you remember?"

"I remember fighting off the cherubs, that's all. But it was it was happening to my double, not to me."

"But when you woke up in the tent, there was just one of you," he said. "Am I correct?"

"Yes. I guess." She pulled the neck of the sweatshirt; it was oversized and stretched enough she could bare a shoulder. "Lock. I guess that explains this bruise."

He leaned forward.

"Can you see close up without your reading glasses?

"I can see fine. I guess I don't need them here," he said, examining her shoulder. "Yes, I see what you mean, but it looks like teeth marks instead of a bruise."

"I have them all over. But I couldn't remember how I got them until you hypnotized me."

"That's another good sign."

"How so? The little shits attacked me and stranded me here."

"Trust me. It's a good sign."

"Why are you being so mysterious? And how did you hypnotize me by the way?"

"When you were little, the first year after you moved out of your father's house, you'd have frequent panic attacks. I didn't want you put on drugs, so I started hypnotizing you. I embedded a hypnotic command phrase to make it easier. Haven't used it for years. I was surprised when it worked just now."

"What's the command?"

Uncle Robert grinned. "I can't tell you without putting you under. Don't worry though, the keywords die with me."

"Somehow, I don't find that all too reassuring."

"Why? I thought you trusted me?"

"I'm not sure I trust anyone that much."

"Come walk with me further," he said, getting to his feet. "I have something important to show you."

She followed him as he picked his way between crystalline cacti and small outcroppings of slate-like rock. The fishing-rod line whispered softly as he reeled it in. They passed between two small hills, and he paused, then pointed silently toward the top of one rise. There, silhouetted by the alien sun, was the same troupe of angels who had sung to her and Uncle Robert in the saucer. They stood silently, still clustered together like a church choir. She couldn't tell if they were watching her and Uncle Robert or even if their eyes were open or closed.

"They're stalking us," she said, half-joking.

Uncle Robert continued walking without answering. On the other side of the hills, they came into a wide depression. Shaped like a shallow bowl but hundreds of yards across, a caldera of sorts, probably formed by the alien equivalent of volcanic action. A small creek coursed through the sand, zigzagging down the gentle slope toward the center of the depression. Uncle Robert walked beside the muddy green stream, which seemed out of place in the strange landscape. Laura looked over her shoulder and found the angels still on the hill. They had turned *en masse* so they were still facing her and Uncle Robert.

Uncle Robert stopped abruptly, and Laura, who was stealing another glance at the angels, bumped into him.

He gripped her by the shoulder, his fingers digging in harder than necessary. There was fear in his eyes. For a terrifying moment, the set of his features, the beads of sweat populating his brow, and the dilation of his eyes reminded her of her father at his most horrible.

"Look," he said, pointing along the course of the stream.

She did as instructed, reaching up and prying his fingers loose as she did so.

They were maybe a hundred yards into the depression, and the course of the stream, nearly a foot-wide swath of muddy water, glistened in the alien light.

"So what am I looking for?" she said, but then saw it. A few yards beyond the edge of the depression a torrent of water gushed from ten or fifteen feet above the ground. The spout, with as much force as an open fire hydrant, came out of thin air. It was the same torrent Samiazaz had pointed out to her.

"I think," Uncle Robert said, "that the gushing coincides with tear in the outer skin of the saucer."

"That's what Samiazaz said. It's Lost Lake leaking in to this world."

"That's my guess too. Look here," he said Setting the rod and reel on the ground, he knelt by the stream and thrust a hand into the water. The stream was deeper than it appeared; his arm went in past his elbow. When he pulled back his hand it held an aluminum can. He turned it upside down to let the muddy water drain out. The blue and white labeling read "Budweiser Lite."

"I doubt this is an alien artifact," he said.

"Maybe Budweiser out-sources to parallel universes," she said.

Uncle Robert smirked but didn't reply. She looked back at the bottom of the depression, to where the stream flowed into bottom of the caldera. "That's a lot of water," she said. "Looks like it would be filling up this place."

"There's a sort of stone grating at the bottom," Uncle Robert said. "The water flows in. The grating keeps the bigger pieces of flotsam from going in. Some of the stuff it catches is ..." He paused, looking up with a thousand-yard gaze, as he were trying to stare into infinity. "Some of the flotsam is rather enlightening."

"Show me," she said, suddenly curious, and started ahead. Now she could see where the water flowed. There was quite a bit of debris. What looked like an old washing machine, large branches and something else, something blue and white that she couldn't quite distinguish.

"Wait!" Uncle Robert shouted. "There's something I have to tell you first."

"Tell me on the way," she said, now really curious.

"Laura, please, do as I say just this once," Uncle Robert said.

The plaintive tone of his voice made her stop. "Okay, shoot," she said. "But I think you should hurry. It looks like it's about to get dark, and I'm not sure I want to be out here at night. Besides, we're being followed. Look behind you."

He turned. The chorus of angels was now standing only about ten yards away, toward the setting sun. Shrouding themselves with their wings made them looke like they were dressed in monk's robes. She had not been aware of them flying or alighting nearby, but there they were.

"Ignore them," Uncle Robert said. "It's the cherubs you have to worry about."

"Tell me about it," she said.

"I think the cherubs are Samiazaz's thoughts become material in a way. Thoughts are actions on the astral plane."

The hair on the nape of her neck rose.

"You're frightening me now, Uncle Robert," she said.

"As well I should," he said. "You see, the little flying bastards made a visit to the manse, right after the sheriff visited me." He dipped the Budweiser can back into the stream, holding it so that it refilled with the murky water.

"My experience was much the same as yours. Except the ones that came after me were much larger than I think yours were. They were too large to come in through a normal-sized window, and they just waddled in through the unlocked front door."

He stood and without warning threw the water-filled beer can at the angel chorus. It landed short, splashing muddy water on their white feet, but they seemed not to have noticed.

"I fought them, as you did, but they were the size of large feral hogs and just as nasty. Four of them carried me back out the door. They pinched and bit me, all the time laughing like demented children."

He started walking now, and she walked beside him. He was still reeling in the silver line. He grabbed the fishing line with one hand as he held the rod in the other, pulling it up off the desert floor. The line stretched directly to the pile of junk at the end of the stream.

"Those damn little wings. I keep remembering them. Despite the pain the little pricks imposed on me, I kept thinking their wings were too small to carry them. But carry them they did all the same, and me too, cursed things buzzing all the time like honeybee wings. They carried me up and over Lost Lake and dropped me from about a hundred feet. They flew alongside me as I fell, laughing at me all the way down!"

They came upon the edge of the detritus, and Uncle Robert positioned himself between it and her. But his body wasn't big enough to block her vision of all of it, and she could see a bare human foot sticking out from the snarl of brush, empty soda cans and other junk.

"So what happened?" she said, her voice quavering.

Uncle Robert stepped closer and gave her a hug, then stepped aside so she could see the pile. "Apparently I died," he said and gave the silver line another tug, pulling up the coat tails of a familiar-looking tweed jacket.

She turned away, afraid to look, fearing she would find.

"The best guess I have," Uncle Robert said, "is this place is some sort of cosmic reservoir. And this body," he patted himself on the head, "is an astral body."

"Astral bodies? That's like theosophy isn't it? You mean ghosts?"

"Madame Blavatsky, you know, the famous Theosophist, wrote about such things, yes. But there are lots of names from different religions about the same phenomenon. In Sanskrit, it's called the *linga sarira*, which translates to something like 'design body.' 'Ethereal double' is a related term. But whatever you call it, it's a nearly exact replica of the physical body, and according to the Theosophists, it often lingers after death as a temporary container for the memories, thoughts and personalities of the physical person.

"The New Age people," he continued, "had some different terms for it. I experimented with astral projection for a while. Once, shortly before your father died, Sophia and I taught you how to enter a trance state. I don't suppose you remember that, though. Sophia was – is still – very proficient at astral projection. She's sort of a guide. It's how I first met her, at an astral projection workshop."

He yanked the line and the tweed flapped up again. She turned her back, looking back up toward the rise. The angels were still there, silent, staring at them, their eyes certainly open now. Her hand came to her face involuntarily, covering her eyes. She didn't want to see either the troupe of angels or the body.

He lightly grasped her wrist and tugged her hand away from her face. "Look at it," he said. "I'm not trying to be cruel, but you need to look at it."

She tried to put her hand back.

"If what the Theosophists said is true, this body, this *linga sarira* is more the 'real me' than that piece of meat lying over there. In fact, the corpse is now and was in life only a crude mirror of this astral body."

She cast his hand away and looked at the corpse, letting out a little half-stifled scream. She had to look away for a moment, detesting her own weakness.

"But I prefer Pythagoras' cosmological theory," he said.

"Pythagoras? The geometry guy?" Was Uncle Robert trying to distract her from the horrible reality at her feet? When she was a child, they used to play question-and-answer games about philosophy and science. She got a quarter for answering the easy questions, a dollar for the hard ones. It was their version of Jeopardy.

Why was she remembering that bit of childhood trivia now?

"He was more than just a mathematician," Uncle Robert said. "He said the ultimate substance of everything – you, me, the Earth, the universe, everything – is 'The Boundless.' That's the phrase he used, 'The Boundless.' What you might call God with a capital G only with a capital B." He chuckled again. "That is, we're all part of God, and individuality is just a temporary separation of a part from the whole."

"What does this have to do with this – whatever it is? This reality?"

"I don't know," Uncle Robert laughed. "My mind obviously wanders as much in death as it did in life."

He smiled at her again in that that way made her feel like a child. "Look at the body again. Study it."

"Why?"

"Always asking 'why.' Always questioning. Always challenging. That's what I love about you more than anything else," he said and paused, scratching his light beard. "Look at it because I'm having a harder time accepting this on a visceral level than you are. Now look at it. Humor me."

The body that was wedged under the edge of the washing machine definitely looked like Uncle Robert. It still wore the tweed jacket that he favored, but the shoes were missing and the baggy, faded seersucker bib overalls were covered in mud and halfway pulled down from the bleach-white buttocks, revealing a plumber's smile. She could only see a partial profile of the corpse's face, but it certainly looked like his.

"Not a very dignified death, is it?" Uncle Robert said.

"Remember I used to work in a nursing home. Death is rarely dignified." She looked back to the astral Uncle Robert. It was twilight now and he seemed to be clothed in a blue aura. The angels had moved closer but were still mute, standing with their eyes again closed.

"I have to ask you another favor – an even more unpleasant one," Uncle Robert said.

She looked at him, waiting for him to finish. He was hard to look at because of the glow; as hard to focus on as before.

"Touch the body," he said finally. "Verify that it is real."

"I can't," she said.

"You've been around corpses before. You're even making love to . . ." He stopped himself, but an understanding passed between them.

"Finish your sentence."

"No," he said. "It would be rude."

"I'm even making love to a corpse," she said. "But that's different. He's not really dead."

"Whatever, but I have to know whether this body here in the ditch is real or an illusion. I can't touch it myself for some reason, but I have to know." He put his hand on her shoulder and gently nudged her forward.

She let him move her, took a step forward out of his reach, and knelt by the corpse. The water made a gurgling sound as the stream flattened out and rushed down the slots in the big stone grate. Tentatively, she used her index finger to brush some soggy hair off the corpse's face. The eyes were cloudy, lifeless, reminder her of a dead fish's. She placed two fingers on the eyelids and pulled them down. The thin skin was clammy and cold, the roundness of the eyeballs beneath stonehard. From the shirt collar a small crawfish emerged, one tiny pincher reaching out as if to wave at her. Overwhelmed by some crawfish anxiety, it scurried back under the collar. She suspected it was feeding on her uncle's soft tissues, perhaps burrowing into the armpit. She resisted the urge to squash it through the fabric. Instead, she tried to give the corpse a little of that dignity they had talked of. She pulled up the pants to cover the buttocks, having to yank hard as the pant's cuffs had hooked on the corpse's heels. Uncle Robert tugged on the silver fishing line again. It disappeared under the corpse's shirt, between two buttons, about where the belly button would be.

She touched the line. Its texture wasn't hard and slick like plastic, but soft and skin-like.

An umbilical cord, a thin, silver umbilical cord.

She stood, turning away from the corpse and back to the now radiant being who looked more like Uncle Robert than the living man ever had.

"It's real. At least as real flesh and sinew as I am, as far as I can tell," she said.

"I thought as much," the apparition who looked like her Uncle said.

"Does this mean I'm dead too?" Laura asked. "Did the cherubs kill me too, and I just don't remember it? Is my mangled corpse lying somewhere out in this weird, effing desert?"

"I don't think so, not now," he said. "Remember, your body is covered in bites and bruises from your encounter with them."

"Yes."

"Well, this body" – he thumped his chest and it resounded like a bongo drum – "shows none of the damage done to that body. I think this body, *the you* I'm talking to now, is your real one – that is, your real physical body. But now that I think about it, the 'you' of the first awakening here, when you talked to Samiazaz, was an astral projection. That's why you didn't get all broken up when you fell from the rock. I'd be willing to bet on that. But the 'you' who is talking to me now is you in your physical body, your Earthly body, not its ethereal double."

"You mean I was asleep when I talked to Samiazaz?"

"More trance-state than sleep, but still where the angels probably deposited you on the Army cot. Remember when I taught you how to relax in a trance, while you were still a teenager?"

She ignored his question; she had too many of her own that needed answering. "If this is my real body, how do I get back? How do I get out of this place?" She suddenly was hungry, famished, in fact. That must be a good sign! Before she could share this observation with the astral Uncle Robert, he interrupted her.

"Two ways come to mind," he said. "One, you could try to convince one of our friends over there . . ." He pointed to the angels. " . . . to give you a ride back to Creedance."

"I don't think I'd have much luck."

"Don't be so sure. I suspect that it's only thanks to the residual humanity of one of them – either May or Marguerite – that you're still alive."

"Why do you think that? Never mind; what's the other option?"

"Wait for the water to stop flowing and crawl back through the gash in the saucer's skin."

"What makes you think it'll stop?"

"Elementary, my dear Watson," Uncle Robert said. "It's draining Lost Lake, and although this place may have an infinite capacity, Lost Lake has only a finite amount of water. And I'd guess the lake is being drained at more than a hundred gallons a minute."

She looked at the spout of water.

"It's only about ten feet above the desert floor," she said.

"Right. When the flow slows down, you could pile some the smaller rocks to climb up on and crawl out on the saucer's exterior."

He gave the fishing line another yank, and it came free of the corpse with a loud click, like a switch being thrown. He reeled in the remaining few feet. The end looked bloody.

There was a rustling of angels' wings. The chorus had formed a semicircle around one of their number – it was May. She squatted, her wings held upright and quivering. The other angels spread their wings, forming an umbrella-like canopy over her.

May's teeth clenched and she screeched like a wild animal, then stood up, leaving a bloody bolus at her feet. May's eyes opened in terror, staring at the egg-shaped bolus as it peeled open and extended flattened arms and legs, so thin as if to be cardboard cutouts. It writhed on the desert floor, the coarse sand sticking to its bloody skin. Then the flattened extremities inflated into fat little arms and legs, and from somewhere a face expanded with a pop; the face was framed by blood-soaked curly locks. It stood on shaky, short pudgy legs: a cherub, a small one, no more than a foot tall.

May leered at the creature, then lunged for it. But though newborn, the tiny creature was too quick for her. It bounded just out of her reach. May reached for its dangling baby feet and nearly caught the, but at the last moment, she doubled over in pain and sank to her knees.

When she rose back to her feet, there was another bolus at her feet. Like its sibling, it also began to unfold like a bloody origami.

May was prepared for this one, and though still grimacing in pain from the birthing, she reached out for it. But the first cherub had only flown beyond her reach. It now buzzed around her head. While she was distracted, the second bolus finished hatching and also took flight.

Now May was tormented by two of her spawn, their little wings buzzing furiously, flinging blood and mucus in the air. The other adult angels made no effort to help her. The two cherubs rose above her head, their bare feet dangling in mid-air just out of her reach, taunting her. May unfolded her own wings as if to launch after them. The two cherubs looked at each other, reached some sort of unspoken consensus, screeched angrily in unison, and flew away impossibly fast, toward Laura.

Laura ducked, catching a glimpse of the creatures' doll-sized faces as they flew over her head toward the horizon. She gasped not out of fear but of recognition.

No, they couldn't have resembled who she thought they did. She must have imagined it! But May had told Wright . . .

May wrapped her wings about her and knelt on one knee as if in shame, as if to shield herself from the judgment of her companion angels. They began to sing, dismally:

Our spawn are our horror
From our flesh, they furrow
Out they hatch into light
Like sparrows sprung from a god's forehead
They must quickly take flight
For his dreams are hungry ghosts
With the mouths of bottomless hosts

The Archangels lied to us
Immortal blessed, yes
But doomed both genders
To give forth and render

Dreamtime of an Alien God

These abominations
Who can eat whole nations

We have been so betrayed
By false demiurges, waylaid
Who spared us from death's door
But made us all bitch whores
And now we are as one
And a new plot has spun

May stood, now none the worse for wear for her birthing ordeal, the shame gone from her face. She and the other angels closed ranks, apparently finished singing. Despite the grossness of the birth, there had been something comical about the presentation, and Laura turned to comment on this, but Uncle Robert was gone. She looked at the drain and saw the corpse still there, but Uncle Robert's astral body – if that's what it really was – was nowhere to be seen.

"Uncle Robert?" she called, afraid again, and was carried into the air.

"Be calm, fly with us, little puss," said May, who had grabbed her left arm. One of May's hands sought out her breast, whether by intent or accident Laura couldn't tell.

"Coffee, tea or thee?" Laura said in a sing-song voice, feeling light-headed. She giggled.

"Don't mind her perverse verse. She's a lovesick slut or worse," chimed Marguerite, primly holding Laura's other arm.

Did Marguerite refer to May or to her?

"No, she's a mother, not a slut," Laura said.

"Mother, smother. I would have killed and eaten the little messenger if I could have caught it," May said.

The moment, though lucid, felt insubstantial, as if she were reading about a character in a post-modernistic novel, an invention of convention. But no, May's and Marguerite's hands gripped her arms, cutting painfully into the skin. The sight of Uncle Robert's body below brought forth a deep pain in her chest. This was all too real to be merely fantasy.

Laura felt her mind clouding over. She didn't know if she would wake up dead, as Uncle Robert had, but as sleep began to take her, she lost the ability to care. She glanced downward to take in the panorama of the caldera. A woman stood ahead near the spewing water. Laura strained to keep awake and could see the woman had big hair, chocolate skin and a pink miniskirt. The woman waved.

Oh, Sophia? Have you been murdered too?

Sleep overtook her before she could learn the answer.

* * *

15.

The Other, Hidden Part of Me

Suzanne.

As Suzanne climbed into truck, Bryan appeared to her in a different light. He had messed with the old pickup truck for more than an hour before he got it running, something about water in a fuel line.

His hands were large and callused like a day laborer's, but last night his touch had been light and sensitive. He was different from the two types men she had known: either college students who rarely seemed to know how to do anything but go to school and party, or working men who mostly were interested only in sex. The college boys had usually been narcissists. The working men – Ben was one of them – usually covered insecurities with bravado.

Bryan seemed to have the better characteristics of both but without the narcissism or bravado.

"I don't see why you can't just stay here with me," Bryan said. "I can make the place safe. We have my grandfather's shotgun. I can take care of you."

The truck's old brown vinyl seat was scarred with cigarette burns that looked like open sores. As she scooted across plastic, the scars felt rough through the thin, flowery sundress she had found in his grandmother's closet. She put her arms around his neck and tried to kiss him, but he turned away and her lips only brushed his cheek.

He smelled of eggs and bacon, the breakfast she had cooked

for him as he bagged up the remains of the giant cherub and mopped up the the bloody ooze. She had enjoyed cooking for him, though she couldn't make herself eat. She wondered how shovel it down after dealing with all the gore, but his appetite seemed boundless. He cleaned his plate, then finished her untouched plate.

"If you just want to get away from me, say so," he said. "You don't have to make up stories about being responsible to your husband." He was more hurt, she realized, than angry.

"Don't be so insecure," she said. "I'd rather hang out with you here, cherubs or no cherubs, but I have obligations."

Though he didn't reply, she could tell by the set of his mouth that he didn't believe her. He impatiently jiggled the gearshift lever, and the transmission growled like a tortured animal. A hollow metallic clunk sounded as the gears engaged. He let out the clutch pedal; the truck shuddered like an old man trying to get to his feet, but managed to get rolling.

As they bounced down the dirt driveway to the main highway, Bryan kept glancing sideways at her and then back to the road. His expression reminded her of a hurt little boy's. He didn't understand and didn't believe her. Her heart might not be beating, but she felt it would break.

Get real; we only spent one night together. We barely know one another. This can't be love.

But it didn't feel like only lust.

The sense of connection, of belonging with him persisted. As they pulled out onto the main road and he coaxed the truck into a higher gear, she thought of the old farm couples still living in rural Harmon County: so melded by decades of sharing of aspirations, fears and opinions they always knew what the other was going to say before he or she said it. She used to believe that such unions were to be avoided, that these couples wound up bored senseless with one another. But now she felt that whatever she said, whatever she did, would be okay and he would accept it. Moreover, he would make her feel good about it. Going with her to see Ben must be very hard for Bryan – if he felt about her as she felt about him – but he was helping her anyway by driving her to Ben's house.

Ben's house. She hadn't thought of it until now, but it had always been "Ben's house." She had repainted the kitchen, wallpapered the living room and picked out new furniture, but it remained his house, not hers.

It was sad, really. In so many ways, Ben had tried to make her love him. She had respected him and felt affection for him, but had never been capable of the romantic love he wanted. And now, with Bryan, here she was hopelessly in love with someone she barely knew.

Maybe undead love is better.

Bryan had propped the shotgun on the seat between them, the end of the barrel resting on the floorboard, and the wooden stock kept sliding against her shoulder. She couldn't scoot closer to him because the gearshift of the ancient truck was mounted on the floorboard and stretched above the level of the seat. He had to keep his right hand on the gearshift to keep the transmission from jumping out of gear. He steered with his left hand – a white-knuckle grip – because the truck did not have power steering. Every so often, he would set his chin on the steering wheel so he could peer up at the sky through the windshield. Her job was to frequently checked the sky from the passenger window. Though the day had warmed up early, he insisted that she keep her side window rolled up in case a cherub tried to fly in. But the drive to the ranch was uneventful.

Bryan stopped the truck at the Ponderosa's front gate and put it in neutral.

"I know it would be smart to drop you off here at the front gate, but I don't want you to go into the house alone," he said.

"Because of the cherubs?"

"That and maybe because of your husband, too," he said. His face was in shadow, making him look older than his years. "Does he have a gun?"

"Yes, but he says he hates guns. It's only to shoot crows."

"He carries that big fucking knife."

"It's a Bowie knife. It's not just a replica, it's more than a hundred years old. He's afraid to use it because he doesn't want to chip the blade."

This bit of trivia seem to settle Bryan and he relaxed his grip on the wheel, his face young again. Her eyes traced along the smooth, masculine curve of his jaw as he set the truck in gear, moving the lever just right so there was barely more than a dull clunk.

He pulled up and stopped in front of the doublewide. Ben's conversion van was parked under the canopy. It looked cleaner than usual. *Cleaner than it had been in her recent dream. Did it still smell like fish inside?*

She got out, he followed with the shotgun slung casually under one arm as if going on a gentleman's skeet shoot. He left the truck's engine running because he said it might not start again if he turned it off.

The first thing she noticed different about doublewide was the windows had been boarded up. Ben must have done this, but why?

"I'm escorting you to the door." He stepped closer to her as they walked toward the porch. "I found you walking on the road this morning. You don't remember how you got there."

This storyline devised, he let her go a step ahead so he was following behind. Oddly, she was comfortable in that moment, with him deciding something that might affect her life so profoundly. For most of her life, she had resisted anyone trying to make decisions for her. Ben gave her, as he said, 'an infinitely long leash,' but however long, a leash was still a shackle. And obligations built from gifts and favors taken without love were the worst kind of leash.

Opening the unlocked door halfway, she called, "Ben? It's me, Suzanne. Are you in there?"

When she heard no answer, she stepped inside. She imagined she could hear Bryan's brain deliberating behind her, grinding into second gear as he followed.

With the windows boarded up, the front living room was in twilight. If the front door were closed it would probably be pitch black. To the left of the door two pairs of Ben's shoes – his work boots and his go-to-town tennis shoes – rested on the mat.

She went to thel hallway, skirting around the floor cushions in the dark. Bryan followed, bumping the barrel of the shotgun against the walls more than once. How much use would the long-barrel gun be in these close quarters?

She peered into the bathroom. The toilet was running. The light was better here because Ben hadn't boarded up the tiny window, maybe because it was only a foot wide and a few inches high and too small to admit any creatures larger than small birds.

"Someone must have been here," Bryan said.

"Why do you say that?"

"The toilet was recently flushed. It's still refilling," he said. He wasn't looking at her, but down the hallway toward the bedroom.

"That's probably just the toilet," she said. "The handle sticks."

She stepped into the tiny bathroom and jiggled the handle, and the sound of the running water changed as the reservoir began to fill.

"See?" she said. "No ghosts; it's just a crappy crapper." And then she looked down to see a set of bulging black eyes staring back at her!

"Yikes!" She stumbled backward into Bryan.

"What is it?" he said.

"Eyes, eyes in the toilet."

Bryan stepped around her and peered into the porcelain bowl.

"What's so funny?"

"I never heard anyone actually use the word 'yikes!' before. It's just a frog."

"It scared the shit out me." And it had; for some reason the slimy little creature had frightened her more that the cherub with the wood-chipper hands. "Are you sure it's just a frog?"

He knelt by the toilet. "It probably got in via the vent pipe on the roof," he said, whatever that meant. "It's awfully large, though. Looks too large to swim up through the toilet drain."

He leaned the shotgun in the corner, looked around, found a toilet brush, and dipped it into the bowl.

"Just leave it alone," she said.

"It's just a harmless frog or toad or something." He swished the brush around as if stirring a stew. "You said you're going to stay here and wait for your husband to come around."

She nodded.

"Then I'd better fish this guy out of here or you won't be able to use the toilet."

"You're not staying with me?"

"That would be too weird," he said. "Come here, you," he said to the creature. "Climb on the toilet brush."

He lifted the brush out of the water. A green and pinkish lump clung to the bristles, staring at him. It blinked at him with transparent eyelids. "That's a good toady," Bryan said.

"Ewww," she said. "Get that thing out of my house."

"You're always welcome to stay at my house," he said, looking back over his shoulder at her. "We could check back here regularly."

"Everyone would think that weird."

"It would be weird to stay here alone," he said.

She started to say that 'weird' was a relative term, but stopped, breathless, as the green clump sprouted little wings and began crawling along the handle of the brush. Bryan was still looking over his shoulder at her, waiting for an answer, and didn't see it the thing open its mouth to reveal teeth where toady gums should have been.

He must have seen the terror in her face and turned back to face the little demon crawling toward his hand. "Shit!" He slammed the brush down on the toilet bowl rim, and the creature lost its grip on the handle. But instead of falling into the water, it took flight with a buzzing that sounded much like cherub wings. It hovered for a moment, veered off to the left, then swerved back toward Bryan's face. He fell back, dropping the plastic brush and brought the shotgun barrel up to swat the creature. The flying obscenity snapped at the barrel; its tiny teeth made screeching sounds on the metal like fingernails on a chalkboard. Bryan swung the barrel down and pinned it against the porcelain sink. It kept biting at the barrel, its black little bulbous eyes never blinking. She could see its face clearly now, a little fetus-like creature that looked like a mixture of human, pig and toad. Bryan leaned forward, putting his weight on the gun. She heard the creature's body crunch. Still biting at the barrel, its little wings flickered in the dim light as Bryan slammed the shotgun barrel down again and again until the creature was a bloody pulp. Finally, its beady eyes went dim and its bite-hold on the gun barrel relaxed.

Bryan scraped the remains off into the sink. The little corpse's blood was black, not red. It didn't seem to have internal organs or bones. It was apparently just a wad of solid, undifferentiated tissue.

"What in the flying hell was that?" he said.

"Another abomination." She had to gasp for air. She had been holding her breath the whole time. If she were undead, she wondered why she had to breathe at all. *Maybe that's what the "un" in undead was all about.*

"Are you sure you want to stay here by yourself?" Bryan said.

When she didn't answer, he shook his head and said, "Come on, you wanted to check out the rest of the house didn't you?"

She led him down the hallway to the master bedroom, neither of them speaking. He was angry with her now, in that silent, sulking way men had that she'd always found hard to decipher.

Ben hadn't done as thorough of a job of boarding over the windows in the smaller rooms, but it still looked as if he had been preparing for a siege. If so, why was the front door unlocked?

She held her breath as she nudged open the door to the main bedroom. A single ray of sunlight streamed through an inch-wide crack in the window boards and spotlighted the blue futon.

The bed was empty, except for a single red and white striped sock with a dirty sole. There was no sign of Ben.

"Obvious question: What now?" Bryan said. He was standing by the dresser, using his free hand to idly poke at the keys of Ben's old Remington manual typewriter: tap, tap, tap. "Hey, it works! What an antique, but I'd like to have one now."

"Stop that!" she said, loud enough to make Bryan jump, and he slammed down a handful of keys, jamming them together. This was Ben's house, his bedroom, his typewriter; it didn't seem right for Bryan to have free reign.

He reached for the clump of jammed keys to pull them apart, but he must have seen something in her face and dropped his hand to his side, looking like a guilty little boy.

And that brought about the other odd impression: that there were two of her, two Suzannes, alike but with divergent personalities, one of which was sane, the other who, due to past obligations and entanglements, was always on the verge of a nervous breakdown.

"I really don't know why you came here with me," she said.

Or know what you see in me at all, as I'm undead.

"So where is he?

"Not in the house; that's obvious." She was still irritated with him over the stupid typewriter.

"He could be out walking around on the ranch."

"You know those two pair of shoes by the door when we came in?"

"Didn't notice," he said.

"Those were the only ones he owned. He wouldn't go outside barefoot. He must be here, but if he wasn't answering . . ."

"How about the van? Could he be it there?"

Good idea, but she didn't say as much. He followed her out of the house and to the van. Once they were outside, she no longer felt tugged this way and that by conflicting emotions. She stopped a few feet away from the vehicle, unsure what to do next.

Bryan stepped in front of her, tried to open the driver's side door and found it locked.

"Why would he lock it up way out here if he didn't bother to lock the front door of the doublewide?" he asked.

"Ben usually kept it locked ever since some drunks from town broke into a neighbor's truck and stole some dynamite. The stupids were using it to blow up cows and ended up blowing up themselves."

"He kept dynamite in the van?"

"No, but he kept his pistol in the glove box."

"Some Buddhist. Ate cattle, kept firearms."

"He didn't eat them. He just raised them to sell the sperm for artificial insemination," she said. Why did she feel it necessary to defend Ben? Why this sudden surge of loyalty for him?

He looked at her, his eyes sad. A silent understanding passed between them.

"You're going to wait for him here, aren't you? Rabid little cherubs or not?"

"I have to," she said. "I'm not afraid of him."

"You're rubbing your new ear. How does it feel?" he said.

"It tingles."

"It would be good for you to have a pistol."

"You're angry."

"No, I'm not." But his voice betrayed him.

"Shit, too bad it's locked."

The large window set in one side of the van was the size of a coffee table and so darkly tinted as to be nearly black. Bryan shaded his eyes with a hand, put his face up to the window and peered inside.

"What's it like inside?" he said.

Before she could answer, the window went THUMP!

They both jumped back – Bryan nearly fell backwards – and stared at the van for what must have been a minute, waiting for whatever had made the assault on the window to do it again.

Nothing.

Bryan looked at her, laughed a little, and said, "Heat expansion," as if that explained everything.

She was going to say that she wasn't so sure, but Bryan stepped back to the van and laid his hand on the window. Nothing happened.

"Morning sun warming up the glass. Just a coincidence," he said. "Courage."

His voice gave him away, as did the slight tremble of his fingers as he touched the grimy surface of the window. All his brave words aside, he was just as afraid as she was.

His fingertips caressed the window like the first tentative kiss of a lover, and he said, "See, nothing."

To make his point, he slapped the window with his open palm.

THUMP! Whatever was inside threw itself against the window again, this time hard enough to make the Plexiglass bow.

"Shit!" Bryan yelped and tried to bring the shotgun up, but the long barrel caught on the edge of the van's undercarriage. The shotgun went BLAM as it discharged into the dirt.

THUMP! A pinkish, amorphous mass pressed against the window, showing huge folds of skin and fat.

THUMP! This time the window creaked, metal against metal, and the upper corner of the frame popped loose.

Suzanne let out, a long, bubbling shriek, then clamped a hand over her mouth. Bryan took a step back, lifting the gun from the undercarriage of the van. Thin wisps of smoke curled from the end of the double barrels.

She moved back too, thinking to run, but decided she couldn't leave Bryan here to face whatever was in the van by himself.

This really must be love, as I'm scared shitless, just like with luminous cherub.

Time stood still. The morning air was quiet, the liquid blue sky a pristine backdrop, as Bryan broke open the gun, then the *click, click* as he fumbled with two bright-red shotgun shells, trying, missing the breech, because his hands shook so badly, then trying again.

She became serenely calm. The fear had left her like a disembodied demon and possessed him. Maybe everyone had a fear-quota, and when that quota is met, they can't be afraid anymore. Whatever, she moved beside him and placed one hand on his shoulders, snatched one of the shells from his hands and, before he could protest, slipped it neatly into the breach. Calmed now, he dropped the other shell in to the second breach and said, "Thanks. Get behind me now."

THUMP! The entire top edge of the window frame came loose from the side of the van. A fetid odor of fish, fetid rotten flesh, mixed in with something as overpoweringly sweet as an old lady's perfume, rushed out of the van.

THUMP! The window sprang loose, projected toward them from the force of its expulsion. Bryan stepped back and Suzanne did too, to avoid being trampled by him. The window fell to the ground, sending up a cloud of dust and stinging her eyes.

I should be doing something other than hiding behind Bryan, she thought, and then the dust settled, and she saw the monstrosity trying to squeeze through the open frame.

Two fat hands gripped the raw edges of the frame where the

window had been. At first glance, the hands seemed human, though puffed up and swollen purplish like those of a bloated corpse. But the arms! The arms were hairless and peppered with huge wart-like bumps.

She gagged. The monstrosity was reminiscent of the warty little creature they had found in the toilet, but this one was as big as a cow. And the smell! God, the smell! As it moved to squeeze further out the window, the odor of rotten fish and cloyingly sweet perfume was magnified a thousand times. It didn't just invade her nostrils, she could actually taste it, and it seemed to sink into her pores. She managed to resist vomiting. Bryan wasn't so lucky. He doubled up, spewing up bits of undigested scrambled eggs.

She grabbed ahold the shotgun and said, "Give it to me!"

Incapacitated, he relinquished the weapon to her, his eyes watering, then went to his knees, still gagging.

The ancient shotgun had double hammers. She pulled back both and hefted the stock up to her shoulder. The gun weighed a ton. The creature was still struggling to pull itself through the opening. It had squeezed through most of its upper body through then became stuck. The calico curtains she had sewn for the van window a year ago were draped over its shoulders. She knew those curtains were three feet wide, which meant the cherub should have been too big to even fit in the van. Huge man-breasts popped through the window now, and she could see the warts on the creature's shoulders were even larger than those on its hands. And the warts were moving, squirming like worms under the skin.

Her finger wrapped around the dual triggers. She wanted to hit the head, but the weight of the gun made it hard to keep the barrel from wavering. Amazed at herself – she usually ran screaming from small bugs and creepy crawly things – she stepped forward and shoved the barrel into the creature's face.

"Lift your head, goddamn it!" she shouted.

The creature obligingly obeyed, raising its head so she could see its face.

And the face was Ben's!

"Illusion spawns illusion within ill. . ." the fake Ben said in a fake-Ben voice before the double-barrel shotgun blast took off its head.

* * *

16.

Calls Come From the Deep

Laura.

Laura found herself sitting on the front steps of her house with no memory of how she had got there.

The last thing she remembered was being carried aloft by angels out of the alien desert caldera. She had ooked down to see a person who might have been her Aunt Sophia standing on the rim of the caldera. Then without a transition of any sort, here she was on the porch.

She had no recollection of leaving the desert or of emerging from the saucer. Nor did she have any memory of being transported over the miles of woods that lay between her house and Lost Lake. One moment she was groggy, worrying about Aunt Sophia and mourning Uncle Robert. The next instant she was here, sitting on the porch, wide awake.

More than just awake: The sky, the trees, even the blades of grass, were all in crystal-clear focus, preternaturally so, while the memories of the saucer, the conversation with Samiazaz and the walk with Uncle Robert's ghost all seemed pale and two-dimensional by comparison.

She was still dressed only in sweatshirt and panties, and the moist, rough concrete of the porch step was chilling her buns. She wondered – hoped – it had all been a dream, and that Uncle Robert was still alive.

Instead of sitting here worrying, the smart thing to do would be to get dressed, walk over and collect her Beetle at John's house, then drive the ten miles or so out to the Jacobsen house. She would probably find Uncle Robert sitting in the library, lamenting as usual, the "ineffableness" of Sophia's "damned feminine mystique."

She relished the image of him there, with his brow screwed up in wrinkles, a twinkle of amusement in his eyes, but she knew on a visceral level that talking with his ghost or astral double or whatever he called it was not a dream. She was sure that her uncle was dead. She knew in her bones that her time in the saucer had been real, as real as anything in this world since the angel saucer slid into Lost Lake and reality became fractured. She just didn't want to believe it.

She began sobbing softly, feeling weak doing so, but it felt luxurious to loll in the tears.

Still crying, she found the inside of her house as sloppy as she had left it. Maybe sloppier. She felt like she had been away a lifetime, and the full impact of the disarray was shocking, even to her.

Still, there was something reassuring about the normalness of the clutter and the sink full of moldy dishes. Through the open door behind her, a small bird chirped happily.

The doorway was empty and the world outside was still blue and green. No pasty white, fat cherubs. She locked the door, padded barefoot to the bedroom and rummaged through the dresser until she found a pair of jeans. They weren't the pair she wanted; those were probably downstairs in the basement. But it was dark and dank downstairs, a bit tomblike, and she wanted to stay in sunlit rooms.

And she wanted a weapon. Before putting on the jeans, she dug deeper in the pants drawer and found it – a .25 caliber pistol wrapped in a sock.

It wasn't exactly a Rambo weapon: The pistol was only about four inches long with a bore smaller in diameter than a pencil. The clip was bound to the handle with a big rubber band.

She pulled back the slide and checked to find the chamber empty. She let the spring-loaded slide go back. The gun was supposedly now cocked. She pointed it at the wall and pulled the trigger. The trigger would not budge.

Shit! She had only fired the thing a few times – she hated guns – and always forgot which way the safety worked. She thumbed it down, fiddling with it, but must have been unconsciously pulling the trigger when she did so, and the hammer clicked.

She had been pointing the gun at her stomach when the hammer fell. *No, this wouldn't do. She was more likely to shoot herself than the effing angel.*

She put the pistol on top the dresser and dug deeper in the drawer until she found a pair clean panties with a cute little Care Bear printed on them. Though they dated years back to high school, they still fit, which pleased her. She dressed quickly in jeans, gym socks and a clean T-shirt. For shoes she had to resort to sandals she found in the closet. The sandals had multicolored sequins glued to the straps and also dated back to her high school days.

She decided to put the gun back in the drawer. She needed a weapon that she wasn't so likely to hurt herself with. She still had her old baseball bat from when she was on the high school baseball team. The only problem was that it was down in the basement, under the bed. She really didn't want to go down there right now.

Maybe later I won't be such a wuss.

As she buried the pistol under some panties, she found the journal.

The cover was some shiny black vinyl material imprinted with neat rows of white skulls and crossbones. Like the sandals, the baseball bat and the underwear, the journal was a remnant of her younger days. She turned it over. On the back was a faded label with a quote from Mark Twain:

Now and then we had a hope
That if we lived and were good
God would permit us to be pirates

She carried the journal into the living room, feeling like a teenager again in the sequined sandals.

Sitting down on the threadbare couch, she undid the book's

magnetic clasp and thumbed to a random place in the middle.

"Aunt Sophia taught me how to do astral projection today," was the first line she read.

A little stick figure was lying on its back in the margin. It had ringlets for hair: a girl, herself, she remembered. Above it was another stick figure, but instead of being done with solid lines it was drawn in dashes and dots. An astral-double stick figure?

She remembered now. It had happened only days before her father's last psychotic episode. The violence at home had been escalating steadily, the shouting, ugly fights, her father's language reflecting an increasingly demented and twisted logic, something about Einstein and Jesus Christ being in cahoots with her mother. Her mother trying to cajole him, demeaning herself. Laura had been so overcome with fear and dread she could no longer cry.

She had moved in with Uncle Robert and Aunt Sophia's after one of the worse episodes – when her father had held a knife to her throat raving about her unibrow. She knew her father had been raving insane, but she was still was haunted with the fear that somehow she was to blame for the tragedy that soon followed.

She had been beyond crying at that time and couldn't stop shaking. Somehow, Uncle Robert had gotten her to relax – was that when he had hypnotized her?

She barely remembered it, but there it was, recorded in her own handwriting, a time when she swirled every letter and used little circles to dot each "i." And she had scratched out or erased whole passages, probably in an attempt to get her thoughts down on paper correctly, but it still was a rambling account.

> September 1- Late Night – Aunt Sophia taught me how to do astral projection today! But maybe it wasn't real. Maybe it was just a dream. I don't know which! But I don't care. I remember flying like a witch in the storm, high over the house!!! It was better than acid. Whatever! It totally stopped me from thinking about slicing my wrists or jumping off the Old Buffalo Road bridge. Uncle Robert is cool. He looks so much like dad, but he's like the

anti-dad. Or maybe my dad is the anti-Uncle Robert, like an anti-Christ. Whatever!!! In my dream or my astro-thing, he was like glowing like a magician. Never mind. It's complicated. Get it? But Sophia is more than cool. If Uncle Robert is a magician, she's like this big sleek black cat, and I don't mean anything like racial you know, even though she is black. She just has the most pounce-to-the-ounce of anyone I've ever met. Oh, I started at the end not at the beginning! Mrs. Moore, my English Skills teacher, says that's cool. She said to start where I want to. In the middle, a flashback, wherever, she said. It's a shame about her getting busted on the maryjane issue. I don't think it's true. I think it was a setup because her bitch daughter-in-law didn't like her. Anyway, back to the beginning. At dinner I was still too freaked out to eat because of the mess going on at home. Uncle Robert and Aunt Sophia talked for a while together outside the dining room. Mostly it was Aunt Sophia doing the talking and Uncle Robert nodding. Good boy! Uncle Robert came back in and sat beside me at the big table. He told me Sophia wanted to teach me a re-lax-a-tion technique. He said it would help me. I said what I needed was a drink. Break out your blended Irish whiskey. I hear you, but take my word, Laura, drinking is a dead end. Especially for the Jacobsens. I should know. And he scratched his beard and looked at the ceiling like he always does when he's unloading some deep stuff. But he didn't have to tell me. Just look at my dad, the anti-Uncle Robert, and you know none of us Jacobsens should be drinking or taking drugs.

He led me back in the living room. Sophia was plumping up some cushions on the couch. She was still wearing those high-heel shoes of hers, the ones that make her look like a hooker. Don't get me wrong. She looks good in them, but when you talk to her, she sounds like someone who should be wearing sandals and hippie beads, not miniskirts and high-heeled red shoes. Lie down. Relax. Breathe normally. Just pay attention to your breath as it comes out your nostrils. Feel it faint and slight on your upper lip. She held my hand, her voice a soft purr. Power shoes. I saw you looking at them. They give me a step up closer to heaven. I hardly knew her at all and then she tells me this crazy stuff about shoes, but coming from her you believe it. She has this way of talking and making the ordinary world go away. I was expecting to see leprechauns at any moment. Ruby slippers. And then I'm up on the ceiling. The ceilings in the living room are high. Ten feet maybe twelve. I'm up there next to the chandelier and I'm down on the couch too. Sophia is holding my hand. Neat. I should be scared but I'm calm, calmer than I ever been. Like I suddenly get it, you know? Sophia looks up and smiles at me. Me on the couch looks up and smiles at me on the ceiling, and I see myself on the ceiling while I'm looking down at me on the couch. Except the ***me*** up on the ceiling is kind of ghostly and it looks better that I ever really look. For a moment I was sick to my stomach and my heart was pounding in my chest. My real chest that is, the chest of me on the couch. Sophia looks up at the ***me*** on the ceiling. Go now. The feedback will make this one sick. And she patted the head of the me on the couch. Just focus on remembering what you see. And she waved toward the ceiling. Scoot off now and go play. She was all smiles. The me on the couch looked a bit green about the gills. Without thinking about it I just floated up back ass-wards through the ceiling. Things darkened for a moment, and I could see the stuff inside the ceiling the space, like a dried-up mouse corpse in between the wood beams. Then I was in the room upstairs, underneath the bed with the dust bunnies. I passed through the bed like it was made of smoke – just like I'd gone through the living room the ceiling. Things dimmed but didn't go completely dark. I could see springs, cotton padding. As I rose over the bed, lightning flashed through the window. Raindrops on the glass sparkled like diamonds. Pretty. And I meant to float there in the room and wait for another flash, but the next thing I knew I was outside the window. Over the roof. Floating in the rain. The drops going right through me. Zing! Zing! The lightning flashed again, and that's when I saw the silver line. I was floating horizontally, my arms outstretched, my legs spread-eagled. The cord dangled out of my blouse and went back between my legs. Like a kite string. I could feel the thing coming out of my navel. As I did a slow somersault so I could see where the cord went. It stretched back through the window and under the bed. I knew without seeing that it was connected to the "real" me on the couch. I added the quote marks around "real" because this me felt "real" too. As real as the couch-me, but a whole lot freer.

Totally free. I looked up to the sky then at one of the brick chimneys on the roof. In a second I was sitting atop the chimney. My ghostly body went wherever I lookedEven without the lightning flashes everything was in super-sharp detail. Not only could I see right down inside the pores in the brick and into the pits in the slate shingle, like I microscope eyes, but I could taste and smell the shingles and the pores in the shingles too. It sounds so gross when I write it, but it wasn't. It's not like I was licking the things. Or sticking my ghostly nose down on the shingles. The smell, taste, and even the history of things came to me if I looked hard enough. I could see the bricklayer who made the chimney. The crew who nailed the shingles to the roof with big square nails. I sat there for what seemed like hours, like a little witch. Thunder and rain. Beautiful and delicious. The craziness going on with dad and mom seemed like a stupid TV soap opera. No canned laughter but a scream queen offstage dubbing in for my mom.

Then as I looked up something huge silver and round filled the sky. The thing was not in anyway hideous or ugly. It was more oval than round and probably many times larger than a football field. But it was hard to say really how big it was. But it was huge. I felt it, and it was evil in some way, I knew in my heart.

As I looked at it, shivering like a little black witch atop the chimney, it opened up like big eyeball and looked right back at me! I fell right off the chimney and was reeled in by the silver line. In seconds I zipped back through the window, through the floor and back down into my body on the couch. For a moment, there were two of me again. The body on the couch and the energy body I was in. Sophia was still there in the room, sitting in the big easy chair next to the couch, knitting. So was Uncle Robert, but he was working a crossword puzzle. Sophia noticed the astral me as I floated down. Uncle Robert didn't notice. Maybe because he was working the crossword.

I had that twist of the stomach again, of infinite numbers of me, like looking into two facing mirrors. Then there was just one of me, but with two sets of memories. Mostly I had just lain there on the couch doing nothing while the other me went soaring, but I still had memory of some things, such as Uncle Robert getting up to get a drink. And Sophia telling me in a soft voice how to remember my experience. But the memory of sitting on the chimney was quickly fading. Sophia leaned forward. Remember what I told you she said. And I started repeating things like she told me to. This is it! I can't wait until tomorrow evening to try it again!

The next entry in the journal was dated September 3. One line:

Blood, blood, blood and murder.

Laura slapped the journal closed. She didn't need any elaboration to remember September 3. Her father had spent the Labor Day weekend drinking and hitting up meth. Then he had murdered her mother and taken his own life.

She had spent years in therapy learning to deal with it, to not bury the rage and terror she felt that day. It was something she would rather forget the whole year it happend, but had been convinced by the therapist that the danger lay in doing just that.

But the account of her astral-projection a couple of days before – that memory had been forgotten. Which was no surprise now that she thought about it. The shock of the murder and suicide had overwhelmed the memory of the astro-projections.

But her opening the book now, to that exact page, was a curious coincidence. If she had found the journal only a day earlier, before her encounter with Uncle Robert's ethereal double in the saucer, she would have discounted the entire account as some sort of fantasy or a hypnotic implant by Aunt Sophia or Uncle Robert.

Now the description of the silver umbilical cord, of the vision of the angel saucer ten years before it actually crash-landed near Creedance, was too similar to be merely serendipitous. Her memory, kick-started by reading the book, was now bringing the immediacy of the experience back to her. She could almost "taste" the pores in the brick again, and she shivered remembering the terror she felt as the huge saucer, the gargantuan eye in the sky, loomed over her.

She ran her hand over the page, feeling the dents in the paper from when she had pressed too hard with the pencil. She remembered all of it, and now she had double the reason to go to the Jacobsen family home. If Uncle Robert wasn't there, if indeed he had permanently passed on to another plane, then maybe it was time to talk to Aunt Sophia. If she hadn't been killed by the angels, too.

She tried the phone before she left but wasn't surprised when she couldn't even get a dial tone. It was going to be a long walk to John Wright's house in her little girl sandals.

She was not ten feet out the door when her undead lover pulled up in his black SUV. As he leaped out of the vehicle, he seemed heroic and beautiful, like something from the cover of a romance novel. She needed a slap in the face to bring her to her senses. He was wearing his sidearm now, though the last time they were together he had told her he'd never wear it again.

With or without the big leather belt and pistol, he looked even sexier than when she had seen him last, if that was possible. His shoulders were broad, his face handsome and unlined but full of character. And he was slim-hipped, flat-bellied. He didn't look dead at all. He didn't look like he was in his forties either; more like his late twenties. She said nothing; it felt so natural just to wrap her arms him and kiss him long and hard. One thought filled her mind: *Lucky me.*

* * *

17.

As We Resurrect Our Lost Souls

Wright.

Wright could barely keep his eyes on the road with Laura sitting beside him as they drove to the Jacobsen mansion. The insatiable pull had weakened, and he had nearly convinced himself that his obsession for her might be fading.

The fact was, that when he was in her presence, it didn't matter if they had been brought together by some hideous strength with alien motives. It just didn't matter. He would die for her this very moment.

The only problem was was that he was dead already. So it would be an empty gesture as he didn't really have much to lose. But what about her? What kind of emotional damage was he doing to a young woman who had been sexually abused by her father, a man about his own age?

He told himself it was only a love engineered by some mystical metaphysics of the archangels. It was dishonorable and just wrong that he should feel this way about a woman in her mid-twenties. Not only that, he was making a fool of himself. This afternoon he had desperately searched for her in the woods near his home, then at the usual haunts in Creedance and on the country roads in between. He told himself that when he found her, he would end it. That he would still be her protector, her confident if she needed, but the love-making would have to end.

Then as he stepped out of the SUV at her house, she ran to him in little girly-girl pink sandals, stood on tip-toe and kissed him. Her hair was unbrushed. She reeked of sweat and pond water and still she smelled delicious. The kiss was an electric rush he felt head to toe.

Though not illegal, his actions certainly smacked of being unethical. Yet it felt so right. It wasn't just lust – or was it? How many times in the last few days had he asked himself this question? No, it was more like a connection, a love so intense that the only way to communicate it was through sex. If he'd been a poet or a musician perhaps he'd be able to express this feeling of the relationship being fated. If he were rich, he'd shower her with gifts. He would steal for her. If there were dragons to be slain, he would be out there, chopping and stabbing away with the best of white knights. But he was only a cop and probably a not very bright one, so all he could do was grab her, hold her. But even this act was more than sex. It was what worship services at church should have been but never were. It was a mystical union.

They bounced along the pothole-riddled road, Laura recounted a disjointed story about first being in the saucer in a kind of a dream and later being there for real. Then there was something about an out-of-body experience when she was a child. She kept going back and forth from the present to the past experience. He wasn't getting the connection, but what disturbed him was the part about Uncle Robert's ethereal double.

"Ethereal double? What's that?"

"That's what I was saying. It's like when I had my out-of-body experience," she said.

He must have looked perplexed, because she said in a vexed tone that an ethereal double "is about the same as a ghost, though not really. It means . . ."

"Does that mean Uncle Robert is dead? That's what I want to know," he interrupted.

"Maybe. I hope not. That's what we'll find out at the house," she said.

"I just talked to him this morning. It's hard to believe."

"He said cherubs kidnapped and killed him right after you visited. I don't know, but what I can't believe is that I only spent a half day in the saucer. It seemed like a week."

They hit a particularly large pothole and she bumped against him. Without thinking about it he patted her thigh, and she kissed him, a quick, wet peck on the side of his mouth because he had to keep his eye on the road.

"I love you," she said, and he said, "Me too," and meant it.

He pulled over into the driveway of an abandoned house. Without speaking, she crawled between the front bucket seats into the back. The rear seat was folded down flat, and the heavy quilt he had taken from Ben Cartwright's house was still there.

She rolled over on her back, lifted her hips and scooted her jeans down to her ankles. He climbed over after her and helped untangle the jeans from her ankles, then slipped down her panties. The words "Lucky Me" were printed underneath a Care Bear. He knelt between her legs and worked his own pants down, which was easy because he had not only lost the flab off his waist but off his butt, too.

She grasped his erect penis with one hand and clasped the other hand on his buns and pulled him into her with one quick motion. She was hot, moist and tight, and he was afraid he was going to cum immediately. But along with the other benefits bestowed on his new body, he seemed to have conscious control over when he came.

She tucked her heels into the crooks at the back of his knees, and they made love like that for a while, a slow tango that neither was in a hurry to finish. She broke the silence with a series of little panting breaths like she was trying to whisper. She came quickly, and he had the incredibly weird but erotic sensation that his penis could actually 'taste' her orgasm, as if his glans was aware of some hormonal change within her, a sense more than just the tactile warmth or fluids. He wasn't done yet, but slowed his thrusts and lay there inside her, poised on the precipice. She brought her legs up and locked them around his waist. He could feel the muscles quiver under the smooth skin of her thighs.

"I love you," she repeated breathlessly. "I don't care if you're alive or dead. I love you."

He wanted to stare into her dark eyes forever, and for the second time today wished himself a poet so he could say so without sounding like an idiot. By her unconditional gift of her love, he felt himself surrender any doubts that his happiness lay with pleasing her.

A rapping on the side window interrupted his thoughts.

He was so deeply into the moment, so drugged by love and passion, it took a moment to realize that they'd been discovered. Shaken, he looked to the window expecting to see a local citizen but instead found a small angel, its face pressed against the window.

Laura saw it too and screamed.

He pulled out and rose to his knees, conscious of his nudity. He could hear the creature's wings buzzing through the glass. It was about the size of a small chihuahua, and there was something familiar about its baby face. It was the first cherub he'd actually seen, and without Laura's description of some of the things they did, he likely would have discounted the creature as mostly harmless and completely ridiculous.

It hooked its fingers over the slightly opened edge of the window glass and claws extended over the edge and began to force the window down. The talons looked razor-sharp and were slightly curved like those of a cat.

"Faaaather," the creature murmured , and Wright recognized the face as a pudgy version of his own.

Tendons strained underneath the baby fat on the cherub's arms as it strained to pull down the window.

"Shoot it!" Laura said in a strained, soft voice on the edge of hysteria. "Shoot the damn thing!"

Wright reached for his sidearm only to slap the bare flesh of his hip; his holster and belt were somewhere near his knees.

"It can't get in," he managed to say. "It's not strong enough to pull down the window. The roll-up gears will hold."

But even as he said this, the SUV leaned as the cherub pushed down on the window. "Faaather," it murmured again, and the wind-up gear did indeed hold, but halfway down the window did not. The safety glass crumbled. The cherub grinned mischievously as it pulled away hand-sized chunks and tossed them over its shoulder.

Wright was paralyzed. Looking at the creature was like looking in a fun-house mirror. It wasn't his face as a child, not even the one he only vaguely recognized as his own in old pictures. The cherub's face was the same face, though quarter-sized, that he had seen in the mirror this morning. Wright tried to make his limbs move as the cherub, its claws still extended, began to scramble through the hole in the window.

Laura was at his knees, pushing on his legs.

"John! Lift your legs!" she shouted.

He obeyed, confused for a moment, then realized she was trying to draw his pistol. The big handgun rasped against the leather holster as she pulled it out. She swung it up in front of his face and pointed it at the cherub, which now had its shoulders inside the vehicle but was having trouble getting its wings through. He saw her finger tighten on the trigger, and he winced, expecting to be deafened and blinded by the muzzle flash, but she had left the safety on and the gun did not fire.

"Shit! What is it with these things?" She began fiddling with the weapon, pointing the barrel at his face for a moment. Staring down the bore of the gun brought him out of his trance, and he took it from her hands. She seemed glad to relinquish it.

"Cover your ears," he said.

"Faather?" the cherub repeated for the third time, showing too many little sharp teeth. It brought both hands up to cover its little pink ears obediently, thinking Wright had been talking to it.

Wright hesitated, but only for a moment, then thumbed off the safety and stuck the end of the barrel right in its mouth past the pigmy teeth. He stole a glance at Laura to make sure she had covered her ears as he had instructed. She had.

He pulled the trigger, and the cherub's head disappeared in a cloud of blood and flying bits of flesh.

"That's over," he said.

"Maybe not," she said. She was splattered with dark blood and bits of pink flesh, as was he. So was much of the back of the SUV.

"I feel sort of stupid," he said but could barely hear his own voice. His ears rang from firing the big pistol inside the closed space of the vehicle, and he was sick at his stomach.

"Why?" she said, picking up an edge of the quilt to wipe away the gruesome muck from around her eyes.

"I should have pushed it outside. Shot it there," he said. "I sort of panicked."

Had she seen the resemblance? He hoped not.

"I understand panic in the presence of those things," she said, and though she was still covered in blood splatters, she began dabbing the goo off his face with a corner of the quilt.

But he doubted she really did understand. Somehow, as threatening as the thing had been, he felt he had just committed infanticide.

He thumbed off the pistol's safety and set the gun on the floor of the SUV. He picked up the other corner of the quilt and started to return the favor, wiping a particularly large chuck of bloody flesh off her neck.

"I think you should hold onto that," she said, nodding toward the pistol.

"I think we need to find someplace where we can hose ourselves off," he said.

"There may be another one," Laura said. She leaned back and began pulling on her jeans.

"Another cherub?"

"Another who looks like you," she said.

She had seen the resemblance too.

"I saw May give birth to two of those things - twins - in the saucer." Tears were streamed down her cheeks.

He turned away from her and struggled to get his pants on. It made sense now, as much sense as anything did in this world. Why did he feel guilty? Was it because the thing had been his freakish child? No, he only felt relief. The thing was a monster. Not a child, and despite the resemblance, he felt no connection with it. No, it wasn't so much guilt he felt as embarrassment. He wanted to explain to her that he had no recollection of having sex with May, but he found himself tongue-tied again.

He had an easier job of getting his pants on than did Laura because his were at least a size too large. Was he going to continue to get younger and younger or would he level out eventually? He helped

Laura on with her jeans, and she kissed his cheek tenderly despite the gore there.

The creature's razor sharp talons were hooked over the edges of the shattered window. He had been right to shoot it, hadn't he? The body just dangled there, the ragged neck seeping black blood.

As Wright struggled to get his shoes on, Laura found a car jack handle and used it to push the body free out of the vehicle.

"Is there anyway we can cover that window?" she asked.

"Not that I can think of. Not out here. If I had a piece of plywood."

He had an overwhelming sense of something being out of kilter, of having made a terrible mistake, and now the consequences were coming home. The hard edges inside the SUV shimmered, becoming incorporeal. And he felt cold, very cold. He looked at Laura and she was still there, but small, diminished by perspective as if she were at the end of a long dark tunnel.

"I love you," she said. "I don't care if you're alive or dead. I love you."

What?

He was back on his knees, between her legs, staring into the dark pools of her loving eyes.

"We're back to where. . . before the cherub," he said, wanting to lose himself in the moment again, but knew something was coming and he had to be ready for it. He withdrew and yanked up his pants. This time, the pistol holster wouldn't be trapped underneath his legs.

He had the pistol out in a moment, but the feeling of something being out of place returned, of a mistake about to happen.

It was the pistol. Something about the pistol.

The tap, tap, tap on the window came again, and Laura screamed as before. But this time he knew what to expect. The fat cherub was there, its head still whole and on its shoulders, the glass still intact, the talons hooked over the edge of the window as before, making the same sound as their razor sharp points screeched across the glass. This wasn't the twin that Laura had spoke about, but the same one whose head he had blown off in what was either a dream or premonition.

It looked him in the eyes and that same moment of mutual recognition passed between them as before.

"Faaather," the creature called, and this time Wright recognized call not as a threat but as plaintive call of pain and alienation.

"Shoot it!" Laura said in a still voice that was more urgent than a scream could ever be. "Shoot the damn thing!"

He started to say that the window mechanism was too rugged to allow it to enter, but it had proved him wrong before.

"Faather," it said again, and it began pushing the window down. Calmer now, Wright saw the cracks in glass begin to spread. He could just lean forward and stick the pistol in the creature's mouth and blow its obscene little head off as before.

Before? Had that before really happened?

He ignored the thought. If he shot it now, most of the gore and the noise would go outside the vehicle. And the window would be left more or less in one piece.

He leaned forward to do just that, still staring into those little eyes that were a perverse reflection of his own.

"Faaather."

And he couldn't do it.

But he had to do something, didn't he? Either it was evil or not. Either it was for him or against him. Either he had to kill it or let it kill him.

Something about this reasoning was inherently flawed. Did this choice have to be so black and white?

He thrust the pistol back into its holster and grabbed at the quilt. Laura looked at him questioning. *What are you doing?*

"Roll off the quilt!" he ordered.

"Faaather. . ." The little abomination was pushing *(again?)* so hard against the window that new cracks spread across the glass.

Wright yanked the quilt hard. Laura tried to roll off the quilt, but it was caught underneath her. She lifted her butt, putting her weight on her heels and arms like a contortionist, and the quilt came free.

"Faaather. . ." the cherub said again in its munchkin voice. It was halfway inside now, its body compressed like a cockroach to slip between the narrow space between the cracked window and the door-frame, but its hips were caught. It stretched out it hands to him, talons now sheathed, like a little child wanting to be picked up. "Faaather . . ."

He tossed the quilt over the creature's face and outstretched arms. It thrashed about violently like a frenzied animal caught in a net. Before it could slash its way through the padding with its talons, Wright wound the quilt around its torso, pinning its arms against its body – at least, he hoped they were pinned. Then he hit the rocker button for the window, winding it down.

"What . . . ?" Laura was shouting.

She didn't finish, but he knew what she was thinking:

What the hell are you doing? Get rid of it. Don't bring it in here.

Which would have been the sensible course of action. What he was doing instead was either stupid or insane – or both. But nothing in this world made sense anyway. He grabbed where he hoped its neck was and pulled it all the way into the cab. Its wings flopped under the quilt behind where his hand clenched on its neck. It pedaled it legs frantically.

"Watch out for the feet!" Laura shouted, startling him so much he nearly let go. But she was right to warn him. The cherub had long talons on its rosy baby feet where the toenails should have been, and they were ripping holes into the door liner. With his free hand, Wright flung the remainder of the blanket around the legs, binding the ankles with the twisted corner.

Now what? He hadn't really thought this far. He had managed to straightjacket thing with a quilt and had a firm hold on its ankles, but the minute he released either of his hands, it would be free shred him or Laura.

Laura was at his side with the roll of crime scene tape he kept in the back. "Will this be strong enough?"

"Not, not even if you go around it several times," he said. "Wait. Wait. Look in that box by the back hatch. There's a roll of clothesline. That's it. The cardboard box."

"Faaather..." came the muffled cry from under the blanket.

"Quiet, you sad little fuck," Wright said. His own profanity surprised him. But profanity suited the thing. "I'll cut you an air hole in a minute."

Laura retrieved the heavy, white plastic-coated cord and methodically wound it around the little beast. As she was doing this, Wright began to doubt the memory of shooting it the first time. Like a dream after awakening, the details of that episode were quickly fading.

Wright used a pair of handcuffs on its ankles. With his pocket knife, he cut a breathing slit for its mouth, then, working between winds of the rope, opened holes for its hands. As soon as it stuck its platypus-like hands out the holes, he had slapped an extra pair of handcuffs on its wrists, careful to avoid the talons.

Now completely immobilized, the cherub stopped calling out *faaather*, but it's playtpus-like hands and feet squirmed.

Wright was reminded of a childhood mischief he and Ben Cartwright had loved doing as boys. They had taped cherry bomb firecrackers to rocks and dropped them into a muddy, abandoned cistern out in the woods, in back of the Jacobsen mansion. The cherry bomb's fuses would burn underwater. When they exploded on the bottom of the cistern, the bombs made dull thumps like depth charges in World War II movies. Standing near the cistern, they could feel the concussion in the soles of their tennis shoes. But the explosion was only half the pleasure. Killed by the concussion, blind, deformed amphibious creatures would sometimes float to the top. They may have once been related to ordinary tadpoles or toads, but trapped there in that lightless, polluted water, they were misshapen and half-formed.

Miniature Gollums.

The cherub, bound in white cord, vaguely ovoid, its rudimentary appendages making awkward swimming motions, reminded him of an over-sized version of one of those sad creations. And it called him "father."

They drove the rest of the way to the mansion without speaking. Wright glanced over his shoulder to the back cargo area at the bound cherub.

Every time the creature made a sound, Laura would jump, and then give him one of those looks. *I love you, but I don't get you.*

Finally he said, "I just could not shoot something that called me 'father.' At least, I couldn't bring myself to do it the second time."

"The second time?" she asked. "You're telling me you've shot one before?"

He started to explain but didn't have the words. If she hadn't experienced the counter-clockwise effect, it was almost impossible to talk about it. Had it been a dream? Had time run backwards, giving him a second chance? He toyed with this idea. The clock had been turned back for him. He was younger yesterday than the day before. Younger again today. But no, that retrograde phenomenon only seemed to apply to him and a few other undead.

Whatever, shooting it the first time had been wrong at some fundamental level. He would say he had felt the damage in his soul – but he didn't believe in souls. He didn't believe in sin, either. And though he didn't know what he was going to do with the perverse bit of flesh in the back of the SUV, at least he didn't have that sour, sick feeling he had done something so bad he'd never be able to rationalize away.

"In a dream," he said. "I shot one in a bad dream, and I was sorry."

She didn't ask for further explanation, which was good because he didn't have one.

Wright didn't know if the second chance was for the cherub or for himself. He suspected it was the latter.

* * *

18.

And It's Over, You Say?

Bryan.

"I'm going," Suzanne had said. "Don't come after me."

Just like that. No explanation, but had she called "I love you" from the open window of the van as she drove away.

He stood there listening to the gravel crunch under the van's tires and considered the contradiction of *don't come after me* and *I love you.*

He also wondered how she could stand the stink of the van. He was ten feet way and upwind from the corpse of the cow-sized cherub, and the smell still made him gag. The stink left a chemical, metallic taste in his mouth, like super-concentrated hair salon air. The smell inside the van had to be many times worse.

He tried to imagine how it could be worse, then the headless corpse let out a long, protracted blubbering fart and he knew. The smell that penetrated his pores, his ears, any open orifice and not just his nostrils, and he had to run away. He only got a couple of yards away before he was brought to his knees by dry heaves. He was saved from another full-fledged vomiting only because he had lost his breakfast a few minutes earlier.

The corpse let out another sigh. Bryan braced for another wave of stink, but now it didn't seem to be farting so much as deflating. Even so, he took a couple of steps back out of caution, but not so far that he couldn't examine the thing in more detail.

Before Suzanne had blasted its head off, he had seen the face of Ben Cartwright's mirrored in its features. That had been the creepiest thing about it. Now there was just a huge headless and sexless spheroidal lump of flesh, deflating in the morning sun.

As it shrank more, its powdery white skin wrinkled, and its shape became vaguely feminine, like a deflated sex doll. Except for the little gossamer wings, it didn't much resemble the cherub that had attacked him in his own house.

The morning breeze picked up, blowing the smell away from him, but toward his truck. He had left it running, but the engine had died when he and Suzanne were inside the doublewide. This was a doubly bad thing because, as things stood now, he doubted he could hold his breath long enough to get to the truck, climb in and get it started — if it would restart at all.

The corpse sagged further, its skin turning from pasty white to black. Why? The one he had shot upstairs in his house had just lain there, oozing, forcing him to roll its remains off Suzanne. It had definitely been made of solid flesh and bone, not a stink-filled bag of skin.

More shrinkage, and the black skin began to crack, and the little bumps on its skin started popping open and expelling lumps of flesh. The lumps hit the ground and began hopping about. Even from this distance he recognized them as the same miniature froggy monstrosities he had found in the toilet bowl inside the house.

The wind picked up. He took a deep breath and made a decision hastened by a dozen of the toady things hopping toward him.

Their wings were wet now, but they will soon dry and be flying. Time to leave.

He sprinted over to a few feet from the corpse and scooped up the shotgun, then jagged to the right and opened the squeaky door of the pickup. He let out his breath with a whoosh as he climbed in the truck. The air had a sticky, rotten taste.

He'd lucked out. The truck's battery still held a charge, and the truck started on the second try. His stomach gradually relaxed as he put a hundred feet, then two hundred, between him and the corpse.

He checked the fuel gauge as he pulled out of the Ponderosa's front gate: a quarter-tank. That would be enough to get him out of the county if he didn't double back to his grandfather's house. He should pick up some clothes and food, but he wanted to leave this place, to get away from memories of Laura and Suzanne as fast as possible.

"I hurt!" he roared to himself.

Suddenly he was angry, and he stomped on the gas pedal, but though the engine roared, it only slowly accelerated. No spun gravel, no g-forces shoving against him. For the first time in his life, he longed for horsepower and bucket seats. Shit, why not wish for .50 caliber machine guns behind retractable headlights while he was at it?

He thought he heard laughter from above as he turned off the dirt road and onto a paved section of Old Buffalo Road.

Not taking any chances, he pulled off on the shoulder and scanned the sky as he slipped his last shells into the shotgun's double-barreled breech. These last shells were only No. 6 birdshot, a load fine for rabbits or quail but of dubious use for six-hundred-pound cherubs from hell. Suzanne had lucked out when she stuck the double barrels in the Ben-cherub's mouth. Maybe he'd luck out and get out of the county without seeing any of the things.

No such luck. He hadn't gone more than a few hundred yards before he came over a rise in the road and saw a cherub about the size of a German sheppard hunched over the gory remains of a large animal, probably a calf, in the middle of the road. Though winged, the creature reminded him of a large raccoon as it tore off chucks of bloody flesh and sinew from the body and stuffed them into its mouth.

Bryan slowed. Should he turn back? He had the shotgun but only two shots. It was bigger than the baby cherubs but not even close to size of the blimp that had attacked Suzanne in the house or the gas-bag in the van. He could roll up the windows and veer around the mess, save his ammunition. If it came after him, he couldn't outrun it, but after all, it was only one cherub. He deliberated, wondering if he had the fuel to make a detour. He could backtrack to the back entrance to Lost Lake State Park. The park entrance on the other side was only a mile from I-40, but he wanted to avoid the Interstate because of carjackers.

What was he thinking? Who'd want this piece of junk?

With that idea lodged in mind, he started a wide U-turn. He was halfway through the turn, the truck crossway in the road, when he saw the white van on its side in the deep ditch to the east.

The Cartwright van? Suzanne?

His eyes went back to the carnage in the middle of the road, his heart pounding in his chest.

Was that a shock of red hair, scalp attached, in the giggling cherub's hands?

He backed up the truck, then jammed it into first gear. The tires spun on the wet grass of the shoulder. In his panic, he had backed up too far. Chunks of grass spun up in the air behind him as he revved the engine in frustration. Then the tires caught and he was speeding toward the feeding cherub at ramming speed.

He slammed on the brakes and the knobby-treaded truck tires half-skipped, half-skidded on the asphalt. The cherub looked up, its bloody smile changing to astonishment, a kind of open-mouth, Shirley Temple, look. *Oh, No, Mr. Buttons!* But it didn't fly away. Instead it toddled rapidly out the path of the truck like a wind-up doll.

He did a little ballet-like move before the truck came to a complete stop, shoving the door open with his shoulder and putting one foot on the running board while keeping the other on the brake. He kept one hand on the steering wheel, the other on the shotgun. His thumb found the dual hammers and cocked them back as the truck came to a full stop. He sprang out and landed on both feet and fired one barrel. Though it was only birdshot, at such close range the creature's chest splattered open in bloody gout.

The cherub stared at him with the same pouty expression as before, and Bryan expected it to wag a finger and scold him.

That was awful naughty of you to murder me so, Mr. Buttons!

Instead it wavered on its feet for a second or so, then just toppled over, its sulky expression unchanged.

Bryan took a deep breath and let it out. Still he could not make himself look directly at the gory mess the cherub had been feeding on. The shooting had happened so quickly and automatically, as as if he had been outside himself, watching someone else leap out of the truck and fire the gun. But now he was back inside his own head, and he didn't want to look.

When he finally did look, the red hair was not hair at all but bloody fur. A leg had been stripped clean of flesh, but that leg ended in a delicate hoof. His first impression had been correct. It wasn't Suzanne, nbut a small white-tailed doe, probably not even weaned yet.

"Bryan!" A voice, Suzanne's voice.

Where?

The sound of breaking glass led his eyes back to the ditch where he'd seen the Cartwright van. Now that he was out of the truck, he couldn't see it down in the ditch.

"Byran!" More urgent now, followed by the sound of glass breaking and the gurgling giggling that was unmistakably cherubs. He jogged over to the edge of the ditch to find two cherubs, the same size as the one he'd just dispatched, perched on the driver's door of the overturned van.

One cherub was peeling away shattered window glass from the door frame while the other, oblivious to jagged shards, was upside down, two little chubby feet in the air, its wings abuzz, as it tried to squirm through a whole in the front window.

"Let go, you little fucker!" Suzanne's voice. "I'm not going anyplace with you!"

The upside-down cherub gripped one of her arms and was trying to pull her out of the van. She was punching at the cherub's head with her free hand but without much effect.

"Hey!" Bryan shouted. The cherub pulling away the remains of the window looked back over its shoulder, but the other one was too busy fighting with Suzanne to notice him.

Bryan brought the shotgun up but was afraid to fire. At this range, the spread of the shot would be wide. He'd hit both of the cherubs and Suzanne too.

He could see her face now as she struggled with the cherub. Her forehead was smeared with blood, but her expression was calm and resolute.

He trotted down the embankment toward the van, veering around scrub oak. Halfway down, his toe caught on an exposed root and he went flying face forward. Time slowed to a crawl as he fell, but he couldn't make his hands let go of the shotgun and use them to stop his fall. A football-size stone embedded in the red clay ground came rushing up to meet his face. But he managed to twist at the last moment and he missed the rock by an inch. He hit hard, but not so hard the wind was knocked out of him. He got to his feet, nearly stumbling again on the steep incline. Both cherubs ignored him as he came up behind them.

"Hey!" He poked the upside-down cherub wrestling with Suzanne in the belly with the shotgun barrel. It ignored him.

The other cherub, which was trying to work the handle of the jammed driver's-side door, turned on him and snarled, then went back to its task.

"Don't make me waste a shotgun shell on you," Bryan said and slapped the side of its head with the barrel. Like its partner, it ignored him.

"Bryan? Is that you?" Suzanne called, a bit breathless.

"Yes. Hang on. I'll rid you of your infestation in a minute."

Or would he with only one shell? He leaned the shotgun against the side of the van and picked among the rocks. Like much of the dirt in this part of Missouri, it seemed to grow rocks better than anything else, and he had lots of choices. He selected an apple-sized piece of limestone, rounded on one side and jagged on the other. Without preamble, he stumbled forward and slammed the ragged side onto the back of cherub's neck.

The impact slammed the cherub's head against the van door. It slid slowly off the van, a huge gash in its neck, the soft skin of its hands squeaking against the muddy paint. Its head turned sideways on the broken neck, and it fell to the ground. It sat up, a popped-out eyeball hanging loosely from threads of tissue on its cheek. The other eye fixed hatefully on him. Then it schlepped face-down in the wet clay, a broken rag doll, its head cocked backwards at nearly a right angle. The ridiculous little wings twitched and were still.

Bryan paused. Killing this one had felt different than with the other two. There had been something familiar about its face, a resemblance he'd only glimpsed as death took it and its rapacious expression relaxed.

He was compelled – and yet repelled by what he might see – to turn it over to examine that face, but he now had the attention of the other cherub. It had let go of Suzanne's arm and backed out of the window, wings humming. It hovered, buzzing like a oversized pink toy helicopter about ten feet over the van. It looked at its dead comrade, then did doubletake back to Byran. Gradually, its expression changed from surprise to anger. Bryan grabbed the shotgun from where he'd leaned it against the van, his heart pounding.

"Bryan," it said in a familiar voice. Its face was familiar too: a small pudgy version of Suzanne's.

"Bryan, don't," it said in a squeaky echo of Suzanne's voice.

He couldn't make his arms bring up the shotgun as the cherub glided toward him, its hands outstretched.

"It's an illusion! Don't let it hypnotize you," yelled Suzanne, the real Suzanne. She had half-climbed out of the window and was leaning on her forearms.

An *illusion* was what the monster Ben-faced cherub had said before she had shot it.

Illusion or not, as the cherub closed the distance, he could feel a breeze stirred by the cherub's buzzing wings. The resemblance to Suzanne's face was unmistakable, and if he hadn't been able to see the real Suzanne only a few feet away, still struggling to free herself from the overturned van, he wouldn't have been able to bring the shotgun to bear.

He pulled the trigger and nothing happened.

It took him a second to realize he had pulled the trigger for the barrel he had discharged earlier. In the delay, the cherub had come close enough to grab the shotgun barrel and begin to push the barrel up and aside – but not enough. Bryan pulled the other trigger, and the cherub's hand as well as part of its skull disappeared in a bloody haze.

Simultaneously, Suzanne shouted "Hey!" and dropped back into the van while the cherub spiraled off in uncontrolled flight and collided with the trunk of a scrub blackjack oak.

Shit! Had she been in the line of fire? No, she'd been off to the right – hadn't she?

She was no longer propped halfway in the van door window. He dropped the shotgun and scrabbled up on the van, dreading what he might find inside. The side of the van was splattered with what he hoped was only the cherub's blood and oyster-like bits of flesh that might have been brains. The gore made the side of the van slippery, and he kept sliding off. Over by the oak tree, the cherub bounced and bumbled about on the ground in obvious death throes.

He got a handhold on the window frame, pulled himself up and found himself face-to-face with Suzanne as she emerged. Her face was bloodier than before, but he could see the blood was not hers but the blackish-red blood of the cherub.

"You're crying," she said.

"No, I'm not," he said, but tears were streaming down his cheeks.

She put both hands on the side of his head and kissed him.

He reached for her, forgetting his handhold kept him from sliding off the van. He slid off, landed on his feet, and teetered a bit, but at least he didn't fall. He still felt stupid for crying, though.

What the fuck was wrong with him? He'd only known her a day. She said she loved him – he was a sucker for that – but she had first left him to go back to her husband, then abandoned him on some sort of mission.

She pulled herself out of the van, and slid off.

"Whee!" she said, as if she were a kid on playground slide.

He turned away from her, but she stepped in front of him and wrapped her arms around him, pinning his arms to his side, saying nothing. For that instant he could feel her love for him as a wave of warmth. It wasn't physical, but a sense of being immersed in a sea of complete, unconditional acceptance.

He felt as if he had come home. It was, he realized, a love he had never experienced before, not even from his mother. Why would anyone want more out of life than this?

"You saved me," she said, a bit coyly, smiling up at him. She released his arms, and he wrapped them around her. They kissed. Her lips were cold as ice, and he remembered she was undead, but he didn't care.

"Not really," he said. "You were doing pretty well for yourself."

"I hit a deer. It ran right in front of me. I think the cherubs were chasing it, tormenting it."

He kissed her again, not wanting the feeling of being immersed in love to fade, but knowing it wasn't sustainable, not at such intensity.

"Is that what drove you off the road? Hitting the deer?"

"I swerved and just sideswiped it. It wasn't big enough to do much damage, but when I swerved I hit one of the cherubs that was chasing it." She traced the line of his jaw with her hand. His day-old beard made a rasping sound under her finger. "It was like slamming into a load of bricks. I think it went through the grill and trashed my power steering. The steering wheel locked up."

"You're freezing."

"I feel okay," she said.

"Come on, the heater still works in the truck," he said. He took her hand and began leading her up the embankment. She followed for a few steps, then stopped, to look back at the van.

"Is there something you need out of the van?"

"No, not really. I just don't know what I'm going to do now."

"Whatever it is you need to do, I'll help you."

"I don't think you can help me. I don't think anyone can."

They climbed the rest of the way up the embankment in silence. All the questions he wanted to ask had already been asked except one.

"Suzanne . . . "

"Yes."

"Do you think that big cherub you shot back at your house was Ben or something that just looked like him?"

She didn't look at him but squeezed his hand. "I don't think it was real. I don't think any of this is real except one thing."

"Except what?"

"Except the love we feel for each other."

He stopped and turned to face her. She looked away. "Maybe you're right. But then why not take what we've got and run with it? And don't give me that obligation crap!"

She looked at him and wiped a tear from her cheek with her free hand. "Now it's my turn to cry," she said. "You don't understand. The obligation I felt was as much toward you as anyone. I wanted to find Ben to make a clean break with him. I owed him that much. And I couldn't be with you without being free of Ben. I'm not a slut. I'm not."

"I never said you were."

"But there was more to it than that. There was something pulling me, like an invisible cord, to go back to the house. Then after we killed the Ben-thing – after *I* killed the Ben-thing – I had to get away. I felt like I was dissolving, fading. I had to get away to think."

"Shit!" Bryan said as they reached the road. Steam was rising from underneath his truck's hood. He had left the engine running while he climbed down the embankment to help Suzanne. It was running still, but barely. It was chugging and making intermittent knocking sounds. He let go of Suzanne's hand and sprinted to the truck. Before he could reach the ignition key, the engine gave a last chug and knock, and died.

As he lifted the hood Suzanne caught up. The overheated engine made popping and cracking noises as a cloud of steam billowed up.

"Is it serious?" she asked.

"With this dinosaur, it's always serious. The good thing is, the engine and everything is so simple I can usually fix it."

But this time it might not be so easy. Unlike modern cars and trucks, this truck had enough room under the hood for him to see exactly what had happened. A freeze plug had popped out, probably rusted from age. The coolant water had spewed out the two-inch diameter hole, and the engine had quickly overheated, then died. The question was, had the engine been hot enough to seize up the bearings before it died? If so, there was no way he could repair it.

Whichever, they were on foot at least for the rest of the day. He scanned the skies. Were there more cherubs up there? Or in the scrawling thicket of blackjack and scrub cedar that bordered both sides of the road? If so, they were so, so screwed. It was miles to the nearest house, and he had used his last shotgun shell.

"Let's go," he said.

"Where?"

"To the Jacobsen Mansion. It's the closest."

"But?"

"Don't argue with me, Suzanne, please."

"But . . ."

"Uncle Robert will help us, and if I can get the truck running tomorrow, you can take it and run off to wherever it is you've got to run off to."

"I was going to say that I wasn't arguing with you."

"Good," he said, but now for some reason he felt angry with her and the mixed signals she was sending him.

Go or don't go. Just don't flip-flop on me.

But as he started walking, she took his arm and his anger dissipated.

They hadn't walked more than an hundred yards before the sound of an engine came from behind them. They turned in unison. It was the sheriff's SUV. The vehicle pulled up beside them and the passenger-side window rolled down. In the front seat were Laura Jacobsen and a man who looked like Sheriff Wright but much, much younger.

"I've been looking for you," the young man said with Sheriff Wright's voice to Suzanne. "We thought you were dead, Mrs. Cartwright."

Bryan didn't tell him that he was half-right.

* * *

19.

You Tragic Waste of Flesh!

Laura.

"Well, Sheriff Wright, she's very much alive," Bryan said.

But Laura could tell Suzanne was undead the moment John pulled up next to her and Bryan.

"Your husband was very worried about you," John said, ignoring Bryan. The sheriff emphisized the word ***husband.***

Suzanne's shoulders slumped noticeably. "Is Ben okay? I've been looking for him. He wasn't at the Ponderosa."

John cleared his throat, avoiding her question. "What are you two doing out here?"

Bryan pointed to a white van on its side in the ditch. "Cherubs ran Suzanne off the road. That's her coversion van is rolled over in the ditch there. I stopped to help, and my truck died."

"I see," John said. "Is that shotgun loaded, by the way?"

"Out of shells," Bryan said.

"Show me," John said.

Bryan glared at him, but flipped a lever that cause the gun to hinge open at the middle and pop out an empty shotgun shell on the ground.

"Sure you're out of shells?" John said.

Laura wanted to kick him for sounding so much like a cop. Obviously, there was more to the issue between the two than just history. Did John know she had Bryan had once been lovers?

Bryan was acting like a dick too. His shoulders were hunched and he had placed himself partially between Suzanne and John. Suzanne had let him do the talking. Why did John feel he had to remind them Suzanne was married? Besides, he had told Laura while they were driving about finding Ben Cartwright dead and that he suspected the big man of having killed his young wife while in a manic state.

"We could use a ride," Bryan said.

The "we" made Laura smile, which surprised her. She had imagined Bryan carrying the torch for her for weeks, maybe months. Now he had found someone else in only a couple of days after she had dumped him, and she felt jealous.

You are being such a bitch.

"Where are you going?" Wright said.

"We just need to get off the road. The cherubs are vicious, you know."

"I know very well."

"Bryan thought we might *both* find shelter for the night at Uncle Robert's house," Suzanne said.

Laura cringed at the mention of Uncle Robert.

"I see," John said. "That happens to be where we're going." His tone was suddenly relaxed, and it took Laura a moment to realize what he was doing. He didn't know if Ben Cartwright had died of natural causes or been murdered. He had suspected Suzanne, which was natural for a cop. It was his job to be suspicious. But Suzanne was not trying to cover up a relationship between her and Bryan. Which meant she didn't know Ben Cartwright was dead. Or did it?

Leaving the engine running, John got out and opened the left rear side door. He rolled the bundled and tied-up cherub to the back of the cargo area, then raised the folded-up rear seats for Suzanne and Bryan.

"What's in the blanket?" Bryan asked as he climbed in. Suzanne got in the other side.

"Don't with mess it," John said. "It doesn't concern you."

The cherub squirmed and said something, probably "father"

again though it was indecipherably muffled by several layers of blanket.

"What is it?" Bryan asked again as John put the SUV in gear and started driving.

"Beg your pardon?"

"What's in the blanket? Is it what I think it is?"

"Son, you don't need to know," John said, and though his tone had softened a little with Bryan, Laura wanted to tell her undead lover that the ***son*** thing seemed affected as he now looked younger than Bryan.

Laura suspected John's refusal to tell Bryan had little to do with discretion and more to do with possessiveness for her. She could feel the tension building between the two men and on impulse she said, "It's a cherub in the quilt. John captured it. He could have shot it but decided to take it alive instead."

Silence ensued, and she resisted the impulse to supply additional details such as the fact that it had called John ***father*** and that its face had resembled his.

Suzanne broke the silence. "Did it – I'm not sure how to say this – did it look like anyone you know?"

John slammed on the breaks hard enough to throw Laura forward against the seat belt. He pulled over to the shoulder. "Sorry," he said to her, then turned to face Suzanne and Bryan in the rear seat. "How did you know?" he shouted. Suzanne was directly behind him and he was only inches from her face.

"Back off, man," Bryan shouted.

"Shut up, college boy," John said and brushed off Bryan's hand. Laura reached out to stop him, but was startled by the appearance of John's arm: It appeared composed of dark blue mists interspersed with thousands of sparkling lights.

Vertigo overtook her, and her vision darkened. Reality – or rather her perspective – shifted and now everyone in the vehicle seemed to be immersed in auras. John was surrounded by a blue-gray aura with red sparks firing off like fireflies around his head. Bryan's aura was black with red flashes. The sparks of each man's aura reached out, ensnarling the other like battling jellyfish.

When Suzanne looked at Bryan, her aura changed from crimson

to a blue-gray. John shoved Bryan back in his seat, but the red tendrils of both men's auras remained engaged across what was now two feet of space.

Without thinking, Laura reached out and chopped with her open hand at the dancing tendrils. Her hand cut through them as if they were mushy spaghetti.

Her vision dimmed again. Then the auras evaporated.

Both men were looking at her curiously. She felt foolish, though she was certain the auras had been real – if not physically real, then at least a reflection of some sort of reality. Had the act of severing the angry red tendrils defused the alpha-male argument? Or was it that a weird act on her part had made them focus more about her? Whatever, the tension between the two men had dissipated for the moment.

"What did you just do?" John asked.

"Things were getting out of control," she replied.

You were getting out of control, my love.

For he was her love even when he was being a shithead.

"I only wanted to ask what she meant," John said. His tone was apologetic now.

"You were in her face, yelling," Bryan said. He put his arm around Suzanne's shoulders.

"Don't get your shorts in a wad. I was just asking." John's voice rose again.

"What did you see, Suze?" Laura interrupted before the two men could get into a new argument.

The redheaded woman looked at her curiously, and Laura wondered if she had not noticed how stunning she was before or if it was the undead effect. Her skin was milk-white, without blemishes, as smooth and nearly pore-less as a newborn's. Her cheekbones were high, almost Slavic, and her eyes a preternatural blue. There was a light blush in her cheeks that Laura had mistaken at first for makeup, but undead or not, hers was the blush of health. There was the usual scattering of the almost orange freckles of a natural redhead, but they were confined to her temples and appeared to be laid out in some kind of order, like a natural tattoo.

Laura realized she had been staring at Suzanne for too long and made herself continue the questioning. "You asked if the cherub looked like anyone? Remember?"

"Yes, oh yes. I did." Suzanne's voice trembled. She looked at Bryan for reassurance.

An understanding passed between Suzanne and Bryan – a silent agreement – she said, "There was one, back at the Ponderosa, a big bloated one, that had Ben's face."

"Ben Cartwright? Your husband?" John butted in, but his voice was calmer now, not abrasive.

"Yes," Suzanne said.

Was there an undercurrent of guilt in her voice?

"But it wasn't him," Suzanne continued. "I – we – Bryan helped me – couldn't find him – Ben – in the house," she stuttered. "But I know the thing was an illusion. Some kind of mind-fuck."

Laura laughed despite herself. Now that Suzanne was dressed in a calico frock instead of her usual combat boots, a miniskirt and a halter top, the obscenity had more impact. It was as if an evangelical church lady had started to cuss like a redneck.

There was one of those moments of silence where the situation demands someone speak but no one wants to go first. Finally, after several seconds, Bryan said, "It came after us. Suzanne blew its head off with the shotgun, and it deflated. It was like a big bag of gas, like a Macy's Thanksgiving Day parade float."

John shook his head. Laura nudged him, but he refused to take the hint, so she said, "The one bound up in the back looks like John."

Both Bryan and Suzanne looked at her uncomprehendingly.

"It looked like him. A Mini-Me John Wright," Laura said.

They laughed at the Mini-Me part.

Now, I've blown my cover too – if I ever had one, Laura thought

"Don't make light of it," John said.

Should she tell them it had called him *father*? Probably not.

"There was another one, one that looked like Suzanne," Bryan said. "I killed it. Like Suzanne said: You can't let them get to you. I don't know if it's a new strategy or if I just hadn't seen enough of them to notice that some looked like people I knew."

John cleared his throat and said, "I have to ask you an awkward question, Mrs. Cartwright."

"It's not Mrs. Cartwright. I mean we were common-law married, but I kept my last name."

"Sorry. I forgot. It's Zimmer – correct?"

"Zimmer-MAN," she corrected.

"Yes, I remember now. Your father was Robert Zimmerman."

"Yes."

"He used to run the furniture store before they built the Walmart?"

She nodded.

"I know this is going to sound weird," John said.

"These are weird times."

"I mean, I don't want you to be offended."

"I don't offend easily."

John drew in a deep breath and let it out. "There's no easy way to ask, so I'll just do it. Have you ever had relations with one of the angels? One of the human hybrids, I mean?"

"What?" she said.

"Did you fuck one?" John said.

"Okay, that's the last goddamn straw!" Bryan was shouting again. "Out of the car!" And he shoved John's shoulder.

John just stared at him, slightly amused.

"What's the matter? Afraid to step out from behind your badge?"

"I'm not wearing a badge, college boy."

"You know what you mean. And don't call me that, you tragic waste of flesh!"

"There you go again. What is that from, some wimpy poem?" John said in a fake southern drawl.

"You mean two-syllable words?"

"Stop it, *boys*!" Laura said.

Ignoring her, John opened his door and stepped out. Bryan did the same.

As childish as it seemed, they were serious about the fight.

Suzanne protested, "Bryan. Stop! It's not worth it."

Bryan and Wright met in front of the vehicle. Bryan acted like he didn't know what to do next. John stood there with a calm smile, then unbuckled his heavy leather belt and dropped it to the ground, holster and all.

Laura knew that as sheriff he had dealt with small-town drunks and druggies for the last twenty years and probably had all sorts of self-defense moves. Bryan, on the other hand, grew up in upscale suburbia. Though he was in shape from all his hard labor harvesting firewood since the fall of the saucer, she doubted he knew much about fighting.

Laura got out of the SUV and Suzanne stepped up beside her. "We need to stop this," she said.

"Well. . .?" John said.

Bryan said nothing. He didn't look so much scared as indecisive.

"What's the matter? Don't know how to get started?"

"You started this with your asshole mouth," Bryan said.

"Now there's a mental image for you. What do you college folks call that? A metaphor?"

"John, would you stop it with the hick-sheriff routine?" Laura said.

He ignored her. "Generally, at this point, one of us spits," John said and demonstrated, cocking his head to one side and letting go a big, whitish glob that made an audible *splat* as it hit the asphalt at Bryan's feet.

"John, Bryan, this isn't proving anything."

"Oh, my dear, but it does," John said. "I proved that the undead can spit."

Bryan laughed nervously and let go a wad of his own. "That would be undead asshole," he said. "The spittin' image of one."

"That's the spirit, college boy," and John closed the distance between them, one leg outstretched, the knee bent, an arm pulled back, fist clenched a waist level, a martial-art move.

Bryan didn't take a defensive stance. Instead, he shifted his weight, moving one foot slightly forward. He raised his arms but only to waist level. Instead of making fists or the flat-palm chopping hands of karate, his fingers were splayed open, as if he was getting ready to catch a huge beach ball.

Suzanne grabbed Bryan's arm and said, "Stop this silliness."

"I have to do this," he said and shrugged off her hand.

"If it's to defend my honor, forget it."

"It's my honor too. I'm tired of taking shit off him, undead or whatever."

Suzanne looked to Laura as if for backup.

"Calm down. You don't have to prove your manhood to me."

"Bryan, if you get in this fight," Suzanne said, "then I'm walking."

That got his attention.

"I mean it. I'm not riding with you – or with the sheriff. I'm walking back to Creedance by myself, cherubs or no cherubs."

Bryan hesitated but only for a second.

"Do what you have to do," he said.

Laura considered making the same threat to John but decided it would be an empty one, and she suspected Suzanne's was a bluff as well. The two men were just going to have to get it out of their systems.

But my poor little intellectual ex-lover is going to get his ass kicked, and it's going to be more than a matter of just a bloody nose!

John brought his rear foot forward, swiveled his shoulders, and punched at Bryan's chest; Suzanne gasped at the same instant. Bryan took a small step to one side, letting the punch fly past him, and in one swift movement, brought up his right palm. Still moving forward by the inertia of his punch, John's chin collided with Bryan's palm. His head snapped backward, and his feet swooped out from under him. He fell hard, his head hitting the pavement with a dull thud.

Bryan seemed to have barely exerted himself at all, but John lay dazed on the pavement.

Bryan took a step back, and John stayed down. Laura ran to his side. His eyes were unfocused, staring at the sky.

"John, John, are you all right?"

"I'm okay. Don't fuss." He struggled to sit up, and she helped him.

"What the hell was that?" he asked Bryan.

"Aikido trumping your shuck-and-jive tae kwon do."

"Aikido, huh? Pretty fancy." John got to his feet. "Where'd you learn that?

"Columbia. There was a dojo led by a Japanese master. My mom and dad's parenting strategy was to keep me really busy in a lot of things to keep me out of their hair: guitar, soccer, martial arts."

"Paid off, I'd say." John straightened up, his spine crackling.

"You say that because you've never heard me play the guitar."

John laughed and rubbed the back of his head. Laura could see a patch of hair missing from where his head had hit the asphalt but no blood. She looked down and saw the patch of scalp – it was about the size of a quarter – stuck to the pavement.

The undead might be able to spit but not bleed.

John picked up his belt, holstered gun and all. Alarmed, Bryan took a step backward. John noticed his alarm and smiled.

"Don't worry. I may be a tragic waste of flesh, maybe even an asshole at times, but I'm not a chickenshit."

As he buckled the belt, he said, "And no matter how bad you play guitar, I don't think I'll heckle you again. Not now."

"Are we done?" Bryan said.

"We're done. You're right. I was acting like an asshole."

"Granted."

"But I had good reasons for asking," John said. "I just asked it wrong."

"I bet you did," Bryan said, still bristling a bit.

Laura felt pride swell for John. Uncle Robert once told her that a man's character can be judged by how willing he is to take responsibility for his own mistakes.

Suzanne said, "To answer your question, Sheriff, no, I haven't had sex with one of the angels. At least not that I remember."

"You don't remember? What's that mean?"

"It means exactly what it sounds like. I don't remember a whole day."

"I found her," Bryan said.

"Hold on a minute. I'm talking to Ms. Zimmerman," Wright said.

"Let him talk," Laura interrupted before he could go into jerk-off cop mode again. So much for character. For about the thousandth time, she thought how ill-matched she and the sheriff were; she knew she should be angry with him, but she found it impossible not to love him.

Obviously, I'm an idiot.

But John smiled at her, and in that moment she knew for certain she had the identical effect on him and that he had the same doubts, too. It was at once a wonderful and fearful perception. He could do no wrong. In his eyes, neither could she. No two people should love each other this much. It was unhealthy.

Bryan cleared his throat. She and John had been staring into each other eyes like love-struck teenagers.

"I was going to explain that yesterday I found Suzanne buried under a pile of brush in the woods. She was unconscious – nearly dead – and she didn't remember how she got there."

"That's disturbing, but what does that have to do with my question?"

"I think the angels dropped her there."

"You don't really think that do you?"

"What?"

"That the angels just dropped her there. That you just happened to find her. Why don't you tell me what really happened?"

"What's with you?" Bryan demanded. "Do we have to go through another aikido demonstration?"

Why was John being such an ass? Laura wondered

And it dawned on her that he was jealous. He knew she had been sleeping with Bryan before him.

She leaned forward and put her hand on the back of his neck and whispered in his ear: "I love YOU, not Bryan."

He turned and smiled at her, his eyes sparkling.

"Chillax," she said. "Please." She wanted to kiss him then and there but felt self-conscious in front of Bryan and Suzanne.

"Okay. Okay," John said, his tone suddenly apologetic. "I guess I'm still kind of ramped up. Tell me what happened."

Bryan glared at him. "I think you owe Suzanne an apology." Suzanne snuck a hand over and squeezed his.

Suzanne was acting as a peacemaker, too. Laura felt an instant kinship to her.

It's up to us to stop these shithead men we love from tearing out each other's livers. Was her love for John as obvious as Suzanne's was for Bryan?

And for about the thousandth time she wondered if it was indeed love she felt or some sort of supernatural sexual attraction.

The hell with it! I'm just going to stop questioning and let it happen.

"It's all right, Bryan," Suzanne said. "The sheriff has obviously been through a lot. Just like us. I think we should move on."

Laura, her hand still resting on the back of John's neck, felt him relax.

Bryan shrugged, leaned against the side of the SUV, and told them of finding Suzanne in the woods, "cold as death," and of taking her back to his grandfather's farmhouse to try to revive and warm her up. Bryan's journalistic training revealed itself as he gave a straightforward, linear recap of the events of the past two days. He told of being surprised by an over-large cherub in the upstairs of his farmhouse and of the creature almost killing Suzanne before he shot it. Then he recounted the other attack at the Ponderosa when they drove over to check on her husband.

"It just looked like Ben," Suzanne interjected. "But I knew in my heart that it was a trick."

Laura knew both of them were leaving out things of a personal nature. It also slowly dawned on Laura that Bryan knew Suzanne was undead. Did he care? If he was as hooked on Suzanne as she was on John, apparently not.

"And that brings us to where you picked us up," Bryan finished.

"Hmmm," John said thoughtfully. "But there was nothing resembling rape?"

"Why do you keep asking that?" Bryan said. "Is there something about the cherubs we need to know?"

When John hesitated, Laura prompted, "Tell them. They've been honest with us. You need to tell them."

It was John's turn to shrug. "The cherub there. . ." He pointed to the squirming bundle in the back. "Called me father."

"It also looked like you, John," Laura added.

"There was that too," he admitted.

"I don't want to get you riled up again, Sheriff," Bryan said.

"Go ahead. I'm over it," John said.

"So am I," Bryan said. "But did you have sex with an angel? Is that why you think it looks like you?"

"Good question," John said. "I wish I knew."

"What does that mean?"

"It means I don't remember."

"How come that wasn't a good enough answer coming from Suzanne?"

"I wouldn't believe it myself, really, but you've got a point. I truly don't remember, but May Tyre said I had sex with her as I lay dying or maybe even after I died."

"Was it maybe immediately after you died?" Suzanne asked.

John's mouth dropped open and he stared at her.

"Well, we need to get this out in the open don't we? I died in that wood pile. I know it. I think Bryan knows it. You're undead. I knew it right away. I sensed it. I think Laura's aware of it too."

Laura nodded.

It was a shocking question, but maybe it was time they talked openly about being undead?

* * *

20.

Transformation Comes Quickly

Bryan.

Sheriff Wright had stopped interrogating Bryan and Suzanne, and was concentrated on driving. If not for the bloodless, hairless, little patch which was plainly visible from the backseat as he drove, the whole fight episode could have been a dream.

Apparently Wright didn't know how to fall, and his head had smacked the pavement hard. He should have suffered a concussion or at least been knocked unconscious.

As if aware of Bryan's stare, Wright reached behind his head and idly scratched at the bald spot as if it were no more than a mosquito bite.

Suzanne smiled at Bryan and scooted closer to him on the back seat. Neither had any reason now to pretend they were only casual friends. Still, it had been a quick transition. A few minutes ago they had all pretended to various degrees of separation. Now it was as if he and Suzanne, and Wright and Laura were on a double date.

A double date to hell! He smirked at his own sophomoric allusion. It had truth to it though. Demonic cherubs were on the prowl, and he was in love with an undead woman who had been a stranger not much more than a day before, while Laura, his ex-lover, was currently ga-ga over the undead sheriff.

He expected Laura to lean over and give Wright a big wet tongue-job kiss at any moment. Having his ex-lover in the front seat should have a chilling effect on romance. Yet here he and Suzanne were, snuggling in the back seat; it was all he could do to not to start a makig out with her.

This was insanity, and it all seemed so normal. He felt happier than he could remember. His life had been constantly in peril since he found Suzanne in the woodpile, but he didn't regret it. Before he'd found her, his life had seemed like shabby place, like a broken-down motel room on the wrong side of town. Now he lived in a world where everything was bright and new. Even with the danger they faced, the world was an exciting place, full of promise.

Suzanne's hand was warm; he found it hard to accept she was undead.

He wasn't sure about they had even talked about the undead issue. For reasons unclear, he felt it was better that Suzanne's condition – or Sheriff Wright's for that matter – went unspoken. It wasn't that he didn't know that Suzanne was undead. It was just that he preferred not to think of it.

Was it love? Funny, he had asked himself that very question about Laura only a couple of days ago. What he felt for her was at once familiar ground – he had loved her, and probably still did at some level.

But with Laura, the love had been built up over time. Although his love for her had started with an initial physical attraction, the bonding had developed gradually. With Suzanne, it had been a nearly instantaneous link. She had filled that hole in his soul left by Laura – overfilled it. From the moment he had touched her deathly cold arm to pull her out of the wood pile, he had entered a new world.

It just didn't make sense. He didn't believe in love at first sight. They said meth was instantly addictive – one dose was all it took to make an addict. It was like that with Suzanne: one touch, not even a kiss, and he was doomed.

"Look! Angels!" Wright called out.

He was pointing upwards beyond the windshield. Bryan rolled

down his side window and stuck his head out.

"Do you see them?" Wright asked.

"Yeah, I see them. There's a whole cluster. They are flying in some sort of formation, like geese."

Canadian geese had a migration route that took them directly over Lost Lake, and they usually flew low at maybe a couple of a hundred feet, just as the angels did now.

"Formation? Are they? I didn't notice," Wright said, swinging the driver's side sun visor aside to get a better look.

"Son of a buck, you're right," he said. "They're in a 'V'."

In the back cargo area of the SUV, the bound-up cherub thrashed about in its quilt. By unspoken consensus, they all ignored it as it if were merely a child throwing a temper tantrum. Maybe it was.

"Looks like they're headed toward the lake," Bryan said. The wind was cool and fresh on his face, and the air smelled of pine and freshly growing hay. He knew how dogs felt. "No cherubs up there that I can see."

"Look out!" Laura screamed.

Suzanne screamed, too, a warble of terror. Then Bryan was thrown against the door as Wright swerved to the right. The headliner crumbled as something large impacted the roof of the SUV.

Wright cursed, and Laura shouted, "There's another one coming from your left!"

Bryan, his head still out the window, looked up to see a cherub flying straight for him. Wright slammed on the brakes, and the cherub, lacking time to adjust its course, collided with the police-style spotlight attached to the front window post. Wings abuzz, it skidded across the front hood of the SUV, the chrome rim of the spotlight lodged atop its head like a crooked, jaunty halo.

Wright accelerated as Bryan pulled his head back in. There was a crash from behind, and he and Suzanne were peppered with flying fragments of glass. He brushed the glass out of his hair and twisted to see what had happened. He was constrained by his shoulder harness, but he managed to turn far enough to see more chaotically buzzing wings.

"There's a cherub in here!" he shouted.

"And another one's coming in!" Suzanne said over the whistling wind. "It's crawling through the window."

"College boy!" Wright yelled. Staring straight ahead he stretched an arm over the front seat to hand Bryan his pistol.

"The gas tank is underneath the back cargo area. Don't shoot down. Keep them off us so I can drive. I'm going to try to get to the Jacobsens," he said and sped up.

"They're getting out," Suzanne warned.

Bryan unfastened his seatbelt with one hand and turned to face the back. The two invading cherubs had their bundled-up comrade in their arms and were trying to leave through the frame of the shattered back window. With each holding an end of the bundled cherub, they were too big to get through the opening at the same time. Bryan thumbed off the safety and raised the gun to fire.

"Shit!" His arm was still entangled in the shoulder strap that had not fully retracted. Like keystone cops, the cherubs kept frenetically tugging on their bundled colleague, banging into the window frame as they did so. Bryan fought with the stubborn strap. One cherub lost its grip on the bundle, allowing the other to exit. As the second cherub followed, Bryan brought the gun up. sighted along the barrel, but decided not to fire.

"Why didn't you shoot it?" Wright called out. His free hand was on the rearview mirror. He had been watching the entire fiasco as he drove.

"What was the point? They were out of the SUV. I think they attacked us only to rescue their buddy."

He didn't say that he had hesitated shooting the cherub because its chubby butt reminded him of a baby's. Stupid, he knew.

"Then it must have been important."

"You couldn't shoot it either."

"I wanted it alive. As it was a kamikaze attack, I think that was the issue: that we had a live one to investigate. They didn't want us to have it."

Bryan was about to tell him he was full of shit, that he had already admitted he couldn't shoot it because it had called him ***father,*** but Laura was shaking her head at him.

Let it go. Just let it go.

"Makes sense," he said but didn't mean it.

Suzanne reached over and re-buckled his seatbelt and kissed him on the cheek. Laura smiled at them. But was sadness in her eyes?

Bryan kept the pistol for the rest of the drive. They all scanned the sky and the brush lining the roadside to the Jacobsen manse. But there were no further ambushes. Wright parked the SUV under the walnut tree next to Uncle Robert's green Land Rover.

They got out and started toward the house. The sky remained clear of either cherubs or the larger angel/human hybrids.

Laura hung back, staring at the Land Rover, a puzzled look on her face.

"What's wrong?" Bryan asked.

"It's the Land Rover," she said and reached over to run her hand over the smooth, glossy emerald green paint.

"What about it?"

"Uncle Robert never drove it. He preferred his bicycle."

"So?"

"It has been parked here under that tree, its paint flaking and its tires rotting, for years. I remember it that way just a week or so ago."

Wright came back and stood by Laura's side.

"You're right. I was out here just yesterday and it was a heap – a very expensive heap. Like Laura, he ran his hand across a bright fender. "Now it's like just out of the showroom."

The hinges of the heavy oak front door squeaked as Sophia Blackstone stepped out on the porch.

"What are y'all standing out there and gawking at that old crate for?" she said. "Come on in. You're late and the vegetarian chili is getting cold."

As usual Sophia was a contradiction – intellectual and homey at the same time, sexy with red stiletto high heels and a blue denim miniskirt, but Martha Stewart-ish in her lacy white blouse and white apron trimmed with daisies.

Laura ran ahead and bounced up the steps to the porch to give her aunt a hug.

"What's a matter, child?" Sophia said, hugging her back. In one hand, she had a large wooden ladle stained red with what must be chili sauce. Bryan was suddenly hungry.

"I thought you might be dead," Laura said, "Like, like. . ."

"Like your uncle?"

"Yes," Laura sobbed.

"Well, don't you fret so, my dear. Around here, dead isn't what it used to be. Is it, John Wright?"

"No ma'am, you've got me there," Wright said in respectful tone.

"And I see you've got another reborn soul with you as Uncle Robert told me you would," she said, nodding toward Suzanne.

"What? He's not really dead? It was a dream, wasn't it?" Laura said.

Bryan wanted to ask Laura what she was talking about, but Sophia said, "Yes and no, my dear." She looked at the sky, hands on her hips.

"These clear azure blue skies and nice little white clouds–don't they look a little too perfect? But as pretty blue as these skies are, they tend to hatch nasty little cupids at a moment's notice. Now y'all come inside. We'll talk about all this over food and hot coffee."

With her arm around Laura's shoulders, Sophia led them inside, through the vestibule and down a hallway to the large dining room. There they found serving dishes sitting on the huge mahogany table. A large crock of steaming chili, a heaping plate of cornbread, a coffee carafe, a bowl of assorted fruit, plates, silverware and cups were all laid out buffet-style at one end.

The table was long enough to accommodate the food at one end and six chairs at the other. Bryan found himself at the head of the line, and he shuffled Suzanne ahead of him. Had she eaten since he had dug her out of the woodpile? He didn't think so.

Overhead was the panoramic mural of a turn-of-the-century harvest scene that Sophia had painted on the ceiling. It really was quite good, rivaling some museum works. All sorts of planting scenes were displayed, collage-style. He had been in the beautiful room before, but something had changed. Now the faces of some of the painted figures look vaguely familiar. Was it just that he hadn't noticed before?

Suzanne ladled some chili into her plate, and he did the same. Vegetarian chili con carne seemed like an oxymoron, but he was so hungry he didn't care. Though it didn't quite look like the chili he was used to, its aroma was delicious. There were a couple of varieties of beans and fragments of what looked suspiciously like hamburger along with chunks of what he hoped were tomatoes. There were also some white cubes he couldn't identify. But this was no time to be picky. He grabbed a couple chunks of cornbread and a banana and sat down beside Suzanne. How long had it been since he'd had any fresh fruit beside locally grown peaches?

Suzanne hand him her plate, got up, and brought back two mugs of hot coffee.

"No reason to hold to Emily Post," Sophia announced. "Y'all go ahead and start eating. I'll serve myself in a moment."

Bryan didn't recall anyone younger than his departed grandmother referring to Emily Post, and he wondered just how old Sophia really was. But no one had to tell him twice to eat. Bryan tasted a spoonful of the chili. It tasted as delicious as it smelled. He relaxed as Suzanne crumbed some cornbread on her chili and took a dainty bite.

She smiled at him and said, "I was afraid I was going to do a vampire thing and not be able to eat real food."

John Wright sat down on the other side of the table. "That's some banana," he said.

"You want it?" Bryan said, feeling friendly toward him now. *Must be the bonding of the weird.*

"Thanks, but there are more in the bowl," he said. "I just wonder where Sophia got them and the other fruit. It's fresh. The stems are even green."

"So?"

"There hasn't been a produce truck come into Creedance for weeks. We're a few thousand miles too far north to grow fresh bananas. I thought it was fake fruit at first."

Bryan peeled the banana and took a bit. "Must be manna – or

rather, banana– from heaven."

Laura sat down beside Wright. She had only fruit and cornbread on her plate. She reached up and touched the back of Wright's head.

"What?" he said.

"It grew back already," she said."

"What grew back? My head?"

"No, silly. You lost a patch of scalp back there on the highway when you two *boys* had your little scuffle. Now the hair has grown back over it."

Wright tapped the spot with two fingers as if he were checking a cantaloupe for ripeness. "Nothing surprises me anymore," he said. "We're all living in a dream."

Sophia coughed ceremoniously and sat to Laura's right. She carried two plates, one she set in front of herself, the other at the empty chair at the head of the table.

"The question is, Sheriff Wright, do we want to wake from the dream?" she said.

Wright said something but his words were mumbled by a mouthful of chili.

"What was that?"

"What I said . . ." He took a noisy slurp of coffee. ". . . is it's your chili dinner that is a dream come true."

"That's not what he said," Laura said. "He said he rather stay in the dream, if this is all a dream, 'cause if he woke up, he might wake up dead."

"I said all that?"

"You were thinking it."

"Are you reading my mind now?"

Laura didn't answer him but continued to explain to the group around the table. "You know, like in *The Matrix*, he would have chosen the blue pill not the red pill. Or did I get that backwards?"

"I have no idea what you're talking about – blue pill, red pill?" Wright said. "I almost said 'wake up dead,' but I meant it as a joke, then thought I might disturb Ms. Zimmerman." He took another sip of coffee. "I'm over it, myself. It is what it is. You know what I mean?"

"You're taking every day, every moment as a gift, aren't you Mr. Wright?" Sophia said.

"You surprise me, Ms. Blackstone. But yes, I've felt more alive these past few days than I ever remember feeling before – at least more alive than I did since being a teenager."

"How about the rest of you?" Sophia said. "Would you rather stay in the dream, or wake from it?"

"You're not going to tell us this is a dream or that the angels are astral projecting themselves into our world again?" Bryan asked. He was thinking of the time, only a few days ago, when Asbeel the archangel had astral-projected right into this room. The scene had been chaotic, with Asbell manifesting himself as a small, screeching tornado, the air electrically charged by his presence.

"And we're all here again except Dr. Jenkins and Uncle Robert. And we're all changed somehow, except maybe you, Aunt Sophia," Laura mused, remembering the same scene.

Bryan remembered Jenkins throwing a fundamentalist fit. He wondered where Sophia was leading them.

"Something akin to that," Sophia said. "And who says I haven't been transformed by all that's happened too? But yes, things are a little more complicated this time." She stroked her chin. The gesture reminded Bryan of something Uncle Robert.

"Perhaps," Sophia said, "it was more complicated before, and Uncle Robert and I only saw half the truth."

"Where is Uncle Robert today?" Bryan asked, looking to the empty place setting.

"He'll make his appearance soon, I imagine," Sophia said.

Laura choked, and Wright patted her on the back. Her eyes watering, she looked questioningly at her aunt.

"All will be explained in good time, dear," Sophia said.

"My love, don't you think now's as good a time as ever?" Uncle Robert's voice startled Bryan; he had not seen the old man enter the room. He was standing in one corner of the room, near a ceiling-high bookcase.

"Come sit down, dear. I've set you a plate."

Uncle Robert strode over to the head of the table and pulled his chair back. He was dressed in one of his standard costumes, a gray tweed jacket and blue bib overalls. Usually the old man was rumpled-looking. Today his jacket was clean-pressed, and his complexion healthier-looking than Bryan had ever seen him.

"Does this mean, we're all . . .?" Laura said.

Wright looked shocked to see the old man, too, despite what he'd said just a minute ago about nothing surprising him anymore.

"Just a minute, dear," Sophia said to Laura. "Let your uncle sit down."

Uncle Robert seated himself in the chair at the head of the table and brought a heaping a spoonful of chili to his mouth while everyone looked on.

Wait a minute. Sophia had set an empty plate and bowl where Uncle Robert was sitting. How had the bowl gotten filled with chili?

Uncle Robert looked content as he tasted the chili. "Heavenly! I can taste all the spices, and there's texture too. Amazing. You are powerful, indeed, my love," he said.

"Laura is an emerging power, I believe. But there's something very powerful indeed about the young man too," Sophia said.

Everyone looked at Sophia, surprised, but no one seemed as surprised as Laura. It gradually dawned on Bryan that he was the young man she spoke of, but was too busy wolfing down the chili to give it much though. Laura was quicker on the uptake.

"Who, me? What are you talking about?" she said.

"I agree," Uncle Robert said as he buttered a piece of cornbread. "Though I can't quite see all the connections."

"I want to know what you mean by 'illusion,'" Bryan said. "Are you saying none of this . . ." He waved his hand over the table. ". . . is real?"

"Or that none of *us* are real?" Wright said.

"Well . . ." Sophia paused. "Simon, you're in a better position to answer that than I."

Uncle Robert cleared his throat. "The answer is yes and no, Bryan. And Wright, we're all real after a fashion, but some of us here at the table are more real than others."

"Oh God, here we go again. Is Mr. Asbeel here again?

"No, he was one of the angels that translated to human/angel hybrid form. You know that. Samiazaz is the only original archangel left on Earth, and he's still stuck in the mud of Lost Lake, though not for long, as the water level is dropping rapidly." He took another heaping spoon of chili, chewed and swallowed. "Damn, this chili is to die for," he laughed.

"Please don't joke about that, Uncle Robert," Laura said.

"First a little recap," Uncle Robert continued. "We all had a very similar meeting here in this very room only a few days ago."

Had it only been a few days? It seemed like months, but yes, it was the day before Marshall and Wright had tried to blow up the angel saucer.

"Knock, knock," came a familiar voice.

"Okay, I'll bite," Uncle Robert said. "Who's there?"

"It's me," Dr. Jenkins said, walking into the room and not taking the bait

"I think missed your straightline," Uncle Robert said.

"What?" Jenkins said.

"Never mind the silly old man," Sophia said. "Though I should have expected you'd be drawn here, sir, I still find your presence a surprise. But now that you're here, please get yourself a plate."

"Don't mind if I do."

"Now attendance of the Citizens of Creedance Conference on the Angel Invasion, the CCCAI, is complete. We're all here, all six of us." Uncle Robert said as Jenkins filled a bowl with chili.

Bryan laughed in spite of himself, then turned to Suzanne and explained that the 'Citizens of Creedance Conference on the Angel Invasion,' was the name for the ad hoc group that had met here before. It had then been composed of six people now present: Laura, Sophia, Wright, Uncle Robert, Jenkins and himself. They hadn't had time to come up with a proper name for the committee, one they could make an acronym of, but they'd only that one meeting. The meeting had been led by Sophia, with Uncle Robert adding exposition. The same formula was being followed now.

"Should I leave?" Suzanne said. "Is this a private meeting?"

"Oh, child, not at all," Sophia said. "Consider yourself part of the family."

"Thank you," Suzanne said. "I really mean it. Thank you."

"Don't thank us yet," Uncle Robert said. "You may not like what you learn here."

"I think I have some clues already," Suzanne said.

"Do you, young lady?"

"Simon," Sophia said in an admonishing tone.

"What? Oh, the 'young lady' part?"

Sophia nodded.

"Well, I don't mean it in a disparaging or patronizing way," he said to Suzanne. "'Lady' used to mean a woman of high moral integrity. And you certainly are younger that I think I ever was. It was meant as a compliment, not in a patronizing way."

"I'm not sure if I fit the 'high moral integrity' part," Suzanne said. "I've done things in the past twenty-four hours that wouldn't make me much of a lady, but you know what?"

"Suzanne, I don't think . . ." Bryan started.

"No, don't hus me. I want to get it out in the open. I don't care if loving Bryan is wrong. I've never known love like this. I didn't suspect such a thing existed, much less that I was capable of feeling it. I don't want it to end."

"Ms. Zimmerman, please," Uncle Robert said. "That's not what I was referring to. I have no intentions of passing any sort of moral judgment on you. No, I was suggesting that the very fact that we're all here in this place has something to do more with our characters - the fundamental elements that make us each who we are — and our sense of some sort of ethical absolutes, than by chance circumstance."

They were all silenced by this proclamation.

"That was the good news," Uncle Robert said. "The bad news is that I think all of our minds are being manipulated by an unseen force. I'm not a C.S. Lewis fan, but I think some hideous strength is at work here, right now."

"Mmmh hmm," Sophia said.

"Then we're lost," Jenkins said. "We can't compete against some higher power."

"I didn't say it was a higher power," Uncle Robert said. "Quite the contrary, I believe it is a denizen of the lower levels."

Jenkins cleared his throat, an unpleasant sound. "Whatever, it sounds like something that's beyond the ken of the puny human mind. I suspect we've all been severely tested over the past few days. I know I have. I've kept my head above water, but I've had to throw out a lot presuppositions of laws I once thought were carved in stone by a loving God. Worse, I used to feel that when I prayed, someone was listening. Now all I've got left is my faith in myself." He scratched his head, either embarrassed or confused. His expressions were usually easy to read, but now his face was a mask. He looked at each of them turned as if expecting confirmation. Getting none from any of them, he paused, shrugged, then spooned in another mouthful of chili.

Bryan noted that though Jenkins' tone was morbid, he had a youthful glow of health. He wore the same clothes he always wore underneath his white lab coat – a dark, not-too-clean, wrinkled sports coat, khaki slacks and a wrinkled shirt – but he seemed taller and broader of shoulder. Was he undead as well? Bryan had come to feel he could sense who was undead and who was not. But he had been slow to recognize Suzanne as being undead. And Wright too; both the sheriff and Suzanne seemed different from the other undead roaming around Creedance. It was a quality he couldn't put his finger on. But Jenkins seemed another case entirely.

"I agree with you about the manipulation part," Uncle Robert said. "We have all been led along some strange garden path by the archangels, myself included."

"Would that be a path to heaven or hell?" Jenkins said. "That's what I want to know."

"What do you feel it is?" Sophia said.

Jenkins held up a hand while he finished chewing and swallowing his bite of chili, then said, "I know I should be terrified about the loss of my immortal soul, but the truth is that like the rest of you, I've recently come to feel so good physically that it's hard to not be happy. All my aches and pains are gone."

"You had a heart condition, too, didn't you?" Laura asked.

"I was bad off, ready for an early grave. I was surprised Mr. Marshall exited this mortal coil before I did. Now I feel fit as a fiddle."

"Same here," Wright said. "Better than fit. I don't remember feeling this healthy even when I was in my teens or twenties."

"How about you, Ms. Zimmerman?" Uncle Robert asked.

"Call me Suzanne, please."

"All right, Suzanne. Do you feel younger, healthier, too?"

"Not much, not physically. My ear grew back." Suzanne recounted how her ear had been missing, apparently bitten off, when Bryan had found her in the woodpile, and how it had grown back overnight.

"But what is really amazing is how I feel emotionally. That's what's really changed. My outlook has changed. My childhood wasn't happy. I was miserable. My father and mother – well, I don't know if any of you understand how a parent can destroy that part of you that allows you to be happy."

"I can understand; believe me, I can understand," Laura said.

"Ben used to call me his black hole, and before you all start coughing, it wasn't a racial remark. He said I was like a collapsed star at times, and I'd suck in all the energy and light in the room. I think he was right, but that part of me, the sadness and despair that I thought all there was to life – that's gone now."

"You've been born again?" Jenkins asked.

"Not in the way I think you mean it," Suzanne said. "I was never very religious; I'm still not. But the world seems filled – that's not the word I want."

"Maybe imbued," Bryan said.

"That's it. The world is imbued with meaning. Everything seems alive; anything is possible." She looked at Uncle Robert for approval.

"We really don't know much more about the archangels than we did the last time we met, do we?" Bryan said.

"You knew, or thought you knew, something about what had happened when we talked in the saucer," Laura said. "Or did I dream that?"

"You were sort of dreaming," Uncle Robert said.

Laura let out a sigh of relief.

"But so was I, and we did talk."

"Oh," Laura said, her voice trembling with emotion. "Does that mean you really are dead?"

"Dead? Yes, this body you see here is not a physical body as you might actually think of being physical in the usual sense. If you reached over now to touch me as a test, as you're probably thinking of doing now, you'd see."

Laura pulled her chair out from the table. To get to the head of the table, she had to walk behind Wright. As her hand brushed his shoulder, Wright patted her hand encouragingly. Evidently, as with Jenkins, the changes in the man went more than skin deep.

When she got to Uncle Robert, she reached out to touch him, but her hand paused, shaking, inches away from his bearded chin.

"What's the matter? Chicken?" Uncle Robert said and reached up to take her hand.

"Ouch! Don't squeeze so hard!" Laura said.

"Sorry. I didn't mean to hurt you, but I wanted to make a point. Now give this old man a nice hug."

She leaned over and hugged him, tears streaming down her face.

"What does this mean, Uncle Robert?" she said. "Are we all dead like you?"

"Again, the answer is complicated. Remember what I told you in the saucer, on the alien desert floor?"

"You said I was real; that is, the body I was in was the physical body I had known in the normal world. However, the 'you' I was talking to was an astral projection or an etheric double. I think they're not quite the same thing. And that the corpse in the big storm drain was your physical body."

"I'm pretty sure that's what's going on."

"Pretty sure?" Wright said.

"As sure as any of us can be about anything since we are all in alien territory."

"So is that the way it is now? Me in an ordinary body, you astral projecting?"

"No, not in this case. Sophia, care to explain?"

"This is not my physical body; this is not the physical plane," she said.

"And this?" Laura said, patting herself on her chest. "Is an astral projection too?"

"Yes, we're all equal here in that respect," Uncle Robert said. "We're all astral projecting at this moment. We're not physical in the usual sense."

"Wait a minute here," Jenkins spoke up. "You mean we're all dreaming?"

"Not exactly," Uncle Robert said.

"Stop saying 'not exactly.' If we're not dreaming, then maybe you mean we're being dreamed up by the angels?"

Uncle Robert was silent.

"Well, for the record, I don't buy any of it," Jenkins said.

"How did you get here, Dr. Jenkins?" Laura said.

"What do you mean, how did I get here?"

"I don't see your car out there." She pointed toward the large picture window. Wright's SUV was in sight, as was Uncle Robert's mysteriously restored Land Rover, but no other vehicle.

Jenkins looked where she pointed. "Well, well, – You know I don't rightly remember. I guess I'm baffled," he said. But he didn't look baffled; he looked amused.

"Doctor, what's the last thing you remember?" Bryan said, feeling sorry for the old man now.

"Walking through the door over there."

"I mean before that."

"I was at the clinic. I was physically tired but my mind was wide awake. I laid down on the couch in the front foyer and – okay, maybe I am dreaming, a particularly vivid dream. But how do I know that I'm not dreaming all of you, all of this?"

"Believe so if it makes you feel more comfortable," Sophia said.

"But the real issue is that some us here have physical bodies to go back to, and some us here don't."

* * *

21.

And She is Now Powerful Indeed

Laura.

"Dead like me?" Uncle Robert said.

"What do you mean, like you?" Jenkins said.

Jenkins' calm demeanor surprised Laura. He may have confessed to having an enlightenment, but in her experience, Jenkins got angry when confronted with evidence that contradicted his preconceptions. Despite his mellowness and their collaboration on the saucer, she felt mildly repelled by him now. Why?

"I don't have a physical body to return to," Uncle Robert said with patience. "That is, not on the plane that you all are used to calling physical."

"Laura tried to explain this to me earlier, but I'm still not getting it," John said.

"I know it's a big leap of faith for all of you except perhaps for Laura, who's had an out-of-body experience before," Uncle Robert said.

"Out-of-body experience?" John asked.

"A large percentage of people have them," Uncle Robert said. "And it's more than just floating about the room watching their sleeping bodies. They journey to other planes, visit departed relatives, learn about their past lives, and encounter spiritual guides. The majority of westerners, including me, must be trained to have the experience. Sorry, I'm lecturing again."

"That's all right, lecture away. Marguerite used to have those dreams," John said. "She would wake up screaming in the night."

"Sounds like Marguerite's dreams were something different from what we're talking about here. These experiences are usually highly pleasant," Uncle Robert said. Then he turned to Jenkins. "I bet you're going to tell us that you've never accepted the occult explanation for the experience."

"No, I don't," Jenkins said, sitting up straighter. "And I would advise everyone here to not allow themselves to be caught up in this group delusion. It's counter-productive bullshit."

"*Folie à plusieurs?*" Sophia asked.

"Beg your pardon?" Jenkins said.

"It's a French phrase; it means a 'shared madness of many.'"

"That's what I said, isn't it? This kind of thinking is contagious. And it can be harmful." "So this is all a dream? A shared dream? A sort of sleeping mass hysteria?" John said. "Is that what you're saying?"

"Exactly," Jenkins said.

"Hmm," Uncle Robert said. "So you're saying we're lost in an illusion, and that we should do nothing. Just let it play out?"

"Yes," Jenkins said. "I'll wake up soon. Find myself in my bed, feeling silly and so will all of you."

"Laura? What do you think? Are we all dreams being dreamt by Dr. Jenkins?"

"Not exactly," she said and laughed. "What Samiazaz told me was that we were all dreamers, dreaming ourselves and each other."

"Samiazaz? The last archangel?" Byran said.

"The one and only."

"You told me about this earlier," John said. "But I was confused. Were you really inside the saucer or just dreaming?"

"It was hard to sort out at first, but I was there both physically and in a dream. I was awake and physically there – in my *real* body when I met Uncle Robert. But earlier, I was asleep in the saucer. The cherubs kidnapped me and took me there. While I was asleep and dreaming, I met and talked with Samiazaz in some sort of alternate reality that just appeared to be inside the saucer."

She took a deep breath, feeling like she was working out a mind-numbing algebraic thought-problem in high school. "I know it's confusing. I find it confusing myself. But Samiazaz told me he was still stuck in the mud at the bottom of Lost Lake and dreaming himself. I think he willed the cherubs to bring me to the saucer so he could talk to me in the dream state. Only he didn't exactly call it a dream."

"That's right. You told me Samiazaz called it dreamtime, which is an interesting parallel to Australian aborigine myth," Uncle Robert said. "What else did he tell you?"

"Assuming he really did tell me, and it wasn't a dream?"

"Let's assume just that for now."

"He said dreamtimes of our species, of our worlds, overlapped there in the saucer. Do you think he was trying to trick me?"

"No, I think it was a lapse on his part," Uncle Robert said.

"Lapse? Why do you say that?" Jenkins said.

"Because he revealed a weakness in his powers. A limit to his manipulation of us."

"How so?" Jenkins sounded angry again.

Before Uncle Robert could answer, Bryan asked, "And how was it you were there in the saucer, Uncle Robert? Did the cherubs bring you there too?"

"In a fashion," Uncle Robert said. "First, they murdered me by dropping me from on high into Lost Lake."

"What!" Wright said. "Laura told me it was your ethereal double she met there!"

"Yes," Uncle Robert said. "The best I can reconstruct is my ethereal double was drawn there to my corpse, which had been sucked into the saucer as water drained in from Lost Lake."

"So you're dead? Really dead?" John said. "Not . . ."

"Not a resurrected undead as you and Suzanne are?"

John sighed. "Yes, why...?"

"Are you sure, Uncle Robert?"

"I'm as sure as I can be sure of anything in this realm. But why my fate was different, I can't be sure. Perhaps it had some connection to the saucer. I've read quite a bit about the occult, as you all might have gathered, and neither your fate nor my exception is discussed in any of the literature. My physical body may have not actually died until after it was sucked into the saucer. However, I think that it's a good bet that saucer is the center of the disturbance, but it might not be the cause."

"What is the cause, then?" Wright said.

"Samiazaz, of course."

"How do you figure?" Wright said. "Does it have something to do with you being here before? I mean *there* before, I mean? Crap, I'm still confused."

"Yes, both are a possibilities," Uncle Robert said. "I'll get to that in a bit, but first let me finish my thought. Sophia and I believe that the archangels are denizens of one of the lower astral planes, and somehow the saucer allowed the incursion of their astral bodies – their design bodies – into our physical plane. Now everything is mish-mashed: Our physical plane and their design-body plane are commingled. Ordinary rules of reality or super-reality don't apply anymore, at least not consistently. That's only our theory, by the way."

"But it's a good theory," Sophia said. "Like the theory of gravity, it accounts for what we've all been experiencing. And as to why Samiazaz is the cause and not the saucer? Think about it. As the lake drained and the water covering him became shallower, the disturbances increased."

"I'm sorry, but I'm still confused," Suzanne said. "Where are we now? Is this a dream, a higher plane, or reality? Am I real or unreal?"

"It's both; you're both," Sophia said. She got up and went around the table, warming up everyone's coffee from a stainless-steel carafe.

"As Samiazaz told Laura," she continued. "The archangels' dreamtime and ours overlap. To the archangels, our reality, our normal walk-around, eating, living and breathing physical reality, is an astral plane – a reality at a different vibrational state from theirs. That's why they can do all the things they do in our physical plane, such as defy the laws of physics, fly about, change shape, and so on."

"I could fly when I projected to the astral plane," Laura said. "You know, that time years ago when you and Uncle Robert hypnotized me."

"Yes, I remember very well," Uncle Robert said. "And we were going to continue your training, but then you started getting stoned all the time."

"Really?" Laura said. "Is that why you stopped?"

"The astral plane is a safe place normally, but if you project under the influence of drugs you can wind up in places where you could be taken advantage of by lower beings," Uncle Robert said. "You were totally out of control for quite some time, you know."

"Whatever. That was then. This is now," she said. "I remember the projection seeming so real at the time that I didn't doubt it. Later, I wondered if it was an illusion. Or if you had drugged me."

Uncle Robert just shook his head.

"So this is not real?" Bryan said, blowing on his cup of coffee to cool it. "I'm imagining the smell, warmth and taste of this coffee and the chili?"

"It's not that it's not real - the real meal deal – but that it's a different reality, with laws peculiar to it," Uncle Robert said. "If you're more comfortable with conjectural science than the occult, you can think of the astral planes as alternate universes. It's not really quite the same concept, as by occult theory, we humans can exist and be conscious on both the physical and astral planes at the same time, though most humans only experience it in their dreams and don't count it as real – at least modern humans don't."

"There are beings, some of them humans, who only exist on what we would call the astral planes, or alternate universe, if you will," Sophia said.

"Think of the astral plane as a world with a different vibrational state, one that we can visit mentally," Uncle Robert said.

"But it's a place where thoughts can have substance. And if you believe the mind or the soul exists after death, then it's not too hard to accept the astral planes, one of which we are inhabiting now, can greatly resemble the physical plane," Sophia said.

"And by some philosophies, these planes are more *real* than the physical plane because the mind lives on here. Myself being a case in point," Uncle Robert said.

"There's an old occult adage: 'Thought is action on the astral plane,'" Sophia said.

"Uncle Robert's Land Rover!" Laura exclaimed.

"What about it?" Uncle Robert said.

"It's brand new here."

"So?" he said. "What's the point of having a projected reality with all the same broken-down junk as in the physical plane?"

"You thought it as restored, so it's restored here, new paint and all? I'm impressed," Bryan said.

"Well, don't be impressed with this old astral fart," he said. "This meal and this version of the mansion are Sophia's doing."

"And the fresh fruit? That's your mind at work too?" Wright said.

"No, Simon is being modest. That was a surprise for me, as well," Sophia said. "I think Simon's responsible for that too."

"Bananas and bright shiny Land Rovers; these are a few of my favorite things. But to be honest, neither was a conscious action. I just always felt so guilty about letting the Rover go to pot, and I've really missed bananas since the Fall," Uncle Robert said. "Besides, bananas contain something that acts as an antidepressant, and I was pretty blue at first, being dead and all."

"Hah!" Jenkins said. "If you all are such advanced creatures, why don't you just imagine yourself not depressed?"

Uncle Robert ignored the doctor. "You see, this reality is a mutually shared consensus. All of us here are contributing to constructing this reality, and though Sophia and I have a lot to do with the accouterments, as I said before, I believe Laura, though she's a novice, is strongly influencing this reality too. I think you're a sort of anchor. And there's something about the young man, as I said, but he seems out of my reach. It's odd…"

"What do you mean by 'anchor,' and what about Bryan?" Laura said. When she looked to Bryan he had leaned back in his chair and appeared to be asleep. Too much astral chili perhaps.

"'Anchor' may not be the best word," Sophia said. "Separately, your uncle and I found ourselves drawn here. I would guess Bryan and Suzanne were on their way here before they met up with you and the sheriff. Am I correct?"

"You're right, but how about everyone stop trying to pin that badge on me? Just call me John," he said. "I resign as sheriff. I'm just as deep in this as any of you. Maybe deeper." Laura took his hand as he spoke.

Sophia smiled at both of them and continued. "Also, there's the fact that Samiazaz invited you to merge with him and disclosed that he will soon be able to be active on the physical plane as the waters recede, which means you are in some way a special case."

"Then why would he allow us to consult here and now if he's so powerful?" Laura said. "Couldn't he just send a flock of cherubs or the human/angel hybrids to disrupt us?"

"Good question," Uncle Robert said. "But I don't think he's in full control of the cherubs. From what we've all described, some of them seem to be projected thoughts of the human/angels, not archangels. As the creatures are thought-formed, our minds affect them, too, warping their shape, projecting our guilt and fear upon them."

Bryan stretched his arms over his head and yawned. "If they are merely thought-formed, how did they pick up your physical body and drop it into the lake?" Bryan said. "Wouldn't they only be able to do those kinds of things while we're on this astral level?"

Had he been really sleeping or just faking it?

"That's why it makes sense only if you accept the theory that the saucer is causing a commingling of the planes," Uncle Robert said.

"Or we could go back to the idea that this all an incredibly vivid dream, and that we're all sleeping somewhere," Jenkins said.

"We could, but do all of you really believe that a dream could seem as real as this?" Uncle Robert said. "It's a choice each of us has to make. It's easier for me to believe this is an alternate reality because under Sophia's guidance I've visited it before many times. So I can imagine how alien you find the concept."

"It still sounds just like so much bullshit to me," Jenkins said.

"Two days ago I would have agreed with you," Wright said. "But now, I want them to be right. I have so much to lose if you're wrong and this is a dream."

"But how do we. . .?" Laura started only to be interrupted by Jenkins: "You all can fly away on broomsticks if you want," he said. "I'm going to stick with my original judgment: It's bullshit."

He stood up as if to leave but found his way blocked by Sophia, stainless-steel coffee carafe still in hand.

"But how do we fight a being as powerful as Samiazaz?" Laura said.

Jenkins took a step to the right, but at the same time Sophia stepped to her left blocking his way.

"We don't fight him per se," Sophia said, placing a hand on Jenkins' shoulder. Was it a trick of perspective or was Sophia now considerably taller than the doctor? Laura couldn't see Jenkins' face because his back was to her, but she imagined he was scowling.

"As impressive as it seems, the archangels' real power is not flight or great strength or the ability to change their physical form," Sophia said, one hand still on Jenkins' shoulder, the other holding the coffee carafe at a curious position, her elbow crooked, as if she were about to punch him with it. "We can fly on broomsticks or skim the aqua blue skies on magic carpets here in this realm if we believe we can. Frankly, I don't know why we haven't magical things already; it may be because of Samiazaz's influence."

"Another name for the astral plane is the 'realm of illusion,'" Uncle Robert said. "Not because it's more illusionary than the physical plane but because of its protean nature, a place of mind over matter."

"If Samiazaz is so powerful, why doesn't he just do as he pleases?" Laura said. "If he wanted to implant his homunculus in me against my will – rape me – there's nothing I could do about it. He can be ten feet tall if he wants. Leap tall buildings, all that."

Jenkins remained curiously immobile, neither trying to shrug off Sophia's hand nor sitting back down.

Sophia continued to talk as if nothing strange were playing out between her and the doctor. "Perhaps it's because even here there are laws," she said. "There are other planes beyond the astral, according to occult theory, and those planes are inhabited by more advanced beings. We've heard them mention the Dreaming God, for example, and there was Bryan's vision of the Blue God, which I think has some portent. The archangels may be able to create a temporary suspension of the laws here, but ultimately they are bound by them – just as we are bound by the ordinary rules of physics and causality when we're in the physical plane."

"You see," Uncle Robert said, "one of our original mistakes was to think of the archangels as higher beings. But they're not. By their own admission they are natives of the lower realms of the astral plane. They are really fallen beings."

"There are different levels?" Bryan said. "Levels within the level? Now I'm really confused."

Bryan stared at Sophia and Dr. Jenkins as he spoke. Suzanne was watching too. The room was charged with an energy focused around Sophia and the doctor.

"It's not that hard to visualize. Just don't think of the astral plane as being either above or below the physical plane. It's not like layers of an onion," Sophia said.

"It's neither heaven nor hell," Uncle Robert said.

"But it can seem like either, depending upon your outlook," she said.

"I repeat," Jenkins said. "Bullshit! You're all acting like idiots." But he remained frozen in place.

"That'll be about enough of you," Sophia said, and she drew back her arm back and walloped Dr. Jenkins full force with the carafe, which made a dull *doink* when it connected with his head.

That's rather harsh, Laura thought. He's an asshole and there had been times when she wanted to slap the good doctor upside the head. But hitting him with a stainless steel carafe still seemed like overkill.

But Sophia must not have thought her initial blow harsh enough. She drew back and whacked the doctor again. This time the thud was louder and the lid popped off the carafe, spraying coffee over everyone at the table and making them jump up from their seats. The impact threw the doctor's head so far to one side that it seemed to lay on his shoulder, but his head immediately popped back up as if his neck was spring-loaded. As Sophia brought the carafe back for another swing Laura could see one whole side of the carafe was caved in. Broken glass rattled about within the carafe as Sophia swung a third time.

Must be a glass-lined thermos, Laura thought, then realized how absurd this thought was. *Sophia has just bashed in the head of the doctor, and here I am thinking what a waste of a good thermos. And stranger still, it wasn't even a real thermos but what? An astral thermos?*

She checked around the table: Everyone except Uncle Robert was looking on in astonishment.

John shook off the spell first and started toward the two, apparently to intercede.

Always the cop, always the hero, no matter what he claims, Laura thought.

"Wait a minute, Ms. Blackstone," he said. Uncle Robert got up too and blocked John's advance.

"Let this play out," Uncle Robert said.

"Astral plane or not," John said. "It's assault."

"Trust me," Uncle Robert said. "It's not as it first seems. Few things here are."

Which seemed an understatement to Laura. Only moments before, Sophia had towered over the doctor in her high heels. Now Jenkins seemed a head taller.

Bryan must have noticed it too, for he stepped backward, knocking over his chair.

Jenkins grew taller still. His shoulders broadened and his hair, which had darkened since his time in the saucer, quickly turned salt and pepper, then went completely snow-white. It wasn't Jenkins who stood there now. A shiver ran up Laura's back. *Could it be who she suspected?*

Because of the entity's increased height, Sophia had to step closer to keep her hand on its shoulder. Sophia's hand glowed iridescent yellow all the way to her wrist.

"Let me go, you mystic monkey," the creature said, still using Jenkins' voice.

In answer, Sophia up-ended the contents of the carafe over its shoulders.

Instead of a few cups of black coffee, what poured out what looked like a gallon of crystal clear water. And it kept on flowing, gallons and more, much too much liquid to be contained within the quart-sized carafe. The water – if that's what it was – washed over the creature's dark sports jacket, stripping it away as if it were acid. But it didn't boil and steam as acid would have. Instead, it seemed to be really just water washing away a thin skim of paint. The substance of the coat ran in streams, revealing marble-white muscles. As the rivulets of color ran down the creature's legs, the trousers and shoes likewise dissolved into a muddy goo at its feet.

"Samiazaz!" Laura said, finally able to vocalize her fears.

Sophia took her hand off the archangel's shoulders and stepped away. Freed from the constraints of the illusionary garments, Samiazaz expanded to at least seven feet tall. His shoulder blades popped through heavy muscles and unfolded like some magic puzzle to fall in a full-length shroud of nearly translucent wings.

Samiazaz turned to face the table, his handsome features transfigured with arrogance, his violet eyes shadowed by the overhead light. The Samiazaz that Laura had met before had vacillated between being passive and patronizing. Now there was no mistaking the arrogance of this manifestation. Here was a being who looked upon humans with contempt from across millennium. But as Samiazaz looked at her, Laura thought that his expression softened. More confusing, there was something all too familiar to his features now, a face she had wanted to forget for most of her life – her father's.

"I remain your last chance to escape this limited existence," he said to her. His booming voice filled the entire room. "If you don't act soon, I will be forced to choose someone else."

"Why her?" Uncle Robert demanded. "Why single out my reluctant niece if it is a matter of free will?"

"Because it is destined to be. She is destined to make the choice. She was created, born into your world, so as to provide a vehicle for me," Samiazaz said.

"Now that is bullshit!" Sophia said. "If it's preordained, then there's no room for free will."

"Your human mind is not able to understand such mysteries. It is in the mind of the Dreaming God."

"You're a liar, Samiazaz," Uncle Robert said. "You can't explain because the only will at work here is your selfish need."

"We know you're hiding something," Sophia said. "I command you to tell me why Laura is so crucial to your plan or leave this place and go back to the lower planes"

"You command *me*?" Samiazaz said. The sneer was in his voice not his face.

"Yes, I do – we do," Uncle Robert said, looking to Sophia for reassurance.

"What power do you imagine you have over me?"

"We don't have power, but someone in this room does," Sophia said and pointed toward the ceiling.

Everyone including Samiazaz looked up. To the right of the crystal chandelier, a black cloud coalesced out of nowhere. It boiled and churned, and was illuminated from within by sporadic red flashes. Laura stifled a laugh for it looked like one of the little black storm clouds that plagued Wiley Coyote in the Roadrunner cartoons.

Any moment now, she thought, *it will start raining on Samiazaz and only on Samiazaz. Then it will send out a bolt of lightning and char him black from head to toe.*

The cloud grew to a couple of feet across and became more opaque, so dark it sucked the light from the room.

The black cloud sank lower until it was only inches above Samiazaz's head. Sophia nodded to Uncle Robert, and they both stood back. Samiazaz continued to stare at the cloud, the amused look on his face replaced with fear and loathing.

Here comes the lightning; any moment now. . .

However, instead of shooting forth a lightning bolt, the cloud sprouted a black cord from its midsection. In an eye blink, the cord grew to several feet in length. Samiazaz raised his arms to ward it off, but cord whipped out between his fanning hands and attached itself to his abdomen. Samiazaz then brought up his wings as if to cocoon himself, but it was too late. The cord began undulating. Underneath its surface, fist-sized gulps of white matter rhythmically traveled up the thick, fleshy-looking cord to the cloud. Samiazaz was lifted from his feet and rapidly shrank. First he was man-sized, then half that. The small cloud was sucking up Samiazaz through the umbilical-like cord. Samiazaz shrank to toddler-size, though his proportions were still those of an adult, not a child. The cord grew shorter, withdrawing into the belly of the cloud. A miniature Samiazaz dangled there for a moment, separated from the underbelly of the cloud by a few inches, his arms outstretched, his wings drooping like wet rags. He twisted as the cord continued to retract and reached out his arms to Laura.

"Laura!" he screamed, then he and the cord disappeared within the cloud.

They all watched, slack-jawed as the cloud moved upward and passed through the ceiling, leaving no mark behind.

Bryan was the first to break the silence. "Okay, now I'm really impressed," he said.

Everyone laughed, though a little nervously.

"I'm impressed too – and astounded," Uncle Robert said.

"Me too," Sophia said, and she was looking at Bryan now, thoughtful.

"You were? I thought it was your doing," Uncle Robert said.

"I don't think I was the one who called it forth," Sophia said. "I've read about such manifestations. Yes, I called on the Universal Mind, but I thought I was bluffing."

"Then who?" Uncle Robert said, "Laura?".

"Me?" Laura said. "I didn't do anything but try not to pee in my pants!"

"Hmm. . ." Uncle Robert mused, stroking his chin.

"But you wanted him gone, didn't you, dear?" Sophia said. "If it wasn't you, then you have some powerful friends in this realm."

"Well, yes," Laura said. "When he got that smirk on his face, he reminded me of someone."

"Who? No don't tell me," Sophia said. "You saw your father in him, didn't you?"

Laura paused, resisting the urge to run out of the room. John stepped closer and wrapped an arm around her. Usually at moments like this, when thinking of her father, she would be repelled by the physical touch of anyone, but she found his hug comforting.

"Yes," she said finally.

"I thought I saw it too," Sophia said.

"I wanted him to go to hell," Laura said.

"And that's where you sent him, I think," Uncle Robert said.

"But it wasn't me who did it, I'm sure," she said. "Besides, you said there is no hell."

"Remember, this is a place where the mind is made real," Uncle Robert said. "There are sublevels of this plane that correspond to something akin to the Christian concept of Hell, but it's not a punishment. It's a place of cruelty, darkness and negativity that entirely radiates from the denizen's minds."

"They can visit the higher realms of the astral plane, but most of the time they are stuck in the muck by their own coarse action and thought," Sophia said.

"It's more like karma than punishment. They're there because of their ignorance of the natural laws. But that doesn't mean they can't visit the other levels of the astral plane – levels such as this one – and mess with us," Uncle Robert said.

"But if they're mostly trapped in a sublevel, a hell of their own making, how could they have interacted with us in the real world?" Laura said.

"By the real world, you mean the physical plane?" Uncle Robert said. "Remember, my death – and most of the physical violence that's occurred – is associated with the saucer. The closer we get to the saucer, the more the rules break down "

"All this doesn't explain me," Wright said. "Or Ms. Zimmerman."

"Oh, but it does in a way, though I don't think either of you want to hear the explanation," Sophia said.

* * *

22.

But Another Level Awaits

There is only one religion, though there are a hundred versions of it. – George Bernard Shaw

"It's all a dream?" Wright said, his voice rising. "How does it explain me or for that matter the other undead walking around Creedance? You're not going to tell me that's all a dream, too?"

"Calm down, John," Laura said. "Don't kill the messenger."

"Impossible. I'm already dead, remember?" Uncle Robert said. "But it would speed things up a little if you'd just let me advance my theory uninterrupted."

"But. . ." Wright said.

"Then you can tell me why you think I'm full of shit," Uncle Robert said. "Think of this as a preliminary hearing."

"Come on, Danger Boy," Laura said, and using both hands, grasped Wright's arm and shook him playfully. "Don't fear the reaper."

Wright laughed. "Go ahead. State your case," he said.

"It's pretty simple really. You and Suzanne are truly dead, at least your physical bodies are, as is mine. Somehow the influence of the saucer has made it possible for your astral bodies to continue to animate and invigorate your dead physical bodies."

"And how did you reach this conclusion?"

"Simple. I'm dead, and I'm here. Both of you are aware of having died – you by your own hand and Suzanne probably at the hands of cherubs. And you're here. *Here* is a kind of staging base for the departed. So it's a pretty good bet that your physical bodies are dead."

"Laura, Bryan and Sophia are *Here* too, as you put it, and they're not dead. You said yourself this is a place of trickery." There was desperation in his voice.

"A place of illusion, not trickery. Thoughts become actions here, and if those thoughts are undisciplined, then things can get very confusing; but I'm getting off track."

Suzanne began crying softly. "It's no use, Sheriff Wright. I'm dead. I feel it here." She put her hand over her heart. "And here." She pointed to her temple. "And I felt it back in the other place, the physical plane or whatever you call it, though things were more real there. I think you feel it too. Don't you?"

"Shit! I guess I do," Wright said and sat down, his shoulders slumping.

"But death is not all that bad," Uncle Robert said.

"Easy for you to say," Wright said. Then he looked and said with a sad smile, "I guess not."

"What I should have said is death is not what you think it is." Uncle Robert reached over and patted Wright on the shoulder. "Sheriff, you were always a straight shooter with me," he said. "Trust me to be the same with you."

"Yeah, sure," Wright said without much enthusiasm.

"No, hear me out. First, we have to rethink what death means."

"I know what's coming," Wright said. "Death is not the end, but you know, Simon, in our conversations over the years, you told me you were an agnostic. You didn't believe in life after death."

"I didn't say I didn't believe. I just said I needed proof – that I don't operate on blind faith, that I don't believe in a big anthropomorphic Zeus-like god. I at least needed something less limited and that didn't force me to turn off my brain, and all organized religions demanded I do just that."

"So what changed your mind?"

"Nothing changed. I've got proof of a transcendental reality. I'm still thinking, moving and feeling alive though I know my physical body is dead. I've seen my dead body. And like you, I feel more alive now that I ever remember feeling before."

"But I think what John is trying to get at," Laura said, "is why didn't your astral body do the same for your physical body as it did for John's and Suzanne's?"

"Good question. But I think it may have something to do with my having made frequent visits to this plane before my death, thanks to Sophia's guidance."

"What does that have to do with it?" Wright asked. When Laura looked at him oddly, he continued, "I'm not challenging you. I'm just asking a question."

"What I knew, and you both need to consider, is that word *death* is a misnomer," Uncle Robert said. "The atheist thinks that death is just the end of a biochemical process. We just biological robots. Wonderfully complex thanks to evolution, but only chemical machines. When the chemical factory stops working, that's it – the end. For the traditional Judeo-Christians and Muslims, upon death of the physical body, the soul leaves and travels to a new place it's never been before, heaven or hell or in some cases, purgatory.

"But other belief systems say the astral body – the design body – resides at different level all the time, and that it projects its pattern – a kind of blueprint – upon those biochemical structures we call bodies on the physical plane. More to the point, death is just a state of not having a physical body for the design body to be attached to."

"Okay, I'll buy this for now, if for no other reason that I'm here talking to you a few days after I blew out my brains out."

"It's all right," Uncle Robert said. "It's conjecture, I think, because I don't know much about either yours or Ms. Zimmerman's death."

"Suzanne," Suzanne said.

"Okay, then, Suzanne it is," Uncle Robert said. "I don't know much about either yours or Suzanne's death experiences. Me, having made the transition to the astral plane many times, I was not only aware of my death but readily able to accept it."

"You see," Sophia said, "this is the first staging place for the recently deceased. Many find death confusing or are in denial, and their astral bodies hang around the physical plane for days or weeks or even longer. Their astral bodies are anchored here, but they cast reflections into the physical plane, often unaware of they are doing so. This confusion of the deceased is the reality behind such things as ghost sightings and hauntings."

The front door squeaked. Evidently, the door hinges in this astral plane needed oiling, too. They all listened as shambling steps sounded in the hallway, and Dr. Jenkins entered the room. Suzanne gasped. Wright stood, and Sophia motioned for him to sit back down.

"Look at Jenkins closely," she said.

The man's eyes were open but unseeing. He moved toward her on unsteady feet, then stopped a few feet away and closed his eyes.

"I think," Sophia whispered, "it's the real Jenkins, that is, it's his actual astral body, not a simulacrum made by Samiazaz."

She stepped up to the doctor, took his left hand and led him to an empty chair. He sat down passively, his eyes still open but unfocused.

"He looks like he's sleepwalking," Laura said.

"In a way, he is. This is the way most of the untrained visit this plane," Sophia said. "If he's aware of us at all, he probably thinks he's just dreaming. When he wakes, he'll only recall vague impressions, and those will fade after a few minutes."

"You know what is so hard to accept?" Bryan said. "It's not the creepy concept that the dead bodies of Suzanne and Sheriff Wright and the others are being animated like puppets by their design bodies. It should be, but it's not. It's that I don't care. I second what the others said. I thought I knew what love was, what lust was, too. I knew the difference. I never felt any connection or desire this strong before. And I don't want it to end either, as weird as that seems to my rational mind."

"I don't understand either," Laura said. "And I don't care. I don't want you to freak and have to hide the razor blades, Aunt Sophia, but I think if someone cut the connection between John and his design body, and his physical body dropped dead in front of me, I mean really dead,

I would have to find a way to follow him to the astral plane."

Bryan looked at Suzanne and realized he felt the same way. Logic and rationality had nothing to do with what he felt.

"I know this sounds even more lame," he said. "But it's like we're under a spell."

"Well, I didn't do it," Suzanne said defensively. "It just seems so unfair. To feel this way and know that it's unreal, unnatural. Why couldn't we have had this in real life?" She covered her face in her hands and began sobbing softly. Bryan put his arm around her shoulders and pulled her close.

"It's not as bad – or as unnatural – as it might first seem," Uncle Robert said. "I'd bet there's a sort of karmic healing going on."

"What?" Bryan said. "You're saying we deserve this?"

"Simon and I agreed about this," Sophia said.

"Before or after Uncle Robert died?" Bryan asked.

"Well, after, as a matter of fact," Sophia said.

"You see," Uncle Robert said, "you need to give up the concept of life after death being a place of either a punishment or reward. Instead, it's meant as a place to heal and learn."

"And that's what we think is happening here, independent of the influence of the archangels," Sophia said. "This was a healing process. It was something you all needed to grow spiritually."

"And that is?" Bryan said. Suzanne had stopped crying and sat up. He handed her a napkin and she dabbed at her eyes.

"Do I have say it?" Uncle Robert looked embarrassed.

"It's all too touchy-feely for Simon," Sophia said. "Laura, John, Suzanne and Bryan, what you all needed was love, both romantic and erotic love. Unselfish, unconditional love, mutually expressed."

"All we needed was love?" Wright said. "Come on now. This sounds like a Beetles' song or a cliché-ridden Hollywood movie."

"The chances are that love is what you all might have experienced on the astral plane, with other spirits in transition. Instead, with the realms merged by the angel saucer, you found it across planes."

"You're saying this is all arbitrary, a kind of toss of the emotional dice?" Wright said.

"If that's all we needed, why didn't it happen between me and Bryan?" Laura said. "We were already seeing each other, fond of each other — more than fond, really."

"No, we're not saying that at all," Uncle Robert said. He shrugged. "It's hard to explain, or accept, unless you understand karma."

"I know what it means," Wright said. "It's sort of like what goes around comes around."

"That's the hillbilly definition, but it's close," Uncle Robert laughed. "Buddhists talk about rebirth and karma, about how one's acts in past lives influence the rebirth in the next life. But their belief system goes further. They also believe that everyone you're involved with in this current life has played other roles in your past lives. Today's lover was a sibling in a past life or parent or enemy or benefactor. They believe that we are bound to a closed circle of acquaintance, particularly people with whom we feel an immediate connection, for an endless cycle of rebirths. Each rebirth we switch roles as in a game of musical chairs, but we repeatedly play out the same drama, though we might be the victim in one life, then the victimizer in the next."

"But why didn't we feel this sense of connection before?" Laura said. "Why did it take John's death to bring us together?"

"I think if you looked back, you'd find you felt the connection, but the age difference blocked you," Uncle Robert said. "And there is sometimes anger and resentment as well as love that carries over from past lives."

"And what about Suzanne and me?" Bryan asked. "I remember seeing her a couple of times in town before all this, but there was no love at first sight – well, maybe just a little."

"Are you certain?"

"Well, there was that time back in Columbia that I tried to pick her up, but she shot me down."

Suzanne laughed. "I'd forgotten that. I wanted to go with you, but I had a big load of guilt about even the thought of cheating on Ben."

"I got drunk afterwards."

"I drove home and had a fight with Ben." She shook her head. "Weird. I wonder what might have happened if the angel saucer hadn't fallen."

"Maybe nothing. Maybe everything. These things take time to play out – sometimes centuries, through multiple reincarnations," Uncle Robert said. "You know, I'm having trouble with all this myself. I used to be what I called a heretical Buddhist. I did the meditation, but I didn't buy into all the reincarnation stuff. Now I guess maybe I do. Maybe I have to."

"Ben really believed it," Suzanne said. "He wanted to believe it, though."

"Have you discovered what happened to him yet?" Uncle Robert asked.

"No, but now I'm wondering if he disappeared when we were in this place – I mean this plane," Suzanne said.

"So you think you might have picked up his astral body and then, when you popped back into the physical plane, it wasn't there?" Uncle Robert said.

"Maybe. It's confusing. If what you're saying is true, I can't even tell when I'm operating on one plane or the other," Bryan said.

"Or how to get from one plane to another," Laura said.

"Well, you're in luck. Sophia is going to show you how."

"Are you going to hypnotize us again?"

"No dear," Sophia said. "That won't be necessary because when the saucer broke down the barriers, it became almost impossible *not* to bounce back and forth between the astral and the physical. Mostly I'm going to teach y'all a few simple techniques to control the transition and how to recognize which level you're operating on."

"Sounds too easy to be true," Wright said.

"It is easy. You have my word on it," she said.

Sophia escorted them to Uncle Robert's den, her stilettos going click, click, click on the hardwood floors. The den was a place of more books, two big overstuffed chairs, and an ornate Persian rug that silenced Sophia's footsteps. Uncle Robert took one of the chairs, and Sophia led Jenkins to the other. Bryan sat beside Suzanne on the sofa, and Laura and Wright sat cross-legged on cushions on the floor.

"Now I know this is an astral plane," Laura said. "In the real world, there would be so many books stacked around that we wouldn't have room to walk."

"You're catching on," Sophia said. "If you look, you should be able to find other inconsistencies. You may notice everything in this room seems cleaner, newer; the edges of things as the coffee tables are sharper, preternaturally so."

"This is not my beautiful house, this is not my beautiful wife," Bryan said.

Suzanne smiled but Wright said, "What?"

"Nothing. Just a bit of a Talking Heads song." Bryan said.

"I don't know the song, but that's basically what we're talking about. For instance, look at this," Uncle Robert said, picking up a small, fat Buddha from the end table next to his chair.

"In the world I remember, this was a laughing Buddha made of teak wood with lots of scratches. Now look at it."

He held it up for them to see. It wasn't made not of wood but of something that looked like lapis lazuli. And it wasn't laughing. It had a serene smile.

"These sorts of discrepancies are what have prompted some to say these places are not an eternal realm at all, but an interior one, created by the mind, a deeper level of dreaming. That's what I used to think," Uncle Robert said.

"The eternal skeptic," Sophia said. "That's why he needed my help to get here."

"But you know, I decided 'what does it matter.' All consciousness is subjective anyway. Not only that, but reality is subject to consensus."

"I'm not following you. Is this place real or not?" Wright said.

"The mind in itself and all that," Uncle Robert said.

"He's referring to Milton's *Paradise Lost*," Bryan said, "That the mind is its own place, and can make a heaven out of hell, a hell out of heaven."

"Exactly, and so what if this level of the astral plane – which, by the way, theosophists call Summerland – might exist in the mind for only the moments between the last heartbeat and death? If to the subjective consciousness it lasts years or centuries or even millennium, then what's the difference?

"Whichever, we're going to try to teach you to pop out of here and back," Sophia said, kicking off her high heels and sitting cross-legged beside Laura on the rug.

"How'd you do that?" Bryan said pointing at the skirt. She had been wearing a denim miniskirt just a moment ago. Now she wore an ankle-length, multicolored peasant dress.

"Well, you didn't really expect me to sit in the lotus position wearing a miniskirt, did you?"

"No, I guess not. But I didn't even see it change."

"That's another clue that you're on the astral plane. Now let's talk about something else before I lose focus and change back. I want you all to start by closing your eyes. Don't clamp them shut, John. Just let the lids relax. Yes, like that. Now, I want you to concentrate on your breathing; you can feel your breath at a small spot just below your nostrils.

"Now, let yourself relax. I want y'all to start mentally scanning your entire bodies, starting with the top of your head, going down your shoulders. Try to feel it, not visualize it, but it's like it's a Xerox machine, and your mind is the light. Go right down to your toes, then come back up again."

Her voice droned on and on, the rhythm changing, her intonation softening, until it sounded like a soft drum, drum, drumming . . .

Laura.

She was sitting on the bed – John Wright's bed. Bright sunlight streaming through the flowery bedroom curtains was of that particular quality of morning light on a clear day.

She didn't remember waking. Sweeping off the blankets, she found herself dressed in an oversized sweatshirt and panties. She swung her feet out of bed and found the floor cold.

She had been here before, hadn't she? There was a memory of a dream that wasn't a dream, of Jenkins, of being inside the angel saucer, of – no, wait. That was another time. The last memory she had was of being in the manse, sitting on the floor with Sophia, John. Or was that a dream too? Her skirt should be here somewhere.

Confused, she pulled the top blanket around herself in toga fashion, which also reminded her of another time and place.

Something fluttered into the room, bouncing about the ceiling, right over her head. She jumped, a scream rising in her throat, but remembered it was just a sparrow.

Remembered?

The visitor chirped in fear and landed on the bed, its wings flapping weakly on the sheet. It was indeed a sparrow. She picked it up, still overwhelmed by déjà vu.

Holding the tiny life in her hand, she stepped to the window and drew back the curtain, thinking to release it outside. The bird's breast rose and fell; she could feel its heartbeat pulsing impossibly fast – and faster. Then the beat stopped and the breast was still.

She opened her palm and looked at the bird in the bright, morning light. This wasn't right. It hadn't died before. Or rather it had died, then had been resurrected.

Before?

It came back to her in a flash, the exploding window, the cruel hands and dirty laughter of the cherubs. She stepped back from the window, expecting it to shatter at that moment.

But nothing happened. She did the reality check Sophia had taught them. Some things did seem preternaturally bright and sharp, but she decided that it was only an effect of the morning light. This was the physical plane. She was pretty sure of that.

But the question was if this reality was before, after the one where she had been abducted by cherubs? Or was that even a legitimate question?

She found her orange waitress skirt and tennis shoes on the floor near the bed. After a quick sponge bath in cold water, she dressed, still keeping an eye on the window.

Outside, she found her Volkswagen where she had left it. Like a decrepit old man, the Beetle started with a death rattle cough, sputtered some gray smoke and lurched forward. She drove to her house without incident, where she dressed in jeans. Then she was off again, hoping she had enough gasoline in the tank to get her to Lost Lake.

She had an appointment to keep.

Wright.

Loblolly pines reached toward a quarter moon in a clear black sky. He was lying on his back, and he was cold and wet. When had he laid down? The last thing he remembered was sitting on the floor next to Laura, his eyes closed, trying to find his breath on his upper lip, then feeling a bit panicky when he realized he wasn't breathing at all. Then this.

A gust of wind made the boughs of the pine trees go *shusssh*. He remembered waking in this exact same spot days ago. Only then, he had awakened confused, with only the memory of the horror of talking to Marguerite and then being possessed by an overwhelming compulsion that dragged him toward Laura's house. Now his last memory was of the conference at the Jacobsen mansion. He had accepted that the meeting had been held in a place of illusion, a place where thought became reality and action. And he knew that this place where he was now was the physical plane. But the Jacobsen mansion memory seemed more real.

He stood and brushed off the dead pine needles. One thing remained the same: He still felt drawn somewhere, only now he knew where. Or rather to whom: Laura.

Though the pull was intense, he resisted it. He had a job to do, and he needed help. Frank Marshall's house was to the south, not far from here, and he set off towards it, knowing somehow he would find the old man there. And they would need Marshall's help.

He consoled himself that he would find Laura at Lost Lake later, though he feared it might be the last time they would be together on this plane.

Bryan.

He became bored with focusing on his breathing, trying to find that delicate tickle on his lip, and wondered if he would be caught if he sneaked a peak. Of course anyone who caught him would be cheating too, or was Sophia watching everyone? The whole scene was beginning to remind him of the Sundays of his childhood, sentenced to the slow torture of Episcopal services back in Columbia. He took a deep breath and let it out slowly, thinking he was getting nowhere. How long had they been doing this? He wanted to peek, if for no other reason, than to see if anyone else had given up. It was all he could do to keep his eyes closed. Then he realized he didn't hear Sophia's voice any longer. She had been guiding this process, reminding them every few minutes to concentrate on their breathing. Her voice was now gone, replaced by the familiar sound of a crackling fire and the smell of wood smoke.

His breath came faster. He knew where he was, but now he didn't want to look, for he knew what he would see, and feared that Suzanne wouldn't be there beside him. He wanted to close his eyes, go back to sleep, and wake with her beside him.

When he finally opened his eyes, he found that as he anticipated, he was not on the couch at the Jacobsen mansion with Suzanne but on the old threadbare sofa at his grandparent's house by himself.

He felt profoundly lonely as he slipped on his boots. His last memory of his pickup truck was leaving it stalled in the middle of the road after rescuing Suzanne from her overturned van. He was only mildly surprised when he found the truck waiting for him outside.

Suzanne.

One moment she was staring at the intricate whorls on the Persian carpet, conscious of the sound of Bryan's breathing beside her. The next, she was standing out behind the Ponderosa doublewide in the pasture under the old dying oak tree.

Wings flapped above, startling her, but it was the usual denizens of the tree: three black buzzards. No cherubs.

She remembered it all now. She had come here just to get out of the house, to think about how to tell Ben she was leaving him. She'd heard wings, had looked up expecting to see the buzzards scattering from the upper branches. Instead she was smothered under a swarm of cherubs. She remembered it all now. Being swept away, dragged through the upper branches of trees, and the stabbing pain as one whispered in her ear and then bit it off.

The memory was so clear. It had been a bright sunny day just like this one. In her mind's eye, she could see the bright red drops of her own blood falling down to the green pastures. She could hear her own screams, a mixture of outrage and terror, but her voice came from far away and belonged to someone else

Her hand went to her ear and found it uninjured. Another thing: When her ear had grown back, it had been without the piercings, a virgin ear. Now the piercings were intact.

So was this a memory, a dream deferred or a vision? Was it an inescapable prophesy or a warning? Was the attack before or after this? If this moment was a prelude to the actual attack, then why did she see it as if she were remembering a past event? If the memory was an illusion, did that mean everything that happened with Bryan, everything she had felt regarding him, was a false memory too? Or had the relationship entirely occurred in that dreamtime of the astral plane, one of those things that lasted only the duration of a heartbeat but seemed like days? If so, did that make it less real? She was being manipulated by forces she couldn't see, comprehend or resist.

She was suddenly angry with her own confusion, her feeling of having no control, of being forced to play out a sequence of events as if merely an actor on a stage. She stomped her foot. No, she wouldn't accept life that way.

Furious, she walked across the pasture to the doublewide. Damn the cherubs! Let them come. She'd bite off their ears this time.

As she expected, there was no sign of Ben at the doublewide. The conversion van was parked in the drive, keys in the ignition, empty of any unwelcome guests. She hadn't expected that.

Twenty minutes later, she was driving into Lost Lake State Park. A beat-up looking white Volkswagen beetle was there, and someone – Laura? – was standing at the edge of the lake. As Suzanne searched for Bryan, a familiar pickup truck pulled up beside her.

Her heart lifted, then fell as she ran to him and he wrappedher in his arms. Would this be the last time they would be together?

* * *

23.

Those She Left Behind

Bryan.

Bryan grunted as he hefted the eighty-pound bag of concrete-mix to his shoulder. Immediately he had to sidestep Wright, who was returning from the barge on the narrow bridge that stretched over thirty feet of the shallow shore-side waters of Lost Lake.

"Bridge" was what its designer, Frank Marshall, called it, but "catwalk" better described the structure. Made of thick wooden boards supported by floating fifty-gallon oil drums, it was about thirty feet long but only about eighteen inches wide. Marshall had been some sort of civil engineer in the Army, and the catwalk certainly had a solid, utilitarian, no-nonsense feel to it, but "bridge" was giving it too much credit.

The catwalk led from the boat dock out to where the water was deep enough for Jenkin's party barge. The idea was to haul enough bags of concrete-mix out to where they believed Samizaz lay and entomb him before the waters retreated enough he was set free. Jenkins' barge was not much more than deck on pontoons, but it should provide them with a large enough working platform to mix and pour the a large volume of concrete. The problem was the lake was too low now to bring the barge to the dock and load it with concrete-mix bags directly.

The concrete-mix bags contained cement, gravel and sand everything needed to make concrete, but they needed a lot of them.

Foiled by low water, they first had tried to load a john boat with a couple of bags of concrete and push it, sled-like, over the twenty feet of mud and sand until the water was deep enough to float it. But the task had proven impossible. Even carrying only one bag of concrete-mix, the john boat became an immovable chunk of aluminum. Marshall had wanted to rig up a powered pulley and cable affair, which would have probably worked, but they didn't have time to implement his alternate plan. The barrels and a scrap lumber had already been at the lake's edge, stacked there before the Fall to build a new pier. So Marshall had built a walkway all the way out to the barge.

Bryan slowed his pace as he passed over the area where the barrels were firmly lodged in mud. The next barrel, and the next step, was a different matter. There was enough water under the barrel to make it float instead of squat in the mud, and the boards under his feet sank a few inches and swayed. It was be perilous going from here on out, but he had to give Marshal credit. In less than a day, undead or whatever, the old man had managed to cobble together a usable if not exactly safe structure from materials on hand. He had worked as if possessed by demons.

Maybe he was.

The bridge swayed with each step Bryan took. Made top heavy with the bag of concrete mix, he wobbled on one foot for a second, holding his breath, the clear cold water of Lost Lake beckoning. Without thinking, he extended his opposite leg, cocked his hip, and regained his balance. He stood still, waiting for the barrels to cease sloshing back and forth. A fall wouldn't have done much more physical harm than to get him cold and wet, but it would have cost time, and time they didn't have.

Samiazaz lay about twenty feet beyond the barge. The tail assembly of the crashed Cessna airplane, white with a red stripe, protruded about four feet above the water. Bryan had recognized it as the wreckage of the plane Samiazaz and Baraqijal had collided with, the same plane that had dragged Samiazaz down as it sank.

No one had rowed out to examine the site; Laura said there was no need as she could sense the archangel there. Marshall had estimated the archangel was now covered by little more than six feet of water. As the water level dropped, they could all feel his influence over this realm growing, and the water level was dropping quickly.

"Bryan, are you okay?" Suzanne called from shore. Her voice had a strange quality as if she were in a deep hole. He did a visual check on the barge, the edges of the boards and the peeling paint of the barrels. Everything looked a bit shabby compared to the preternaturally sharp perfection of the astral plane. This must be real. This must be the Earthly plane and not an astral one.

"Yeah," he said, and took a deep breath and started toward the barge again.

Little steps. Only ten feet to go.

He made it to the barge without further incident and stacked the bag on its deck. Behind him, he could hear Wright's footfalls clumping along the catwalk. The sheriff didn't have to pick his way carefully or even walk normally – he trotted. Bryan wondered if he'd been so gracefully agile before he died.

"Coming at cha'," Wright called. Like Suzanne's, his voice seemed to come from a long ways off.

Bryan stepped out of the way as the man made an elegant leap onto the deck.

"Smooth move," Bryan said. "All you need is a top hat and a cane."

"Yeah, I'm a regular Fred Astaire," Wright said, not meeting his eyes.

Actually, Bryan had been thinking Gene Kelly, whom Wright now somewhat physicallly resembled, but he let Wright's interpretation go. It was good Wright was keeping his morale up, but Bryan suspected it was put on. Since the session with Sophia and Uncle Robert, both Wright and Suzanne had been emotionally distant, disconnected. Little wonder. No one knew for certain what would happen once they entombed Samiazaz. Would Suzanne's and Wright's undead bodies become unanimated, really dead? Would they go on as before, only more mortal? Would they simply disappear? The concrete they planned to entomb Samiazaz with might or might not block his influence as effectively as deep water.

Wright stood with hands in pockets, staring back at the beach. Looking like an orphaned child, he was staring at Laura, who was on the beach talking to Suzanne.

Bryan knew how he felt. If Samiazaz really was the center of the influence, he would lose Suzanne on this plane. Supposedly he would still be able to visit her on the astral plane, even make love to her there, but that seemed a poor substitute to having her here. His sorrow was tangible, a dull, deep ache in his chest. He understood now that heartbreak was more that just an expression.

"How many more bags will we need?" he managed to ask Wright.

"How many we got out here already?"

"About twenty by my count."

"That's only about six cubic feet of concrete. We'll need a lot more. But here comes Marshall now."

A yellow dump truck, spewing black smoke from its stacks, roared and rattled into the park. Without slowing down, the driver, Marshall, did a tight U-turn. The truck's oversized tires slung gravel and small stones. He braked and backed up to the edge of the ramp. Stacked in the truck bed was a concrete-encrusted cement mixer, and a large cardboard tube about eighteen inches in diameter and maybe ten feet long. But it was the bags of concrete mix that Bryan focused on. He inwardly groaned at the thought of lugging even one more bag to the barge. There must be at least forty in the pile. Marshall climbed out of the truck. He didn't wave or shout.

Without a word, Wright leaped back on the ramp and trotted back to the beach and Marshall. Bryan followed carefully.

As Bryan reached the beach, Wright, Marshall, Laura and Suzanne had gathered together and Marshall was talking. "It's taking too long," he was saying.

"Taking too long for what?" Bryan asked.

"Mr. Marshall said the dropping of the water level is more dramatic than we originally thought," Laura explained.

"In the hour or so I was gone, you can really see the difference," he said.

Bryan had been hesitant to include Marshall in the effort. Doing so had been Wright's decision, and he vouched for him, but Bryan thought the retired military man too reckless. After all, it had been his plan to use a fertilizer bomb to destroy the alien saucer, an action that had only marginally damaged the saucer and was now responsible for the draining of the lake and the restoration of Samiazaz's powers. Of all the undead, Marshall was the most unhappy with his situation. He wanted to move on, to leave his reanimated body behind. He probably saw this project as a kind of kamikaze way out.

"The bottleneck is lugging those bags of concrete-mix out to the barge," Bryan said. "If we're going to finish before sunset, we need a new plan."

"Samiazaz could be high and dry before tomorrow morning, maybe even by this evening," Wright said.

"I think I've got an alternative," Marshall said, and without explaining, got back behind the dump truck steering wheel.

"What's going on?" Wright said.

Marshall ignored him, slammed the door, and put the truck in gear.

"Talk to me, Frank," Wright said.

"All of you had better get out of the way," Marshall said. "I'd recommend over there by the merry-go-round." Without further explanation, he put the truck in gear and drove up the hill, leaving everyone else behind coughing in a cloud of dust.

"What's he doing?" Laura asked.

"I don't know for sure," Bryan said. "But I think we ought to get out of the way like he said."

Marshall drove to the top of the hill, stopped, dropped the truck into reverse, then revved the engine like it a dragster and he was waiting for the starting light.

"Run!" Wright said and gave Laura a little push toward the merry-go-round.

"I think we'd better run, too," Bryan said to Suzanne, realizing what the old man was up to. Marshall revved the engine one more time, then popped the clutch. The truck began rolling backward down the hill, picking up speed every second. Bryan grabbed Suzanne's hand, and they double-timed toward the playground behind Laura and Wright.

In a dirty yellow blur, the dump truck sped by them going thirty or forty miles per hour before they were halfway to the merry-go-round. As it roared past them, they all turned to watch. It hit the edge of the shore and straddled the catwalk like a train on a track. The truck's tires slung chunks of mud and wood splinters twenty feet in the air. The barrels popped out behind the truck bed like big blue turds. Both side doors sprang open, and Bryan expected to see Marshall projected on the next bounce. But though the man must have been ricocheting inside like a bean inside a maraca, he somehow managed to stay inside the cab.

"The crazy son of a bitch is going to hit the barge!" Wright yelled.

The truck slowed as it plowed into the deeper water, and the bridge sank completely underneath it. The water wake rocked the barge as the truck continued sinking. For a brief moment Bryan thought the water would rise over the cab, but the tires found the lake bottom before the water reached the bed. Still above water, the engine continued running, and the truck churned toward the boat. As the rear of the truck bed bumped against the barge's rear pontoon, the engine either died or was shut down by Marshall.

"I'll be damned," Wright said. "The crazy bastard did it."

Marshall rolled down the side window, climbed out, and crawled up to stand triumphantly on top of the cab. "What are you all standing there gawking about?" he called. "Time's a-wastin'!"

Less than hour later, Marshall, Wright and Bryan had transferred the last bags of concrete to the barge. Laura and Suzanne, carrying a bag between them, distributed the weight around the deck so as to capsize the barge. For a while they worried the extra weight would bottom-out the boat. But it had been a party boat before being drafted into duty as a barge and was capable of hosting twenty or more revelers; now the water level barely reached halfway up the pontoons. Finally, Marshall and Wright unloaded shovels and cinder blocks.

The idea of entombing the angel had seemed simple at first, but had turned into a major construction project. But Wright and Marshall were up to it. Their endurance and plain brute strength was amazing. Bryan, on the other hand, was exhausted. Wright was nearly twice Bryan's age; Marshall closer to three times. Yet they both out-lifted and out-endured him. He felt like a wuss. He grew dizzy when the time came to unload the gasoline-powered cement mixer, a piece of iron and sheet metal that must have weighed hundreds of pounds. No matter. Wright and Marshall wrestled the thing onto the deck from the back of the truck without so much as breathing hard. Bryan still wasn't sure if they breathed at all. He began to suspect now that Wright must have let him win the fight back on the highway. But why? The Sheriff was obviously a more complicated man than the bigot Bryan had first thought he was.

Marshall set two five-gallon lidded white pails at his feet.

"Make yourself useful, boy" he said. "Get off our pansy ass and put these over by the mixer."

Marshall, on the otherhand, remained a true-to-form asshole.

Bryan struggled to his feet and tried to lift the pails with no avail. They must have weighed a hundred pounds each.

"What's in these things? Lead?"

"Pretty close. Iron and steel shavings from Kelly's welding shop."

"Why?"

"I saw a movie once about vampires. Something about leaded iron stopping them. I'm going to mix it in with the concrete."

"I'm not sure archangels and vampires are of the same stuff."

"Whatever, a little bit won't hurt the concrete. Maybe give it strength. Here, I'll take them." The old man picked up both buckets as if they were filled with air. Which made Bryan do the check for being on an astral level once again. Despite Marshall's feat, nothing much looked preternatural, so he decided they were probably still on the physical plane. The clincher was being wet, cold and muddy up his waist. The footbridge had been a collateral casualty of Marshall's crash landing the dump truck into the lake, and they had been forced to wade out to the barge. The only way he and Laura could stay warm was by working hard. Now Wright and Marshall insisted they squat in the middle of the deck and to discuss their next move. The cold began to seep into

Bryan's muscles.

"We don't have much time to lose," Laura said. She looked as tired as Bryan felt. Aside from being dirty, Suzanne, like Wright and Marshall, didn't seem worse for wear at all. He studied Suzanne's face for a moment as she searched the sky. Even in the now bright sunlight, her face seemed without pores. Her features – her nose, freckles, lips, cheekbones, and eyes – were in no way individually extraordinary. She should register as merely a pretty woman. But when he just looked at her as holistic whole, she was beautiful. *Must be love.*

But what about Wright? He too seemed to be a too-perfect John Wright. The man had that male model quality. Marshall, when he kept his mouth shut, was the image of the picturesque kindly gentleman. Bryan examined his feelings. Did it matter that Suzanne, like Wright and Marshall, appeared to have been Photoshopped into a normal, shabby reality? Did he care that Suzanne was an illusion, an entity airbrushed and beautified by some supernatural power?

The answer was no. He still loved her.

Chunks of mud had peeled off their pants and littered the deck around them. Wright picked up a saucer-sized piece of mud and pitched it into Lost Lake. "So, what are we waiting for? Let's do it," he said.

"No, we need to be organized," Laura said. "We can take five minutes to decide who does what."

"What's to decide?" Marshall said. "We cruise over to where the fucking angel is stuck in the mud. We build a form and seal up the bastard in concrete."

"I'm still unclear on how we can pour concrete under water," Bryan said.

"It's done all the time for boat piers and the like, even here in the sticks," Marshall said. "And here we don't have to worry about it carrying a load. The problem is going to be mixing big enough batches to keep the 'crete from being watered down."

"Frank, just tell us what to do," Wright said. "You're in charge."

Marshall nodded. For the first time today, perhaps ever, Bryan detected a smile on the old man's face.

They pulled up the anchors and cast off. The barge had two

outboard motors but Marshall didn't want to cloud up the water any more than they had already had, so they used long pieces of PVC pipe to push the barge away from the dump truck. The bottom there allowed only a few feet of clearance for pontoons. Any one of them could probably stand on the bottom and keep his or her head above water. In a few minutes they were far enough away from the stirred up mud that the water of Lost Lake became clear enough to see the bottom again.

Laura's claim she could *sense* the angel's location made Bryan think of Mina in *Dracula* – what was her last name? It didn't matter, but Bryan remembered that after the vampire had bitten her, she could be put into a hypnotic trance and see what he was seeing, even across continents. Finding Samiazaz was a lot easier because his watery resting place was marked by the remains of the plane's fuselage. And they didn't have to travel even across a continent, only a few yards from where they had loaded the barge.

Laura stood on the prow, yelling directions as the men, like muddied gondoliers, pushed the boat along with long pieces of pipe. The crystal clear water swished across the sides of the pontoons. The wood planks of the barge's deck creaked softly under Bryan's feet. Far off, a farmer's cow bellowed a mournful moo. The air was cooling, and he savored one of those moments of timelessness, a slice of *right now*, with him and the world perfectly enmeshed.

Laura shouted in alarm when they found the demiurge. They had nearly overridden his submersed body, and they had a minute of frantic back poling before they settled alongside him.

Completely naked, he lay on his back under about six or seven feet of water. His long white hair flowed in the current. Like Marshall, Wright and Suzanne, he didn't seem a part of this world.

Very little remained of the plane, at least that was visible. The fuselage was embedded in the mud. A piece of the main wing lay flat on the bottom a few feet away. There was no sign of the plane's cabin or the remains of its human pilot. Samiazaz had supposedly been dragged down to the bottom with the wreckage while the other archangel in the collision, not so entangled, had floated to the surface and been revived when towed to shore. But Samiazaz lay a good ten feet away from the fuselage; there was no evidence of him being held down in any way. It was another mystery among many, but it bothered Bryan.

"He's watching us," Suzanne said.

Indeed, the archangel's eyes were open and tracked Laura as she moved from the prow to beside Wright.

"I wonder what would happen if I shoved this piece of pipe down the bastard's throat," Wright said angrily.

"Probably nothing. Some people tried shooting the archangels when they first arrived. Remember?"

Bryan remembered those reports. The bullets hadn't bounced off of the angels. Instead, it was as though the angels weren't there, and if Sophia and Uncle Robert were correct, they weren't.

"Besides," Laura added, "if it wasn't for Samiazaz, you and I would have never found each other."

"True," Wright said, but his tone was bittersweet.

Under Marshall's supervision, they set up the concrete mixer and started its little putt-putt gasoline engine. They put in several buckets of water but no concrete-mix yet. Marshall explained that the concrete-mix he had procured was a fast-set type. They would have to work quickly to make the entombment strong. The cinder blocks were to build the form.

"How are we going to set the blocks underwater?" Bryan asked. "Just drop them around him?"

"I'm going in," Marshall said.

Bryan studied Marshall. He was taller than Wright, but still only about five feet eight. The water would be over his head here. "I don't see an aqualung or even a snorkel," he said.

"So you think I'll drown and die?"

Bryan shrugged.

"Well, I won't."

"How do you know for sure?"

"Because I've tried to drown myself. Right over there by the playground. Yesterday evening, I walked into the lake and sat down. My lungs filled with water, but nothing happened. I just sat there watching, my eyes wide open like a dead fish. When I got bored, I walked out and coughed up all the water and muck."

Marshall looped the end of what looked like white clothesline through the hollow cinder block, tied a knot, then slung the block over his shoulder. "Ballast," he explained.

Wright had been listening. "I'll help," he said. "Got more rope?"

"Over there by the concrete mixer, but I can handle it," Marshall said.

"The college boy and the two women can pitch enough blocks to keep up with both of us."

"Whatever. Don't expect me to hold your hand when your lungs fill up."

"Don't worry about me," Wright said, rubbing the top of his head. "I've dealt with worse lately."

"Just remember, it's only scary the first time," Marshall said, then turned to Bryan. "Keep the blocks coming quick, but don't bean me with one. Understand, boy?"

Before Bryan could answer that he might drop one on the old soldier's head intentionally if he called him *boy* again, Marshall jumped feet first into the water. The bottom was more sandy than muddy this far out, and water cleared quickly. Marshall stood beside the angel, in over his head by at least a foot, looking up them expectantly. Air bubbles the size of tennis balls escaped from his mouth as he tried to say something. Bryan shook his head, wondering what it felt like to drown when one was dead already.

Marshall leaned over Samiazaz's body and plucked at something. Visibly straining, he lifted a steel cable about the diameter of a pencil away from Samiazaz's midsection. Apparently the cable was a guy wire from the plane's wings. Painted white, it hadn't been easily visible against the archangel's body. The cable stretched to the fuselage on one side of Samiazaz and disappeared into mud on the other, and it must be what was holding the creature on the bottom. Mystery solved, which should have made him feel better, but he knew that when the water dropped and Samiazaz's powers returned, he would be able to snap the cable like a kite string and free himself.

Laura pointed to the west and the setting sun. Bryan's sense of urgency increased.

Marshall let go of the cable and it snapped back taunt against Samiazaz's stomach. Then Marshall waved at Bryan as if to say 'come on.'

Bryan shook his head uncomprehending.

Marshall shook his head impatiently, then held out his hands out as if to play catch. Bryan took the hint and dropped a block over the side. It gurgled as water filled the hollows. Marshall caught it before it hit bottom. The old man set this first block parallel to the angel's body and only a few inches away from his shoulder. He twisted the block to work it into the sandy bottom. By the time Bryan had another block in hand, Marshall was ready for it. Then Wright was in the water, coughing up big bubbles of air as Marshall had a minute before.

In no time at all, the two men had boxed in angel with a rectangular wall four cinder blocks high. Then Marshall had Wright boost him up until his head was above the surface. He had to cough up great gushes of water before he could talk.

"Give us about ten bags of mix. Don't break the bags. Just give them to us whole," he said this between coughing up quarts of water.

By now Bryan was ready to collapse. But the water level had dropped noticeably since they had started laying blocks. He summoned some more energy, and with Suzanne's and Laura's help, managed to do as Marshall asked. The two underwater workers leaned the bags on end around the blocks to prop them up, then both climbed back on deck.

Bryan cast a glance toward the angel. Laura had been creeped out by Samiazaz's eyes following her everywhere and now stood away from the edge of the boat. The water within the cinder block walls had cleared and the angel now stared blankly through the clear water at the sky.

"What next?" Bryan asked.

Wright and Marshall bent over, their hands on their knees, still coughing up great gouts of water.

As his lungs cleared, Marshall said, "Now we mix concrete like the crazy men we are."

"What about us crazy women?" Laura said, but Marshall just

shook his head.

The large cardboard tube, which was a wax-coated concrete form, was to be used to funnel the concrete to the bottom of the pour. If they just dumped the freshly mixed concrete in and let it settle down, it would absorb too much water, Marshall explained. By pouring the concrete down the tube, they would amass fresh concrete from the lake bottom up, displacing the water within the cinder block cage as they went.

"The Romans did it this way thousands of years ago, but they used volcanic ash with their cement. We'll have to do with this premix," Wright said. "It would be better if we could mix enough concrete to fill it in one dump, but maybe it won't have to be strong enough to hold up a Roman highway."

They worked at a fevered pace. No one was spared. Bryan, Suzanne and Laura took turns holding the tube and ferrying buckets of water from the lake. Only Marshall and Wright had both the strength and reserve energy to quickly heft a bag of concrete to the mouth of the mixer, slash the bag with a utility knife, and dump it in. All of them were soon covered in a film of concrete dust and fine sand, making them look like gray zombie corpses.

The concrete they poured gradually immersed Samiazaz. The water above became clouded with gray particles as the concrete rose over his legs and arms. Only his face and barrel chest remained uncovered. Bryan expected to see something in his expression – hatred, arrogance, panic – but there was nothing. Samiazaz's face remained immobile, as unresponsive as the marble it appeared to be. *Wait! Did the lips curl in a faint smile? Was there a glimmer of irony in the eyes?*

For about the thousandth time, he obsessed about what would happen when the angel was completely entombed. If Samiazaz's influence had trapped the souls of Wright, Marshall and Suzanne in their dead bodies, what would happen as they encased him in concrete? Another thought, a crazy stupid thought, possessed him. Maybe it would be like the Rapture. Maybe Suzanne and the rest would be whisked out of their clothes and into heaven as he watched?

"Ready to go," Wright called.

In his exhausted state, Bryan needed a few seconds to realize that Wright was talking about having another batch of cement ready.

"Come on! Right now! We're running out of light," Wright said.

Bryan looked to the west. The sun was a large orange globe setting behind the loblolly pines. Suzanne stood behind him, her hand on his shoulder, silhouetted by the setting sun.

"He's smiling now," Laura said. She had to use both hands to help him steady the cardboard tube, so she nodded toward Samiazaz.

Samiazaz appeared not to be smiling but grinning arrogantly. Without turning Samiazaz his head – perhaps Samizaz was unable to do even that – his eyes flickered toward the west, then back toward the boat. Laura had been careful to position herself so she was out of his line of sight, but he obviously was staring toward her, seeming to sense her as she sensed him.

"Look, incoming!" Marshall shouted, pointing toward the setting sun.

Though the light was failing quickly, there was no mistaking the flying figures. A cluster of flying cherubs was silhouetted by the setting sun. They were too far away for the buzzing wings to be heard, but they were coming on fast.

"I thought the archangels were powerless over water," Bryan said.

"Marguerite could fly over water," Wright said. "So could the other angel/human hybrids."

"The cherubs could be Samiazaz's thoughts in action. That's what Uncle Robert said," Laura said.

"Marshall, Bryan, Laura," Wright called. "You take care of the concrete. I'll keep them off us." He picked up a shovel by the end of the handle, his hands close together as if it were a baseball bat.

"I knew I should have brought a goddamn gun!" Marshall said, but he grabbed another bag of concrete and began dumping it into the mixer. More gray dust settled around them.

Suzanne picked up one of the ten-foot pieces of PVC pipe and held it out in front of her like a medieval foot soldier's pike. It looked like an ineffectual weapon until Bryan noticed the outward-facing end had been cut at an angle, making a sharp-looking lopsided point.

The cherubs – close enough now to reveal there were five – swooped down to about eight feet above the water and came straight at the boat. Were more coming from behind or from the flank? Bryan chanced a quick glance; no, there was only the one squadron.

"They're flying in a V-formation," Suzanne shouted.

Evidently cherubs had studied geese, not military strategy. So they were a flock not a squadron.

The lead cherub was at a Wright's head level; the sheriff tucked in his chin and shoulder, took a short step forward and swung, connecting the broad, flat side of the shovel blade with its grinning face. The impact made a *bong* sound, the shovel handle snapped off where it joined the blade, and the cherub spun off, flipping head over heels to splash down in the lake.

Suzanne rose up on her toes and thrust the sharp end of the PVC into the mouth of the following cherub. The pipe was two inches in diameter, much larger than the cherub's puckered mouth, but the combined force of Suzanne's thrust and the piglet-sized creature's flight drove the PVC through the back of its head.

Suzanne swung the skewered cherub over her head and down on the deck.

Then the remaining three cherubs were upon them. Suzanne pulled the PVC out of the dead cherub to swing at another one. The flying obscenity dodged in midair and overshot the boat. Wright stabbed at another with the sharp end of of the broken-off shovel handle and slashed a wing. The cherub skidded on the deck of the boat like a plane crash-landing on an aircraft carrier. The remaining cherub landed on its feet on the deck a few feet from Bryan.

The buzz of the cherub's wings rose and fell; the one that overshot the boat must have made a U-turn over the water and was coming back.

"More concrete coming!" Marshall shouted, and the cardboard tube became heavy again.

With silent consensus, Bryan and Laura moved the underwater end of the tube above Samiazaz's chest. The movement caused the cloudy water to swirl out the way, and for a brief moment they saw his face through clear water, but his expression was unreadable.

"Argh!" Marshall yelled. The crash-landed cherub had wrapped its arms and legs around his leg, and was sinking its teeth into his knee. Bryan moved to help Marshall, but the damn thing face turned its head to reveal a face that mirrored Bryan's own, and he hesitated.

"Keep pouring!" Marshall commanded as he tried to kick off the cherub.

The gray slurry gushed over the archangel's face and chest. As the mush settled, obscuring the demiurge, the sun dipped below the horizon and they were suddenly working in twilight. There was enough light to see the concrete settling like cold lava over the archangel. Samiazaz was became completely immersed. The cherub with Bryan's face released its hold on Marshall's leg, took a step away, then dissolved into a colorless mist that drifted away. Marshall collapsed on the deck.

Somewhere behind Bryan was a splash.

Bryan was about to ask if there would be another batch of concrete when he saw the expression on Laura's face. He looked over this shoulder to see Wright had fallen to the deck too.

Suzanne?

He dropped the tube and stood up to look for her. She was nowhere on deck!

He remembered the splash and looked over the edge. There was a glimmer of white and red under the darkening water, and he jumped in feet first without thinking. The water was a cold shock, but it wakened his fatigue-drugged mind, and his hands found her in the darkening water.

With one arm around her waist, he managed to pull his head above water by grabbing a pontoon with his free hand.

"Help!" he cried.

And Laura was there, reaching out to help him drag Suzanne back onto the deck. The lake water had turned the concrete dust on Suzanne to a gray slime. He pulled off his shirt and turned it inside out so he would have something to clean her with.

He shivered as he squatted next to Suzanne's lifeless body. Her face was serene, her eyes closed. Her skin no longer looked poreless, and he saw a mole he'd never noticed before and the beginnings of fine wrinkles near her eyes. Still, he had never seen her more beautiful, more human, though he knew that what lay before him was truly lifeless now. That essence of Suzanne – whatever it was called, soul, astral body, design body, whatever the occult term was – that essence was gone. This was just a dead image of her.

Laura sat beside the body of John Wright. She was sobbing softly. Her tears were cutting lines through the layers of dirt and concrete dust on her cheeks. He felt his own tears doing the same.

* * *

24.

Last Thoughts of the living

Bryan.

As twilight ended, Laura and Bryan mixed one more batch of concrete and poured it into Samiazaz's tomb. The full moon rising in the east gave them enough light to finish. Together, they dragged the three lifeless bodies to the center of the deck. They had nothing to cover the corpses with, but they hauled buckets of water and washed the dust and grime off Suzanne, Wright and Marshall. When they finished, the faces of the dead were still gray under the moonlight, but it was the grayness of death, not of concrete dust and mud.

They examined Samiazaz's concrete tomb. The final batch had brought the slurry up over the top of the cinder blocks. The water level now covered the top of the concrete by only a few inches. Metal shavings in the concrete sparkled like stars in the bright moonlight. Otherwise, the tomb looked like a slipshod job, lopsided, asymmetrical. But Samiazaz remained immobile beneath it.

"Before, I could feel him searching for me with his mind," Laura said. "As soon as we covered his face, I didn't feel it me anymore. It was like a searchlight was turned off."

Bryan knelt on the deck, stuck his hand in the water and touched the top of the concrete mound. The quick-curing concrete was hot and already firm to the touch. Alive or undead, Marshall had known his stuff, and maybe the metal filings had turned the trick.

“According to Uncle Robert, Samiazaz is trapped back on the astral plane, too, but in a tomb made of his own fears and arrogance, not concrete and steel.” Laura said.

“It’s a fitting end for the bastard,” Bryan said.

They poled the barge as close to the shore as they could. Both were physically and emotionally exhausted. The pontoons bottomed out on the silt when they were still twenty feet away from the beach. They wanted to take the bodies with them, but didn’t want to drag them through the mud, even if they had possessed any remaining strength to do so. Instead, they took refuge in Laura’s Volkswagen Beetle. The rattletrap car, old enough to qualify as an antique, started right up. In minutes, the heater was going, and they both felt somewhat better.

“It’s like an undead car,” Laura tried to joke, but he could tell her heart wasn’t in it, and her eyes welled with tears.

“I thought that when Wright moved on, the spell would be broken, but it isn’t,” she said. “I miss him terribly. I miss that mystical bond we had shared worse than ever, so much I want to die.”

Bryan climbed out of the car without a word and looked at the stars. She got out too, and said, “I’m sorry.”

“For what?” he asked.

“For everything. For what I did to you. For your loss. Everything.”

“It wasn’t your fault,” he said, patting her shoulder. “I understand what happened between you and Wright. The same happened to me with Suzanne.”

“What are we going to do about them?” Laura said, nodding toward the barge.

“I’m so tired I’m about to fall down right now, but I hate to leave them out there on the boat in the open.”

“Me, too. I’ve got a queen-sized blanket in the back of the Volks. Could you help me take it back out to the boat and cover them up?”

"Yeah. But then I've got to get something to eat or I'm going to pass out. Look." He held out his hand. It was shaking.

They walked back out to the boat with the blanket. The three lifeless bodies were still there on the deck. Some residual hope, like that of a child not wanting to give up believing in Santa Claus, had made Bryan dream they would have revived. Or at the bodies could have had the good grace to have disappeared. If they had vanished, there would be hope they were resurrected somewhere else. But all three lay there, their dull eyes open but unaware of the heavens.

Laura unfolded the blanket and together they draped it over the bodies. The blanket was actually a thick and heavy quilt, and it reminded Bryan of his grandmother's quilt, the one he had wrapped Suzanne in after he had brought her back from the woods. This blanket's maker had made a sort of mandala of differently colored triangles converging on the center. It was a mixture of Americana and the Occidental, a fitting shroud. A light breeze had picked up and whipped the corners of the quilt, so they weighed it down with chunks of now-hardened concrete that lay around the deck.

Though two cherubs had been killed on the deck, there was no sign of their blood. Evidently the blood had dissipated with the bodies when Samiazaz's influence in this physical realm ended. It was still hard to accept, however that the seemingly solid blood, bone and flesh of the cherubs had been just a manifestation of Samiazaz's tortured soul.

Back in the Beetle, Laura said, "Where should we go?"

"Someplace where there is food."

"I have no food at my house."

"The cupboards are bare back at my grandfather's, too."

"Then our choice is to go into town or back out to Sophia's."

"I wonder if her real-world food will be as good as her astral cooking," Bryan said.

Laura laughed, but it was forced. "At least it will be hot."

"What if she isn't there?"

"I can cook – sort of – if I have to. Sophia taught me."

They drove for a while without speaking, then Laura said, "I feel bad about leaving them there like that."

"Me too," he said, hesitant to tell her what he was thinking. "I'm not thinking straight right now, but you know what?"

"What?"

"I thought of gathering up driftwood and making a pyre right there on the boat. Set it afire and push it out in the middle of the lake like the Vikings did," he said.

"I had visions of fire, too, but I thought of Indians."

"About the same difference. Cleansing of grief through fire."

"Yeah." She smiled at him. You weren't thinking about throwing yourself on Suzanne's pyre, Viking fashion, were you?"

"Only the wives did that," he said.

She laughed at this, but it he wondered if it had crossed her mind. *Surely not.*

She clutched and downshifted as they climbed a little hill. The car ran but its old engine was weak. As twilight gave way to night, Laura had to turn on the headlights. The beams were dim yellow and flickered dimly with every bump.

"I was afraid if we set them afire they might rise up again in agony," Bryan said.

They topped the hill and came onto the long level stretch of road preceding the manse.

"Here's what we could do," Bryan said. "Eat something. Talk to Sophia. Then go back to the lake. If the bodies are decaying, then we burn them or bury them or do something."

She nodded. Neither of them cared for the finality of it all, but at least they had made a decision.

Laura parked her Volks next to Uncle Robert's Land Rover. Two of its tires were flat and the paint was peeling, testimony to their still being on the physical plane.

Inside the house, Laura called out, "Aunt Sophia?"

"In the kitchen, dear," came the reply. They both relaxed. It was like coming home.

Sophia set a plate of hotcakes down on the table as they came in.

"I know it's a breakfast meal, but here in the physical world you got to work with what you have. You know, if life gives you lemons and all that," she said. "Get your own plates out of the cupboard."

Bryan must have been staring, because Sophia said, "What cha' looking at?

"You usually dress – differently," Bryan said.

Sophia wore paint-dabbed bib overalls over a T-shirt and flip-flops.

"I've started painting again. A new mural. You wouldn't expect me to do that in a miniskirt and high heels, would you?"

"I guess not."

"Besides, just between us mortals, I dressed like that mainly for Simon," she said.

"I thought it embarrassed him," Laura said.

"No, dear. He pretended it did, but he secretly loved it. He liked that it upset the local status quo."

"Is there coffee?" Bryan asked.

"This late?"

"Doesn't seem normal to eat pancakes without coffee."

"I have some old grounds. I can re-brew them."

Sophia sat down with them as they ate. "You two look like you've been to a funeral."

"We have," Laura said. She started to tell Sophia what had happened at the lake, but her aunt stopped her.

"I know, dear. I know all about it."

Laura began crying again. "He's gone, Sophia. They're all gone." She rubbed away the tears with the back of her hand. "I'm sorry. I'm sorry. I'm acting like a baby. We suspected this would happen."

Sophia stepped closer, bent over and gave her a hug, then dabbed away the tears with a dishtowel.

"Come. Follow me. I want to show you my latest work in progress," she said.

She led them into the dining room where they had encountered Samiazaz. Stacks of books were everywhere and dust was on the table. Along one wall, leaning against the bookshelves that stretched to the ceiling, was a canvas that easily measured eight-feet high and twelve feet long.

"I moved it from my studio because the light is better in here," she explained.

She had started an elaborate panorama in charcoal, and though large sections of the painting were still little more than charcoal sketches, the story it told was clear. Uncle Robert was there, larger than life, a ghost in translucent color. He was dressed in a monk's robes complete with a knotted rope for a belt, a thick tome one hand and a fifth of whiskey wedged under his arm. With his free hand he pointed toward five people in golden medieval armor: John Wright, Frank Marshall, Suzanne, Laura and Bryan. Instead of swords or pikes, they held shovels in various poses.

The blue sky was filled with flying cherubs. No, wait. They weren't flying but tumbling down as if from some precipitous height.

Beneath their feet, the canvas darkened. Here, on the upper walls, were cherubs too, but in various stages of ruin and disfigurement. There was the bloated dirigible of a cherub with its Ben Cartwright mask, rupturing under the downward thrust of Suzanne's shovel. A multitude of tiny toads burst forth from the fissure, echoing Bryan's memory of the encounter. Facing the other way, he and Laura were shoveling parts of cherubs – arms, legs and decapitated heads – off to the side. Wright and Marshall were the most heroic of all. Their faces were firm with resolve as they swung their shovels to bat at the tumbling cherubs.

Under their feet lay an archangel, probably Samiazaz, but it was hard to say for sure, as his features were unfinished. He was on his back with a blank stare as Bryan remembered him at Lost Lake, though he wasn't preserved under water but faded and disfigured. His upper body was white, marbled Apollonian muscle, but below the waist he was all scales and claws, and the folded wings that peaked out from his broad shoulders were those of a dragon.

The complicated battle of humans, angels and demonically bloated cherubs swirled about a common center, a whirlpool, a vortex, whose center was anchored on what looked like a gash in the canvas itself, but was instead a painted illusion. Pieces of cherubs were being sucked into that gash, and even the archangel seemed to stretch, his very fabric of being distorted as it was drawn toward the black hole of the gash.

Bryan recognized the gash: It was the one in the angel saucer.

"It's a bit of a cheat, you know," Sophia said.

"How did you do it?" Laura asked.

"Do what?"

"There are things happening in your painting that mirror what happened to me. Things I've never told you or anyone else about!"

Sophia laughed softly. "Well what's the good of being a psychic artist if you can't freak out people once in a while?"

"You said it was a cheat," Bryan said."What did you mean?"

"Oh, it's not wholly original. It's derived from Bruegel's *The Fall of the Rebel Angels,*" she said. "But I didn't realize I had unconsciously parodied it until yesterday."

"Yesterday? How long have you been working on it," Bryan asked.

"For about three months," she answered.

"That would mean you started it only about a month after the saucer fell. Long before the archangels began mating with humans, months before we started seeing cherubs," Laura said incredulously.

"I had it charcoaled in, everything, even the cherubs, in detail the first day," she said. "Most of the faces came next, and Wright's armor. I had a lot of trouble with that. He and I weren't getting along then. I thought him a racist bigot. I don't know what he thought of me, but we were always uncomfortable in each other's presence. And as for Suzanne, she and I had never met when I started her face. Many times I wanted to paint someone else because I have trouble with the skin tones of Irish redheads, but something in me made me scrape off the paint and start over until I got her right. I puzzled over the shovels, but whatever was directing my hand wouldn't let me paint the swords I thought needed to be in their hands anymore than it would let me paint anyone but Suzanne."

She took a deep breath and let it out.

"And painting Simon as a translucent ghost upset me most of all." Her voice wavered a bit, and she frowned. Bryan was afraid she was going to cry. Laura looked weepy too. He wanted to hug both of them, but it didn't seem proper.

"It's beautiful and horrible at the same time," Laura said, wiping away tears with the back of her hand.

Bryan, missing Suzanne now more than ever, said. "So, Sophia, have you visited Uncle Robert – I mean Simon – on the astral plane yet?"

"That's another thing I wanted to talk to you about," she said.

"You said you would show us how to visit them there."

"I'll guide you to the astral plane, but first I want you both to get cleaned up and get some rest."

"But . . ."

"No buts about it. You're both filthy and obviously exhausted."

They both protested, but Sophia wouldn't take no for an answer. She led them upstairs to the large bedroom that had cherubs - the harmless, playful kind – painted on the ceiling. The king-size bed was freshly made up. Bryan entered the room with mixed feelings.

Only a few days ago he and Laura had made love in the bed. In the brief interim, Laura had met John Wright and fallen hopelessly in love with him, and Bryan dug a dead woman out of a woodpile and lost his heart to her.

"There's hot water and clean towels. You leave your clothes out in the hall, and I'll wash them while you bathe," Sophia said.

The unease in their faces must have been obvious. "What's the matter?"

"We're not, not . . ." Laura started.

"Not together?"

"Yes," Bryan said. "It's kind of complicated."

"Well, but do you hate each other now?"

Laura looked to Bryan.

"No, of course not – not at all," he said.

"Can't stand the sight of each other?"

"You don't understand." Laura said.

"Oh, I think I do. You feel it would be unfaithful to John Wright and Suzanne Zimmerman if you saw each other naked now."

"Something like that. It's as if we've gone from being lovers to being like brother and sister," Bryan said.

Laura nodded in agreement.

"Well, this is the only room that's heated today, and its bathroom is the only one with hot water. I suggest you look the other way while undressing. Besides, your undead lovers are beyond such petty concerns now."

Before Bryan or Laura could argue further, she shut the door, leaving them alone with each other.

Laura opened the door of the walk-in closet and stepped into the darkness. She rattled hangers about, then she stepped out with two sports jackets draped over her arm, one corduroy, the other gray tweed. She pitched the tweed jacket on the bed.

"Here," she said, avoiding his eyes. "We can wear these in place of bathrobes coming out of the bath. I'll go first."

She went into the bathroom and closed the door. A minute later, she opened it wide enough to dump her dirty clothes outside. He took them and threw them in the hallway outside the bedroom door as she ran water in the tub. He added his dirty socks and T-shirt to the pile but kept on his jeans.

In about fifteen minutes, she stepped out, shrouded in steam, her face clean and flushed from the hot water. Then it was his turn. He stripped off the wet jeans as the tub refilled, and threw them out of the bathroom as she had done.

His bath was only lukewarm, but it still felt wonderful. *Just like a sister to use all the hot water.*

The water turned dark brown in seconds, and he became sleepy as he soaked. The sandy grit seemed to have crept into every nook and cranny.

He dried himself while standing on wobbly feet and buttoned up the tweed jacket. He was taller than Uncle Robert had been and he would have to be careful how he sat.

Stepping out of the bathroom he found Laura already tucked in the big bed. The corduroy jacket hung on a bedpost and the room was lit dimly by a single kerosene lantern. She was sleeping with the counterpane pulled up so it covered part of her face.

She had turned down the covers on the other side of the bed.

Quietly, he turned the knob on the lantern that adjusted the wick until the feeble light flickered and went out. Then he hung the tweed jacket on the other bedpost at the foot of the bed, climbed in, and pulled the blanket up around his neck. He laid there, his back to her, listening to her snore softly. The bed was large enough that they needn't touch each other.

It began raining, softly at first, then rising to a torrent, tides of rain rattling the thick window panes. He worried the downpour might wash the quilt off the bodies of Suzanne and the others, worried that as the deck of the barge didn't have a rail, the deluge might even sweep the bodies into Lost Lake. His worry receded down a dark tunnel of exhaustion, and as sleep overtook him, one of Laura's feet found his leg and rested there.

The room was filled with daylight when he awoke, but it took him a good minute to remember where he was. Laura was gone but her scent remained. He found his jeans, T-shirt and underwear – clean, dried but not pressed – laid out on a chair.

How long had he slept? It could be anytime from midmorning to midafternoon.

He dressed and went downstairs in sock feet. No one was in the kitchen, though the remains of a country breakfast were still on the table. He grabbed a piece of toast and sipped some leftover tea, sweetened with honey and browned with cream – cat's potion – the way Laura liked hers. The sound of voices drifted down the hall as he munched on the toast, and he moved toward them, toast and cup in hand.

He found Laura and Sophia sitting across from each other at the big oak table in the dining room.

"But I don't understand," Laura was saying as he walked in. "You said I would be able to find John on the astral plane."

"I don't understand either, child," Sophia said. "Either they don't want to be found – which I doubt – or it's something to do with the angels."

Bryan sat down at the table. Laura looked angry or hurt or both. "Sophia and I astrally projected to Summerland. We couldn't find anyone from Creedance who had died since the crash of the saucer. Even

Uncle Robert."

"It's like a curse," Bryan said. He meant it as a statement of the absurd, but Sophia nodded.

"That's one way to think about it," she said.

"So are they lost to us forever?" Laura said.

"I don't know. Sometimes the design bodies will hang around their earthly corpses or where they used to live for days, weeks or even years, but usually that only happens for those who died violently or were in denial about being dead. I don't think that's the case here."

"Could it be something to do with the saucer?" Bryan asked.

"I don't know. There's nothing in any of the books I've read about demiurges from another astral plane shanghaiing the recently departed."

She smiled and clasped her hands on the table. "I'm sorry. I didn't mean to mislead you. Neither did Simon. I'm as confused as you are, and I wanted to see Simon again as much as you wanted to see your lovers. Maybe the saucer still has an influence. I just don't know what to tell you do next."

"I think I know one thing we can do," Laura said. "Can we borrow some gasoline?"

It early evening when Laura's Beetle clattered and coughed its way to the beach of Lost Lake. The full moon, though low in the west, still gave Bryan and her enough light to unload the Army surplus jerry cans of gasoline from the Beetle's back seat. The water had sunk a little lower. The pontoon boat now crouched about waist high above the water. The edge of the saucer, seen edge on, jutted from the water. Its mirror reflection was bent on the still water, so two saucers floated there, one real, the other an illusion. Bryan got to the boat first and hefted his can onto the deck. Laura struggled with hers in the ankle-deep mud.

"Let me help," Bryan called.

"No!" Laura said, and he left her alone as she half-carried, half-dragged her jerry can through the mud to the boat. Her determination and resolve weren't enough to help her get the can up on deck, so finally she relented and let him lift it for her.

Except for one of Suzanne's bare feet, the bodies had remained covered by the quilt. They didn't pull back the quilt because it was obvious from the smell that the bodies were beginning to decompose.

Bryan covered Suzanne's foot, and they doused the quilt with gasoline. The quilt was quickly soaked, and the overflow ran around their feet and off the deck onto the water. Lighter than water, the gasoline floated, painting an oily iridescent film.

"Won't the gas just go up in a flash before the bodies are burned?" Laura coughed. The gasoline's strong fumes burned their lungs.

"The deck boards are thick wood. They'll make a good fire. What's left of the barge will sink into the silt."

"Are you sure?"

"No, not really."

"I guess it doesn't matter does it?"

"No. What matters is that we did something. I'm going to leave my can here. Save some gasoline in yours. We'll have to make a trail back to the shore and light it there unless. . ."

"Unless what?

"Unless you want to burn up too."

They both knew it wasn't a rhetorical question. He suspected part of her really wanted to stay on the barge. Part of him wanted to do the same.

"I'll survive," she said finally. "I'll live and I'll survive. I have to. I have things to go on and do before I die. You know what I'm talking about."

"I feel the same way," he said.

The sun was just dipping below the horizon as he tossed a torch into the gasoline pooling on the edge of the shore. The gasoline leaking from the barge floated on top of the water, and the flame, blue and cold-looking, raced to the boat. When it reached the barge, the flame roared and lit up the lake in a yellow blaze that seemed to reach to the stars.

By the firelight, they could see the mound of concrete that was Samiazaz's tomb. The flecks of metal hadn't had time to rust and reflected the golden flames of the funeral pyre, making Bryan think of Samiazaz's prison as a misshapen whore sprinkled a ballroom dancer's glitter makeup.

The light from the fire also highlighted the ragged wound in the saucer's side.

"The waterline is below the gash," Laura said. "The lake won't drain in any more."

"We have an audience." He pointed.

Two winged figures had emerged from the gash. They had to be angel/human hybrids because all the archangels except Samiazaz had merged with humans.

"I was hoping the saucer would just fade away once Samiazaz was deactivated," he said.

"I wonder what we'd find if we went back in, now that the archangels are all gone," she said. "Do May and Marguerite and the other hyrbid angels own the saucer now?"

"Don't know."

The sound of the fire changed from a roar to crackling as the deck boards caught.

"Want to go with me to find out?" she asked. She stood close enough that her shoulder brushed against his. The fire changed color from clear yellow to red.

"I guess. Why not? Why the hell not," he said finally.

A loon called sadly across the lake as the two angels took flight, leaving Bryan and Laura alone to watch the bodies of their lovers burn.

Author's Note: This concludes the second book of the Messengers trilogy. In the next and final book, *Dreamtime of an Alien God*, Laura and Byran explore the other worlds to which the angel saucer is a portal, looking for their lost loves, and finding much more than they could have expected. The status of all three books and links to their Amazon pages may be found at http://magichatbooks.com/ .

http://magichatbooks.com/

R. Douglas Burns

www.ingramcontent.com/pod-product-compliance
Lightning Source LLC
Chambersburg PA
CBHW020327180626
46812CB00001B/85

* 9 7 8 0 6 1 5 7 0 2 3 8 4 *